THE WALL
The Refugees' Path to a New Republic

THE WALL
The Refugees' Path to a New Republic

PROLOGUE

Day was just beginning to break.

The desert sands were stained red, like a sea of blood. Hidden within stood an assemblage of over five thousand individuals.

Through the radio one Army man held to his ear, a female reporter's voice continued describing the situation in breathless tones: "A week has passed since the caravan has set up their campsite. They have applied for asylum with the US government, but have yet to receive any reply, and are clearly reaching the end of their ropes. As we speak, reports keep coming in of refugees climbing over the wall to reach the States. America, and the world, continue to watch closely."

At that moment, close to ten media helicopters were flitting about, the air as intensely charged as ever.

The partition at the border between America and Mexico, dubbed "The Wall," stood nearly twenty-three feet high and spanned dozens of miles, with steel piles (nearly four inches in height and just over one inch in thickness) placed at around six-inch intervals.

" . . . Citizens of the Central American country of Cordova are fleeing the dictatorship of President Gumersindo Cortázar, as well as the brutality of José Moreno and his narcotics cartel, Los Eternos, with no end in sight for the mass exodus. Over ten thousand have fled this year alone, and that figure will only increase. In response to overwhelming pressure from America's far right, US President Robert Copeland is refusing to allow them entry. Troops have been dispatched in order to prevent them from setting foot on American soil . . ."

The copters overhead dipped lower.

US Army Captain Jadon Green, commander of the troops guarding The Wall, set the radio away from his ear and raised the volume. The tension was excruciating; the young men of arms were teetering on the brink. One faint spark could be all it took to light the powder keg.

Gazing ahead, they could see the expanse of the Mexican desert between The Wall's giant steel piles. The scene on the ground was reminiscent of a Middle Eastern refugee camp, with countless tents large and small. The asylum seekers had already been eking out a life there for a week, and their numbers were growing.

What Jadon had seen in Turkey flashed to mind. The camps of Syrian refugees fleeing the Islamic State. The folks whose hopes for the future had all been swallowed by starvation and fear. The crude tents lined up on the low ground. The all-but-barefoot children begging for food, even amidst the mud on rainy days and nights. Occasionally, the residents of the site would flock to some United Nations or private charity truck carrying relief supplies. The only purpose driving the displaced was to survive another day.

The reporter's voice jolted Jadon out of his train of thought: " . . . Refugees are surging closer and closer toward the border, having walked around 2,500 miles since leaving their home country of Cordova one month prior. Many of them are women and children, and many are elderly. Originally, what they're calling the caravan numbered a little more than a thousand, but its ranks swelled when they were joined by Mexican migrants, and now they're thought to exceed the

five thousand mark. Meanwhile, five hundred American soldiers are stationed to face them. The soldiers have their firearms at the ready, yet the refugees continue to advance toward the wall at the border with no sign of being cowed . . ."

As the dawn encroached, a heavy, rumbling moan rose from the distance as the stark shadows were stretching at the red sands' horizon. An altogether new band of refugees that had marched throughout the night was approaching. Soon enough, they'd drawn close enough for the soldiers to ascertain their individual appearances.

The nervous energy seizing the soldiers grew yet more potent. They once again pointed their guns.

"Fingers off your triggers, soldiers," said Jadon. "We're just trying to scare them. Remember, they're not armed. No harm will come to you, so calm down." It did serve to soothe some nerves for the time being, but how long would he be able to keep that up?

The crowd, which was dyed as red as the desert, kept closing the distance toward The Wall, planting fear into the young soldiers' hearts. Before they knew it, the refugees who they thought were still asleep had gotten onto their feet too. In a blink, the scarlet sunlight from beyond the dunes had given way, and a great throng was flooding the other side of The Wall.

Several men ran up to the partition and began climbing. The number of refugees sticking by The Wall kept increasing, until they outnumbered the soldiers many times over. They held ladders and ropes with grappling hooks by the plenty.

"The people at the head of the Caravan are advancing up The Wall," stated the radio excitedly.

"Masks on, soldiers," said Jadon. "Use the tear gas."

At his orders, dozens of tear-gas bombs were launched. Angry roars came flying, but the refugees were not deterred. Instead, they ran toward The Wall, clinging to it in their thousands and setting upon the ascent. The soldiers defending The Wall were ready to defend their country, while hoping it would not come to a confrontation.

Then, a gunshot pierced the air. Every soul stopped in its tracks. The only commotion, the whir of the copters. Yet before the ringing of the first shot had even gone, it was joined by a whole host of automatic weapons. The gunfight was now underway.

"Hold your fire. That's an order!" screamed Jadon, but his voice was drowned out by an unholy combination of wrathful bellowing, anguished cries, and bullets unrelenting.

The soldiers were flustered, and in the confusion, all too many just kept firing. The refugees were beating panicked retreats now, but the hail of bullets felled women and children without mercy.

"Stop! Stop firing!"

Behind the soldiers, Jadon fired a handgun into the sky. Just like that, the storm ceased.

Firearms still hot in their grips, the soldiers gaped dumbfounded. It seemed they'd returned to sanity.

It had taken a little over ten minutes for the Mexican side of The Wall to be drenched in the blood of the hundreds who now lay prone on the grit. Everywhere there was weeping, moaning, shrieking. One of the cries rang out over the din; a man raised an infant girl up for the sentries to see. Blood was dripping from her head, tinging the man's own head in red.

"America's killed my wife and daughter," he cried. "They are the devil. I will have my revenge. I will kill you all."

A woman was crumpled at his feet, bleeding from the chest and abdomen. Jadon could only stare in disbelief.

Meanwhile, at the Oval Office . . .

President Copeland was looking over the script of a speech he'd be reciting at a dinner party to which the UK ambassador was invited. Would it be a bit gauche to add a joke about how leaving the EU would definitely solve the immigration and refugee problem?

That was when Chief of Staff Albert Campbell barged in, passing by the president's desk without a word to turn on the TV.

"What the . . ." the president found himself murmuring. Then, he turned pale.

"It's the bit of The Wall 12 miles east of El Paso. CNN's got the footage." Campbell raised the volume. Gunshots resounded in rapid succession, while thousands on the Mexican side ran away in all directions, and hundreds lay bloodied and broken. "There's been a shoot-out at The Wall. The body count is suspected to be over a hundred."

"Have them stop firing this instant. I ordered nothing of the sort!"

"This isn't live. It's already over."

The president looked back at the screen. They were now showing medical orderlies frantically running around, with voices audible from the studio.

"The acting commander ordered them to cease firing the second they started. But the fire lasted over ten minutes."

"Who shot first?"

"We're looking into it."

If we fired first, then . . . Then everything's going to spin out of control. But Bob swallowed those words. He was going to get blasted by his constituents, his rivals, and the international community. This was a massacre, plain and simple.

"Call the secretaries of defense and state. We're holding an NSC meeting," said Bob, rising from his chair.

But he froze when he saw who was at the door. It was his daughter Patricia—who'd recently turned thirteen—stiff as a board, eyes glued to the screen. No doubt she'd overheard their conversation too. Her gaze turned to her father.

"Go to your room. I told you not to come here; I work here." He didn't mean to sound that harsh, but that was how the words came out.

Patricia dropped the file she'd been holding, and the photo of the puppy born just last week fell to the floor. That jogged his memory: She'd told him all about it over breakfast, and he'd asked her to show

him. She snapped out of her dazed silence and broke into a run. "I hate you!"

That remark stabbed deep into his heart. He saw the tears welling in her eyes. She was a smart one, with an interest in politics. The full gravity of the situation couldn't have eluded her.

The "Tragedy at The Wall" was made known to the world in real time. One hundred fifteen Cordovans were dead, 332 injured. Zero Americans were dead, eight injured.

The media and press were unanimous in decrying Washington. In addition, Captain Jadon Green was now the object of scorn and ridicule, reviled as the Border Butcher and the Killer Commander. Had he been court-martialed, he would have faced the distinct possibility of a life sentence, but he was able to secure a plea bargain at the inquiry commission thanks to his old superior, Colonel Stewart Gobel. Jadon acknowledged his own folly and his lack of experience. The military wanted Jadon disposed of as quickly as possible, so they slapped him with a dishonorable discharge. Now that that was on his record, depending on the state, he couldn't vote or bear arms. In short order, the Tragedy had been chalked up to the grave error of a single captain, absolving the military as a whole.

The White House promptly conducted polling to better grasp the extent of the fallout. In a day's time, President Copeland's approval rating had plummeted 15 percent (from 52 percent to 37 percent). And the only reason it wasn't even lower was because of the press conference he set up right on the incident's heels, wherein he expressed his condolences to the victims and declared he would get to the bottom of the whole affair. At the same time, he stressed the rule of law in not allowing entry to the refugees who'd tried to storm their way over.

The invective that had dug under his skin the deepest remained Patricia's "I hate you!" Even now, he could see the tears glistening in her accusing eyes.

* * *

Meanwhile, over in Cordova, dictator Gumersindo Cortázar wasted no time addressing his nation after he was apprised of the first reports: "Don't run from your country. The Americans will just slaughter you. The only country for Cordovans is Cordova. The only country for Cordovans is right here. This is your heartland."

Following that speech, almost no one dared leave the dictatorship anymore.

■ ■ ■

1

THE DESERT WAR ROOM

No sooner had Jadon entered the room than his phone rang.

He gave the screen a once-over before putting it on the table and disrobing his mud-stained outerwear. Then he pulled a can of beer out of the drugstore paper bag and chugged it all down. His body absorbed the alcohol. His muscles were tired, but he didn't feel like falling asleep. He'd just wake from his nightmares in another cold sweat.

The room was in a motel in the LA burbs. Voices from the neighboring rooms passed through the walls as if they were made of cardboard. He turned on the TV and put it on mute.

A week had passed since he started working construction at this place. Ten-hour days, $170 a day. It was the only job he could come by while keeping his identity hidden. Such was the fate of former US Army Captain Jadon Green, ten months and counting since he left the military.

The moniker of Border Butcher had gained more traction than he'd expected. He'd been forced to change jobs nine times now.

One place, he'd even gotten canned the day after he started working. The boss there simply placed a paper on his office desk, giving Jadon a defiant look all the while. Needless to say, the paper featured an article with Jadon's photo. Jadon had to swallow the sudden urge to punch his lights out, but he balled his fists and bore it.

The internet was virtually plastered with photos and articles. Hundreds of the dead and injured, splayed and fallen before The Wall's steel piles, and more than half of them were women and children. Some of the corpses even had bullet wounds through their heads. And behind the soldiers stood Jadon Green with his handgun, shooting into the sky. To the world, it looked as though he'd been *encouraging* them to fire.

They'd needed a scapegoat to pin the blame on, naturally. And he just happened to fit the bill. Still, he didn't care to make excuses. Or rather, he *couldn't* make excuses. He'd been the captain there. That was the plain truth.

After draining another beer, he grabbed a bottle of whiskey off the table and partook. Only, he didn't really "partake" so much as he used it to wash it all down. Maybe it was the soldierly discipline, or whatever was left of it, that kept him from drowning in more than a certain amount. Maybe it was more out of consideration for his four-year-old daughter . . . and the child support he needed to dole out.

Ever since the day of the incident, the media and morbidly curious onlookers alike camped around the Green family home, waiting for their prey to exit. Trolls and harassers made sure their phones rang nonstop, night and day, while their tires kept getting slashed. Some nights, a stone or two would be thrown through the windows in the wee hours. Paulina had been three at the time. Every night, she'd cry. Every night.

That wasn't even getting into the swarm of countless letters and emails. Some of the mail contained box-cutter blades. The paranoia was intense. The slightest bump in the night would cause Paulina to jolt awake and burst into tears. Shirley would hold her tight and cower with her in a corner of the room.

Eventually, Jadon had the two take refuge in his in-laws' home. The first two months, he called every day. All the while, memories of that day would attack unbidden whenever he had a moment to think in his own home. And his insomnia only grew worse and worse. In his dreams, claws would reach out from between the gaps of The Wall. There had even been times he'd wake himself up shouting, begging them to stop.

It wasn't long until he turned to booze. And the phone calls, they went from once every other day, to once a week, to zero from his end.

Six months later, the divorce notice came in. He couldn't blame Shirley. He signed it and delivered it the very next day.

The smartphone on the table began ringing again. This time, he grabbed it reflexively.

"Finally picked up, huh?" Shirley said. "I called more than ten times. The child support bank transfer still hasn't come in yet. Are you still sending it to your old friend? Because let me tell you, it's the military that made our lives such a mess. And it's Paulina who pays the price. Not that I don't, either. You want to see her, don't you? Then take responsibility and . . ."

Shirley kept talking his ear off. Jadon took the phone from his ear and found he could still hear her. This was not speakerphone.

Then, the doorbell rang.

Jadon set the phone on his bed and threw on his jacket, looked through the peephole, and opened the door. There stood a gray-haired, tall-figured man in Army uniform. His face was sun-beaten, with a scar from his right cheek down to his neck thanks to a bullet in Iraq.

"Do me a favor and put away the gun, would you?" he said, his voice deep.

Jadon dropped the pistol's hammer, and stashed the gun in his belt.

Colonel Stewart Gobel was Jadon's former superior. For whatever reason, he'd held Jadon in high esteem since the young man joined, keeping in touch even after changes in unit makeups. He went so far as to defend Jadon, pulling strings so he could avoid getting court-martialed, on the condition he be discharged.

"Nobody who comes a-knocking means me well."

"Has it been three attempts on your life, now? You handled them all pretty well, seeing as the police never got involved."

The first time, he was attacked in a back alley. The second, in a restaurant restroom. A bunch of young men had gotten all worked up, declaring in their rage that they'd kill America's mark of shame, the Border Butcher. One got his right arm broken, while another lost a few teeth from a trip to the toilet bowl. The rest ran scared. The third attempt, the most brutal of them all, took place two months prior. He'd been eating at a coffee shop when, suddenly, a guy came at him with a steak knife. He'd gotten gashed in the arm, but managed to steal the knife and thrust it at his assailant's throat. He was an old man. A very old man.

"Go ahead, do me in. That way you'll get the chair, Border Butcher!" he'd crowed hoarsely. Jadon tossed the knife, paid his bill, and left.

"What do you need?" said Jadon.

Stewart was scanning the room. "You should've given me a shout. I could've helped you out."

"You already know plenty about me and my post-retirement lifestyle. You're always watching over me so I don't screw up again, aren't you?"

"Don't feel so sorry for yourself. I know full well you're stronger than that."

"You're giving me too much credit. I wasn't qualified to be a captain. That's why it happened. So I'll keep staying out of the Army's hair."

"You need money."

"So you know about the child support too."

"And how you're sending money to an injured subordinate. Your being broke is what's behind the divorce, if I'm not wrong." Stewart heaved a light sigh and looked square at Jadon. "We're talking $25,000."

"You really do know everything about everything."

"That's why the US military is the strongest in the world. And why it's here to stay."

"Well, you may be under the impression the military is high-grade goods, but you know the name of the guy who kicked down its market value."

"Some rich lady stuck it onto a teddy bear. Some have even said they'd try to buy it back. The US military's high honor, stomped on by money."

He was referring to how Jadon had sold his Silver Star Medal online, sending all the money to his injured subordinate. That was another inciting factor for the divorce.

"It was just a hunk of metal."

"But what it represents is sacred."

"Is that why you bought it back?"

"I was against it. You used the Silver Star to the maximum benefit it could provide. Instead of showing it off for the sake of your own honor, you tried to save a friend. It's one of the reasons I've always believed in you. And no matter what form it may take, honor should be granted to all who have devoted themselves to their country," said Stewart, staring.

"The Army must have way too much time on its hands, if you know this much."

"If you come here tomorrow morning at eight, $100,000 will be transferred to your account. If you complete the work, that's another $500,000. It'll be a twenty-day gig."

Stewart took out some memo paper. Jadon didn't extend a hand, so the colonel stowed it in the breast pocket of the work shirt Jadon had on.

"I'm not a soldier anymore, colonel. I'm not taking your orders."

"Just hear me out. You can turn it down if you want. And you won't have to send back the 100 grand, either."

"I lost everything because of orders from on high."

"Not everything. You've got a head on your shoulders and muscles to work with. Both of which I whipped into shape."

"Why don't you do it, then?"

"I would if I could."

Stewart raised the cuff of his pants, showing his prosthetic leg. Jadon had heard the man had gotten wrapped up in a terror attack in Europe. Stewart patted Jadon on the shoulder, and then left.

Jadon closed the door and tossed the memo paper in the bin. He checked his phone. Voicemail.

". . . not listening to me anyway. Hope you're ready to never see Paulina again, then. Don't bother calling, either."

"I'm working as hard as I can to send—goddammit!"

Jadon threw the phone at the bed.

He went to the window and peeked through the curtain gap at the parking lot. Stewart was strolling over to a black sedan. Before getting in, he shot his room another glance. Flustered, Jadon hid.

Sitting on the bed, he mulled it all over. Then he got up and fished the paper out of the trash.

■ ■ ■

The next morning, he was at the designated airport, Van Nuys. When Jadon arrived at the boarding gate for private jets, a man in a dark blue suit drew near. He tried to pick up Jadon's bag, but he rebuffed him. Jadon followed him out onto the landing strip, where, sure enough, a jet was idling, ready to take off at a moment's notice. Standing next to the boarding ramp was Stewart.

When he caught sight of Jadon, Stewart began climbing up the steps without a word. Jadon followed suit.

After Jadon settled in his seat, a cabin attendant carried a tray his way. On it lay a can of soda, a proof of bank transfer, and a receipt.

"No more alcohol for you. I sent Shirley $100,000 in your name. Just sign your name on the receipt. The Boss is the methodical type."

Stewart knew Shirley. When the two got married, Stewart had been in Paris, so he sent a bottle of champagne.

After graduating from West Point, Stewart Gobel served extensively in Afghanistan and Iran before he ended up working at NATO Headquarters in Brussels. It was on vacation in Nice that he got caught in a terrorist blast. At present, he was working for the Army chief of staff in DC.

Jadon stopped himself from asking who the Boss might be. It had nothing to do with him, surely.

"Hand over the phone, please. The operation's already started."

"I never said I'd take it up."

"It's just so that we don't give away our position. I'll give it back to you once we return. Think of it as being part of the $100,000."

The jet was flying east. Beyond Los Angeles, the desert sands sprawled in all directions. In about an hour's time, they began the descent.

"This airport . . ."

"It's called Basin Sands. Hasn't been in use since Las Vegas Airport started operating. It's largely unknown," said Stewart.

Jadon looked surprised. "I've seen photos of it, back when I was looking for a place to do desert training exercises."

Stepping onto the exit ramp, Jadon was instantly enveloped by that distinctive desert heat. A limo was idling in wait below.

The car zoomed along a stretch of road, one that would have led to Las Vegas in thirty miles going straight, but at one point they veered south. Sometime later, a fairly dilapidated hotel loomed ahead.

Soon, they entered an underground lot, where dozens of other cars were parked. Among them a large fuel tanker and two in-service electric generator cars.

They took an elevator to the first floor, and when the doors opened, Jadon froze. The space was a huge dome, bustling with both people and the latest electronics. And in front, a 100-inch screen, displaying a vista of gorgeous greenery. An aerial photo? No—it was a satellite hookup.

The dome was divided into two sections. Over in one end, a giant, U-shaped table was situated, with around twenty seats and a small monitor set up at each of them. Over in the other end sat dozens of personal-use desks in a line, each laden with piles of documents and a computer.

Two sets of three zeroes were displayed in the digital readout above the large central screen.

"It's a digital clock that started when the operation did. It's got the date and the hour," said Stewart, noting where Jadon was looking.

At the colonel's prompting, Jadon set foot inside the dome.

Some maps and a scale model lay atop the U-shaped table.

"They're maps of Cordova and its capital, La Caridad, right? And that model's the Presidential Residence."

"I imagine that, in your eyes, Cordova took everything from you, and thinking about it can't be terribly pleasant."

"What're you up to here?" said Jadon, turning to face him.

"Welcome to the War Room." A young man in a T-shirt and jeans (and some files in hand) called out to him, stopping next to him. "Hey, you're not the Border Butcher, by any chance?"

After the young man hollered behind him, Jadon could feel stares from all around the room.

"So the main player's finally showed up. Guess the operation's starting in earnest."

Stewart gave a very confused Jadon a push on the back, and together they strode forward.

"That idiot's Billy Ganaway. They let him out of prison while he was still serving time, just for this mission."

The man had been arrested three times for hacking institutions such as banks, IT companies, and even the FBI—which was his third strike. Stewart explained how, after Billy got a sentence of seven years behind bars following the FBI hacking, the man had come here on a deal offered by the Department of Justice.

Jadon had heard the name before. He remembered the headlines. "Mad Lad Billy." "Billy the Brain."

Jadon subsequently followed Stewart up to the second floor. Once there, he could see down the entire hallway.

"We actually started in earnest about two months back. Finding you was what took the most time."

Jadon turned to look behind him; the source of that voice was a man in a wheelchair. A man whose face rang some bells. He wore a well-tailored suit that fit his frame to a tee, but the creased trousers and sneakers were out of place.

"Wait, I know you . . ."

"Hello, Captain Green. My name is John Olson."

John offered his hand. Jadon shook it, only to find the man's grip was weak.

John Olson was the CEO of the world-famous ICT juggernaut, PathNet, and while he'd once been all over TV and magazines, he seemed reclusive as of late. Was his health declining? The John Olson that Jadon recalled was a fearless and intrepid man—a talented IT technician, global-scale businessman, and consummate athlete all in one. He'd even heard John used to play tennis with President Copeland, and that they were very good friends.

"I take it PathNet's moved house to the middle of the desert?" said Jadon.

PathNet, headquartered in San Jose, was a developer of database software for businesses. Its main office tower had been used in several Hollywood movies for exterior shots of a futuristic-looking building. John had founded the corporation while in his twenties. Through its innovative lineup of products, it gained enough market share to constitute half of the database market by the early 2000s. PathNet currently ranked second in terms of software company size. Its annual sales had reached the 40 billion dollar mark, and it employed 120,000 people worldwide. John himself, meanwhile, possessed total assets in excess of 32 billion dollars, making him the fifth richest person on the planet.

"Six months ago, I retired and became the Adviser to the CEO. They call me the Boss around here."

"Well, I'm not a captain anymore. Just a laborer."

"Just call me John, then. I never cared to go by the Boss. I'll call you Jadon," he smiled. The man was still in his late thirties, but over half of his hair had grayed, making him look as old as fifty. And there was always something doleful and depressive in his expression.

"What are you here to do? The central screen is satellite footage. That's military-level stuff. Accessing that doesn't come easy."

John didn't answer his question. He just shifted his gaze down the stairs. "The middle-aged guy in the glasses, that's Professor Eugene Kowalchuk. He won the Nobel Prize in economics five years ago. The blonde lady by him is a UC Berkeley psychologist named Liz Watson. The guy making a pass at her is a political aide to the former president, Tim Daniels. The muscley one in front is—"

"Nick Beasley. I know him, he's got a training company for mercs. I've seen him around, but we've never spoken," interrupted Jadon.

"Yes, he's the mercenary man. And we have communications, infrastructure, and education experts here, to name a few. Their staffs are here too . . . all assembled for this little project."

"Yeah, well, it looks like a zoo to me. You've got all the hot and trending new species. Though I guess you've got some moldy oldies cooped up in here too. What's this mismatched menagerie plotting, anyway?"

At that, John shot Stewart a quizzical look, before his eyes squared back on Jadon.

"We're going to take down the Cordovan dictatorship, and help build a new nation there." John straightened out his back a little, and stared right into Jadon's soul. "We're not just going to run roughshod over the country. We're going to leave it better than it was before. Create a better future. This is the Revolution Project for a new age, and I want you to lend a hand."

"I'm just a soldier. Or rather, I used to be. And from where I'm standing, you people are nothing more than a wrecking crew. Surely this zoo has no need of an endangered species like me."

"A wrecking crew is only ever there to pave the way toward progress. And you'll be one of our key men."

"That glorious war of yours exists only in your head. Meanwhile, it's the men in the field who fight and die."

"That's why we need you. You're the one who can keep that tragic reality to a minimum."

John just kept boring a hole through him. Jadon could sense something in those eyes . . . some higher cause that went past mere commercial gain.

"I want you to hold the reins at the field of operations. According to Colonel Gobel, you're the most capable and dependable of all the men he's trained. With your help, we'll train the Cordovan Revolutionary Army, defeat President Cortázar and the drug lord Moreno, and establish a new nation. Plans have already been made for the reconstruction phase. To that end, we must rescue revolutionary leader Luis Escárcega from the detention center—"

Jadon put his pointer finger to his lips. "Shh. Stop. I've heard enough. I'm not onboard, and I'm going home now. I only came to begin with because I was told I'd be given 100K to hang for a day."

John looked surprised. Stewart just silently looked Jadon's way.

"According to Colonel Gobel, you're the most patriotic guy around. America believes in justice, and sticks to its principles. Help us help America."

"I lost everything for the justice that America preaches. I've lost my friends, my convictions, my money, my family, and myself. So if you ask me, I've already fulfilled my duty as a US Army officer."

Jadon turned to look at Stewart with defiance in his eyes. Stewart lifted his shoulders in an exaggerated shrug, and looked down at the floor.

"You mean to say you have no interest in saving the people of Cordova?" came John's deep voice.

"The people of Cordova are on their own. Look how readily they abandoned their home for the promise of a better living, never sparing a thought to how that might impose on other countries. America gets hit by another hundred thousand or more undocumented immigrants every single year. And the same thing's happening all over Europe too. They just come flooding into richer countries, soaking up taxpayer money while the citizens bear all the strain. Can you blame people for being angry?"

"Cheap labor and diversity are what prop America up. They're why America has come to such prosperity. Also, I don't know if you know this, but part of the reason those immigrants' countries are in turmoil is thanks to the fight for hegemony by Russia, China, the powers in Europe, and yes, America itself. There have been countless proxy wars, where each side was funded, armed, and egged on by a different competing faction on the world stage, all for the sake of their own national interests. You've got to be humbler, more generous. Otherwise war will never vanish from the face of the Earth."

Jadon had no comeback. All of those things were already in the back of his mind. He vividly recalled those rows of tents in that barren moor. He recalled the single tent where a family of nine (the grandparents, the married couple, and that couple's kids) lived day to day. All they'd ever been provided was a little water and food to survive for the next few days. Half of which they had to sell in order to cover living expenses. When the food inevitably grew scarce, the children would go perpetually hungry. He remembered the people begging for United Nations food aid. The United Nations officials throwing bags of food off the tops of trucks. The folks pushing away children in order

to wrestle for the bags. Jadon had always viewed that desperation from the sidelines, but not without a measure of discomfort.

I'd never let my children or family starve. I'm not like them.

Jadon shook his head slightly and banished those thoughts. "War drives men mad and robs them of their reason. I've had enough for a lifetime," he muttered.

"Do you know how many refugees there are in the world?" asked John calmly.

"I'll be just fine if the ones at The Wall are the only ones I ever know."

"Seventy million. And that number's only getting bigger by the year. Persecution and dissension all over the world are driving people out of their hometowns and countries."

"I wouldn't run. I'd fight."

"Do you want the women and children to fight too? Without weapons or organization? If they fought, all they'd succeed in doing is die in greater numbers. But I'm with you—instead of focusing on taking them in, we should focus on giving them their homelands. Secure, reborn homelands where nobody starves." John's staring eyes brimmed with sincerity. "Please help us, if for no other reason. We want to help them build a homeland they don't have to abandon. A homeland they can live in with safety and pride."

Again, Jadon had no response. Was all that possible? *I'm nothing more than a powerless former Army man. I can't protect my own family, let alone sway the fates of nations.*

Then, a man with an eyepatch and crutches drew near. He had keloids over half his face. "I'm Antonio Alvarado. I fought alongside Professor Escárcega on the front lines of the revolution as a member of Nueva Cordova. Then I escaped from Cordova after Professor Escárcega was captured by the government half a year ago, and left for the States. President Copeland has acknowledged my asylum," he said, before heaving a deep sigh. He'd managed to get all of that out at once,

in spite of the pain evident on his face. "My family was tortured and killed, and I lost my right leg and eye. The bastards even murdered my daughter. She would have turned four years old the next day."

Four. The same age as Jadon's daughter, Paulina.

"Don't you know who I am? I'm the Border Butcher. I couldn't put a stop to the massacre. I'm not qualified as a captain. I'm just so tired of playing soldier. I don't want to see any more bloodshed. It's your country. Fight for it yourselves."

"I agree with you. People should always fight before running. If they didn't run, you might not have ended up with a name like the Border Butcher. But people have their reasons. The Tragedy at The Wall was a terrible massacre, but that doesn't mean I hate you. You tried to stop it."

Jadon remained silent. He could sense the conviction in Antonio's eyes.

"I fought for my country with everything I had," he continued. Then he thrust his right hand toward Jadon. It was missing three fingers. "We love our country too. For the sake of our children and the next generation, we want to make it a safe and prosperous place, where there's no need to escape to begin with. And we'll stake our lives and bodies to do it."

"Building a country where the kids don't need to run, huh? Sounds like a fine idea. Do your best out there." Jadon shifted his gaze to John. The man in the wheelchair looked dauntless and fierce, his features sharp, but at the same time, his expression radiated a gloom that didn't scream "former CEO of a global-scale corporation" or "super billionaire."

"Something tells me you're not giving me the full picture. Not when you've got thirty billion in the bank. You're sponsoring and spearheading the operation, but why? What's in it for you? It's dirty work, and it's not exactly in your business empire wheelhouse, either. Yet here you are, going out of your way to sink money into some third-world country."

"If I tell you it's out of sympathy for Antonio, you're not going to believe me, are you?"

"Damn straight I'm not. This whole thing is too big to be some billionaire's pet project—not to mention dangerous. We're talking about overturning an entire country."

"A task I was given by President Copeland, who's an old friend of mine. Ever since the Tragedy at The Wall, he's been hurting a great deal. I'll bet it's the same for you. So many were injured and killed by America's indiscretion—and you're one of its victims too. There's only one way to prevent such an atrocity from ever happening again—we free the people of Cordova from the dictatorship and the cartel. And despite the righteousness of our cause, we can't go public with the operation."

John's already pallid face turned whiter and his breathing grew heavier. Try as he might to continue making his case, Stewart wheeled him aside and stood in front to face Jadon directly.

"Half a year ago, several people who'd fled Cordova came to see the president. Antonio's one of them."

Antonio had been one of Professor Escárcega's pupils, as well as a lecturer of political science at Cordova University. He held Luis in high esteem, and joined him in the struggle against the dictatorship.

"They're the ones who asked President Copeland to help them build their Nueva Cordova, and he was deeply moved by their plight. But he can't mobilize his own country's military to intervene in another country's affairs. Loads of people and governments don't think kindly of American interventionism. That's why President Copeland had to ask John."

The plan to revitalize and regenerate Cordova, named Operation Caravan, was proceeding by covert order of the president.

The events of the last year flashed before Jadon's mind.

"Ever since the Arab Spring," said John, "dictatorships have fallen, but left quagmires in their wake."

Beginning with the Jasmine Revolution in Tunisia in December 2010, the movement to topple dictatorships rippled throughout the

Arab world. Up until that point, monarchies such as Saudi Arabia, Morocco, and Jordan—as well as the republics of Egypt, Syria, and Libya—had been subject to the politics of dictatorships backed by military force as a matter of course. The offending governments had maintained power through surveillance and suppression, resulting in ever-widening income disparity. The protests and demonstrations of the Arab Spring managed to take down some oppressive regimes, but without much by way of a philosophy for what the new nations should look like in place of those regimes, a power vacuum emerged, and with it, chaos and confusion.

"To avoid anarchy and unrest, and to prevent the rise of some other dictator, we need to lay the groundwork for the new nation that's to be built in place of the old. A new nation based in freedom, democracy, and economic independence. That is the new revolution, and the aim of this mission."

"It's just never gonna work out that way. You're not a politician. You're an engineer and a corporate manager. A country ain't the same as a business."

"They are the same. The plan is as tight and precise as it is elaborate, and the implementation will be equally so, all thanks to the latest AI technology. It won't be difficult."

Hearing that ironclad confidence pop out of John's mouth, an uneasy feeling seized Jadon's heart. The war in their heads would not be the war that played out on the ground. The war in their heads didn't show all the blood, the bodies, the pain.

"There must be more qualified people than me."

"I'm sorry to hear you say that. I'll have them send you back to LA tomorrow. Please stay the night. The place used to be a hotel. Not a three-star hotel, but it's got hot water."

John extended a hand. His handshake was as feeble as before.

After eating, Jadon and Stewart stepped out on the balcony. Jadon simply looked out over the desert in silence. Red-tinted sands as far as the

eye could see. For a moment, the scene at The Wall floated to mind. It had been the break of dawn, but apart from that the red sand vista was similar. Red.

Red.

Jadon shook his head, and faced Stewart. "What's John hiding?"

"Nothing. He told you everything."

"Look, I've got nothing to lose, so I've got nothing to fear. Meanwhile, he's got way too much to lose. Why's he going ahead with this silly little plan? Why's he starting a war? If I'm gonna be taking on this job, I want to know everything. I don't wanna have any doubt in my mind, dragging me down," he said, staring him down.

Stewart returned the stare. After a slight sigh: "Do you remember the Islamic extremist terror attack in France?"

"Which one?"

On July 14, 2016, a man in a truck in Nice recklessly zigzagged over the road for over a mile, killing eighty-six and injuring more than four hundred. He was a French resident born in Tunisia. Eight months earlier, several attacks took place simultaneously in Paris, where shootings and suicide bombings by suspected Islamic State terrorists killed 130 and injured over 350 people. After a string of such incidents, the blowback against refugees and immigrants turned severe.

"The one in Nice. John lost his wife Catrina and his daughter Rose. John himself lost both legs. Those legs are prosthetic. The culprit was a man who'd fled to France."

"What are you hiding? What's your connection to John?"

"Catrina was my daughter. Rose was my granddaughter. When the attack happened, my wife and I were there. Though I got off with just a leg."

"And your wife?"

"Unharmed. But losing her daughter and granddaughter at the same time did a number on her. She kept blaming herself for not being able to save them. Six months later, she overdosed on sleeping pills and died in the bathtub."

For a while, the two looked at the red sands without another word. Jadon could swear the particles of sand were flowing into his body and dyeing it an altogether different hue than his namesake.

"You really want to build a country that doesn't give rise to refugees?"

"I think it's worth trying."

"But we're not obligated to butt into another country either."

"Had it not been for the refugee crisis, my daughter and granddaughter would be alive today. My wife too. John and I have both lost the ones we loved the most, same as you. I just have to hope it never happens again," said Stewart, in hushed tones.

Stewart's words spoke to him.

Before Jadon knew it, the light baking the sands had given way to the dark of night.

"Is this the reason you saved me from the court-martial? Why I'm not in prison right now?"

Stewart didn't answer. They just kept staring into the black.

"Even if you die, the money will go toward your family. It's too cold out here. Let's tuck in early. The operation starts tomorrow."

At that, they returned to their rooms.

Jadon couldn't sleep. Every time he was about to nod off, a giant wall would appear in the darkness . . . along with the corpses of women and children with bullet holes through the head, lying in piles alongside his own family's bodies. He got out of bed, sat at the computer desk, and pulled up satellite photos of Cordova.

Tropic vegetation covered over half of the country's land, shining bright in the sunlight. The Pacific lay to the west, and the jungles to the east. It only took about six miles walking across a neighboring country to reach the Caribbean Sea.

Click. The screen now showed research documents detailing information on everything there was to know about Cordova. Though the rainforest's resources and the underground minerals (including rare earth metals) had yet to be gauged with much accuracy, they appeared

to be quite promising. According to some sources, if the political situation were to stabilize, and public order restored, companies the world over would rush in. Jadon looked up details on the country's economics, industry, education, and various other fields.

Before heading the dictatorship, Cortázar had been an elite soldier who graduated from the Military Academy of Cordova. When he was a major general, at the age of forty-two, he took over in a military coup, and his rule had persisted for over a decade. Furthermore, he'd consolidated even more power in the subsequent years.

According to the psychoanalysis section, signed off on by psychologist Liz Watson: "He's a brilliant mind, with a high capacity for analysis and judgment, and a steady hand, but he's also deeply suspicious by nature, and he does have his impulsive side. Those inclinations have only grown stronger and stronger in recent years."

■ ■ ■

Jadon reached out a desperate hand. His body drifted back, back into the clutching darkness.

Help me. Save me!

But all that leaked from his throat was a hoarse groan.

He was in the desert now, standing, baking. A man materialized, a blood-soaked child held high in his hands. The woman lying at his feet was perhaps the wife and mother. The shouting was most likely excoriating America and the Butcher.

The blackness proceeded to swallow Jadon whole, its dark particles permeating every single cell in his body in the hopes of converting his mass into yet more shadow.

Good. Just drag me to hell already.

A noise reverberated from the bowels of the void, startling him awake. He got up and grabbed the receiver from the desk.

"Did you get a good night's sleep?"

It took Jadon a beat to realize it was John. "Nope. Barely caught a wink, actually. I was thinking about your plan. And about my role in it."

No noise. The man on the other end must have stopped in his tracks. ". . . I'll send someone. Please come with us to the War Room."

Less than five minutes later, he heard a knock on the door. It was the wheelchair-bound man himself. And judging by the sweat on his brow, he'd made haste.

"It ended up being me. Have you packed your things? Let's get out of here."

A few dozen men and women were already gathered in the dome-style hall.

John spoke to a captive audience through a mic: "The last piece of the puzzle is here with us. Today, Operation Caravan is officially a go. I'd like each one of you to carry out your mission without forgetting the weight on your shoulders. And never let your guard down. Together we'll establish a new nation, from which the children will never need to flee. May God bless us all."

The digital clock on the wall began to tick. The eclectic team of specialists was seated at the U-shaped table, with John at its head.

"In twenty days' time, we will have retaken Cordova, setting upon the creation of a new nation."

The people who had been summoned here were dressed as they pleased. Some were in white lab coats, some in suits and ties, and some in jeans and T-shirts. Jadon was in the jeans camp, though he had a work shirt on. When he'd been discharged, he'd burned all of his ACUs to cinders. All he had left were his combat boots. They were perfectly natural on him, like extensions of his feet.

The Republic of Cordova was a small country in northern Central America, about sixty square miles in size. It had a handful of islands off its Pacific coast, and its total population was just under eight million. It had obtained independence from Spain in the late 1800s, but the most widely spoken language was still Spanish. Its capital was named

La Caridad, and its main industry was agriculture. Its GDP was below 20 billion USD, less than half the yearly revenue of John's corporation, PathNet. As one of the most destitute nations in Central America, it was designated by the IMF as an HIPC (heavily indebted poor country). Though nominally a republic with a president as head of state, political affairs had been unstable for decades upon decades, with successive military governments coming into power since 1930. In 2010, the president at that time declared a constitutional referendum, aiming to remain president for life. On the day of the election, however, the military sprang a coup, with then-Major General Cortázar instated as interim president. The military currently employed twelve thousand troops, seven thousand of which comprised the Cordovan Army. There was also a presidential elite guard regiment that reported directly to Cortázar.

"Cordova is ruled over by former military darling Gumersindo Cortázar," stated Stewart, using the diagrams and photos projected on the giant screen as aids. "More than half of the nation's budget goes toward strengthening the military by way of arms purchases. In terms of force of arms, Cordova has its bordering nations beat. Those nations, fearing retaliation, refuse to allow in fleeing Cordovans."

"With regard to his mental state," came Liz Watson's voice through the speaker, "Cortázar's the paranoid sort. He's unforgiving and vindictive, and he doesn't trust his subordinates as far as he can throw them. He's already executed twenty or so close associates, and he always surrounds himself with blood relatives. As you might expect from maintaining power for this long, he's no dummy, and he knows how to get things done. He is attentive, and not to be underestimated."

The night before, Jadon had looked her up on Wikipedia. She was a UCLA professor, specializing in war psych.

"Like Cortázar," she continued, "José Moreno, the head of the cartel Los Eternos, has great sway over Cordova—"

"The Eternals, huh," said Billy Ganaway.

"That's what they fancy themselves as. Makes you laugh, doesn't it? Anyway, the punks are channeling large amounts of cocaine into the American heartland. There's been no major conflict between the dictatorship and the cartel. They're essentially keeping each other in check, each unable to get a grasp of the extent of the other's power. But it's definitely a touch-and-go situation."

"A mother lode of tin has been discovered in the mountains," said Professor Eugene Kowalchuk. "Many companies from all over the world would jump at the opportunity if the country solicited for development assistance, with political stability and lasting public order as the conditions of doing business. The hope is that they can eventually develop by their own power at some point. There's actually a bunch more underground resources that are promising too. They'll be needing foreign investment and technical assistance for sure though."

Next to speak was former presidential aide Tim Daniels. "Just talking poli sci here, but I think the next president ought to be Luis Escárcega. The guy's a class act, and everybody in the country loves and respects him. But he's being held prisoner as the rebel ringleader. If we spring him and put him on top of the revolution, we can secure the support of the people and the other anti-government forces."

Daniels filled them in on the makeup of said anti-government forces. At present, the largest was the Revolutionary Army, also known as Nueva Cordova, which was headed by former Army Captain Sebastian Loyola. Six years prior, he'd grown disillusioned with the direction of the country under Cortázar, escaped from the military (taking several of his subordinates with him), and formed the Revolutionary Army. While a stern man, he was also a man of integrity who said what he meant and meant what he said, and more than worthy of their trust— or so vouched Antonio Alvarado.

Nueva Cordova comprised around two hundred people, but it enjoyed wide support among all regions of the country, and could presumably multiply its ranks tenfold if called for.

Various voices streamed in through the mic.

"Professor Escárcega is loved and believed in by the whole

populace. If he calls out to Cordova, the people will rise up. There's a fair number of his former students in the military, and lots besides who support him in secret. That's why Cortázar's got him behind bars—and his head on the chopping block."

"So we break him out and set him up as the leader of Nueva. That's the easiest way."

"But we don't know if Luis is up to it. Going by the intel I've gathered, he's been in shackles for so long he's gotten weaker both mentally and physically."

Suddenly, Jadon got on his feet. Now everyone's eyes were on him.

"I get the gist of Cordova's situation. And I know what you people are trying to do—using AI. So how many boots on the ground and guns in holsters is it gonna take to topple Cortázar and wipe out the cartel? You just gotta run some numbers through the AI and you'll have your answer, right?"

Their eyes roamed in search of someone who'd reply to Jadon's question. It was Nick Beasley who spoke up. The merc training company consultant had a scar running from the back of his left hand up his arm. He was famous in the industry, and a friend of Stewart's.

"Los Eternos have an estimated 1,500 combatants. They've got the latest weapons too. No other group can hold a candle to them. The military is 12,000 strong. The president's guard will be a much tougher nut to crack. They're not elite by any stretch, but it's got three hundred people. By comparison, Nueva's got maybe two hundred."

"That's pathetic. What the hell strategy can we even use?"

"That's why we need to pick the brain of a top-notch commander. Though maybe you aren't up to the task after all," said Nick, shooting Jadon a prodding look.

Moreno, the kingpin of Los Eternos, was once a vice commander of the president's guard. In addition to former colleagues and subordinates, he employed soldiers and police officers at high salaries. Their main source of funding was through the production, refinement, and sale of drugs—mostly cocaine. They also profited through ransoming and selling stolen goods. Los Eternos clawed their way to supremacy in Cordova's underworld on a mound of corpses, with more than a thousand total casualties on both sides of the war against their erstwhile rival cartel. Their monthly revenue often reached the 60 million USD range, and Moreno himself possessed $4 billion. Los Eternos were known for their various acts of cruelty, like the kidnapping, torture, and murder of peasant farmers who declined to grow narcotics. Needless to say, both the US and Mexican governments had prices on Moreno's head.

"The crux of the operation isn't just taking the government by force. Our ultimate objective is democratic nation building," said John, standing up to calm the two down.

The central screen displayed descriptions of Cordova's manufacturing, agriculture, and other industries, as well as detailed figures on production and the country's existing conditions. John and the specialists from each relevant field had worked together to analyze and quantify every corner of Cordova, and to run a simulation for a functioning, independent state. They were among the world's top experts.

"They're actually making lots of money, surprisingly. What's failing Cordovans is production and distribution," said John, as he glared at his computer.

"In just Moreno's and Cortázar's bank accounts, two years' worth of the national budget is stockpiled," said Tim Daniels, amazed.

The meeting ended in around two hours. It mostly involved going over the whats and wheres of Cordova, and the time schedule they were to follow.

The second Jadon returned to his room and hit the hay, he heard a knock.

In entered Stewart and a nurse. Stewart took out a new smartphone.

"I'll be holding onto your phone until after the end of the operation. I transferred all of your data into this one. It's tap-proof."

"It's not just Cordova that's affected, huh? There are other countries who'd be interested enough to intercept our communications?"

"It's for assurance's sake. We can't be slapping more stuff to worry about on the president's desk."

Stewart signaled the nurse. Brandishing a syringe, she drew closer to Jadon. "Your arm, please. Every participant in the operation's accepted the shot." A cylindrical capsule, 0.4 inches long and 0.08 inches in diameter. "It's a transmitter. It'll tell us where you are, and the status of your vitals."

"And once the operation's complete?"

"We'll take it right back out of you, of course."

Jadon gave her his arm.

■ ■ ■

In a room at the FBI Academy stood a fresh new face for the force, Adán Solano. The special agent was training in video analysis under the guidance of his superior, Vanessa Smith. He'd also learned the ins and outs of how to use facial recognition software.

Recruitment exams for the FBI were said to be more challenging than the bar exam in many states, demanding applicants to have skills on par with holders of advanced degrees—such as Juris Doctor.

"This isn't what I became an agent to do. I want to arrest serial killers and kidnappers. I want to take down evil crime syndicates," he told her.

He'd already been glowering at the computer display for nearly three hours now, and he was fed up. A twenty-six-year-old second-generation immigrant from Chile, Adán graduated from MIT's Department of Electrical Engineering and Computer Science, before attending a State University of New York law school. Focusing much of his interest on the issue of immigrant crime, he'd spent thirty minutes in his interview about his opinions on the subject, including illegal immigration. *The government and related organizations should work together to fight against the issue on a more fundamental level.* It wasn't exactly a new take, but his enthusiasm and earnest desire to persuade the listeners earned him points. Vanessa, a thirty-five-year-old black woman, had been one of his interviewers.

"Good detective work's always just a series of low-profile inquiries stacked together, so I need you to do what your boss tells you to do. Your supervisor's nothing if not competent."

"Well, apparently having competent supervisors isn't reducing America's crime rate any. We need more active agents—"

"Real-life agents and police officers aren't like the ones you see in movies and TV. The vast majority go through their entire careers without firing a bullet at a single soul. I haven't had to, either—not yet. And that's something to be grateful for. We've reached the age of science-based forensics, computers, and AI. Leave the cuffing to bigger, beefier guys. We'll be here using our heads over our guns."

"And staring at hours of video footage is using our heads?"

"This is so you recognize how useful artificial intelligence can be. But you can't leave it all to robots just yet; you've got your human pride to uphold."

For this training exercise, he had to make use of facial recognition software based on the most cutting-edge AI advancements to pinpoint a wanted criminal in the crowd at JFK Airport—a task nigh on impossible for the unaided eye. In two hours of staring, he just couldn't find someone who fit the description. If he didn't know better, he'd call this training an excuse to bully him, because Vanessa had tracked down the perp in three minutes using AI.

Vanessa's phone rang, and she glanced his way as she got up. "Find the guy before I get back. Don't throw in the towel against the AI," she said, giving him a pat on the shoulder before taking her leave.

Just as Vanessa had instructed, he looked into the vicinity of the international arrivals gate using his own eyes, as well as conventional facial recognition software not loaded with AI.

Thirty minutes passed, and he was nearing the limits of his patience. He stretched, only for the screen to display the file list of past recordings. He clicked on one of the files more or less at random. It just so happened to be *The Tragedy at The Wall.*

A year ago, when Adán had been a law school student, he'd glued himself to the TV watching news of the sorry affair unfold. As a second-generation immigrant himself, the incident hit a little close to home.

"Jesus Christ," he muttered, without meaning to.

It was helicopter footage of the soldiers firing on the refugees rushing up The Wall. The audio consisted of the whir of propellers and gunfire, lots and lots of gunfire. A shriek from a female reporter could also be heard. And at the base of The Wall, countless bodies, most of which belonged to women, children, and the elderly.

A man was standing up, holding a girl in his hands and screaming. Adán switched the vantage point to a worm's-eye view. The man was speaking in Spanish: "America's killed my wife and daughter. They are the devil. I will have my revenge. I will kill you all."

They weren't words to live by, but with that level of carnage, Adán could understand.

He clicked replay. Something was nagging at him about the video. It was *different*, somehow, from what the media had put out. Was this footage never made public?

The first gunshot . . .

Adán opened the other files, leaning closer to the screen. "I've never seen *that*," he exclaimed.

While FBI Headquarters were run out of the J. Edgar Hoover Building in DC, the Laboratory Division and the Operational Technology Division were across the Potomac in Quantico, Virginia, as was the FBI Academy, located within Quantico's Marine Corps Base. With many branches (namely, the Intelligence, National Security, Science and Technology, Information and Technology, and Human Resources branches, as well as the Criminal, Cyber, Response, and Services Branch) and with fifty-six field offices, the FBI had the wherewithal to investigate terrorism, espionage, federal corruption, cases involving multiple states, and large-scale burglaries, among other crimes.

The Oval Office was situated in the White House's West Wing. The president's family lived in the East Wing.

President Copeland tapped his smartphone, but only after making sure no one was around.

Bob was fifty-two years old, and a Democrat. His daughter, Patricia, was born when he'd been nearly forty, and he doted on her with abiding affection. It had already been a year since she'd told him she hated him. He believed their relationship was mended, at least on the surface, but the Tragedy at The Wall was now taboo.

"Is this line safe?"

"Our security's perfect, Mr. President. If there's ever a problem, it's on the White House's end."

"We're using you for our security. And please, John, when it's just us, call me Bob."

"Understood, Mr. Pres—Bob."

The president got up off the sofa and sat back down on his desk's swivel chair. "I wanted to ask you about Operation Caravan. You messaged me that the last piece of the puzzle's in place, and that the operation's a go?"

"Captain Green arrived yesterday. He refused at first, but we convinced him to join."

"I read up on his army track record. I feel guilty that his life turned into a mess after the Tragedy too. I mean, to get hit with a dishonorable discharge . . . But is it really wise to send him to Cordova? He was the captain when the Tragedy happened."

"I have no idea. It was my father-in-law, his former superior, who recommended him. The colonel believes in him."

"I still remember Catrina and Rose. It was such a crushing loss. Is it because of that attack that you're supporting me now?"

"The world we live in is full of contradictions and absurdities. That was one of them. The Tragedy at The Wall was another. People with their whole lives ahead of them can die out of nowhere, just like that. And if there's one absurdity I'd like to fix, it's that one."

"Usually, we'd send in the Army, but . . ."

"That's not an option. That is, unless you're willing to give up on reelection in favor of congressional hearings."

Bob was at a loss for what to say. There were times he honestly thought he *should* do just that. But it wasn't as though America had won every fight it'd been in. In fact, the country had racked up more failures than victories—Vietnam and Afghanistan came to mind. And why?

It was the guy before me who built The Wall. And it didn't just divide nations. It also divided people.

"This operation will be in the hands of Cordovan nationals. We're just providing an assist. It won't surface."

"Right, you're right. America's time to shine comes later. We're going to aid the new Cordova—not through weapons, but through the spirit of economic development and peace."

"The preparations to make that happen have already been made, Bob. Besides, this operation isn't just Cordova's. It's also for America's sake."

In recent years, the number of illegal immigrants had exceeded seventy thousand. Cases where people turned themselves into the border guards after crossing and applied for refugee status were on the rise. The US legal system allowed people to stay and work in the United States during their screening process after applying. In addition, more than half of the people or groups had children with them. The presence of children made their detention periods shorter.

Most illegal immigrants came from Central America, and the Texas facilities boarding them had been exceeding capacity for a long time. They were pulling through thanks to the efforts of churches and volunteer organizations offering the meals, clothes, and transportation methods they needed.

"It's as you say. And ultimately, it'll benefit the whole world. New measures will be taken against the global refugee crisis too."

The global refugee count was now at nearly thirty million, including Syria, Afghanistan, South Sudan, Somalia, the Democratic Republic of Congo, and Myanmar. And if one added people who couldn't cross any borders—remaining within their countries of citizenship in camps after losing their homes due to civil war, violence, or disasters—that figure more than doubled. More than 370,000 had been killed in Syria, and thirteen million were roaming the war-torn country. Of these, five million had fled their hometowns and lived as refugees in foreign lands like Turkey, Jordan, and Iraq. Many had crossed borders on foot, or crossed the Mediterranean by boat to reach Europe. Iraq, the new home of many of those refugees, was nearing its breaking point, with internal strife lasting years and years. Approximately a third of the refugees were children. Malnutrition, forced marriage, and violence at evacuation destinations were often brought up as serious issues around the globe.

"I'm grateful, and I pray that you and your fellow fighters will be rewarded for your bravery."

With that, he dropped the line. The president looked out on the yard for a few moments.

The scene from a year earlier came unbidden to mind once again. Patricia watching the footage with tears in her eyes. The words "I hate you!" hanging sadistically in the air. Never would he forget her expression, her tone.

At present, Patricia was behaving no differently from how she had before the incident, but she did turn a dubious eye toward him from time to time. He knew it wasn't just his imagination.

The southernmost region of the United States shared the same climate and geology as Mexico, and yet there was great economic disparity between the two. Many Mexicans and Central Americans were in the United States in search of work. The former president had erected The Wall based on the idea that illegal immigrants were taking jobs from American citizens and committing crimes, but The Wall had done nothing to curb the numbers. The root causes—economic inequality and political instability—remained unaddressed.

Eliminating illegal immigration, then, required the stabilization of the respective political realms of Latin America, and an across-the-board increase in the countries' economic power. In Cordova's case, they needed to destroy the cartel and rescue the citizens from the pit of fear and brutality. Then they'd have to remove the dictatorship and release the people from its tyranny. But neither the United States nor the United Nations could actively intervene in the nation's domestic affairs.

During the Arab Spring, dictatorships had collapsed almost by chance, but several new powers soon swooped in to fill the vacuum, sparking yet more pain and strife. John and the others were trying to raise Cordova to its full potential, down to creating a new system and revitalizing its economy. If they succeeded, it would serve as a model to forever look back on.

The president's eyes turned to the desk calendar to check the date. John had told him the operation would span twenty days. He took a pen and marked the date.

■ ■ ■

2

THE ROAD TO CORDOVA

In the previous year, more than a thousand political prisoners had been arrested and detained in Cordova. With a total lack of freedom of speech in effect, Cortázar's power over the military became absolute. In addition, nearly a thousand murders kept occurring each year, alongside myriad assaults, kidnappings, cases of extortion, and rapes. Much of it had to do with Los Eternos. And those were just the crimes that came to light—the tip of the iceberg. Cordova was in a vice grip of poverty and fear, but the preparations necessary to liberate the nation from the dictatorship and cartel were underway.

The first stage of the plan constituted a military campaign centered on Stewart Gobel, Jadon Green, Nick Beasley, and Antonio Alvarado. They would send mercs and weapons to Cordova as advance troops, as well as train up the soldiers of the Revolutionary Army, while the minds in the War Room formulated concrete operation plans to take down Los Eternos and the Cortázar regime. The second stage involved sending a combat unit commanded by Jadon to rescue Luis Escárcega, currently held captive by government forces. Luis would then serve as the Revolutionary Army's leader, aid in defeating the regime, and set up a new government in its place. Meanwhile, John was spearheading the preparations for the nation-building that would take place after the new administration's founding. The lead players had to be Cordovans, such as Luis, Antonio, and their allies.

Many a meeting took place in the War Room discussing the new Cordova.

"This will be a new form of nation-building that makes free use of AI tech. Taking into account info from all the relevant fields— geology, topology, resources, climate, population figures, demographics, education levels, national history, and current industry metrics— we can create an optimal framework for the country. We're now able to immediately identify where the infrastructure is lacking, what forms of transportation are needed, what the most suitable crops are, and what industries ought to be promoted. It'll show us Cordova's ideal form," stated for the first time Professor Kowalchuk, an economist.

"It all seems a bit, I don't know, *dull* to be leaving it all up to robots," said Liz Watson, "but I guess that's the best method we've got at the moment. For the time being, let's just focus on making a country where residents can retain their humanity. Then the people there can and should make their own decisions. I can analyze the psychology of the nation and give advice on that front."

"Professor Escárcega's a political scholar, and an economist too. He himself must have a vision for Cordova. If we leave it up to him, the people are sure to rally behind him."

"Sounds like the birth of an American puppet state," quipped Billy Ganaway.

"Not so. President Copeland has no involvement whatsoever."

"It's true this revolution business failed in the Arab world. Tunisia, Egypt, Libya . . . their dictatorships all collapsed, only for their situations to get even worse. Syria's a quagmire. Ever since the major powers like America, China, and Russia stuck their hands in, and new regional powers like the IS came to be, it's tough to imagine how it could get any worse. In order to prevent that mess from happening again, we'll be working out the details of the nation-building well in advance of the actual shift in power."

"First things first, we make sure it becomes a country its citizens don't need to be fleeing for parts unknown. A land of peace and security beloved by the people, where the children's bellies are full."

Jadon was simply listening to the others' back-and-forth. From what he'd heard so far, this was just a room of experts *talking* at each other. They had yet to see the hell that was to come. The *real* hell. Taking down two ruthless organizations and constructing a new Cordova in their ashes? That was easy enough to say, but the devil was in the doing. Sacrifices and suffering would be inevitable. Blood would be shed, and lives lost.

"I want to know more about the rebel forces within Cordova," Jadon told Antonio.

"Since Professor Escárcega's capture, Nueva Cordova has been in a state of collapse; it wasn't a large force to begin with. The professor was always reluctant to take part in armed conflict. He was trying to raise public awareness by calling out to the people, including the people in the government. He even seemed to think there were soldiers in the military who had heard his words and believed in him. But I think he had to face reality when they took him in."

"No, it wasn't because no one believed in him. The regime apprehended him and took him out of the public eye because they saw him as a threat," said John forcefully. "Our first objective is springing the professor. He'll be the one to direct the rebel forces. Without him, we can't win this fight. The leading players need to be Cordovans and Cordovans only. All we are is a helping hand. The international community won't approve of any meddling on our part. Even after the people have retaken the country, rebuilding is the job of Cordovans and the United Nations. We're staying covert throughout."

"Cortázar is getting cozy with Russia," said Antonio. "They're thinking of doing joint development of their underground resources with Russia's military assistance. But it seems he's a bit too overwhelmed dealing with Los Eternos for now." Antonio worked the computer using his mobility-impaired hand and pulled up the map of Cordova.

After the meeting, Jadon heard more about the situation in the country from him; checking that info against the American military's intel was all in order to hatch a plan to recapture Cordova's halls of power. Directly involved in the military operation were Stewart, Jadon, Antonio, and mercenary training company consultant Nick Beasley. The other specialists would be on the sidelines to capitalize on their expertise and lend their indirect aid.

"Before anything else, we need mercs and weapons. We breach the Cordovan border with the mercs, join up with the revolutionaries, and train them."

Antonio was nodding, but there was no telling how much he understood.

"I want you to be in touch with the locals, and make preparations to receive them. We'll gather the soldiers and secure a space for training. We'll send in a preliminary wave of ten mercs. They'll train your comrades into real soldiers."

"We can shoot guns too. What we need is weapons."

"You people don't know a damned thing. That's why you ended up in such a sorry state. War is about which side is the best at killing, and the enemy's a well-trained force of pros. You need provisions and training in equal measure. You need the mercs."

Stewart and Nick were listening, but didn't say a word. Nick was a friend of Stewart's, and an expert on mercenary training. Jadon had heard the two were contemporaries at West Point.

A vista of gentle desert hills stretched before their eyes. Jadon came with Nick to a merc training company in the deserts of eastern California. Jadon used to go there all the time when he was still commissioned.

"I was told by John to collect only the best mercs and weapons. Looks like money's no issue."

"Don't go talking about how money's no issue to anyone besides me. The people we'll be meeting are selling stuff without a list price. They decide the price after sizing up the buyer. They could easily tack on a few zeroes on the price if they think the client's good for it. It feels better to get money than to spend it. And buyers don't know how good the product is until they use it. That can be said for both mercs and weapons. That's how we've always negotiated. But now we're the ones spending. Make cost-effectiveness your number one priority," said Nick, his eyes still on the hills.

The two were standing in front of the window of the room they'd been escorted to, watching the training exercises play out on the hills. Tanks were trundling across the hillside, infantry running in the vicinity. A cloud of sand and dust rose up from the hill ahead, and they could feel the mellow rumbling of the fired shells in their guts. At the sound of an automatic rifle, the infantry started running.

"What do you think of the plan? Give it to me straight," said Jadon.

Nick's gaze didn't stray from the training exercises unfolding on the faraway hills. "What do you think? You took the job because you figured the plan can work."

"No, I took it because I had no other choice. There's no way it actually works."

Nick glanced his way. "You drew the shortest stick. We backup guys won't have to shed a single drop of sweat, or witness any bloodshed."

"You're not going?"

"At my age? Stewart wanted to go, but I stopped him. With his body in that state, he'd just be a liability. We'll be helping you and the mercs from the War Room. That way you can make it back alive."

"You'd better give me decent enough logistics support."

"I looked at your military record. You were so close to making it big. Your achievements in Afghanistan and Iraq were impressive. You even got a Silver Star. If that border incident hadn't happened—"

"I want to forget all about it. Don't tell me there's nothing *you'd* rather forget."

"Oh, I've got nothing." Nick's line of sight shifted back toward the hills.

After an hour of waiting, a man in a suit and tie appeared. His shoes were so shiny they almost reflected his face. Behind him stood a man in camo, but by his looks, he wasn't one of the soldiers from the training zone. There wasn't a single grain of sand on his boots. Behind both men, another man who was around six feet five was watching with his arms crossed.

The man in the suit strode over to Jadon's and Nick's side. "They're doing battle training in two groups. One group's the mercs, the other's the enemy."

"Are you using live ammo?" asked Jadon.

"Only when necessary. Today's ammo is . . ."

He looked at the man in camo behind him.

". . . rubber bullets. Live ammo leads to both government suits and trainees complaining. It's only used for dedicated firearms training."

"You're here to procure mercs and weapons, if I recall. What kind of manpower do you need? What types of weapons, and how many of each type?"

Jadon handed the suit a list. He took it and perused.

"How many soldiers do you have with battle experience who can speak Spanish? They need to speak English, too, of course."

The man looked behind him and asked the fellow in camo. "Not many. We don't get too many straight-A linguistics enthusiasts here."

"We could do with thirty or so," said Nick over Jadon's shoulder.

"We can give you ten at most."

Nick patted Jadon on said shoulder. "Let's go back."

The tall one stood between Nick and the door. Nick stomped on the man's foot; he bent over, and Nick raised his shin aiming for the man's face. Soon he was rolling on the floor groaning. Nick proceeded toward the door without missing a beat. Jadon hurriedly followed.

The two exited the building, and headed for the airport. Nick drove.

"Where'd you find that company, anyway?"

"I was still in the Army when that deal went down."

"So the military's been involved with an outfit that sloppy? No wonder the quality of troops has dropped."

"I just watch how the training's going and write reports. It's a government official who makes the final decisions."

"How was it? Are you sticking by the contract?"

"I'm not sure. Where else do I get mercs and weapons? Maybe I should hit up a veterans association."

Jadon didn't respond to that nugget of sarcasm.

"I'll come up with thirty Spanish-speaking mercs and the weapons on the list in two days."

Nick pulled out the weapons list from Jadon's chest pocket. Automatic rifles, grenades, mortars, explosives, and other small arms were written alongside numbers, as was their ammo. All bound for Cordova. They were mainly American military standard M16 rifles, with more than a few MP5 submachine guns to boot.

"These are how the rebel forces we're training fight the good fight."

"We're having them fight against a whole country's military with *these*? They'll get wiped out on day one."

"The rebel soldiers have weapons of their own." Nick crossed out some of the weapons on the list with a pen, and added some alternatives. "Like this, it'll be easier to get a hold of all of them. And it makes more sense like this too. These, you can use both in the jungle and on the streets. But if you think the old list is better, I'll go ahead with that."

"I've got a feeling you're the better judge of that," said Jadon, skimming the new list.

"What do we do with these mercs and weapons?" Nick asked.

"We put ten of them on a civilian aircraft as soon as possible so they can start training the rebels. The plane will fly toward the Cordovan border, and they will make the rest of the way to the destination by car and by foot. That'll get them nice and used to the terrain and climate by the time they reach the camp. I've asked Antonio to send a guide."

"The problem is transporting the rest of the mercs and weapons. They won't fit on civilian planes."

"We'll stow them onto military transport planes, hiding them in plain sight. Transport planes fly out to the US base in Colombia on a daily basis. We'll have them drop off the mercs and weapons on their way over. Revolutionary Army trucks will be waiting at the drop-off points. They'll be close enough to the rebel camp to arrive the next morning. Antonio's seen to it."

"It's a nice stroke of luck, having the military at our disposal. I knew that Silver Star of yours wasn't a fluke. Your subordinates must've placed a lot of faith in you. But won't the military find out?"

"The second they find out, the operation's done for. John's bearing all the responsibility so that the president isn't affected."

Nick nodded. Jadon had been in the military for more than a decade, but he'd never met a man quite like Nick. The man didn't care much for the military, but he sure was well-versed as to its inner workings.

■ ■ ■

That evening, Jadon and Nick returned to the War Room, deep in the Nevada desert. John had invited the two to dinner, but they turned him down and retired to their rooms. Jadon called an old subordinate of his, Sergeant Jason Rooker. Nick was right—there were still plenty in the armed forces who thought the world of old Captain Green, and Sergeant Rooker was one of them.

The Silver Star was awarded to those who saved the lives of their brothers and sisters in arms, and quite a few people regarded Jadon as the reason they were alive and kicking.

"Is that you, captain, sir?" Jason lowered his voice the second he realized it was Jadon on the other end. "Where have you been all this time? I kept asking around, but no one seemed to know, and you even went and changed your number. Not to mention how all the mail I sent kept coming back to me."

"I've got a favor to ask. And it's not the kind you can refuse. Do you want to hear it?"

"Not at all. Let me guess, it's only barely aboveboard legally."

"Oh, no, it's totally illegal. That said, it's for the sake of the country. And it'd be helping people in need."

"All right, I'll bite. I'm intrigued now."

"I repeat: once you hear it, you can't refuse."

Jason paused for a moment, before lowering his voice even more. "That's hardly fair, sir. Now if I turn you down, I won't be able to catch a night's sleep in who knows how long. Okay, I'm ready. Hit me with it."

Jadon told Jason about the plan to transport the mercenaries and weapons. Jason absorbed it all without so much as a peep. "I won't cause you too much trouble, I promise," said Jadon.

"This alone's more than enough 'trouble' already, sir. If I get found out, I'm not getting off with a military discharge. I'd get court-martialed and thrown behind bars at the lockup."

"I'll come visit you. And I'll bring you loads of goodies from the outside."

"Don't forget to bring some ladies in with you. You know my type."

"One more thing, Jason. You still got that in with the Defense Intelligence Agency?"

Jason heaved an effusive sigh. "Sorry to tell you, but we broke up. She resigned and got hitched. But you're not going to let that stop you, are you, captain?"

"So you finally get me, I see. I want you to look into something for me."

Jadon listed off the place and a handful of names. Jason listened silently.

"I know what the official release says. I want to know what's beyond that."

"There's something beyond that? I'll try and do what I can. I just need time," said Jason. He was palpably relieved; Jadon's request wasn't so bad.

"How much time?"

"Three days."

"Do it in two. Send the info to the place I tell you."

With a hushed "yes, sir," the call was dropped.

An hour later, Jason called back, and the time and place of the rendez-vous four days from now were disclosed.

"It's a military aircraft doing cargo shipping runs. It makes a stop at Choiba Airport in Colombia to refuel and load more freight. That's where we'll drop off the unregistered soldiers and weapons. We'll tell people this is a top-secret government operation. Top-secret missions of that ilk do happen from time to time."

"How many times have missions like that happened?"

"This operation would be the second time, sir. Also, the meeting time needs to be strictly adhered to. Being a single solitary second late means not getting to board. If something happens, I'll say I don't know a thing. I ask you to do the same, captain."

"Roger. I owe you one."

"Hold on, sir. We're talking twenty soldiers and 1.5 tons of cargo That can only be weapons and ammo, right? Who are we waging war against?"

"If you don't know a thing and you want it to stay that way, then don't ask me."

"Please, you've got to win this thing, sir. If you take another L, there'll be nowhere left to go for you."

Jason wished him good luck and hung up. Jadon exhaled and reseated himself. Jason's words echoed in his mind.

* * *

In 2018, the Kurdish paramilitary group backed by the American military carried out an operation to clear out Islamic State remnants in the east of Syria. The IS had set its sights on attacking the al-Tanak oilfield, and commenced attacks on al-Bahra and Gharanij, villages where two of the bases of the paramilitary group in the vicinity were located.

Jadon was rushing alongside five subordinates in a military vehicle. His whole body was banging against the body of the car from the high impacts. It charged into the rubble by the side of the road, and came to a stop at a slant, its tires elevated on one side. The stench of gasoline pervaded the inside of the car.

"We got hit. Car's not responding. Everyone get off, it's gonna blow."

The doors refused to open. Pounding gunfire ripped through the air. A soldier by his side had his head hanging down. Jadon pulled him up by the hair. Half of his face was missing. He pulled out the subordinate sitting behind him. He was still breathing, but he kept coughing blood. His lungs had been sprayed.

Jadon shouldered the last remaining subordinate who was still alive and ran like mad. Intense pain stabbed at his side, and he nearly buckled at the knees, but he regained his bearings and made a last dash for a bombarded building.

An explosion caused a gale of heated wind to pelt at his back. He glanced back to find the car blown to bits, now home only to roaring flames and a shroud of black billowing smoke. It had eaten a rocket.

Jadon endured enemy attacks for two hours before the rescue copter finally made it to the scene. The man he saved managed to survive, and he was none other than Jason Rooker.

The US military-led coalition supported paramilitary groups for airstrikes and land operations, but nearly fifty people died in the space of two days, with an additional thirty-nine dead on the IS side.

Just as he'd promised, Nick had secured thirty Spanish-speaking mercs and the weapons on the list by the crack of dawn. "Ten Spanish-speaking mercs will be gathered at Van Nuys this afternoon to board the plane for Colombia. There'll be people there to greet them, right?"

"They'll be waiting for them at Choiba. Antonio arranged for the trucks."

"The weapons will be stored in a warehouse in downtown LA later today. We can carry them out of there whenever we're ordered."

"And the other twenty mercs?"

"We're mustering them from all over the country. They'll be assembled and ready to go by sometime tomorrow. The people who've already arrived are in different places across LA."

"The military plane's ready to go. It'll leave for Cordova once the mercs and weapons are aboard."

"The secret's not going to get out internally within the military?"

"Looks like there are sometimes special missions that go unrecorded. Every operation stands apart, so there's no inter-communication. They're men we can trust. Let's just leave it to them."

"I hope you're right about them," said Nick under his breath.

That evening, Jadon and Nick were in the War Room discussing the remaining mercs. Antonio came in with news that the first wave of mercs had joined the Cordovan rebels and they were now headed to the Revolutionary Army camp together.

"Next is us."

"Not us. You. I told you I don't like being on-site. We'll support you and the mercs from here." Nick stared at Jadon with a grim look.

"I'm so grateful, I could cry," Jadon fired back.

■ ■ ■

The satellite phone call was placed on speaker, though the audio was staticky. Through Antonio, they had established contact with the Revolutionary Army members inside Cordova. The first wave of ten mercs had evidently arrived at the revolutionaries' camp.

"Nueva Cordova currently has about two hundred troops, all of whom possess a strong will to take their country in a new direction. Morale is high. But most of them are farmers who've never fired a gun in their lives. Their weapons are old and subpar, and two hundred men aren't nearly enough," said Bryan Fuller, leader of the mercs sent to Cordova.

"They aren't up to snuff. How much can they improve? The training period won't last that long."

"Don't worry, we'll whip them into shape, just you wait and see. Otherwise we won't live to see another day," answered Bryan.

"Check in on Professor Escárcega, would you? The success of this operation hinges on him. How many Cordovans will rise up if the professor calls the country to action?" Jadon ordered.

"I'll look into it right away, sir. But we need real-time footage of the capital, La Caridad, and the detention facility where the political prisoners are being held. We also need a grasp of the positioning of the regime's troops, and the security levels of the detention center."

"We're working on it here in the War Room. We'll obtain that info, mark my words."

Jadon hung up.

"Basic training for US Army recruits lasts six months. Haste makes waste," said Nick, in a relatively easygoing tone. He'd been listening in on the call from behind.

"All they need to learn is how to shoot and how to take cover. The enemy will mostly be on the same level, give or take a handful of pros. Cordova's military may be backed by the state, but at the end of the day it's still cobbled together and held aloft purely by money. Whereas we've got the latest, most state-of-the-art weaponry lined up. Our guys just have to get close, aim at the enemy, and pull the trigger, and they'll hit their marks."

Jadon returned to his room and took out a picture of Professor Escárcega from an envelope John had handed him.

Luis sported a white beard and head of hair. His dark blue eyes and taut mouth radiated a no-nonsense aura of willpower, but there were hints of kindness somewhere in his face too. If this man raised the call, there could even be some Cordovan military soldiers who sympathized. Jadon could tell the man oozed charisma—the charisma the operation depended on.

Jadon shoved the photo back into the envelope and went to bed.

"I'm surprised. The Boss was telling the truth—I was able to keep the satellite stationed over Cordova." Billy Ganaway stood up and raised his voice so that everybody cast their eyes on the central screen against the wall.

"Looks like the same old image to me. Where's the surprise?"

"Look carefully. We're watching real-time satellite footage. This isn't some recording or photo—this is Cordova *right now*. And that's pretty incredible," said Billy, his eyes still on the footage on screen—a range of dark, lush green, and a lake. "Beautiful. Scenery like this makes a guy think twice about just ditching the Earth quite yet. But this beauty will go the way of the dodo, if Cortázar gets his way and clears out the jungle for his development projects. He's planning to deforest and construct a tin mining and smelting plant, and he's negotiating with Russia and China to make it happen." Billy moved the cursor, and the green turned gray. They were buildings. "This is La Caridad. There's Cortázar's official residence and the buildings of the central government nearly smack-dab in the middle, with the National Foundation Plaza out in front. There's also the military parade. The city's main thoroughfares lead to this plaza." The screen zoomed in on the city. "Compare this to the map on the table. There are military facilities all around the central government buildings."

"Is this sturdy-looking building the detention camp?"

"Ten years ago, that was a premier luxury hotel. Then it got battered in a battle against the Revolutionary Army. The revolutionaries concentrated their fire on it because it was playing host to foreign weapons merchants and local government officials," said Stewart. "The hotel has indeed been converted into a camp for political prisoners. Cortázar wants them dead, but he intends to make his debut on the international stage, so he can't outright execute them."

"There are more than ten military barracks surrounding the perimeter of the city, each with over three hundred soldiers at the ready. No matter what happens to Cortázar's residence or the central government, a truck full of fully armed soldiers can make it there in ten minutes."

"Zoom in some more," said Jadon.

The central screen zoomed in on the buildings. The overall image suddenly took on a greenish hue, with red shadows shifting throughout.

"I switched it to infrared. Now we can capture things that are around three square feet in size." Billy kept singing the technology's praises as he moved the image on screen along the Foundation Plaza.

"Does this mean we've got twenty-four-hour surveillance of every inch of people's homes? Will there be no bathroom privacy in all of Cordova for the next twenty days?"

"All we've got is an overhead view. And if we go over the contract period by even just a second, the Pentagon will know, and our location will be identified. After which the FBI will bust down our door, and we'll be arrested for treason."

"You'd better be on your guard. His words are words of experience."

"As it stands, we're at the helm of a state-approved crime. We can't afford any slip-ups," said Billy, scanning the room with an expression that screamed *got anything to say about it?*

That afternoon, while Jadon and John were discussing things, news came in from Bryan that Professor Escárcega's execution had been set for a week from now. Jadon put the satellite phone on speakerphone and placed it on his desk.

"I was told it was set for a *month* from now. How reliable is this intel?"

"It seems to be accurate. The camp's in an uproar over it. The Revolutionary Army's planning to go it alone and save him."

"They can't. They'll just get slaughtered."

"What else can be done?"

"The remaining troops and I will head there tomorrow. We'll carry the weapons with us too. We'll come to everything else once we cross that bridge. Don't let them rush off a cliff like that."

"Is 'tomorrow' going to be fast enough?"

"I'll get ready today. You quell Nueva Cordova in the meantime." Jadon hung up the call.

John had been on the other end, listening in as the two conversed. He called everyone to the War Room and informed them how Luis's date of execution was suddenly much closer at hand. The tension was thick.

"Rescuing the professor is the crux of our entire plan. If he gets offed, we won't have a leg to stand on, and the operation's all but done for."

"We have no choice but to ask Nueva Cordova to go save the poor bastard. But—"

Antonio yowled with distress. He knew how reckless that would be. Nueva Cordova marching to their deaths was the last thing he wanted.

"I'll head for LA in two hours. By sometime tomorrow, I'll be at the camp in Cordova."

Jadon looked at Nick.

"Are the mercs and weapons okay?"

"The twenty mercs are waiting in LA. The weapons will be stashed onto the trucks today, and I'll make sure they can roll out at a moment's notice," Nick replied calmly.

"And we don't have to worry about them getting themselves caught? It took two days for the first wave of mercs to reach the camp."

"Tomorrow, while on the regular US military flight headed for the base in Colombia, we'll get off at an airfield near the border of

Cordova. At night, we'll transfer to a helicopter to enter Cordova and land near the camp. If we keep to the shadows, we won't get spotted."

"Please, whatever you do, make it to the camp. Without you, the operation's a fiasco," said John, staring at Jadon.

"I'll give it my best shot."

"That's what everyone says. But if you don't succeed, then it's game over. There's no restarting this thing. And the consequences of failure are too massive to contemplate. We'd be wresting any and all hope from the Cordovan people. This isn't just about some company making a buck. There's so much more on the line. The fate of an entire nation hangs in the balance," said Nick, his expression more serious than Jadon had ever witnessed.

Jadon returned to his room and called Jason.

"I'm leaving tomorrow. Tell me when and where to rendezvous in LA."

"Pushing it too far again, I see. But I'm ready for you, captain. You're always using me, but this is the last time," Jason carped before giving him the time and place.

"Did you look into the thing for me?"

"It wasn't too difficult, much to my surprise. I just wonder why they never mentioned it in the official release. I don't get what's running through the minds of the higher-ups," he said, lowering his voice even more. A load on Jadon's heart flew away, just like that. "But why do you need to know about it, anyway? Isn't this ancient history? You know what, never mind. I forgot, it's better that I don't know, right?"

"You have my eternal gratitude. I'll never bother you again."

A beat passed before Jason replied, his tone different. "I've been in the military for quite some time too. I know you well enough to have a general idea of what you're trying to do. And I believe in you, captain."

The line dropped.

Just then, a knock on the door. Jadon opened it to find John in his wheelchair.

"The success of this operation revolves around you. I'm counting on you," said John, squeezing Jadon's hand. His grip felt a tad stronger than when they'd first met. Jadon squeezed back.

"The copter's ready. It's on the hotel's roof. Please take it and transfer to a jet at Basin Sands Airport."

John had summoned a helicopter from Las Vegas.

"I'll give it my all, Boss," said Jadon, the words coming quite naturally.

That evening, after John saw Jadon off at the roof, he hailed Stewart. Then, the two made for John's room.

"Tell me what's really on your mind. What are the chances this operation succeeds? You're my father-in-law. I won't get upset, so lay it on me," said John, giving Stewart a whiskey.

Stewart gave it some thought for a long while. Then, at last, he spoke.

"To tell you the truth, even as we were planning the thing together, I thought it was a foolhardy endeavor. Working as individuals to send in mercenaries to topple a country's administration? Granted, it's a small country, but the point stands. And then, on top of that, we're supposed to help rebuild a new nation to replace the old. That's interference in a country's domestic affairs, no matter how you slice it. And the plan is linked to the US president. If the press catches wind of this, it won't leave the headlines for ages. There's no question he'll be pressured to resign."

"And the chances we succeed?" John repeated, fixing his gaze on Stewart.

"The chances are zero, John. Or at least, extremely close to it. But I intend to expend every last ounce of effort to try and make it a success. I seem to recall you said much the same," he replied, returning the stare.

The two stood by the window, and turned to look out upon the vista. The sun was setting, the vast sandy expanse glinting in the moonlight.

■ ■ ■

Meanwhile, at the image analysis training room of the FBI Academy, Adán was showing Vanessa the video he'd come across.

"The first gunshot wasn't fired from the American side, but from the refugees' side. And if that's the case, then the American military's actions were justifiable. This is completely crazy; did no one else notice?"

"When it comes to the Tragedy at The Wall, it's always the end result that people focus on. More than three hundred refugees from the caravan were killed or wounded. That's a stone-cold fact that's not going anywhere. America took heat from the whole world, and the president's approval ratings took a more-than-15-percent nosedive," she replied, as she stared at the computer screen. "If the media circus over the whole affair didn't abate at some point, his approval ratings would plunge even more. That's what the White House must have figured, anyway. In any case, they wanted the tragedy behind them, and fast. The military was of the same mind. That's why they court-martialed the commanding officer at the scene and expelled him from the Army. Dishonorably discharged."

"But what if the truth about which side shot first were to come to light?"

Vanessa looked up from the display to face Adán.

"Don't be so naïve. Everyone's already reached the agreed-upon conclusion, and the hubbub around the massacre's dying down. Actually, it's already more or less off people's minds. If you throw the case upside down, you'll be stirring some serious shit. The effects will be too profound to predict."

"But the truth is getting twisted. Think about the lives that got ruined over the injuries they sustained, not to mention the hundred or more people who died. Think about the Army captain—I'm sure his life is in shambles too. Don't they deserve justice? And isn't the FBI's job to uncover the truth and right wrongs?"

"You really are wet behind the ears. It was the military that conducted the investigation. Neither the local police nor the FBI could stick their noses in. It was all just too big. The eyes of the world were trained on DC. Unless you want to go fighting the world? We just don't have the authority."

"But a truth of this magnitude can't just be ignored."

"So you want to make an enemy of the military, then. Of the federal government. Well, I hope you're ready for whatever's coming your way. Besides, a video or two isn't going to cut it—"

"All right, ma'am. All I ask is that you keep mum while I gather incontrovertible proof to blow this wide open."

"It all went down nearly a year ago. I've heard that since then, there've been wide-scale personnel shakeups of those involved within the military. You'd have a ton of trouble just finding them if you insist on working alone."

"I'll see how far I can get. And I won't ask you to help me. I'd just be grateful if you don't rat me out."

"Do as you like. I have nothing to do with it, no matter where this might take you." She played up a big shrug before exiting the room.

Adán proceeded to replay the video for the umpteenth time, straining his ears to catch the audio. About an hour later, Vanessa returned to the office. Behind her stood Executive Assistant Director Bart Benton.

"I just couldn't keep silent. Everything I told him was for your sake."

"Save the excuses. I just worked out something else: *multiple* people fired the first shots from the refugees' side."

"Are you saying there were two first-shooters?"

"Try ten or more. I analyzed the gunfire audio and the bullets on

camera. I narrowed them down to M16 and Kalashnikov ammo. The M16 bullets are obviously the Army's. The Kalashnikov bullets were fired by outside agents. Of course, the sound Kalashnikovs make varies slightly depending on the gun. So we have *twelve* different-sounding instances of Kalashnikov fire."

Bart pushed Adán aside and replayed the video. First, he watched without a word, then turned to face him.

"Have any ballistics tests been run on the Kalashnikovs that were discovered at the scene?"

"I inquired. They haven't, or so I'm told. But the military's storing the photos. I already had them send them over. Told them it was for in-service training. I also asked the FBI crime lab to check if they were fired from the same gun."

"Any results yet?"

"They asked me to fill in a formal request form first. I'm writing one now."

Bart picked up the desk phone. "Put me through to the crime lab." He put a hand over the mouthpiece. "Who'd you ask?"

"Cedric."

"Yes, this is Bart Benton. Let me speak to Cedric."

Bart put it on speakerphone and returned the receiver. When Cedric came on the line, Bart stated his name and title. Cedric's tone of voice changed.

"The ballistics test Adán asked you to do, did you do it?"

"Oh, that? There's more than a hundred files. I'll get you the results over the next few days—"

"I want to know by tomorrow morning. I'm afraid you're not sleeping tonight."

Bart hung up without even waiting for a reply.

"Thank you, sir. I'm lucky you came to the rescue."

"I don't know about *lucky.* If nothing comes of this, then a certain someone will be quitting the agency. Make that two certain someones, actually."

"You can't be serious, sir. All I did was report what I heard," said Vanessa, who was still looking at the screen.

President Copeland had been pacing around the Oval Office for almost half an hour. It was 9 p.m. in DC, 8 p.m. in Cordova, and 6 p.m. in Nevada, where John was. The operation to free a nation took shape in both the sands of Nevada and the jungles of Central America. It would be a war cut off from the light of day, a war unknown to the annals of history. This was hardly the only such instance up until now, but there would be one key difference: this time, when the war ended, the construction of a new nation would begin.

"Is there anything I can do?" asked the president into his smartphone.

"Please, don't be silly, Mr. President. Ahem, Bob," came a calm and composed voice.

"Of course. You're right. I can't help with an operation that doesn't exist."

"That's right. Absolutely nothing is happening."

"I'm the president of these United States. I think it's safe to say I'm the kind of guy who comes through for people. I know there's something far more important than the title of president. So if something disastrous happens by your people's hands, do tell me."

"I know the strength of your character. And how you'll never be able to refuse any request we might make. But rest assured we're working day and night to make sure nothing like that happens," he said quietly, before the line dropped.

The president gripped his phone for a while. Then, he placed it in his chest pocket and called his secretary. He was slated to start discussing trade negotiations with China in ten minutes' time.

■ ■ ■

3

THE REVOLUTIONARY ARMY

Jadon returned to LA the night after he was informed Luis would be executed in a mere week.

He thought twice about calling Shirley—she should have gotten her $100,000 by now. And she'd doubtless pepper him with questions before letting him talk to Paulina.

The hotel that Nick directed him to was located near Van Nuys. He tucked himself into bed, but his mind was racing with the events of the past few days, and what he would be attempting in the weeks to come. No way he was catching a wink of sleep tonight.

A knock on the door.

According to his watch, the date would flip over in just ten minutes. Gun in hand, Jadon looked through the peephole. Standing there was a young man in jeans and a baseball cap. He looked Asian. Chinese, maybe, or Japanese. He was holding a six-pack of Budweiser and a box of pizza. "Nick told me you were here. Said I needed to see you today or never," he said cheerily.

Jadon opened the door for him.

"Put away the gun, please. Name's Tsutomu. Third-generation Japanese immigrant, born and raised in America. I don't give out my last name to people I haven't worked with for at least a month. You're Jadon Green, right? The Border Butcher? I heard all about it from Nick," he said, scanning the room as he spoke with a winning smile. By the looks of him, he was in his twenties. Yet it was clear from how he carried himself that his poise and agility were effortless. And he was probably older than he looked.

"Were you Delta Force?" asked Jadon.

"How did you know? Nick didn't tell you, did he? He's not supposed to."

"Oh, I can tell," said Jadon. "Had a friend, back in the day."

The Delta Force, a special operations force of the US Army, was founded in 1977 as a counterterrorism unit. Its existence went unacknowledged by DC, and no official information had been made publicly available as of yet. It was headquartered in Fort Bragg, North Carolina, under the Joint Special Operations Command. Selection training was conducted twice per year, demanding that hopefuls not only be airborne-qualified and pass physical examinations, but also excel at various other skills, such as close quarters combat or speaking multiple languages. Since members were often disguised as civilians, they enjoyed a high amount of freedom with regard to their clothes, hairstyles, and general appearances. The Delta Force was divided into three combat squadrons (a support squadron, a signal squadron, and an aviation platoon), and in principle, members operated in groups of four. They exuded a different aura altogether, compared to other Army soldiers. Or at least, that was what Stewart had told Jadon.

"I'm on orders to serve as your aide. The other nineteen are bosom buddies. We've worked together on operations loads of times, and they're pretty damn proficient. You're in good hands."

"Why'd you go Delta Force, though? Nick told me Navy SEALs are the real movers and shakers."

"The Army, the Navy, it made no difference to me. They both train to kill." Tsutomu handed him a beer.

A man of medium build and with an affable smile, one might take him for an ordinary college-age guy. But he moved his body with a practiced efficiency, and his eyes could turn from warm to piercing on a dime. This Tsutomu had seen—and survived—his fair share of carnage.

"Why'd you leave? You must've been outstanding, to make it into Delta Force."

"My pay's so much better now. By switching to this I tacked another zero onto my yearly income. You know how it is. Besides, I don't want to—"

"On second thought, let's not ask each other these kinds of things." Jadon opened a bottle against the edge of the table and took a swig. Then he transferred the pizza from the table to the bed and unfurled a map.

"Have you heard the plan?"

"Operation Caravan, right? I was concentrating on choosing the people for the job, so I haven't had the time. I was told to ask you about the details."

Jadon gave Tsutomu a summarized overview. But Tsutomu probably already knew. Only the fickle and unreliable would stake their lives on a mission they weren't clear on.

"What a crazy mission. I should've asked more before responding."

"Would you have turned it down?"

"I'd have asked for twice as much money. Some of my colleagues have got families to feed."

"Let's just say our boss has very deep pockets and doesn't mind parting with it. And he offers insurance too."

"Nick didn't breathe a word about any of that. I need to yell at him later over who's the beneficiary of the insurance."

"In any case, you have to get home alive before you can worry about that. We've got two enemies to crush—the dictatorship and the cartel. To do that, we . . ."

"Make them fight each other," said Tsutomu, at the same time as Jadon, and they clinked beer bottles to toast. "Is there a way to pit them against each other like that?"

"We won't know till we try."

Jadon filled Tsutomu in on the War Room, and how the combined expertise at their disposal—from matters of war to economics and even psychology—would assist the campaign. He also divulged how a brilliant hacker now working with the War Room had gotten a grasp of Cordova's and Los Eternos' financial information, and how they had access to real-time footage through an American military satellite. Furthermore, while he didn't tell Tsutomu about President Copeland's peripheral involvement, with an operation of this scope, Tsutomu must have inferred.

"The Boss isn't just thinking about tearing the place down and leaving it at that. He's aiming to tear it down only so it can be built back up. We'll destroy the oppressive regime, and the people will construct a new nation in its wake, while making use of the plan the minds at the War Room whipped up. Together, we'll create a safe and stable country that doesn't generate refugees. A country its kids can take pride in," said Jadon, repeating John's mission statement. As he spoke the words, his once-fuzzy grasp of those ideals became more concrete, surfacing from his subconscious mind.

The two continued to talk over beers until, suddenly, Tsutomu stood up. "Please get some rest. We're meeting at five o'clock in the morning at Point A."

Jadon checked his watch. Two hours until the allotted time.

Tsutomu had his hand on the doorknob, but he turned to look back at Jadon. "Do you have any jungle combat experience?"

"No."

At that, Tsutomu shrugged. Jadon had received jungle combat training, but the battlefields in Afghanistan and Syria were composed of rock and sand. In Syria, he'd had to fight IS militants lurking inside towns and villages.

"In the jungle, human soldiers won't be your only enemies. People's lives can be taken as easily by a snake, a scorpion, or even an ant or a spider, as by a stray bullet," said Tsutomu matter-of-factly.

"We're training our troops in the jungle, but the main battlefield will be La Caridad, where Cortázar lives. We'll be engaging in urban warfare. Fighting the country's military head-on would spell disaster for the Revolutionary Army. We need to run straight up to the snake's head and slice it off."

"Our objective is to apprehend Cortázar, or failing that . . . Well, we're gunning for regime change," Tsutomu said with a wink before closing the door behind him.

When Jadon arrived at the designated point, he encountered nineteen young men in civilian clothes alongside Tsutomu. The building was akin to a warehouse, but the atmosphere was quite convivial; the mercs were laughing and joking, and some of them were even sitting on the floor. None had firearms on them, but they did have small backpacks and US military barracks bags. If he didn't know better, he'd swear they were going on some holiday trek.

Tsutomu noticed Jadon there and got on his feet to stand at attention. The rest followed suit. They moved like well-oiled machines—were they all former Delta Force operators?

"All twenty of the men participating in this operation are here."

"Guess you all know each other. Well, it's good to work with you."

Tsutomu gave him a salute, prompting the others to do likewise. Jadon found himself returning the salute.

Then they all got on the small bus that had been arranged for them. An hour later, they arrived at Edwards Air Force Base, where a medium-sized military transport propeller plane awaited. The engine was already running.

"The weapons are already aboard. The rest will go down exactly like I told you earlier."

A great number of wooden boxes were loaded inside.

"Here's your ACUs, Captain. I'm told Nick was asked by Colonel Gobel to make sure you got them."

It was a US Army combat uniform, all right, but it lacked any insignia. After Jadon changed clothes, the fully armed young mercs proceeded to board. They, too, were wearing ACUs, in addition to well-worn vests (derived from all kinds of units, including the Delta Force and the Navy SEALs), which contained magazines, hand grenades, knives, and their warrior pasts.

"What is all this?" Next to Tsutomu lay two large suitcases and a golf bag-looking backpack containing a sniper rifle.

"I'm headed to the jungles down south. The more clothes I bring, the better." He eyed the suitcases with a look that said *feel free to open them.*

Jadon ambled toward the boxes that had been tossed on board in untidy heaps.

"A hundred M16s; thirty thousand rounds. Plus three hundred grenades, twenty mortars, and fifty bazookas, each with their own sets of ammo. They've already been looked at," stated the soldier who had fastened the boxes down.

The plane took off as scheduled. Around a half hour later, they'd flown over the border from California to Mexico. They could see the sprawling sands and colorful towns they associated with Mexico, but soon enough, that scenery gave way to green jungle. Jadon had his eyes on his phone's GPS and the map on hand. "While you've all probably worked in Central America before, this operation's going to blow those out of the water. Prepare for danger, and lots of it. I want you so prepared you could fly into combat right as we're speaking," said Jadon.

Everyone listened to Jadon's words with grim but earnest expressions. Gone was the brotherly banter from hours prior. Tsutomu must have apprised them of just how fraught with peril Operation Caravan would be.

"We won't be entering Cordova directly by plane. We'll touch outside their tents. It was more reminiscent of a refugee camp than the camp of revolutionaries.

The command center was located behind the camp, in a thirty-square-foot cave at the bottom of the steep cliff. There was enough room inside to store the weapons. As for the décor, there was one low-quality table made of low-quality wood, and zero chairs. Some threadbare blankets were laid over the floor.

Bryan led Jadon into the cave command center.

"How's the training going?"

"Some of them are really excellent. But half of them can't read, and the majority of them don't speak English. It'll be tough for them to use the weaponry we're giving them to the fullest," replied Bryan.

"The US military was the same way fifty years ago. And even now, only a select few soldiers can use more high-tech weapons. It's all in the training," said Jadon, but at the same time, he knew there wasn't nearly enough time to train them properly.

They exited the command center to be greeted by the cold stares of the assembled revolutionary soldiers.

"Be careful, okay? Some of them know you're the commander from the Tragedy at The Wall," Bryan whispered in his ear.

"Is there anyone in the Revolutionary Army who can speak English and take command?"

Bryan cast a glance at the thin, sharp-eyed man, who was holding a Kalashnikov that could only have been stolen from a Cordovan Army soldier. Jadon walked up to him.

"What's your name?"

"Arsenio. Arsenio Fernández."

"You be our go-between with the revolutionaries." Jadon took Arsenio's gun and switched on its safety. "Never have the safety off outside the battlefield."

"That guy's the Border Butcher!" The man staring at Jadon tossed away his smoke and stood up with gun in hand. The eyes of the men in the vicinity pointed Jadon's way.

them in fluent English. "My name is Sebastian Loyola, and I am the captain of Nueva Cordova."

With black hair covering his ears, a thick beard, and a gaunt and chiseled face, the man made a stark impression. Jadon recalled Sebastian's war record, which he'd been given access to in the War Room. He was a former Cordovan Army captain. He had also received instruction at an American military training center.

"I heard all about you from Antonio," he said under his breath, upon drawing closer to Jadon. "You'd better keep an eye out—everyone here hates your guts. And I'm not particularly fond of you, either. But right now, I need whatever help you can give me."

"I didn't exactly come here to make friends, bud. I came to shake off my bad dreams. Once I accomplish my objective, I no longer have any use for this place."

"That's funny. We're fighting to get rid of a nightmare too."

Tsutomu silently listened as the two exchanged greetings.

"How many soldiers and weapons are here?"

"There are ninety-eight soldiers in the Revolutionary Army, and we have the hundred automatic rifles you people brought."

That was around half the figure Jadon had been given. Only a hundred men? But Jadon didn't voice his concerns.

"And your ammo?"

"We don't have much. That's why we can't train nearly as many as we'd like."

A big sun-bronzed man with a GI crew cut pushed his way through the soldiers to get to Jadon. It was Bryan Fuller. "I've been waiting for you this whole time. Nick Beasley told me about you. You're here early."

"I just want to get this done and over with as quickly as possible. It doesn't seem like I'm welcome here, anyway."

Bryan smiled grimly and glanced at Sebastian. More than a hundred people lived at the camp—the soldiers and their families. They were all lank and thin, with shabby clothing. Some were cooking

Jadon shook his head to clear his thoughts. The point of descent was a narrow patch of grass with a small red light at the center.

"We can't all land at the same time. We have to land one by one."

Jadon's copter was the first of the five to touch down. The Nueva Cordova liaison rushed up, as the copter immediately took to the night once again. The next to land was Tsutomu's.

"Everyone's accounted for. And the duffel bags have been shoved onto the trucks," Tsutomu reported.

Jadon called Bryan Fuller (of the advance unit) using his satellite phone, informing him they'd made it into Cordova. "We're headed for the revolutionaries' camp now. We'll need to cut across Cordovan forces to do so. If something happens to one of the trucks, we'll do our best to back you up with the other."

The twenty-one men split into two groups, one per truck, and spared no time setting out for the Nueva Cordova camp.

"Two hours from now, we're getting off and carrying the duffel bags on foot the rest of the way. We'll reach the camp at the crack of dawn."

And so the trucks pushed deeper, rolling down the jungle roads. At one point, they hid the trucks in the jungle itself, and advanced on foot from there (while still heavily equipped). By the time the day was getting appreciably brighter, a guide was taking them up a hill. At the top of the hill, they could see about thirty tents in the depression on the slope, a sheer cliff in back.

■ ■ ■

When they entered camp, they were surrounded by soldiers. Revolutionary Army soldiers. The faces of Nueva Cordova. And their guns, Kalashnikovs all, were pointed at Jadon, Tsutomu, and the rest. Tsutomu and his soldiers made to brandish their own guns, but Jadon stopped them.

A tall man came out in front of the soldiers and began speaking to down right near the border and transfer to a chopper from there," said Tsutomu, relaying what Jadon had told him the night before.

Not long past noon, the plane began its descent. Spanning the sun-drenched overgrowth, a runway could be seen.

"This was an airfield for the cartels until just last year. Now it's being managed by a military industry. They're making a stop here for us," said Jadon as he peered out the window.

Moments after the soldiers and their duffel bags got off the plane, it took off again, flying for the US base in Colombia.

Five old CH-47 helicopters were waiting for them at the airfield's edge. The military had sold them off to the private sector, their original affiliations becoming unclear in the resale process. Nick had arranged for everything from this point on.

The soldiers loaded the large quantities of duffel bags onto the copters with skill and efficiency.

"We're flying into Cordova after sundown. Then we're touching down at the rendezvous point with our liaison and heading for the Nueva Cordova revolutionaries' camp," confirmed Tsutomu, assuring Jadon things were going as planned.

Darkness had fallen, and before they knew it, the five choppers took off in formation, breaching the border into Cordova in no time. They were literally flying under the radar.

"Put on your NVGs, soldiers. No lights whatsoever."

At Jadon's command, they strapped on their night-vision goggles. The whirling of the rotors in the nighttime sounded eerie when the rest was silence. Memories of his days in Iraq flashed to mind. A rocket had ripped out of nowhere, damaging the copter's tail and sending it crashing down into the desert. Jadon had needed to carry an injured subordinate, walking long hours into the night to rejoin their allies.

"In five minutes we're there. I've been ordered to take off the minute you and your things are unloaded," came the pilot's voice.

the first time anybody in Jadon's position had been so blunt and straightforward with him.

The four of them discussed the current state of the camp and how they could rescue the professor. After Sebastian and Bryan left their side, Jadon asked Tsutomu: "Are those two not getting along, or what? Has Bryan told you anything?"

"I'm guessing they're just feeling antsy because the training isn't going as expected," said Tsutomu.

"Then why don't you do something about that?"

"You've just got to beat those two up in front of everyone."

"Which one of them should I beat up first? I want to go about this in the most effective way. I'd have a hell of a time beating both of them at the same time."

"Sebastian trained for around six months at a US military training center, before Cortázar came to power. He must know US military training methods. I bet that's why he's so agitated and impatient."

"What do you mean?"

"US recruits and Cordovan peasants are fundamentally different. We have to teach them English, and how to handle guns. They're currently under the impression that if they just hold their guns and pull the trigger, they'll hit their targets. They're too used to seeing people get shot to death. It hasn't even occurred to them that if they don't aim, they won't score kills. Or that they might inadvertently commit friendly fire."

"But the level of zeal is different between US soldiers and the Cordovans too. Americans become soldiers to earn a living. These guys are doing it to survive," said Jadon.

Tsutomu nodded and shrugged.

The next morning, Sebastian and Bryan gave Jadon a tour through the camp. The soldiers of Nueva Cordova were already receiving combat training at the hands of the advance party of mercenaries, including marksmanship, mano a mano, and marching while fully equipped.

"Well, well. Now I see why Nick told me to follow you, captain," he said, his voice a little louder than before.

That night, Sebastian and Bryan came to Jadon and Tsutomu's tent for a meeting.

"Professor Escárcega's execution is right around the corner. We'll spring him before his head touches the chopping block. Contact him as soon as humanly possible. I want to bring someone who's familiar with the geography of La Caridad, and who knows a thing or two about the detention facility. That way the rescue operation will go smoother," said Jadon.

"I've sent a contact of ours to La Caridad. He'll be back with some intel for us shortly. Do us a favor and get a move on with the training. The faster, the better. Also, are those all the weapons we've got? Peashooters and grenades?" said Sebastian.

"We're not weapon couriers. Tell the soldiers they need to get serious about this if they want to win," said Bryan, glaring back.

"They may not be enough, but we did give you an arsenal to work with. We'll teach them how to use them and turn them into soldiers that can hold their own against the regime. Our only enemies here are the Cordovan military and Los Eternos," said Tsutomu.

Sebastian turned toward Jadon. "The major powers always have us dancing in the palm of their hands. The prior administration was cozying up to China for a hefty chunk of aid money. Then Cortázar took over, using weapons given to him by the US, which helped him build his little dictatorship. Not long after, the US decides to give Cordova the cold shoulder. And now that Cortázar's decided to get closer to China and Russia, the US is suddenly all about giving us a boost. So tell me, who do we believe?"

"Believe in me. I've got nothing to do with America anymore," said Jadon, staring Sebastian in the eyes.

Sebastian was startled for a moment but nodded. This was perhaps

Now there was a big crowd of people surrounding him.

"Anybody else have any grievances to air? Step right up."

But they all just looked on wordlessly.

"I'm only going to say this once, so get it into your thick skulls. You know Antonio Alvarado, don't you? He used to be a comrade of yours. His family got tortured and killed by the regime, and he himself lost his right eye and right leg. He even lost three fingers. It was Antonio who asked me to save your homeland."

The soldiers were suddenly dead silent, rapt with attention.

"You know what Antonio asked me to do? He asked me to make Cordova a country the children wouldn't *need* to escape. And the rest of the mercenaries here? They came to give you people a hand. And the way we can do that is by toughening you up. We'll turn you into lean, mean fighting machines that can stand up to Los Eternos without batting an eye. And by the time we're finished with you, you'll be walking all over those regime soldiers. But the training will be tough. Real tough. So those of you who aren't man enough can seize this opportunity to blow out of here. Those who remain will be the men who fight for their homeland. Because it'll be you fighting, not us. Now shout if you wanna remake the country. Shout if you want the children of Cordova to spend their days on Cordovan soil with pride!"

"For the children!" some among them shouted.

"I can't hear you. Guess you don't really care about your country after all. I wanna hear you, loud and clear!"

Again, some of the soldiers did shout, but their eyes were filled with hate. The majority just glared at him without a word.

Jadon gave them a final look before clearing off.

"I'm surprised. I didn't know you could speak Spanish," said Tsutomu, striding after him.

Jadon showed him the paper he'd read off of. Then he crumpled it, popped it in his mouth, and swallowed. "That's the whole speech. Antonio translated it for me."

Tsutomu and the others encircled Jadon. Jadon pushed Tsutomu aside, stepped forward, and glared at the man. "My mission is to train you people. I came to this shithole as a favor to somebody. If you've got something to say, say it now," said Jadon in Spanish, looking around at the men. "You can do whatever you want, and I'll look the other way. But do it now. Because from now on, my orders are absolute. Got it?"

A big man at the front lunged for Jadon, who dodged and swept his legs. His would-be assailant rolled headfirst onto the hard ground. The man attempted to clamber back up, only to be met by a boot to the gut that sent him sailing through the air, body bent like a jumbo shrimp. But Jadon made sure that kick wasn't as harmful as it looked.

"You people are just a bunch of spineless rats. You'd flee your country just to scrape together a little more money? Just because you can't fill your bellies? Where's your pride? And what kind of example are you setting for your children? Fight, goddammit! Fight, and take back your homeland!" he shouted.

The soldiers bit their lips and clenched their fists, clearly dying to pounce on him.

"Anyone else got something to say?"

Suddenly, the man he'd kicked down came at him with a knife. Jadon sidestepped the knife and punched him square in the face. Blood sprayed from his nose, but he was undeterred, holding the knife toward Jadon once more.

Jadon grabbed the thrusting knife arm and slammed the man's elbow joint against his shin. The knife clattered to the earth. Jadon then dropped him down, picked up the knife, and held it against his throat.

"Hope you enjoyed this last dance because next time I won't be so merciful. I will stick this into your throat, and you will die. Got it?" Jadon spoke into the man's ear in Spanish. He whimpered.

Jadon lifted him back up and shoved him aside. "You forgot this." He threw the knife at the tree right beside the man. It quivered menacingly.

when I was ten. A veteran taught me," said Tsutomu, who'd been eavesdropping.

"You look after him then. And don't shy away from disciplining him either."

Gerardo flipped him yet another bird, but Arsenio clocked him on the head.

There was an ocean of things they had left to do, but only three days remained until Professor Escárcega's execution. And still no contact—no new information.

Whenever the opportunity presented itself, Jadon would reemphasize the need to create a new nation for the children. Gradually, the local soldiers started heeding his words with increasingly serious expressions.

Jadon got in touch with the War Room via his satellite phone. Securing the necessary power by running a generator, he booted up his computer and downloaded the latest info from the War Room. He had real-time aerial footage of La Caridad, the positions of government troops, and more, all at his fingertips.

The revolutionary soldiers may have loathed the Border Butcher, but they couldn't deny how tough he was. Their morale had improved considerably, and the fruits of their training grew more evident. Their hostility and resentment toward Jadon were centering their focus. And he was aware of it too. He kept the drill-sergeant energy going, laying into them unrelentingly.

"Still no word back from Professor Escárcega? I want to know if he's down with all of this," he reiterated.

That night, he finally got his wish.

"The professor apparently said he doesn't want to see any more blood and that he's powerless. He's lost the will to fight."

"Can the new government function without the guy?" Jadon asked Sebastian.

"It wouldn't be easy. He's Cordova's father figure. He looms large in the hearts and minds of the people. There must be more than a few of his followers even in the military."

"What do we do then?"

"The only thing we can do—convince him. Unfortunately, he said he doesn't want to see anyone. That he's made up his mind."

"Has he got a wife, or kids?"

"His wife, Pamela, died seven years ago. His daughter, Penelope, lives and works in La Caridad as a Cordova University Medical School professor."

"Can we get her to convince him?"

"I heard they're not on good terms, so they don't talk much at all. Which is why Cortázar hasn't locked her up. But he is keeping an eye on her."

"Her father is going to get executed in two days. We've got to do whatever it takes to get him out of there in time."

"The security around the detention center's getting heavier."

"I don't care if he doesn't like it; we'll drag him out by force," he said, irritation bleeding into his voice.

That night, Jadon reread the file on Luis. Sixty-seven years old, and with the finely chiseled features of a philosopher, he stared at Jadon with his gentle eyes. The photo radiated with an avuncular warmth that wrapped around him like a scarf. The man had been a professor of political science and economics at Cordova University, as well as the university's principal. But he was even more popular among the citizenry, and it wasn't hard to see why. He was a moderate who had been pushing for elections and democracy for the country.

Meanwhile, in La Caridad . . .

In the near-exact center of town lay Foundation Plaza, to which all of the main roads led. Legend had it the city started from this square.

The Presidential Residence, an imposing stone building in Spanish style, was located at the end of the plaza. One could view the entire square from its balconies.

President Gumersindo Cortázar was in his office. The side facing the balcony used to have a wide glass window, but now it was a marble wall except for the door to the balcony. Cortázar had it remodeled the year he came into power. Death by sniper was not on his agenda.

Near the wall right in front of the entrance was an office desk, and in front of the desk, a sofa. In front of Cortázar sat one "Raminez Dourne."

"The poppies produced in this country are refined in underground factories and shipped to the States. And it's the cartel, Los Eternos, and its kingpin, José Moreno, who control that trade. If we can bring down Los Eternos, we can take over the Latin American narcotics outfits," said Dourne, with sky-high confidence. Dourne had been a military advisor to Cortázar for two years now.

"A few years ago, the military and Los Eternos were countervailing forces. But ever since you've arrived, my troops have been winning ground against Los Eternos, and it's all because we started employing strategies based on sound logic rather than just relying on firepower. But the cartel still controls a third of Cordova." Cortázar looked Dourne's way. "You were right."

Cortázar was glad he'd hired Dourne. He'd followed his counsel, regarding how to deal with the refugees and how to fight against Los Eternos, and he'd been rewarded for it so far. Yet he had to wonder who this man was, exactly. He was something of an enigma. No way he was just some terrorist who'd fled Europe. "Six months from now, we'll be able to wipe Los Eternos off the map for good."

"I wouldn't underestimate them or you'll get burned. The real fight starts now. They must be getting panicked, after all. Tell me, do Cordovans have the saying, 'a cornered fox is more dangerous than a jackal'?" asked Dourne, in fluent Spanish. But he wasn't Spanish or Hispanic himself. Cortázar had overheard him speaking in fluent English on the phone, too, but that wasn't his native language either.

Cortázar had asked for his résumé, but Dourne had told him he'd rather not take the job if he insisted. That notwithstanding, his prowess as a military and political adviser was indisputable. By following his words of advice, Cortázar had gained a level of influence and military might that dwarfed Cordova's neighbors.

"It would be best to keep some of the cartel's drug factories operational. If you're not getting high and steady tax revenue, then they'll make for an easy and constant source of income," added Dourne.

"Drugs will eventually destroy America. If we channel five or ten times as much coke into the States, we can increase the number of addicts and sow internal discord, which would leave the country in a weakened state," said Cortázar.

"I'd like to take the reins of a factory."

"So you're planning to quit being my military adviser and get into drug trafficking?"

"It'll serve as a powerful foothold to push back against the United States. I'll hook America on drugs," he spat. It was plain to see he was driven by an overflowing animosity toward the United States.

"Well, I couldn't agree more with the idea. We'll produce it in Cordova and send it to America. I'll let you be the one to take over Los Eternos' operations."

"To that end, I need you to leave the factories unscathed. I'll need the distribution network too." Dourne's eyes turned toward the map on the desk.

■ ■ ■

Jadon hit up the War Room for information on Luis's daughter, Penelope. She was thirty-two years old, and a practicing surgeon in addition to a medical professor. She was as beloved as her father, as she worked hard to better public health and education, and even helped construct new hospitals and schools. Her popularity was another reason Cortázar was reluctant to lay a hand on her. Her hair was trimmed short, and she had a sophisticated look about her eyes. Her no-nonsense lips resembled her father's.

Jadon went to have a word with Sebastian. "You tell her about Nueva Cordova? She's got to convince her father."

"We're trying to get in touch with her, but she's refusing contact. Says she doesn't want to get wrapped up in a political struggle."

According to the War Room's intel, Penelope believed her mother died in poverty and disillusionment because her husband, Luis, only ever had time for Cordova and its people. She hadn't seen her father in person in many years.

"How's the training coming along?" asked Jadon.

"The camp's changed since you got here. I don't doubt they'll be excellent soldiers," replied Sebastian.

"Good. I'll be leaving camp today."

"But now's the critical period. My subordinates are starting to gain hope, and it's thanks to you."

"What, they don't hate me anymore?"

Sebastian looked rattled for a fleeting moment, before he calmly stated, "Even so, they've changed. And they've begun to believe that if they change, the country will change too."

"I'm going to La Caridad to see Penelope. I'm going to ask her to talk some sense into the dear professor."

"No, it's too dangerous. The place is crawling with government troops. There's no need for you to go there."

"The most important thing for this plan to succeed is that the professor will stand with us. And for that to happen, I need to be there."

"You haven't got any real idea of just how dangerous this country is. If you die, the plan goes down with you."

"And if I don't go, the plan dies anyway. No professor, no victory."

"Then at least go with some escorts. I'll pick out some guards for you."

"I don't want to stand out. Give me as few men as possible." Jadon ordered Sebastian to finish preparing to head to La Caridad forthwith. Half an hour later, Sebastian came back with Arsenio in tow.

"He's worked in La Caridad before. He's also in touch with some friends who live there. He's your best choice for an escort."

"If we're going to La Caridad, we need to make it there before sundown," said Arsenio, pointing here and there on a map. "The city may be filled to the gills with soldiers and policemen during the day, but once it's dark, there's not a single soul left out on the streets. Even the police find it too dangerous to patrol, so they leave it to fully armored military vehicles."

"Where do we find Penelope?"

"There's a restaurant she's a regular at. She gets some tea there on the way home from the university."

"How high-class of her."

"That's how she's fighting the power. She's selling the people on her ideas. She's telling them to carry on with their lives, even in the middle of all this strife."

"So she shares her father's beliefs, but is still on the outs with him?"

"We're not privy to the baggage between parent and child— between father and daughter," said Arsenio detachedly, his expression unchanging. The man was highly competent, but he was also quite distant. Jadon could only imagine the hell Arsenio had witnessed in his life.

Jadon was reminded of his own daughter, Paulina. When was the last time he'd seen her? She always used to jump up to him when she caught sight of him. But before he knew it, Paulina was hiding behind her mother and looking at him with troubled eyes.

"We need Professor Escárcega. And the professor needs his daughter," said Jadon with conviction.

Walking in the enveloping heat of day, they were a cascade of sweat. Nearly five hours of continuous walking had gone by since they left the jungle camp. Once they cleared out of the trees, they still had to go down the road leading to La Caridad. The road kept alternating between paved stretches and bare red soil. Cars kicked up clouds of dust as they zoomed by. Arsenio stopped a pickup truck, and together they climbed into its cargo bed. They got off before reaching the city proper, to avoid the rumored military checkpoint inspection. Once again on their feet, they saw some slums on one side of the road. A multitude of small, cramped hovels, they were just frameworks for houses with sheet iron and pieces of wood nailed on.

Beside the slums were the trash heaps. The accumulated garbage carried here from La Caridad had formed big hills. Half-clothed children were fishing for scraps of metal and plastic from the mountains and mountains of refuse. The wind held the distinctive shantytown stench of rot.

Jadon found himself standing in place, staring.

"Let's pick up the pace," urged Arsenio, visibly nervous. He didn't want an American like Jadon to see this squalid underside of his country. It was a source of shame.

After another hour of walking, they had made it into the city. Arsenio's expression relaxed. Citizens were strolling about, and the markets were bustling.

Jadon remembered what John had told him. The country was not naturally destitute. John had made it abundantly clear that he believed they were just helping realize Cordova's true potential.

Around four hundred thousand people called La Caridad home, a good 10 percent of Cordova's total population. Foundation Plaza (or "la Plaza Fundadores") was at the center of the city. Surrounding the plaza were several government buildings, including the Presidential Residence ("el Palacio Presidencial") and the House of Assembly ("la Cámara de la Asamblea"). La Caridad's main roads extended radially from the plaza to the suburbs. The city was dotted by many commercial establishments and markets, which were crowded with customers and passersby.

Military facilities were lined up behind the Presidential Residence, with government troops stationed to protect the Residence from any antigovernment forces or cartel terrorists. Soldiers were positioned to be able to counterattack at a moment's notice.

On the busy streets, a fully armed government soldier stood out from the civilians.

"Wasn't expecting so many people. This doesn't look so different from a city in Mexico. Is the city that dangerous?" asked Jadon.

"It's not like they can hole up in their homes all day. But take a good look at their faces. I think you'll find they're different from the people in your country."

Jadon covertly scanned the vicinity. Sure enough, they all looked rather dead in the eyes.

"The people, they're fatigued. They're tired of the fear, tired of being poor. But still, they must live their lives."

"Is Penelope safe? She's Luis's daughter."

"Which is exactly why no one can touch her. Though she's not totally safe either."

Even as they spoke, Arsenio was keeping a constant, watchful eye over their surroundings. There were familiar faces from the camp blending in with the residents, along with two mercs. They were the guards appointed by Sebastian.

"Penelope is methodical by nature. If nothing out of the ordinary happens, she'll be around here, near the university, this time at night. Call it an evening break on the way back from work."

Arsenio stopped in his tracks. A slender woman with chiseled features and short black hair that left her ears uncovered was reading a book while drinking some tea at a table outside a restaurant.

"That's Penelope. What should we do? Should we go up to her together?"

"I'll go up to her by myself. She's a university professor and a medical doctor. She must speak English, right?"

"Be careful. There are government troops all over the place."

Jadon unbuttoned his outerwear to show he wasn't concealing any weapons. Some soldiers were eyeing the pair.

Jadon sat down next to Penelope.

"If you get on my nerves, I will scream," she said.

"Is that how you greet someone you've just met?"

"I know you're a Revolutionary Army person. Revolutionaries have been harassing me constantly these past few days. I believe I told you people I have no interest in politics or my father."

"I don't care what you're interested in. You don't want to save your father? Because we'll help you do it."

"If you don't mind, leave me alone. You must know what happens to people who associate with revolutionaries in this country."

"The people of this country adore and miss your father. You should be proud of him. Why do you hate the thought of seeing him again?"

"None of that has anything to do with you. I just want to preserve my own lifestyle."

"Which I don't mind. But give the people of Cordova a chance. You don't have to think of him as your father. Just give us an opportunity to speak with Professor Luis Escárcega."

Jadon peered into Penelope's eyes. She averted her gaze and bit her lip. After pausing for a moment's thought, she said: "My mother didn't have a husband, and I didn't have a father. He was always walking his own path. And why shouldn't he continue to do so? I don't want him around me."

"He's a great man. You ought to be honored to have him as your father."

Penelope glared at him. There was anger there. She took a deep breath and exhaled, choosing her words.

"All my mother and I had were each other. Whenever he decided to show up, he was out the door moments later with her money. Even teaching at college, he'd stay the night elsewhere more often than at home. My mother was forced to hold down several jobs to make ends meet, all while killing herself to raise me. She died of overwork, destitute and full of despair. And you know what? The guy didn't even attend her funeral. So what do you even want me to do?"

"I want you to talk some sense into Professor Escárcega. To tell him all of Cordova's waiting for him."

"Don't be stupid. I'm a Cordovan, too, and I'm not waiting for the bastard."

"He's going to get executed in two days."

Penelope froze. She tried her best to seem calm but couldn't hide her shock.

"And that's my problem how? I'll say it one more time: Don't show your face again. If you don't leave right now, I will scream," she vowed.

Just then, a bearded man came running out of the restaurant. And on his belt . . .

Jadon instinctively tackled Penelope to the ground and shielded her. A large blast sent him rolling along the road with Penelope in his arms.

The table, chairs, and fragments of glasses and plates pelted his body. Jadon lay on the ground, protecting her all the while.

A girl burst into tears. Jadon looked in the direction of the wailing to find the poor child kneeling by the bloody form of a woman who could only be her mother.

Jadon told Penelope to hide behind a car and ran toward the girl, who was splattered with blood herself. He picked her up and sprinted back to Penelope.

A large van screeched to a halt nearby. The doors were flung open and a cadre of men leapt out, pointing their automatic rifles at both government troops and fleeing civilians, commencing fire.

"They're Los Eternos goons. They bombed the restaurant and are shooting up the place."

Jadon managed to get back on his feet. His arm felt heavy, like a sack of bricks. Looking down, he saw it had a piece of shrapnel in it. After making sure his blood vessels weren't damaged, he started taking it out.

"Stop!" he heard Penelope shriek. A cartel man shot the girl Penelope had in her arms and grabbed her by the arm in an attempt to drag her away.

Jadon scanned the area and took a handgun from a fallen government soldier and aimed it at Penelope's assailant. "Hands off her. The military will be here in no time."

The thug thrust her away and pointed his rifle at Jadon. A gunshot pierced the air, and the man collapsed.

They could hear gunfire ripping through adjacent streets; this was a shoot-out now, and a savage one at that. They could even hear the combatants screaming at each other. The government troops who had rushed to the scene had begun firing on the cartel men. They gunned the men down, seized civilians indiscriminately, and even started turning bullets loose on those civilians who were trying to flee.

"This way!" Penelope grabbed Jadon's arm and ran. "If the military arrests you, all you'll have in store for you is a public execution. You're the Border Butcher, aren't you?"

They entered a side street, and after running for a while longer, they arrived at a quiet residential area. Eventually, they stopped in front of a house.

"This is my place. Come on, get inside. If they find you with me, you're not the only one who will be in trouble."

And so Jadon was pulled into her home.

"Take off your clothes. You need first aid."

"It's nothing. Barely a scratch. We'll get me sorted after getting back to camp—"

"Oh, are you a doctor now? Because I am." She promptly retrieved a med kit from her closet. "You need proper treatment now because it's going to heal in no time. They've got these handy tapes now."

She wasted no time disinfecting the wound and applying the adhesive wound closure strips.

"Are you okay?" asked Jadon.

"This blood isn't mine. It's the little girl's. She died in my stead."

"No, she didn't. Los Eternos killed her. And don't forget that *this* is the reality of this country."

"What do you want me to do, huh? I'm powerless. I couldn't even save that girl!"

"You saw it with your own eyes. Los Eternos and the military have no qualms capturing and slaughtering innocent civilians."

Penelope put her index finger to her lips to shush him.

A handful of soldier-filled military trucks were driving along the road.

"This is what your father is trying to get rid of. He loves Cordova. And he was giving it his all to turn his homeland into a country to be proud of. All you have to do is talk to him."

"I told you, I haven't seen him in years. I want nothing to do with him."

"Don't let today's Tragedy happen again. Or do you want that girl's death to be in vain?"

A single tear streaked down her cheek as she bit her lip. She was left speechless, until: "I'll go see him. But that's it. I don't expect anything from him, and I don't have anything to say to him."

A gunshot rang in the distance, mixed with panicked screaming.

■ ■ ■

"I'm in," said Billy Ganaway, his voice hitting every corner of the War Room. "And I'm filthy rich! I could probably give the Boss a run for his money."

The people nearby came to look at the display screen. It showed an account number, along with the account holder's name and the amount of money deposited.

"Guess this guy's a big-money depositor at Westalpen Bank. And, boy, is that a lot of moolah. I'd love to make this public for the world to see. Just think of the panic it'd kick up. But that's somebody on the FBI's Most Wanted List for ya."

Stewart and John, who'd been notified of this spectacle of Billy the Brain's not a moment earlier, came to see the display for themselves. Billy typed in the name of Gumersindo Cortázar. More than a few people by that name came up, but only one of them had as much money in the bank. No doubt that was the secret account of the Gumersindo Cortázar they were after. With this, Billy's hacking of the Swiss bank was a total success.

"Looks like even the world's leading security measures are paper-thin before Billy's hacker skills," quipped Stewart.

"If I'd been working alone, it'd have taken me half a year. I only managed it in three months because of PathNet's full cooperation. The Boss gave me all the software and hardware I could ever need. Of course, while I did get a little advice from some programmers, it was all me for the most part."

Billy bowed his head in John's direction with an uncharacteristically straight face.

"We're only messing with Cortázar's account. The money needs to be transferred to a new account in Cordova. Everyone's watching you," said Stewart, putting a hand on his shoulder while eyeing the screen.

"I know, I know. You've really got zero faith in me, huh?"

"Not with your record I don't. And don't leave any traces."

"Obviously. I won't make that mistake again!"

When he'd hacked the FBI, agents had his home surrounded within two hours' time. Billy had stolen a march on the FBI before, but the bureau had been waiting for him to slip up. They'd tracked him through a pathway of entry.

"Cortázar's got $7.5 billion in his personal account. Moreno's got $3.8 billion in his. They were really pinching their pennies, the both of them, and now that's biting them in the ass. Time to transfer a total of $11.3 billion into the new account."

Three days prior, Billy had infiltrated a Cayman Islands bank named Grand Caribbean Bank, which was where the kingpin Moreno had set up his slush fund account.

Several people in the room started airing their opinions.

"The new account will serve as the economic wellspring for the new administration. It could even cover a year's worth of the national budget for a country of Cordova's size."

"If the new administration comes to power, they can use that money to start up a revitalization program. Ask for help from aid companies. Companies that have plenty of employment opportunities for Cordovans."

"Let's ask the United Nations for aid too. The only problem is we don't know when the regime will get replaced by Nueva Cordova."

"Now then," said Billy. "With the stroke of a finger, Cortázar will be penniless, and Cordova wealthy."

And just like that, the number at the top of the screen vanished.

"There goes all their money. I did leave trace though, which will make it seem like Cortázar and Moreno stole from *each other.* Now they'll really go for each other's throats. We could be looking at full-blown combat by tomorrow. And no matter which side wins, it just means we'll have one less enemy to worry about."

"Please inform Jadon that we've entered the next phase," said John, the mirth in his voice a match for Billy's.

"Why the long face, Stewie? It's times like these you've gotta smile and be happy," Billy told Stewart.

"This isn't what real war is like. There will be blood on the streets. Many innocent people will suffer and die. I can't smile, not after what I've seen and experienced as a serviceman."

That was when Nick piped in. "Everybody focus on the central screen. There's been a bombing in La Caridad, and a shoot-out's developed. They're saying it was a terrorist attack. Get in touch with Jadon ASAP."

In the middle of the screen, they saw red-hot flames scorch the street.

"Enhance the image, I want to see the situation up close," ordered John.

The flaming portion of the footage zoomed larger. Everyone in the room crowded around the screen to get a closer look at the burning building.

"Make the image sharper, it's too blurry."

"The bombing happened at a restaurant. What's going on there?"

"Quiet, everyone. I've got a Defense Department friend on the line," said Stewart. He just listened, nodding at points, before hanging up with a "thank you."

"A restaurant near the Presidential Residence got blown up. They're saying the culprit's a cartel man. The shoot-out's between government troops and Los Eternos stooges. There's been civilian casualties too. As such, there's a chance the military puts La Caridad under martial law."

"If Los Eternos are behind the bombing, this might be Moreno's retribution for his Cayman account getting emptied. He must think Cortázar stole the money," said Billy, voice cracking with emotion.

"Just as planned. Their clash is only going to heat up from here, which is perfect for us."

"I can't get through to Jadon. He should be in La Caridad; he said he was going to see Penelope Escárcega!" said Nick, the satellite phone still glued to his ear. It was ringing, but Jadon wasn't picking up.

A flurry of voices erupted as the assorted specialists of the War Room attempted to gather information.

"Jadon's MIA. Is there any way we can reach him?"

"Did he not have any guards around him? He must've gone there in a group. Contact the other revolutionaries and find Jadon!"

"The military has barred entry into La Caridad and arrested the Los Eternos members."

"Shh! It's him!" shouted Nick, putting the satellite phone on speakerphone and placing it on the table.

"I'm with Penelope. She's agreed to persuade the professor."

"I just said I'd go see him!" said a female voice in the background.

"Are you all right? We heard a restaurant got bombed."

"We managed to make it out alive by the skin of our teeth. Now the town's really crawling with soldiers. Right in front of our eyes, there are army trucks going up and down the road. I'm heading to the professor, so I need an up-to-date diagram of the dissident detention center, plus all the details on its security setup. Get me all the info you possibly can."

"We're asking the Pentagon, the CIA, and other agencies for all the help we can get. You'll get the info you need the minute we do."

"Okay. Tell me whenever something comes to light." Jadon ended the call.

"That's all we'll get out of Cordova right now," said John. "Back to your battle stations, everybody."

Quiet returned to the War Room. Then, Antonio's satellite phone began ringing. The whole room's eyes were on him as he hung up, his face white as a ghost.

"That was Sebastian Loyola, the Revolutionary Army commander. Professor Escárcega's execution has been moved up a day. Now it's scheduled for noon tomorrow. That bombing must have lit quite the fire under their asses."

"Tell Jadon immediately. I know he can pull it off in time." Stewart picked up the satellite phone.

■ ■ ■

At the FBI Academy, Adán and Vanessa were leaning so close to the screen they were nearly touching foreheads. Three hours had passed since they started analyzing. Adán was trying to identify the American soldier who'd fired the first shot from the American side.

"The first shot came out of this car from the Mexican side. It was a Kalashnikov, the gun of choice for tons of terrorists and guerrilla fighters the world over, including guerrillas in the Middle East."

"Then are you saying Islamic terror groups were involved?" said Vanessa.

"I want to look into any and all possibilities. Anti-American countries in Central America use Kalashnikovs, too, just like in Cuba. And Cordova's no exception."

"Even Cordova's military uses Kalashnikovs, if I'm not mistaken," she replied.

"The American soldiers started firing the instant the first shot was fired. From there it's a hail of bullets, and the tear grenades. Smoke candles were tossed from the Mexican side too."

"This is ridiculous. What the hell did the military's investigation look into? Look at all the crazy stuff we're uncovering," she sighed. "Is this what was broadcast?"

"This is the original we got from the TV station, yeah. I think any video of the incident that wasn't broadcast live was edited. They might've even changed around the order of events."

"The will of the government and the military must have influenced the editing too. The media's so easily swayed." Vanessa drew away from the screen, stretched her body, and faced Adán. "The military was so busy trying to bury the debacle at their doorstep that they rushed to label the incident settled and accounted for, all so Americans would forget about it sooner rather than later."

"And that's why the military discharged Captain Green?"

"The president must have been okay with it. Though he probably didn't say so outright."

"So the people around him just judged for themselves how he wanted the affair handled?"

"Not just that. Nobody had to say a word for them to feel the pressure coming at them from all sides. From the president, from the government, and of course from the military too. That's why the police and the FBI were forced out. Or rather, why they weren't even allowed in the ring," she said, choosing her words carefully. "And then, they declare the investigation's over without any fanfare. Their plan succeeded too. Nobody would ever know—until a newbie FBI agent stumbled on the video."

"So they prioritized getting the news blitz over and done with. The whole world was raking America over the coals."

"But there's really no excuse. We're talking about a damn massacre. So many *died*. There needed to have been a proper criminal investigation aiming to find the real killers and arrest them. And that's the job of the police or the FBI," she asserted firmly.

"This whole tragedy was purposefully instigated. It's clear to see a lot of the gunfire was from the Mexican side, and from a wide range of positions, at that. They were artificially creating a bloodbath. No wonder the US soldiers would be firing their hearts out. And that's also why the body count's so high."

Adán worked the keyboard. A man in American ACUs appeared on the neighboring monitor. He was firing from behind the sandbags piled up in front of The Wall. "This Latino soldier was the first to fire from the American side." Adán zoomed in on the soldier in question, brightened up the image, and printed out the screenshot. "The military must be aware of that too. But they haven't breathed a word about it to the public."

"The official line is that the soldiers saw the oncoming wave of refugees as a threat and fired in response. All they released to the public was the name of the commanding officer—Captain Jadon Green."

"Find out who the Latino soldier is. I want to meet him and look into what exactly happened there," said Vanessa.

Adán sent an inquiry to the Defense Department about the garrison that was sent to The Wall. The First Corps at Joint Base Lewis-McChord. Around five hundred were stationed there. They found the private in the photo easily enough.

Private Ricardo Sepúlveda was from Nevada, and his parents were immigrants from Mexico. One month after the Tragedy at The Wall, he left the military, citing an inability to withstand the duties of the job due to mental instability. After the incident, several media organizations interviewed him, which had to have played a part as well.

"We need to pay Sepúlveda a visit to ask him what was going on," said Adán, poring over Sepúlveda's photo and data.

"Where does he live?"

"New York. I can make it there today if I leave now." Adán headed for the door.

"Well, if you're going, I suppose I am too," called Vanessa. "Don't forget your badge and gun. You may be in training, but you're still an FBI special agent."

Adán hastily fished his gun holder from underneath the documents on the desk and put it on.

The two went to Stafford, Virginia, to catch a train to New York. Sepúlveda's address was in the crime-ridden Brooklyn neighborhood of East Bay, where men were loitering idly in the streets. Once they stepped out of their taxi, Adán and Vanessa went right up the stairs of the aging apartment building. On the way to Sepúlveda's place, they heard a couple in one of the rooms hurling abuse at each other, along with some ominous smashing noises.

"It's a dangerous neighborhood. Keep your wits about you," said Vanessa, taking out her gun. Adán followed suit.

"What do we do? Should we call for backup? There was a patrol car parked a block away. We can get there in five minutes. It'd be faster than phoning."

"You want the FBI to be asking local police for backup?"

"I take it that'd be weird?"

"It's fine, I'll go. Whatever you do, do not do anything without me, got it?" Vanessa went down the stairs.

Gun still in hand, he put his back to the wall and watched the door. Time slowed to a crawl. He glanced at his watch every minute.

The door of an adjacent room opened, and a man entered the hallway. Upon seeing Adán and his gun, he hurriedly jumped back inside and closed the door behind him with the click of the lock.

Adán heard the footfalls of multiple people running up the stairs. Vanessa had brought two NYC police officers, and together, the four of them stood in front of the door to Sepúlveda's apartment, guns at the ready.

"Private Ricardo Sepúlveda, this is the FBI, with the police. We just want to ask you some questions. Please open the door," said Vanessa.

No reply.

One of the policemen bade Vanessa stand back and kicked the

door with all his might. It swung open without resistance. The officer signaled for her to enter, and she did, her gun never leaving her hands.

Adán stopped breathing—the stench of death hung in the air. Vanessa scrunched her face and held her nose.

A man's corpse was lying in an empty bathtub. He was already halfway to being a mummy. He must have died several months ago. Every inch of the room smelled putrid.

"Someone slit his throat. He died instantly, unable to cry out," stated one of the officers. Sure enough, there was a dried-up four-inch gash across his throat. The other officer was reporting to HQ with his walkie-talkie. A half hour later, the room was full of cops.

"How did no one notice? The whole place reeks to high heaven. And it had to have been even worse before."

"The rooms around here are all like this. Also, his rent got paid on time every month. Via bank transfer, which is unusual," said the officer nonchalantly.

Adán and Vanessa left the corpse for the police to examine and headed for the NYPD, since possible evidence had been taken out of the room by police detectives.

"Look into Sepúlveda's credit card history."

"I plan to." Adán snapped photos of absolutely everything that seemed useful with his phone, after which he sent the pictures to his FBI computer.

By the time they got back to the FBI Academy, it was ten to midnight. They entered the room with Adán's computer and turned it on, opening up all of the photos he'd taken. It didn't take long to dig up Sepúlveda's bank deposit records. They'd used the name of their boss, Bart Benton, to get some agents working on it.

"A year ago, he got a payment of ten thousand dollars and another of twenty thousand transferred to his account. The first payment happened the day before the Tragedy at The Wall, and the second the day after. And that's when his rent started coming directly from his account."

"What the hell was this guy mixed up in?" Vanessa stared at Private Sepúlveda's photo on the screen. He was smiling in his Army uniform.

■ ■ ■

For the umpteenth time, President Copeland muttered some variation of "great" or "excellent."

"We've taken the money from Cortázar's personal account," said John, "and transferred it to a new account for use as Cordovan revitalization funding."

"It's that much money?"

"It's $11.3 billion, adding in the money we took from Moreno's account."

The president whistled. "Wouldn't have guessed they were richer than me by that many zeroes. America ought to spare some more thought to its president's salary too. Not that you could pay me to be president of Cordova."

"You can stockpile as much money as you like, but you can't take it into the grave with you. And if you leave it behind, people will fight to get their hands on it. Now their money will be used for the right reasons."

"When you put it that way, I get it. Though I don't think eleven billion's enough to rebuild Cordova."

"We're talking about rebuilding a whole country. No amount of money is ever really going to be enough. But we do have a finance person, and a person who's a pro at attracting companies. And I have a hunch Cordova will be getting major economic aid from Washington too."

"Oh, I promise you the president of the United States of America will help in any way he can."

"Hearing that is a huge relief. In due time, we'll be making the revitalization plan public to the world, in the name of the new administration of Cordova."

"Did Captain Green make it into Cordova okay? Is he moving forward with the plan?"

"He has infiltrated La Caridad as part of a strategy to save Professor Luis Escárcega, who we're tapping to be the next president of Cordova."

"I heard there was a bombing at a restaurant a few hours ago. Are you sure he's okay? I got reports saying the town's in a state of chaos."

"He's hiding in Professor Escárcega's daughter's home. The moment we send over the necessary details regarding the dissident detention center, the rescue plan will commence."

"Talk about frustrating. We've got the world's most powerful military, yet we're stuck having to rely on all of you."

"That's just politics. This operation is top secret; on the surface, the coup will be carried out entirely by the strength and will of the Cordovan people. We can't afford for the name of the president of the United States to crop up."

"I know that. You guys have my thanks. And soon, all of Cordova's." And with a heavy sigh, the president dropped the call. He stared at the lawn for a while.

An aide entered with a knock on the door. "Please hurry, sir. The French ambassador is waiting for you. And don't forget to take the EU files."

■ ■ ■

4

OF FATHER AND DAUGHTER

An hour past sundown, the world was seized by darkness. And Jadon was still hiding in Penelope's home.

The intel on the dissident detention center, including both the floor plan and infrared photos taken via satellite, had been sent to his phone, courtesy of the War Room. The red shadows pinpointed all the matter that was exuding heat—which was to say, people. There was internet access in La Caridad, so there was no need to use the satellite phone to obtain the relevant info.

Tsutomu had told Jadon two hours earlier that thanks to the Los Eternos restaurant bombing, Professor Escárcega's execution was slated for noon the next day—a day sooner than the mercs and revolutionaries expected.

Jadon called Tsutomu via satellite phone. "There are twenty-five guys guarding the place. Last I heard, there were more of them. The bombing must've caused them to shift personnel around. If we're going to save the professor, now's our only shot."

"It's too soon to attempt it tonight. If we gather the troops and head there now, then—"

"How many escorts were assigned to me?"

"Five. Including Arsenio."

"Can you get in touch with them? I lost track of them after the bombing."

"They fled to an ally's house for refuge. I told them you're okay. They said they'd head back to camp after things calmed down a little."

"We're going to rescue the professor tonight. I had the War Room send me details on the detention center's layout and security setup. I'm with his daughter Penelope at the moment."

"I guess tonight's the only time we could make it happen. La Caridad is swarming with soldiers. Nobody would expect the detention center to get attacked on the day of a Los Eternos bombing, not now that the city's on high alert. I'll call Arsenio right away and get back to you in half an hour."

Jadon hung up. A stray dog was barking outside, while an irate man was shouting at a crying woman. This distressing soundscape was punctuated by the occasional gunshot. La Caridad was now a lawless zone.

They heard an explosion in the distance and the world turned dark. The power was out. They looked out the window; no light anywhere.

"The power plant got blown up or the grid got wrecked. Happens all the time," Penelope informed him.

A dim light illuminated her. She was standing with a candle in her hand. Penelope made them some sandwiches. They ate and stared at the flame until the call from Tsutomu came, right on time.

"Arsenio took the four subordinates to a bar behind the detention center named Destino. They've got some equipment ready. Please meet up with them," said Tsutomu before hanging up.

"Do you know a bar named Destino?" Jadon asked Penelope.

"Everyone knows it. And I can't imagine a better name for a place where the country's fate will be decided," she replied.

The streets were deathly quiet when they left Penelope's home. Military cars were patrolling, while pairs of soldiers were standing at each corner. Martial law hadn't been declared but talking heads on the TV and radio were cautioning citizens nonstop not to go outside.

Penelope suddenly came to a halt, pushing Jadon against a wall with her. Their faces close together, they could feel each other's warm breath as their lips touched.

A small group of soldiers walked by. They'd noticed the two, but they just clucked their tongues and continued on their way.

"Don't get the wrong idea. I'm just saving myself some trouble. If they caught sight of an American walking around in the middle of the night on a day like this, you'd better believe they'd take him away—and the lady with him too," she said matter-of-factly.

The two made it to Destino. The bar had about ten customers, who were apparently treating the day like any other. Arsenio and two revolutionary soldiers were there waiting with their small backpacks.

"Where are the other two? The mercs?"

"They took down the two guards at the entrance of the facility. I kept them there in the guards' places, so we can enter easily. You have the building plans, right?"

Using his phone, Jadon showed Arsenio and the other two all the info the War Room had sent him. Arsenio gave him a handgun and some spare magazines.

The city's power was out, but only about half of the detention center's lights were off, thanks to its in-house generator. Jadon, Penelope, Arsenio, and the two revolutionaries entered the facility and proceeded down its dimly lit passageways. The layout was almost mazelike, perhaps to put a stop to potential escapes or attacks.

"There are three guards on the professor's floor," said Jadon, checking the info on his phone.

"Even more guards are getting shuffled away from the detention center to increase the security of the city itself. The power substation got blown up, and they don't want any more damage on their hands. Looks like luck's on our side."

The place was utterly silent. Sebastian had told them that, according to a man who'd been released from the prison, if detainees made noise after dark, they would go without breakfast the next day.

As they pressed through the halls, Arsenio and his subordinates took down another five guards.

Eventually, they ran into an iron door that wouldn't have existed when the place was a hotel. Looking through the peephole, they saw two seated soldiers playing cards at a table.

"Put your head down and relax your shoulders. We can't miss this chance." Arsenio stuck a gun to Jadon's head and pounded on the door. "I'm taking this American to the one-man cell in the back. Open the door, would you?"

"We received no such orders."

"Only because of all this ruckus. They must not have gotten to you yet. You're the only ones who can skate by playing cards."

The smaller of the two soldiers peeked through the peephole and opened up for them. Jadon whipped out his gun and he and Arsenio fired at the same time. Silencers muffled their shots as the guards collapsed onto the table and down to the floor.

"Professor Escárcega's being held in the back. Do NOT make a sound."

There were one-man cells on both sides of the passage leading toward the back. They were occupied by the major political dissidents.

"His cell is all the way at the end."

Turning the key they'd taken from the guards, they swung open the door of his cell, and found him lying in bed. Six months behind bars had without a doubt made him much weaker than before. They figured Luis wouldn't be able to move terribly fast on his own, so they'd have to help him.

The room was ill-lit, but Jadon could tell Penelope caught her breath upon seeing her father. He flashed a light in Luis's face. It was swollen with dark-red abscesses and the outer corners of his eyes had blood-matted cuts on them. This came as no shock to Jadon, but it did to Penelope.

The professor knew she was his daughter the second he laid eyes on her.

"I came here because these people asked me to talk to you about the revolution, but I don't know what I should say. Just do what you want. You are a perfect stranger to me."

"Building a new nation is for the benefit of the people. And I believed you and your mother were of the people. That . . . That's why . . ."

"You think somebody who can't even provide for his own family can provide for a nation?" she said, quietly but firmly.

"It's just as you say. I wasn't able to provide for anyone, in the end. Just know that I love you and your mother with all my heart, like I love the people of Cordova."

"Well, the woman you loved died. And you're the one who all but killed her."

Luis's cheeks were shining in the dim light. He was crying.

"You two can hash it out later. You heard her, didn't you? We're here to spring you. We're taking you to the Revolutionary Army's camp to help us make a new Cordova," said Jadon, who helped the professor to his feet.

"Let's go, while they still haven't spotted us," said Arsenio, who also provided support for Luis.

"If I escape, my allies will be killed in my place."

"Then you should die with them," said Penelope, glaring at him.

"Forget about them. Taking just you out of here is dangerous enough. How many allies are we talking?"

"Five," said Luis. "If you're serious about rebuilding the country, you'll need more than just me. You'll need them too."

"You must be joking. Do you know what you're asking?"

"Please, I'm begging you. Free them too."

"Unlock all of the cells. We're taking everyone with us," said Jadon with a hushed tone.

"Are you kidding me? Getting out of here with the professor alone will be hard enough." Arsenio looked at Luis once more. He sighed, took the keys off the table, and went about unlocking all of the cells.

"Make no noise. If they spot us, we die."

The group swelled with the additional dissidents—all in their late sixties and all just as enervated as Luis. Together they escaped the compound.

Arsenio had arranged for a medium-sized truck to wait for them, and they spotted it once they made it out of the compound. The six freed dissidents were placed onto the cargo bed, unable to climb aboard by themselves. The moment Jadon and the rest got in, the truck took off.

They rushed through a pitch-dark La Caridad at breakneck speed. Military vehicles were parked all over town, with countless fully armed, gun-holding soldiers patrolling the streets. The truck weaved through all of the obstacles, at times blasting the horn to scare groups of troops out of the way. Only when they reached the city outskirts did they slow down and park someplace safe.

"This is as far as we go," said a young man who got off the truck. "There's a security checkpoint up ahead. Normally it'd take ten minutes on foot to get to the jungle from here, but you've got those six gentlemen with you. It may take a whole hour to get there."

Arsenio paid the driver, and the truck returned to the city center. Jadon and his group began walking toward the jungle.

Professor Escárcega and his dissident allies were bone-tired, but they trudged forward—their lives depended on it. Over an hour later, they'd reached the cover of the trees. Although the old men were exhausted, Arsenio led the group deeper into the jungle.

* * *

Cortázar was at the desk in the office of the Presidential Residence. Raminez Dourne was seated on the couch in front, and before them stood three military commanders.

Cortázar sighed. The investigation of the Los Eternos restaurant bombing was ongoing. To date, the regime's forces had killed forty-nine cartel militants and captured nine. That there were so few in custody was due to the soldiers' orders to shoot anyone who resisted arrest.

Counting the dead among the government troops and the police, a total of thirty-three had lost their lives.

"Thirty-seven civilians died and more than a hundred are injured, all thanks to Los Eternos. Tomorrow I'll be announcing to the world that we will eradicate Los Eternos," said Cortázar.

"How about we say the Revolutionary Army was partially involved in the act of terrorism?" said Dourne.

"No reason not to. We can even give that as the reason we offed Luis. And it'll lower the revolutionaries' morale."

Then, a knock on the door. In came the liaison officer.

He looked at the commanding officer for a fleeting moment before training his eyes on Cortázar, who nodded.

"Professor Escárcega has escaped. The other dissidents as well," he reported.

Cortázar's face twisted and he struck the officer. The fallen officer bled from his mouth, and his face looked pale with fear. "What the hell were the guards doing!?"

"They were all killed. Over half of the guards had been called away to suppress Los Eternos."

Cortázar froze and stared at everyone in the room. Then his eyes landed on Dourne. Cortázar looked dubious.

"What interest would Los Eternos have in someone like Luis? I think it's possible some revolutionaries snuck into the detention center, killed the guards, and rescued him."

"The Revolutionary Army doesn't have the wherewithal," said one of the commanders, voice quivering.

Dourne gave the liaison officer a hand up. "Who else would need him, though? They attacked the prison because they need the professor. Were the soldiers in the facility shot? If guns were fired, why was there no commotion?"

"They mostly either got their throats slit or their necks snapped. Only a few were shot. They must have used silencers," said the liaison officer tremulously.

"This was the work of pros," said Dourne. "One or more men who received formal training infiltrated the facility and stole Luis away. Nueva Cordova is nothing more than a gaggle of peasants and vagrants. And if it was the revolutionaries, then—"

Cortázar gave it some thought. "It's Sebastian. He received American military training. I took him under my wing, and he repaid me by slipping away and founding the Revolutionary Army. I'm going to catch him and rip him limb from limb," he muttered, before pulling himself together and lifting his head. "They want to use Luis as a tool. Get him back by tomorrow's execution."

"We're already on it," replied Dourne, who looked at the liaison officer. "An operation is currently in the works. There are soldiers patrolling every street, and there's been no report they passed through a checkpoint. They must be headed back into the jungle. We'll track them down as soon as possible."

"To think Luis still had the energy to cross the jungle. And alongside the other dissidents, to boot. They can't be going very fast; we'll catch up to them in no time. Now hurry!"

At that, the commanders left the office in a mad rush.

Luis's condition had deteriorated at a remarkable clip these past few weeks. Cortázar kicked himself for not following Dourne's advice and executing him when he had the chance. He supposed he was at fault for wanting to exploit Luis's execution for political points. He kicked the table, his anxiety reaching unprecedented peaks. He kicked it again, but the anxiety didn't ebb.

Dourne's cold eyes simply watched.

■ ■ ■

They had been walking through the jungle for two hours now.

Penelope was lending her father a shoulder to lean on. He was walking as best he could, but he was visibly struggling.

Jadon dialed up the War Room using his satellite phone. They could use the chip they'd embedded inside his body to determine their location.

"Look to see if there's anything that'd hamper us if we continue straight in this direction," he requested.

"You're going in the right direction, but government forces are on your tail. I'll call back with more in a bit."

"We can't walk any longer. Just leave us and go."

The dissidents were sitting at the base of a tree.

"You get a ten-minute break. The second your break's over, we move. Everyone, I want you to keep walking even if it kills you. All of us will pitch in to help anyone who physically can't walk. US Army soldiers like me never leave anyone behind. We make it back together, or else."

The words "US Army soldiers like me" had inadvertently slipped out of Jadon's mouth.

Penelope, who was also sitting, kept looking at her feet.

"Let me see," said Jadon.

"Leave me alone."

Jadon grabbed her by the ankle, despite her protests. The sole of her sneaker had come unstuck, and her big toe, chafed and bleeding, was peeking out. She had been walking through mountain trails and rocky areas of the jungle with her father in tow, and the strain had proven too great for her shoes.

"Treat your foot. You're a doctor, aren't you?"

Penelope took some tape out of her bag and put it over the wound. Jadon mended her shoe by securing the sole in two places using nylon zip ties.

"That should hold for the time being. Walk carefully."

Within ten minutes, the War Room called.

"The enemy's on your heels. There's around twenty of them. They'll catch up to you in thirty minutes," came Stewart's voice.

"That fast? How are they even chasing us? I made sure we left no trace." Jadon scanned their surroundings. All he saw was yet denser rainforest. "Maybe they're viewing us via satellite? With Russia's or China's assistance, maybe?" Jadon speculated.

"The only satellite over Cordova is ours."

"Are there drones flying over us? Search the skies."

"There's some weak radio signals. Check the belongings of everyone there."

Jadon had Arsenio pat down the dissidents, but he didn't find anything on them. They all knew each other from over a decade ago. No one stood out, except the oldest-looking man who had a watch on. The others had had theirs taken by government troops.

"My wife gave me this watch when I retired from being a professor. She died a year ago. It's a memento of her. They took it from me when they apprehended me, but they gave it back when I explained what it meant to me."

Jadon tossed the watch into a ravine perpendicular to their path.

"They're not soft enough to be doing you favors out of the kindness of their hearts. They put a tracker in it. Now hurry! Otherwise our pursuers will catch up to us!" said Jadon.

An hour later, and no government troops were to be seen. Jadon called the War Room.

"Are they still following us?"

"They were thrown off the trail, but they're closing in on you again. Can you pick up the pace?"

"It's no use. We're escorting a group of elderly men whose strength has diminished after years of incarceration. Some of them can barely even walk. At this rate, we won't make it to the camp in time."

"Figure something out. We'll keep track through the satellite, and send you info when we can," said Stewart, hanging up.

"Hurry them up. The enemy's getting closer and closer. They must have excellent scouts."

"We're just too slow," said Arsenio quietly. "Going over the mountains with the whole group is not possible. And Professor Escárcega is severely weakened." He was panicking too—he could sense the government forces were approaching. "I knew taking all of the dissidents would be too much for us to handle. I can take Professor Escárcega, but just him."

"You'd better not let anybody else hear your whining. I promised I'd return to camp without a single man down." Jadon ordered the group to move out. Luis attempted to get on his feet, but his legs wobbled. Penelope swooped in to support his body.

"Let's go."

They slugged through the woods, Arsenio leading the way.

Meanwhile, President Cortázar was in the military communications room.

While it was hardly sufficient, he had, through the military tech assistance of anti-American nations, scored an exhaustive assortment of the latest telecommunication devices, which Dourne had secured through his web of connections.

"Give the tracking team the positions of Luis's group. He is to be captured alive. I want to have him executed as the mastermind behind the bombing."

"We've discovered a dissident's wristwatch. It seems they noticed the transmitter and tossed it away."

"Scan the vicinity. They must be nearby. Luis and the other dissidents have no energy. They can't keep walking for very long. Bring me Luis by any means necessary!" Cortázar exclaimed. Nearly ten hours had passed since the prison break.

"Don't turn off the radio. Look to the north and the west. Do you see any footprints? There can't be fewer than ten of them. They must be leaving traces," said Dourne, speaking calmly into the mic.

"Hurry! They're traveling slowly; sprint and we'll catch them in no time," came the increasingly agitated voices of the tracking soldiers. "Eyes on the ground; you don't want to trip on any branches!"

"We've found their trail. We're giving chase." With that, the line dropped.

Cortázar and the others held their breaths as they watched the blip of light on the display. The tracking unit holding the transmitter-embedded wristwatch was on the move. They were headed for the jungle depths.

Twenty minutes later, voices came through the speaker. "We've spotted the revolutionaries. We'll catch up to them in an hour. They're moving faster than before. They're aware we're pursuing them."

"Hurry! Get me Luis no matter what. I don't mind if you kill the spares," Cortázar yelled into the mic.

Rough breathing could be heard from the trackers. "Looks like Luis hasn't noticed our presence yet. Over and out."

Cortázar collapsed into a chair. Ever since the restaurant bombing, he hadn't caught a wink of sleep. If he closed his eyes, he'd likely fall asleep on the spot.

"Why don't you go rest, sir? I'm here," said Dourne.

"Very well. Tell me when they make contact." Cortázar left the communications room.

In the War Room, everyone below John was watching the satellite footage. The blip representing Jadon's transmitter was wending its way through the jungle. The other marker represented the unit of government troops chasing the revolutionaries. The distance between the two groups was growing shorter and shorter.

"Is there anything we can do to save them? At this rate, the enemy will catch up in no time," pleaded John, words came out of his mouth unthinkingly. "There are about twenty government troops on their tails. Jadon's group has six elderly men and a woman, with only six combatants including Jadon himself."

"Even if they manage to slip away, the enemy will still discover the camp's location. They need to intercept the enemy someplace."

"They'd just get wiped out. You heard Jadon's report. They have no choice but to leave behind the six dissidents and run," said Nick as he watched the satellite video.

"Can we send a rescue unit from the camp?"

"It'd take them four hours to get there, and that's if they're fast. Meanwhile, the enemy will catch up in thirty minutes. And they'll then have a fight on their hands."

The tension in the War Room was thick.

"There's an aircraft carrier sailing near Cordova. The onboard rescue choppers ought to be able to reach them in twenty minutes!" shouted Billy, who looked up from the computer he was using.

"Send the carrier's command channel to my computer," barked Stewart before rushing to his own room.

Upon closing the door, Stewart pondered for a few seconds and then called the Pentagon.

I'll call on Navy Operations Headquarters. I know a few vice admirals, but they'll ask me for my reasons no matter what I request.

He called his secretary from when he worked at the Defense Department a few years back. After a few words of greeting, Stewart warned that what he was about to say was to be kept confidential. "It's an emergency. Some idiots got stranded in Cordova and are being chased by government troops. All of them are American citizens. There's no time to go through diplomatic routes. What can I do to get some choppers to rescue them while bypassing all the procedures?"

"We can't intentionally violate a country's airspace on just a captain's orders. Only the president can order something like that. But the president can't just give the okay without a lot of persuasion. Congress might grill him over it."

John knocked on the door and entered. Stewart said thanks and hung up.

"We need the president to order the carrier to send in the choppers."

"That's what I thought, which is why I'm here." John got out his smartphone.

The USS *Truman* was navigating the waters thirty miles west of Cordova, whose landmass stood out in sharp relief on the bridge's radar. Captain Otis Dalton had been nodding and repeating "yes."

"Send some rescue copters; there are civilians who need saving right now. This operation is top secret. The destination is . . ."

The captain put down the receiver and relayed his instructions to his vice commander.

"That would be an airspace violation. We'd need permission from the president."

"It's the president that ordered the operation. Avoid combat if at all possible, but if you are attacked, I give you permission to fire back. Now hurry. We've got no time to waste."

Three rescue helicopters departed the carrier for Cordova, their mission to save thirteen civilians.

When Jadon's group stepped onto the ridge, gunfire reverberated through the air. A revolutionary soldier walking in front of the pack fell backward, bleeding bullet holes in his chest.

"It's them! Everyone get back!" shouted Jadon, getting low to the ground. He felt the fallen revolutionary's neck—no pulse. "They found us. Get the dissidents out of here; three of you go with them. The rest of us will keep the enemy at bay. You've got to make it back to camp in the time we'll be buying you. North from here—"

But the soldiers came firing before Jadon could finish his sentence. He and his group retreated from the ridge to take cover behind trees. Leaves took the brunt of the spray of bullets.

The satellite phone started ringing. "I sent some rescue choppers," came Stewart's voice. "We've pinpointed your exact location, and they'll be there in twenty. Just hang in there."

"There's a depression in the east side of the ridge. We'll go there, and fire a flare when we see the choppers," said Jadon.

"Got it. I'll tell the pilots."

"I'll fight too," said Penelope, reaching for the dead revolutionary's gun. Then she slipped, only to be caught by the arm by Jadon.

Her shoe was beginning to come off, her bare foot exposed. Only one of the zip ties was left. Jadon took a shoe off the soldier's corpse and gave it to her.

"It's a little big, but you can use it."

"No way. Give it back to that poor man."

"He'd tell you to wear it. You have to live on for his sake too."

Penelope looked confused for a moment, but she took the shoe and put it on.

Arsenio and his men had begun to fire back at the government troops.

"Look! Ten o'clock!" shouted Arsenio.

He looked toward the ocean. Three helicopters were flying their way.

"The rescue choppers! Take the dissidents to the basin, then light the flare and guide the choppers to your location."

The government troops started coming into view. They were ascending the mountain while shooting their automatic rifles. Jadon tossed a grenade and a roaring explosion tore through the trees while sending earth and sand flying. But the opposing fire only abated for an instant. Soon they were back to shooting, and with even greater intensity.

A powerful explosion ripped a few yards from Jadon's position, blowing him backward into a tree. It was a rocket. The enemy was using RPGs.

A revolutionary soldier was lying beside him, stomach pooling with blood. Jadon grimaced slightly at the sight. The man was still conscious. Jadon placed one of the soldier's hands onto his wound and told him to apply pressure to stop the bleeding.

The red smoke of the flare rose up toward the sky. Arsenio's group had reached the basin and signaled the choppers.

Another explosion, this time behind Jadon. Debris soared through the battlefield. A mortar shell?

The government soldiers, some wielding RPGs, were rushing toward the basin. They intended to stop the copters from landing. Jadon got back on his feet and unleashed a barrage of fire at the enemy troops.

One of the choppers approached and rapidly shed altitude. Machine gun fire soon pelted the eardrums. Missiles and bullets alike were now mowing down Cortázar's forces. Bullets smashed into the ground and into the trees, while the impact of the missiles shrouded the war zone in smoke and flame.

The government unit was routed. They'd never considered the possibility of a helicopter attack.

"The choppers are landing. Put the dissidents on board," said Arsenio.

Penelope helped Luis and the other dissidents up onto the helicopters.

"Hurry, they're coming!" shouted the Navy soldier who got off the chopper.

Jadon carried the revolutionary soldier shot in the stomach on his back—he had never left a man behind and certainly wouldn't start now. He ordered his subordinates to recover the bodies of the fallen as well. Meanwhile, the helicopters' gunners continued firing at the government troops.

Jadon's group ran for the choppers while carrying the dead and wounded.

When everyone made it aboard, the choppers took off and quickly gained altitude. Looking down, they could see government soldiers impotently shooting their rifles up at them.

"I'm returning to the aircraft carrier," yelled the pilot, eyes fixed forward.

"Drop us off where I tell you," said Jadon, coming up behind the pilot's seat. He told him the course he should take and where to land.

"We're currently violating a country's airspace, and you're telling me to go back to the danger zone? I'm under no such orders. Let me call the brass." The pilot reached for the radio.

"Why don't we skip the hassle," said Jadon, pointing his handgun at the pilot. "Tell the other pilots to follow you. You'll be saving American citizens, and you're just taking those citizens to the place they want. Then your mission will be complete. The aircraft carrier's already been contacted. If there's a problem, just tell them you had to obey me since I had you at gunpoint."

The pilot looked at him and silently withdrew his hand from the radio. Jadon lowered his pistol.

Approximately twenty minutes later, the camp came into view. Jadon told him to land on a vacant lot nearby.

The chopper lowered itself, and Revolutionary Army members flocked to the lot. He could make out Sebastian and Tsutomu in the crowd. The Nueva Cordova soldiers came dashing up to the chopper as soon as it touched land. Penelope helped her father off.

The soldiers cheered in welcome. The copters' pilots and crews looked on, clearly surprised. After watching Arsenio and his men lay down the casualties, Jadon went up to the crews.

"Thank you, you saved us. Your courage and sound judgment are laudable."

"Good luck, Border Butcher." The pilot suddenly straightened up and saluted him. The crews did likewise. They must have cottoned onto the situation. Before he even realized it, Jadon saluted back.

Luis and his dissident allies, kept on their feet by Penelope and the other soldiers, made their way into the camp to cheers and cries of jubilation. The man of the hour was soon surrounded on all sides. Penelope looked at her father and the soldiers with an expression of confusion.

"Your father is loved and respected by the people," Jadon told Penelope, who had stepped away from the crowd of soldiers.

"Yeah, well, he was hated by his family. He never spared his family any thought."

"Did your mother ever say she hated him?"

Penelope didn't answer and turned her gaze to the man at the center of the cheering revolutionaries.

"I think your mother probably believed in his mission. And she raised you into a fine, outstanding woman."

"What do I do now? My job here is done."

"We're going to build a new Cordova together, with Professor Luis Escárcega at the core. We're going to make Cordova a place where no one needs to run from gun-toting maniacs," he replied, staring into her perplexed face.

That night, Jadon summoned Sebastian and Tsutomu to the command tent.

"We're in trouble. The military has followed us to a point just twelve and a half miles from here. They know it was Nueva Cordova that rescued Professor Escárcega. They're no doubt searching for the camp as we speak."

"According to Arsenio," said Sebastian, tracing the helicopter's path on a map, "the choppers flew from the sea to the pickup point. After it saved your hides, they flew toward the sea and wrapped around and returned to camp. Cortázar's men won't find this place *that* quickly."

"I'm the one who told the choppers to fly in that pattern. But Cortázar's more cautious and cunning than I expected. He'd placed a transmitter on one of the dissidents we freed and used that to chase us through the jungle."

"Starting tonight, we'll double the number of lookouts."

"Let's move camp as soon as we're ready."

Outside the tents, underneath the moonlight trickling down between the trees, a welcome party was held for Luis and the others.

Before long, almost everyone—except Penelope—was asleep, too tired to even think.

Still conflicted, Penelope was hugging her knees, watching her father sleep under his blanket. He probably wasn't asleep either.

Jadon put some clothes on her lap.

"You should change. It'll be easier to move in these. We're going to move camp soon. We'll be walking through the jungle again."

"Did you take them from a dead body?"

"They're meant for a rookie soldier, and they're your size. You can take new shoes there yourself."

"These fit perfectly with my socks on," she said quietly.

The stillness of the jungle was broken only by the cries of animals. The starlight dimly illuminated the clearing, and in that near darkness, over a hundred soldiers slept alongside their families.

President Cortázar exhaled deeply. He'd lain down on the sofa, hoping to get some shut-eye, but there was no way he was falling asleep.

I should have kept one of the men here. He wouldn't have been a conversation partner, but he would have made a nice target for my rage.

He'd banished all of his subordinates upon returning to his office.

Just as Cortázar reached for the phone receiver, an officer from the communications room came in.

"We've lost contact with the tracking unit."

"Is it a radio malfunction?"

"The last thing we heard was someone saying helicopters had arrived, followed by gunfire. Then the audio cut off."

Cortázar froze, his eyes focused on the officer. "The revolutionaries don't have damned *helicopters*. Are you sure you heard right?"

"I'm not sure. That's just what I heard. You're right . . . They can't, there's no way . . ." The officer's voice was trembling.

"Where's Dourne?"

"In the communications room, sir. He told me to tell you about the helicopters."

Cortázar stood up, exited, and headed for the communications room. The officer followed hurriedly in the president's wake.

The communications room was in a state of confusion. Dourne was watching the scene from the back with his arms folded.

"Didn't you have Luis and his group cornered? You were supposed to kill everyone but take Luis alive."

"A few choppers appeared, and gunfire was all we heard before the signal cut out."

"So the cartel used a copter and—no. No, the cartel doesn't have copters. It must be from another country's military. They must be American choppers."

"Copeland's far too spineless to be behind such a violation of our airspace. I gave orders to find out where the choppers landed," said Dourne, the picture of composure.

"Bring me Luis. *Alive.* I'll rip him apart before the watching eyes of the public and hang him from a pole. He'll serve as an example to anyone who wants to get in my way!" shouted Cortázar.

"Blow the rest of them to bits. Kill them all, you hear me?"

"I know that's what you want, but—"

"Reestablish contact with the tracking unit. Make them get a move on." Cortázar plopped into his chair, while Dourne remained standing behind him.

■ ■ ■

In front of Adán was FBI Deputy Director Douglas Fellure.

Vanessa urged Adán with her eyes: *Answer the man's questions honestly and politely.*

"Who was the captain of the unit guarding The Wall?"

"Captain Jadon Green, sir."

"What division is he with now?"

"He left the military after the incident. Or rather, he was made to leave. Dishonorable discharge. Everyone was calling him the Border Butcher. Some of his subordinates were injured too." Adán was dangerously close to adding *the military's awfully inept at hiding things.*

"Where is he now?"

"We're searching, but at the moment it's not clear. We know he was working at a construction site in Texas at one point, but he quit that job half a year ago."

"Find him. I want to hear his story from his own mouth."

"I believe the military is already investigating. Jurisdiction for this case has been transferred from the local police to the military police. I think the MP might have it on record."

"The FBI hasn't even spoken to the man. It's important that we uncover the truth, especially in light of how many people the incident hurt, and all the heat the country took on the world stage. The president's approval ratings tanked as a result as well. The shadow of the massacre still looms over the American people. The midterms are half a year from now, and the president wants reelection. If we realize the truth is at odds with the official line, the ramifications will be huge. Get on it," said Doug. "But keep it confidential. If we relitigate this and end up with nothing to show for it, the FBI will be a laughingstock. Am I clear?" He glared at them and left.

"Captain Green had a wife and daughter—Shirley and Paulina. That's what his Army file says. Do we know where they are?" asked Vanessa.

"They got divorced a while after it happened."

"Just because they're divorced doesn't mean they're totally estranged. It also says Jadon doted on his daughter a great deal."

"Shirley Goodrum-Green is living with her parents in San Francisco." Adán showed Vanessa a memo pad.

She turned to her computer and ran a search for morning flights from Dulles International to San Francisco.

During the flight, Adán read aloud the documents he'd hastily dug up on Jadon's ex-wife. "Shirley Goodrum-Green lives in her mother's home. Her daughter Paulina is four years old. Shirley has custody. Jadon Green visits once a month. Jadon and Shirley first met when . . ."

Six hours later, the two disembarked at San Francisco International, where it was three in the afternoon. They rented a car and drove to Shirley's home.

It was in a residential area in town, but not an upscale one—many illegal immigrants from Mexico were among the Hispanic population here.

Shirley was a tall woman with blond hair. She raised an eyebrow and eyed the two suspiciously. A little girl nestled up close, hands gripping her skirt. Her eyes resembled Jadon Green's. So this was Paulina.

Adán showed Shirley his FBI badge, and her expression morphed. She had the look of a woman who anticipated something like this might happen one day.

"All right. What did he do?"

"By he you mean Captain Jadon Green, right? Well, that's actually what we came to ask you."

For a moment, she looked confused, but she drew her daughter closer and told the two to enter.

The late-afternoon Californian sun shone its rays through the light blue curtains. An old woman—likely Shirley's mother—appeared to lead Paulina away to another room. Shirley pondered fretfully for a few moments. Then, finally, she'd worked up her resolve, and spoke. "I got a $100K deposit in my account. For the past half year I got seven hundred a month in child support, and it'd come late all the time. And now I get a hundred thousand? I tried calling, but the line doesn't go through. I know something must've happened."

"When was this?"

"About a week ago. I was so surprised—just the day before, we'd gotten into a big fight about the child support payments. From then on, his phone stopped receiving calls."

"Where do you think Captain Green might be right now?"

"I've honestly got no idea. From what I understand, he's always staying at hotels or motels." She didn't seem to be lying.

"Does Captain Green have any friends he could ask for help?"

"He used to have loads of friends, but ever since the Tragedy and his dishonorable discharge, most of those friendships evaporated. And he never had a friend with a hundred thousand dollars to spare, that's for sure."

"Have any of his past or current friends contacted you?"

"Our shared friends were aware of our situation, so they left us be. Or that's just the charitable interpretation. They probably just didn't want to get mixed up in our woes. People were calling him the Border Butcher. And we were the Border Butcher's wife and child."

Tears were streaming from her eyes, but she continued speaking without wiping them.

She recounted how Jadon drowned himself in alcohol, and how he had to jump from job to job. She told them how recently it looked as though he'd reached the end of his tether.

"I don't want to think about the possibility he's gotten himself involved in crime. But he might have, if for nothing else than for his daughter. Just the thought of it upsets me." Shirley lifted her head and looked at the two agents.

Vanessa and Adán listened to Shirley for around two hours, after which they took their leave. They managed to make it in time for the final flight to Dulles, which was scheduled to touch down at a little past six in the morning. On the plane, neither of them uttered a single word for some time.

Shirley's parting words echoed in Adán's mind. "The Tragedy at The Wall was a tragedy for us too. Our family was torn apart. And Jadon, he *changed*. The Wall destroyed our lives. I despise it."

About an hour into the flight, Vanessa broke the silence. "Did you look into his credit card history? The last place he used it?"

"Yeah. He used it in LA to pay for a cab ride, which took him close to Van Nuys. He hasn't used that card in the past week. He only has a hundred dollars left in his bank account anyway. I inquired with the airport, but there's no record of him buying a ticket or leaving the country. He's vanished without a trace."

"He was constantly late paying child support but then sends her $100K. There's no question something's at play here. Something huge."

"And I bet it has something to do with Sepúlveda's death, too, though that's just a hunch."

"I agree. Looks like our first order of business is looking for where Sepúlveda's thirty thousand bucks came from."

"It came from a company based in Florida named Azure Ocean. I tried to find out what kind of company it is, but no dice. I called them, but no answer."

"You should've told me that sooner! And don't you dare say it's because I didn't ask."

"Shall we go to Florida?"

"Director Benton won't give us permission. We just flew to San Francisco with nothing to show for it."

"We have some new leads though. I mean, Shirley got a payment of a hundred thousand as child support. That's eye-opening, to say the least. That means Captain Green did a job that netted him that much money. He might even still be doing that job. That's important info."

"But where will that take us? Maybe we should have stayed longer in Cali."

"But the director asked us to be back ASAP."

"Guess Azure Ocean's our only lead for now. You couldn't reach them by phone, right? Then we have no choice but to go in person. Oh, wait, there's an FBI field office there. There's no need for us to go there. I know an agent named Tony who works there. Let's have him look into it," she mumbled, half to herself.

The two arrived at Dulles an hour ahead of schedule, at 5 a.m. Neither of them had slept much.

But Adán didn't even feel tired, nor did Vanessa.

Fresh off the plane, they went straight to Quantico and the FBI Academy, where Vanessa called her old acquaintance from their trainee days, Tony Iadanza, to ask him to take a look at Azure Ocean.

"What do you want me to find out for you? I can't look into anything if you don't give me the skinny." said Tony. "Also, calling me at this hour? Consider this a favor."

"I want you to look into everything. What does the company do? How big is it? What scale does it operate on? How many people does it employ? There's plenty there to find out. Oh, and the CEO. What kind of guy is he?" She ended the call with, "I owe you one, by the way. We may be onto something pretty big here."

Three hours later, Tony called back. Vanessa exchanged glances with Adán and put the call on speaker. "I tried calling Azure Ocean, but it never went through, so I went there in person. It's a shell corporation, and it was founded by one Enrique Tenedor."

"Who's that?" asked Vanessa.

"He's a businessman from Colombia—an importer and exporter of general goods."

"Any red flags?"

"He's nothing but red flags. He was a Cordovan national. I looked into his bank account, and he's worth at least two too many zeroes for a business of that size. Also, guess who he's cousins with?"

"This ain't a quiz; spit it out already!"

"His cousin is Gumersindo Cortázar. The president of Cordova."

"The president of Cordova!?" they blurted simultaneously.

"Has Cortázar given Tenedor's business money?" asked Vanessa.

"I think that's safe to assume. There are loads of other suspicious large-sum transactions too."

Iadanza rattled off a list of names of both individuals and corporate enterprises.

"So the president of Cordova sent money to Tenedor's company," said Adán, who had been listening silently until now, "and Tenedor's company sent money to Sepúlveda's account. Sepúlveda was, from what the video of the Tragedy shows us, the first shooter at The Wall from the US side. Is there anything else that draws a link between Sepúlveda and the rest of this?"

"I don't know yet," replied Iadanza. "I'll get back to you once I find anything." And so he ended the call.

"We have no choice but to look further into the video. Finding out what order the shooters from both sides of The Wall fired shots has changed the case. All three of the first three shooters are from Latin America," said Adán.

"Are you saying those three are all acquainted?"

"I'm saying they might be connected in some way." Adán sat straight in his chair and booted up the computer. He watched the footage of the Tragedy, occasionally casting a glance at the muted TV screen set to CNN.

Without meaning to, President Copeland was speaking under his breath. "This is bad. Vice President Hanna's onto us."

"What's all this about?" asked John calmly over the phone.

Bob had never seen this man get worked up. He did, however, hear of the one time when John became distraught—after the act of terror in Nice. When he snapped awake in the hospital, he'd asked about his wife and daughter before he thought to ask about his legs. And then . . .

"I don't know what's what. That's why I'm panicking."

"Your voice sounds fairly composed to me, Mr. President."

"Mr. President," as opposed to "Bob." John was talking to him not as his best friend, but as the leader of the United States of America.

"He's been sniffing around, John. Though he hasn't gotten a solid grip on goings-on just yet."

"It may be about the rescue-by-chopper operation you ordered. More than a few people were involved; it's not hard to see how there could be leaks."

"It shouldn't matter how many people were involved. None of the people connected to the military had any way of knowing what the operation's true purpose was. As far as they're concerned, we rescued a bunch of wannabe explorers who were in over their heads."

"It soothes my heart to hear that. We're also being extra careful, so please remain vigilant. I've said it before but allow me to say it again: he's more ambitious than you think, sir."

When he'd consulted with John over who to pick as VP, John had crossed Hanna's name out. When Bob asked why, he said it was because Hanna's heart was actually set on the office of the presidency.

"Looks like you were right. But I can't exactly just step aside, not after I've made it this far. I'm sure history will look back on our actions with thanks and praise."

"We very much share that view, sir. It's no exaggeration to say your decisions will save an entire country."

"But there will be those who decry the operation as the self-centered arrogance of a superpower. In a way, they'd be right, but sometimes both God and the people are better served by thinking simple."

"Absolutely. There are people who need saving, so we'll save them. We'll do our best to curb any unreasonable circumstances. It was just the method that had a few problems with it."

"You always know just what to say to ease my mind. How're Jadon and the rest doing?"

"I'm grateful to you, Mr. President. Thanks to your determination, they've completed the rescue mission without a hitch. But Vice President Hanna may know something. It is true that an unofficial project is unfolding under their noses. We'll pay even closer attention to secrecy from now on." The call dropped.

So Jadon had managed to rescue Professor Escárcega after all. Bob felt at once relieved and conflicted.

Eight months had already passed since he'd met with the Cordovan exile Antonio Alvarado. If the Tragedy at The Wall had never happened, it might have been possible to present Cortázar's tyranny to the United Nations and apply pressure that way. Yet, he realized, that wouldn't have changed anything. In fact, it would have made it worse since

Cordova's feeling of isolation from the rest of the world would only grow. And the more insular the country became, the more intense the oppression.

I can't let the world know of my involvement. Because if I'm involved, they'll take it as all of America being involved. But if this plan succeeds, a new country will be born. That's what I need to hope for. Patricia will understand, one day.

Ever since the Tragedy, his relationship with his daughter had been cordial on the surface, but something was definitely amiss.

Bob gazed at Patricia's photo on his desk.

■ ■ ■

5

THE DICTATOR AND
THE DRUG LORD

A tense atmosphere gripped the Cordovan president's office.

"Moreno thinks he's a drug lord? He's no lord. He's just a filthy thief!" said Cortázar.

He threw the wine glass in his hand against the wall. It shattered.

His asset manager stood pale-faced before him. Poor Benicio had just informed the president what had become of his Swiss bank account.

"How could something like that happen? Don't tell me this was the work of a bank robber? Westalpen's supposed to be the safest bank in the world! Have you called their number? What did the bank say?"

"It seems your remaining balance is $10, sir. It was apparently done via a normal withdrawal."

"Who did the withdrawing? You must know that much."

"They wouldn't say, sir. They said it would damage the bank's credibility. That's why Swiss banks have so many major clients. They did suggest we look into the Cayman Islands, though."

"Moreno has a Cayman Islands account," said Dourne, who had been listening quietly. "It's worth looking into."

"There's no concrete proof Moreno took the money, sir. Just circumstantial evidence. We need time to—"

Benicio never got to finish his sentence. He flew backward onto the floor, blood draining from his head. He'd been shot between the eyes.

"I don't know how many times I told you—manage my money like your life depends on it. Now find out where my money's gone and make it snappy! And gather my top brass while you're at it. Prepare to launch a counterattack against Los Eternos. Search Moreno's hideout and raid it. I want you to spare no effort crafting the perfect attack plan. Bring me Moreno alive, if it's the last thing you do!"

"Not so hasty," said Dourne. "I can't imagine Los Eternos successfully hacked a Swiss bank. There's no way they have the brains."

Cortázar glanced at him briefly and got right back to yelling his head off.

"Get me my money back. Find his bank account and rob him for all he's worth. Attack the cocaine production factories too. And kill all of his men. But don't damage the factories themselves."

Cortázar tried to calm himself down with deep breaths. First the Los Eternos terror attack, then Luis's escape, and now this. His head was swimming.

I never expected Luis to slip from my grasp. Last I checked, the man was half-dead. When I shot one of his comrades, Luis groveled at my feet, begging for his allies' lives. And that pathetic wretch escaped from prison on the day before his execution? A prison with extremely tight security. But now every one of those guards has been killed.

But that's not all. The soldiers who'd chased after them have gotten mowed down by some helicopters, with a mere handful left alive. Some force is moving behind the scenes, in my country. But the first order of business is getting my money back and annihilating the cartel. Subduing Luis and his feeble insurgents has to come later.

"Bring Moreno to me. I'll have him singing like a canary in no time, just you wait. He'll tell me where my money is himself."

"I'm more worried about Luis," muttered Dourne. "I didn't think he had the power to summon helicopters." With that, he exited the office.

Cortázar emptied the rest of his gun into the bleeding corpse and ordered the grisly spectacle to be taken care of.

Clashes between the cartel and government troops flared up throughout the country. Up until now, they had been keeping each other in check, but that unsteady standoff was out the window . . . just as the War Room had schemed.

The Cordovan military was the favorite to win due to its superior numbers of both soldiers and weapons. In battle after battle, Cortázar's forces slew Los Eternos fighters mercilessly. Executives were arrested, tortured for the whereabouts of the money, and summarily executed. Nobody knew anything about Cortázar's stolen fortune. Eventually, cartel members began fleeing the ranks.

Through the media, the official line Cortázar fed the country and the world was that he was "wiping off the face of Cordova the cartel vermin that are undermining all humanity, with the help of ordinary Cordovans."

"Cordova vows to break away from drug abuse, and we are willing to make any and all sacrifices to accomplish that goal. I would like the international community to aid me and Cordova in our efforts. I promise I will bring peace and safety to my glorious homeland," he said. His aim was to secure support and financing from the outside world.

It only took a few days for Los Eternos' power to wane drastically. Yet the military had also sustained losses. In every major city, including La Caridad, back-to-back Los Eternos terror attacks rocked the nation.

In one such instance, more than ten people were killed and many times that number were injured when a truck loaded with explosives rammed into a military base. The number of drive-by shootings against government troops on patrol had reached the double digits. La Caridad was virtually under martial law. Armored vehicles made the rounds at all hours of the day. A strict curfew was enforced by the fully armed soldiers on the streets. Any individuals who aroused their suspicion were arrested, detained, and ruthlessly tortured. The government troops that attacked Los Eternos hideouts were frequently ambushed and wiped out as intel on the military kept leaking.

Global news outlets hadn't failed to notice the chaos in Cordova. One CNN news crawl stated: "In Cordova, a combat unit comprised of agents from a drug cartel named Los Eternos struck a local government military base, resulting in a large number of weapons being taken from the armory. Hostilities are expected to heighten going forward."

That news made its way to the jungle as well. The War Room had contacted the Revolutionary Army about it via satellite phone.

Meanwhile, the revolutionary soldiers' training was continuing apace. Now that Luis was there, the goal of rebuilding the country had taken on a greater sense of possibility, and morale had skyrocketed accordingly. Moreover, the dissidents were beginning to recover their physical strength. Since they were all university instructors, journalists, and intellectuals, they took to educating the soldiers at the camp while discussing how to rebuild and reshape Cordova. Penelope was always by Luis's side, tending to his needs.

Early one morning, the Revolutionary Army higher-ups convened a meeting inside the command tent. Luis and the other dissidents took part in the discussion. Together, they would determine Nueva Cordova's plans for the future. Jadon relayed John's Cordova revitalization plan to those in attendance, including how they would use state-of-the-art AI to lay out the ideal path for Cordova once the revolutionaries took back the reins.

"Once you're back in power, we're leaving this country," said Jadon. "The future of the country is up to you, the people of Cordova. It's your responsibility to organize a new administration and step forward into a brave new Cordova. John Olson will provide economic support the second you request it. And it'll be the job of the Revolutionary Army to seize control of Cortázar's forces and safeguard Professor Escárcega and the other heroes of Cordova."

Sebastian and the rest listened solemnly.

"It is the people, not the military, that will aid the Cordovan government to come," objected Luis, who was still against the idea of taking the country back by force of arms. "Peace will not last when safeguarded by guns and violence. You can give your citizens bread and water, or bullets to the chest, but never both. Getting rid of famine and the fear of state violence starts with person-to-person reconciliation."

"But peace and security do lead to access to bread and water. We can't do anything without taking down Cortázar and retaking the country first. Don't go abandoning your country again. It's vital that you participate."

"Everyone fears death, and they fear their children's or family's deaths more than their own. To the people, protecting the lives of their loved ones is their highest priority. That is why people abandon their country. No one can blame them for that."

Jadon had no reply. Luis's words went straight to his heart. He knew now the impossible situation Cordovans had been placed in. But there was no getting around the fact they needed to topple Cortázar. John himself had underscored its importance.

"John and his friends will pitch in, but he agrees that it needs to be Cordovan people who stand at the forefront of the revolution. And you're the one who can rally them, Professor Escárcega."

"I can't handle the burden. I'm too old to be giving my all to the country anymore. We need the strength and enthusiasm of the young."

"But first we need to establish a country where they can study and learn without fear. A country they can be proud of. And you can make that happen. The people love and respect you."

"They *used* to. But now I'm just a powerless old man," he murmured quietly, averting his gaze.

The photo of Luis Escárcega that Jadon had first seen was that of an old man, yes, but he wasn't the utterly exhausted man he saw before him. How cruelly had they treated him at the detention center?

Penelope was listening with a grim look on her face. It seemed as though she'd come to see her father through new eyes.

When the meeting concluded, Jadon told Tsutomu to stick around. "After we sprang them, the government caught wind of the camp's existence. Cortázar is throwing troops at his Los Eternos problem right now, but once that's over with, he'll focus on eliminating Nueva Cordova. It's only a matter of time before the camp's exact location is identified and they come to raid us. We need to move camp ASAP."

"We've doubled the number of lookouts, and I'm consulting with Sebastian on where to go."

"I'd like to further weaken the military, before they come for us."

"I agree. If Cortázar keeps scoring victories against the cartel, he'll only gain momentum. We need to give him a nice sucker punch," said Tsutomu, leaning over Jadon's shoulder. Jadon turned the computer screen to face him.

"These are satellite images of Cordova. You can see the locations of the Los Eternos cocaine refineries," said Jadon.

"If only these were higher-res, we'd be able to figure out their scale and personnel. And we'd be better off if we knew their security situation too. We have to tell Los Eternos where the government troops are positioned, and where they're going. If we leak the size and the path of each government combat unit that's on the attack, then the damage on both sides will increase."

"The War Room's already disseminating some intel on the Cordovan soldiers' movements to Los Eternos, but if we add all the disaffected farmers to our forces, we'll amass a formidable army. And soon we'll be mobilizing for La Caridad too. We can't compete with the military at the moment."

"But we don't have enough weapons for them. We don't even have enough for *us*. We need to obtain weapons somehow." Tsutomu's gaze fell upon a corner of the command center. Almost all of the ammunition they'd brought here was gone, and the firearms had been handed to Nueva Cordova's newest recruits. Sebastian and all of his men were more than aware they lacked firepower.

■ ■ ■

At the command center, Jadon and Tsutomu were discussing where to move camp and how they might get their hands on more weapons.

"The sooner we move camp, the better. Cortázar's troops are on the hunt for Professor Escárcega as we speak. And once they find him, they won't hesitate to attack. We need to procure more weapons ourselves, rather than rely on the War Room," said Tsutomu.

Jadon listened attentively to what his comrade in arms had to say. Then Sebastian and Arsenio entered the command center.

"According to Chad, there's a Los Eternos armory three miles south of here. He says he saw dozens of Kalashnikovs and ammo boxes there."

Chad was a young man who'd fled the cartel about a week prior. Many of the Revolutionary Army's soldiers were escapees from Los Eternos and the government military, which they only joined to escape poverty. When asked how old he was, Chad replied that he didn't know—he was probably in his mid-twenties. He knew his way around firearms, and Sebastian took a liking to him.

Most of them hadn't even gone to elementary school. When they weren't training, they were being taught how to read and write, English, and basic mathematics.

"If there was a Los Eternos armory, then the War Room would have already spotted it," said Jadon.

"Not if it's expertly camouflaged. Satellite cameras wouldn't help on that front, especially if it's an underground facility."

"How'd the cartel amass so much weaponry, anyway?"

"Los Eternos also make money selling weapons to guerrillas and criminal organizations in neighboring countries. They use the money they earn through the coke trade to buy from arms dealers, and they sell the weapons they steal from Cordovan soldiers. That's how the cartel's grown so huge in so little time. They've got collection sites for weapons all over Cordova. It's not just a stroke of luck one happened to be nearby," said Sebastian, looking at Jadon and Tsutomu alternately as he spoke.

"The security will be tight. We're no match for them right now."

"Actually, he said there aren't that many soldiers guarding the armory. Since they've recently been beset by military aggression, most of the cartel fighters have been sent to escort the higher-ups."

"Are you sure we can trust this Chad? He said he escaped from Los Eternos, but . . ."

"We can't know for sure. But a Los Eternos armory is there for the picking. How can we resist?" Jadon asked Tsutomu, who just shrugged in response. "Let's scout it out. Gather us some soldiers, on the double."

Ten minutes later, Tsutomu returned with his equipment on. When the two were alone in the tent, he handed Jadon a bulletproof vest.

"Please put it on. It's not military-issue; it's police-issue. If you wear your ACUs over it, no one will know. This is a dangerous operation; we don't know when we'll get attacked."

"The other soldiers don't have the luxury of bulletproof vests."

"Don't be stupid. Bulletproof vests are standard in the US military. Besides, you're the captain. If you die, the operation's all but over." Tsutomu pulled the collar of his ACUs, revealing the bulletproof vest underneath. "Nick Beasley told me to have you put one on when the fighting got serious. And I nearly let you get killed when you went to La Caridad without one."

Jadon gave it some thought, but ultimately, he decided to put it on.

* * *

Jadon had Chad lead him, Tsutomu, Arsenio, and ten other soldiers to the Los Eternos armory. After about two hours of walking through the jungle, Chad stopped in his tracks, telling them that the armory was near the mountainside.

"But I don't see anything. And where are the guards?"

"They all ran away. The military's been hitting the cartel hard." Chad brandished his gun and scanned the surroundings.

Jadon was getting anxious. "I'm worried about the camp. Let's go back."

"Wait. It's around here for sure. I came here two months ago."

"Two months ago? They must have moved operations ages ago." Arsenio pointed his muzzle at Chad.

"Hold on. It's near those trees."

They went up to the big trees Chad was pointing at. After removing dead leaves and soil, they found a wooden hatch. Carefully, they opened it to find a cavity that stretched underground. With Chad at the front, they descended the hole. The place was spacious, with dozens of different-sized boxes piled up here and there. Taking the lid off one of the boxes, they stumbled across a set of five Kalashnikovs. There were twenty such boxes, plus boxes containing hand grenades, mortars, mines, rockets, and ammo.

"Inform the camp to send more men. The guns, ammo, and other weapons are to be taken out of the boxes and stuffed inside backpacks to carry back."

They sent a messenger to the camp, and three hours later, more than thirty soldiers of the Revolutionary Army had arrived.

"Hurry it up. I'm worried about the camp."

Jadon had the soldiers without guns arm themselves and ordered the revolutionaries to carry the rest with them. On their way to the camp, when visibility was good, Tsutomu stopped walking and stood still. The mountain where the camp was could be seen between the trees.

"I've got a bad feeling."

"Me too. The mountain's too quiet."

Jadon noticed young Gerardo by his side. He was looking at the mountain too.

"What are *you* doing here? This place is dangerous."

"I can fight too. I'm a soldier of Nueva Cordova. But never mind that. I can't hear birds chirping, or any other animals."

The jungle was eerily silent. "Double the number of lookouts on both sides of the unit. If you sense anything out of the ordinary, be sure to tell me," ordered Jadon.

If they went down the valley and followed the river, logically they should be able to spot the camp.

"Send some scouts. The rest will wait here on standby. Be ready to fight at all times."

Tsutomu sent a merc and a revolutionary as scouts. That moment, they heard gunfire. Several of the soldiers stood up and looked toward the camp.

"Heads down! It's an ambush! Everyone—"

But the soldier standing at Jadon's side fell backward before he could finish his sentence. Instinctively, Jadon huddled around Gerardo and took cover behind some rocks. The fallen soldier had taken a bullet to the head. His death was instant.

"That was a sniper shot. Keep your heads low to the ground. We're being aimed at."

Gunfire. Jadon poked his gun out from behind his cover and fired continuously in the direction of the noise.

"Go back into the jungle. Find the sniper!"

They dashed deeper into the cover of the trees as they kept returning fire.

"Are they Los Eternos or are they Cortázar's men?"

"Likely the latter. Their aim is spot on. They've received military training for sure," said Tsutomu, eyes on the mountain in the distance.

"How did they find us?"

"Maybe they were shadowing us and lying in ambush in a spot

where they've got the upper hand. Or maybe they were chasing after Los Eternos and just happened across the camp." Tsutomu started pulling the trigger. Had he spotted the enemy?

"Or maybe . . ." *Maybe somebody at the camp ratted us out to the government.* But Jadon swallowed his words.

"Where are they shooting from, and how many of them are there?"

"The main force is hiding in the shade of the rocks on the mountainside. There's thirty to forty of them, and they've got Kalashnikovs. They're Cortázar's guys all right," said Tsutomu, his eyes on the prize as he carried on firing.

Jadon used his satellite phone to reach the War Room and explained the situation.

"I want to know the enemy's location," said Jadon. "Send video."

"Be careful!" shouted Tsutomu. "There's a sniper at nine o'clock." The War Room must have heard him too.

"They're mid-level soldiers, but the more they shoot the higher the chance they hit their targets. Take them down quickly!"

"You've got enemies behind you too," said Stewart through the phone. "No idea how many. Things aren't looking great. I'd like to send video, but I can't. There's an issue with the connection." The commotion going on in the War Room was audible.

"You can at least tell us which direction to run, can't you?"

"Wait five minutes. We're adjusting the satellite."

"What happened to the twenty-four-hour surveillance of Cordova? The shoot-out's gotten intense, and the enemy's approaching. We need to move."

"There's a waterfall to your left—"

Stewart's voice cut out.

"I see the waterfall, but what do we do with it? Do we run toward it? Or are there enemy soldiers there? Tell me!" No response. "Dammit! The line's severed!"

The gunfire scaled ever higher in intensity. The enemy was closing in, and they spotted soldiers wielding RPGs rushing up the mountain trail.

In the War Room, everyone's eyes were on the central screen. A shoot-out was transpiring in the mountains of Cordova, plus the occasional explosion courtesy of hand grenades and rockets.

"What's going on out there? Are Jadon and his men all right!?" shouted John, leaning in from his wheelchair.

"It's a communication blackout, sir. There's nothing wrong on our end. Jadon's satellite phone might have seized up."

"Find out what's causing this at once. If it's a mechanical failure or glitch, fix it!" said Stewart. "Don't lose track of Jadon's position. Switch to infrared."

John stared at the satellite image on the screen, within which a blue dot appeared. It was Jadon. The reddish dots were the other soldiers, both of the Revolutionary Army and the Cordovan military.

"The Revolutionary Army's numbers are decreasing. Half of them aren't moving."

"Which of those dots are our men, and which ones are the enemy? Enhance the resolution. Is Jadon okay?"

John was now next to Stewart. "Please save Jadon's group at all costs."

"There's nothing wrong with Jadon's satellite phone," said Billy.

"Then why can't we get through?" asked Stewart.

"The satellite phone's getting radio interference. Someone nearby may be jamming the signal."

A hush fell over the War Room. It was John's voice that broke the silence.

"Can we restore it?"

"We can, but it'll take time. Around two hours."

"Do it in half an hour. You can use PathNet's engineering department!" shouted John.

* * *

A pall of silence hung over the jungle. The gunfire had suddenly ceased. The bodies of Revolutionary Army soldiers lay all around.

"We can't get where we need to go unless we come within the sniper's range. I'll serve as a decoy, so move when I give the signal," said Tsutomu, never averting his gaze from the direction of the gunfire.

"Be careful. The sniper's not amazing, but he's not bad either. Now that we're aware of his presence, he'll aim for his target's body to stop him from moving and then land the killer head shot. That's what I'd do. The sniper's taking aim and the only reason the others have stopped shooting is because they're leaving it all to him."

Cautiously, Tsutomu moved in the direction opposite Jadon. At that very moment, a gunshot pealed through the air, then another, then another . . . the impact points were getting closer to Tsutomu. With each shot, the sniper got a better grasp of his timing and adjusted accordingly.

Snipers usually worked in pairs—the shooter and the eyes. A high-caliber team could hit their mark from more than half a mile away. The observer collected data on the target and other factors—such as the area's wind speeds—determined the point of impact and adjusted it if necessary. Tsutomu deliberately moved in a way that upset the sniper's timing. Jadon wondered whether Tsutomu had been a sniper himself at one point.

In a battle, the sniper was acting alone, picking off the soldiers in his sights one by one. He was pulling the trigger as soon as his scope found a target.

Tsutomu disappeared. He'd taken cover in the underbrush. His every movement was calculated and purposeful. The sniper was supposed to have killed him by now—he was probably less than five hundred yards away.

Jadon shifted position. That instant, he took a shot to the chest. He hurtled backward, rolling down the cliff.

Then another shot.

"Don't die, Jadon!" he heard Arsenio say.

But soon he lost consciousness.

When he opened his eyes, he saw Arsenio's face.

"It's okay. The bullet hit your vest. Your ribs might be cracked, but there's nothing life-threatening."

"My head . . ."

"You've had a concussion. You tumbled for a hundred yards and hit your head on something. Any normal person would've died. You should thank your mother for making you so hard-headed."

He took Arsenio's hand and sat up. His head and chest hurt when he moved. He looked way up and saw the rocks that had provided cover earlier. He tried to take off his vest, but Arsenio grabbed one of his arms.

"Keep it on. It saved your life."

"Where's the sniper?"

"Tsutomu shot him dead. He took his chance when the sniper shot you. Another military attack will happen soon."

"Let's go back up the mountain and join Tsutomu's group."

"We can't climb up. Let's go down to the valley. If we walk by the river, we'll get back together one way or another."

Jadon tried to stand, but he staggered. His whole body was in pain.

"Get up. Don't you dare die on us and leave us with all the work. The only one allowed to finish you off is . . ."

Jadon looked up at Arsenio. *"Who are you?* You've always struck me as suspicious. You're always giving me that odd look. But you don't seem to be a government spy either."

There was an unmistakable murderous urge in Arsenio's eyes whenever he looked at Jadon.

"I was at The Wall that day. Together with my family."

A year had passed since the Tragedy, but Jadon could still see the scene. The countless mangled and bloody bodies at the base of the rusty steel piles. He revisited that hell in his dreams. The moaning mass of casualties. The screams and wailing. The never-ending gunfire. Then, a blood-soaked shadow would shoot from the darkness and seize him in its clutches. It would sink its maw into Jadon's throat and rake its sharp talons over his face. *Stop*, he'd say. *Just let me go!*

"I haven't gone a single day without thinking about that day. But I didn't know you—"

"You don't remember me, huh. My wife and child died. They got shot in the head and stomach by US soldiers' bullets and died in pools of their own blood."

"It's my fault. I couldn't stop my soldiers from firing. I might as well have killed your family myself." Jadon's face twisted, and he whimpered. Tears welled in his eyes.

Arsenio regarded the man with some surprise.

"Just kill me now. I deserve it." Jadon struggled to get up. Pain stabbed at his chest. When he stopped breathing, the pain receded.

"I hate your guts, and I hate America. You're the man who killed my wife and daughter, and so many other Cordovans. And America is the country that made that happen. But I believe in your vision for the country. I want to make a country no one needs to flee ever again."

They heard more gunfire in the distance. The government troops had started attacking again.

Arsenio helped Jadon up and kept him on his feet.

"I don't forgive you. Once the Revolutionary Army wins, I *will* kill you." Arsenio pulled out his knife and ran it along his neck.

"I'm worried about the camp. If you've got cojones, start walking."

Jadon took a step, his knees wobbly. Arsenio supported his body.

The gunfire was getting closer. The two of them descended to the river.

In the War Room, John's wheelchair was slowly circling the room along the wall. At times he would stop and look at the screen in front. This happened whenever he was lost in thought.

The central screen was a window into Jadon's patch of the jungle, but trees were blocking the view of the soldiers. The only proof of Jadon's activity was the moving dot of light that represented him.

"If that blue dot is him, then he's safe and on the move."

"We can't see him, though. Communications are down."

A communications hiccup had occurred in the process of sending satellite photos of escape routes. Billy and the engineers were doing everything in their power to fix it.

"The line still hasn't been restored? But it's already been two hours." John's wording was as cordial as ever, but he couldn't hide his irritation.

"The issue doesn't seem to be on our end," said Billy, clicking his mouse with evident annoyance. "Either it's the devices on the Cordovan side that are malfunctioning, or there's some radio interference. Or maybe the satellite is temporarily on the fritz. There's a whole lot of little things that can go wrong."

"How many more hours must I wait until I can talk to Jadon?"

"You can talk to him in about three hours if it's audio-only. We can't send video. We'll be activating other electronic devices after running virus scans on them."

"Let me talk to him in one hour. You're the best hacker in the world, aren't you? And you said you were a wiz when it comes to electronics too. Well, if that's the case, then prove it. I'm fed up with this whole situation."

"Fine. You're distracting me, so why don't you make yourself scarce for the time being?"

The secretary beside John looked taken aback. John letting his emotions come to the surface was a rare sight indeed, but even more shocking was how someone had talked back to him.

■ ■ ■

As they walked along the bank of the river, Jadon stumbled countless times, and each time Arsenio helped him.

Jadon tripped over a fallen tree. His chest and shoulders were searing, and he couldn't stand.

"Are you in pain?" asked Arsenio.

Jadon didn't answer; he just gritted his teeth.

"Bite on this. It's coca leaf." He pushed the vivid green leaf into Jadon's mouth. It tasted extremely tart. After a while, the pain eased, eventually disappearing altogether, replaced by a whole-body numbness.

Arsenio put Jadon's arm over his shoulder and stood him up. Together, they moved forward.

Just before sunset, Jadon and Arsenio neared the camp. Jadon stopped walking. Something was amiss. The air felt strange. Arsenio had the same reaction as he looked around.

Suddenly, Arsenio dashed forward, leaving Jadon to follow him. They cleared out of the jungle, and the sight that greeted them made Jadon stop breathing. Arsenio stood stock-still.

The smells of burnt tree, gunpowder, and blood made for an unholy mixture. Dozens of tents were toppled and trampled flat. Some were still burning. And amid it all lay bodies of Revolutionary Army soldiers.

The two went farther into the charred, ash-black ruins of the camp. Gerardo was lugging bodies alongside the rest of the surviving soldiers. They'd each made it back to camp in one piece.

Tsutomu was there to welcome Jadon and Arsenio. "I was thinking we should conduct a funeral for you."

"Arsenio saved me. But . . . but this . . ." He was at a loss for words.

"It was like this when we got back. When the military attacked, all we could do was run."

"Where's the professor?"

"He went into the jungle to hide, but he's in shock. I haven't been given the detailed lowdown on what happened yet. Right now he's with the injured. Penelope's looking after them."

The attack came without warning. Over a hundred government soldiers came at the camp from three different sides. After laying the place to waste, Cortázar's men left before dusk.

"They must have figured they'd lose their advantage come nightfall," said Tsutomu, as he watched the soldiers carry the dead.

"Let's bury the bodies. We can think about the rest later."

The survivors gathered around. Bryan Fuller was in command. Sebastian was injured and receiving treatment. Bryan reported that they'd lost half their forces in the attack.

"What happened to the rest of the soldiers?"

"Either killed or missing. Some also turned tail and ran. The weapons we brought were blown up so the enemy couldn't take them."

"Did the government troops come here looking for Luis, and come across the camp?" Jadon asked Bryan under his breath.

"I don't know. The enemy troops were awfully familiar with the camp's situation. They shut down all avenues of escape, and attacked from advantageous positions. They may have known that a lot of the soldiers had left camp to transport the weapons," said Bryan. He lowered his voice even more: "There's a traitor in our midst. That's the only way to explain how efficiently we got demolished."

"How bad are Sebastian's injuries?"

"They're not too bad. Penelope's tending to them. What do we do now?"

"I can't seem to contact the War Room. And Cortázar's men will come back to finish the job."

They heard voices welcoming the soldiers who were returning from the jungle. As time passed, the number of soldiers increased.

"Tonight we make camp here, but we'll get out before dawn. Because make no mistake, they're still watching us from who knows where."

"We should move camp tonight. They might attack whenever it gets bright enough."

"We have women and children and many wounded. Taking them

through the jungle at night would be even more dangerous. Double the number of lookouts," Jadon ordered Bryan.

That night, everyone slept wherever they could. Jadon looked on the ruins of the camp while leaning against a tree on the outer edge. The smell had only gotten worse. It was the aroma of burnt bark and charred flesh.

He was dead tired, and every time he moved, his whole body was racked with pain, but so much more was swimming through his mind. What had happened here? What ought they to do?

He recalled Arsenio's words, and the atrocity that altered his fate forever . . . the Tragedy at The Wall. Until today, he'd tried to seal it in the recesses of his soul. He wanted to forget it ever happened, to erase every second of it. And the more time he spent knocking that notion around in his mind, the more a single scene from that awful day came bubbing back up. The countless corpses splayed over a wide expanse of sand, and Jadon Green standing there staring. And now he had to accept that Arsenio's wife and daughter were among them.

"Let me look at your injuries."

Jadon looked up. It was Penelope, with her med kit.

"They're no big deal."

"I thought I told you you're not the doctor here. Arsenio asked me to check on you. You got shot by a sniper and tumbled down a cliff. He said you were lucky to come out of it with such minor wounds. Guess the Border Butcher has the devil's luck." Penelope pressed on his chest. Jadon grimaced, and she pushed harder.

"If that's your only reaction, you'll be fine. I don't think your ribs are broken. Some may be fractured though. I don't have much medicine in this thing. I'll apply a poultice. If the pain doesn't get any better, then you'll need X-rays and proper treatment," she said, applying ointment to the cuts on his hands and face. "I'm thankful to you, you know. For bringing me together with my father. I don't forgive him, but I am trying to understand him."

"How's he looking? He seems very defeated. Both physically and emotionally."

"He keeps saying too many have died. That he might've been the one who ushered them to their deaths."

"But my boss keeps telling us that without him, this revolution would never succeed. He's taken the post-revolution period into account as well. Cordova's renaissance will happen under a President Luis Escárcega. You'll persuade him, won't you? We went through so much to save him."

Penelope had no reply, but Jadon could swear she nodded ever so slightly. She'd felt the soldiers' love and admiration for him.

Then, suddenly, she stood up.

"Sorry, am I interrupting something?"

It was Tsutomu. He was smiling, looking at the two of them.

Penelope just stared back at him before stomping off.

"If you're going to talk to me, don't pop out of nowhere like that," said Jadon, lowering the hammer of his pistol and telling him to sit. "Something's off. They didn't just stumble upon us while searching for Luis. They *knew* where everyone was. They struck when our main force left camp to stock up on weapons. Plus, my satellite phone isn't working anymore."

Tsutomu's smile disappeared. "There's a spy among us. From now on, we should be limiting knowledge of the important stuff to a select few."

Tsutomu and Bryan were saying the same thing. "Does Sebastian know?"

"Most likely. But he probably doesn't want to believe it either. Having a traitor among your subordinates? That's a tough pill to swallow."

Jadon put a hand to his chest. His rubs hurt when he moved.

"It's thanks to you that I'm alive. If it weren't for the vest you gave me, I wouldn't be here. And you shot the sniper before he could bean me in the head," said Jadon. But even as he spoke, Tsutomu's words crossed his mind. Tsutomu played decoy because he knew the sniper would aim for the chest first. He knew it would give him an opening. But Jadon flicked that thought away.

Jadon cast his eyes on the camp. He curled his body up under the starlight and stared at the black shadows that were nestled close together as they slept.

Cortázar was looking at the plaza through the window.

La Plaza Fundadores was a symbol of Cordova. It was made around fifty years ago to commemorate the founding of the nation, in the hopes that citizens and tourists alike would come and visit. But now it was nearly empty and all too quiet.

Behind him, several aides were awaiting his orders.

Already, two hours had passed since he issued the order to commence the assault. He'd been told that one-third of the Revolutionary Army's elite troops were absent from their base, and most of the people who were left at the camp were women, children, and new recruits.

"Looks like you called it. The camp was near where the helicopters landed. And with their main force out of the picture, our assault unit could get in close without any trouble," said Cortázar, who was holding Dourne by the shoulders.

Dourne was gazing expressionlessly at the map on the table. There was a big red X on a point in the jungle.

A soldier was led by a secretary into the room.

"The attack was a success, sir. We burned the Revolutionary Army camp to the ground."

"Did you get hold of Luis?" said Cortázar, anxiously leaning forward.

"He wasn't there, sir. He might be at another camp."

"This is the first I've heard of *another camp!* Keep searching. Capture him. I'll have him dragged across the plaza alongside Moreno as terrorists and I'll slice them to bits in front of the public!" he spat, incensed.

On the War Room's central screen, they could see where in Cordova all of Los Eternos' drug refineries were located. There were eight in total. Five of them had already been destroyed by the Cordovan military. The other three were large facilities closer to La Caridad. Their camouflage and surveillance were suitably stricter, and as such, they had yet to be spotted by the regime's forces.

"Please enhance the satellite photos' resolution. That way, we can get more detailed information, including their security setups," said John.

"American military satellites can distinguish topography on a roughly yard-by-yard basis," replied Billy. "I managed to improve the program and raised the resolution by thirty percent. The rest is for a photo analysis expert to decipher."

After the bank account transfer they pulled on Cortázar and Moreno, Billy had used the computers to wade into military operations as well.

"Then please go kick the photo analysis expert in the butt and get them on the case. Jadon's soldiers and the revolutionaries' lives are on the line," said John, exasperated. He was leaning from his wheelchair toward the central screen.

Stewart calmed him down and pulled him back upright. "Are there no other cocaine refineries? Expand the scope of the search."

The red dots on the screen multiplied.

"There are three places on our radar," said Antonio.

"Get all of this information to the Cordovan military. They'll decide which to attack."

Billy looked at John, but the man's eyes were fixed on the central screen. Billy just shrugged and faced his own screen again.

Ever since the camp was stormed, Jadon and the rest were moving location every few days. Their forces had been cut in half and transporting all of the food and weapons through the jungle was extremely exhausting. Some had started to complain that their health was taking a turn for the worse. Still others deserted the revolution. Morale was on a steady daily decline.

Luis was not just advanced in age, but also in poor health due to the harsh existence he'd had to endure. Meanwhile, Penelope devoted herself to treating the wounds and illnesses and managing the overall health of the dissidents and soldiers, most of all her father's.

"We need to stock back up on weapons and mercenaries, but there's no way to know when we'll get that opportunity again." Tsutomu was usually an optimistic sort, but when he and Jadon were alone together, he could be a complainer too.

After setting up a new camp, Jadon stared at the map on the table. Cordova was a country blessed by abundant forests and rare minerals. The only ones who didn't seem to know that were Cordovans themselves.

"I just wanted to take the time to say thank you."

Jadon turned his head. Standing there was Professor Escárcega, without Penelope.

"I'm afraid I may have done you a disservice." Jadon took Luis by the arm and sat him down on a chair.

"You brought my daughter back to me. She was my biggest concern."

"All I did was use her to my own ends. I used her to get to you."

"That may be true, but it's also true that in doing so, you saved my soul," said Luis, looking up at the man. It was the gentle sort of gaze that wrapped a person in a cloak of warmth.

For a long while, neither spoke. The keens of jungle beasts punctuated the silence.

Jadon spoke up first. "I was the captain at The Wall."

Luis's placid expression didn't change. "I know. Cordova has TV and internet, too, you know. I recognized you the moment we first met in the detention center."

"But then, why—"

"Sometimes, when I look at you, I feel sad," Luis stated quietly. "You mustn't beat yourself up over it. The refugees tried to scale The Wall in order to survive, yes. But you had your own duties to fulfill. I don't think either side was necessarily in the wrong. But there's no doubt the end result was a tragedy. I've given it a lot of thought myself. The massacre killed and injured so many and it altered fate for the worse. But you're one of those victims. I can tell from observing you. You came here to save Cordova so you could atone."

Jadon had no response. What Luis said hadn't occurred to his conscious mind, but it could very well be true.

"Like you said, everyone loves the country they were born and raised in. But there are those who, faced with poverty, terror, and—worst of all—despair, must go through the anguish of abandoning their homeland. The people who formed part of the caravan and attempted to cross The Wall were looking for a ray of hope for themselves and their children. And now you've given us that hope, here in Cordova." Luis sighed. His face got slightly red. "Most would throw aside their countries to survive and out of love for their children. But that sad reality cannot stand. We must rise up, stand proud, and make our homelands safe places to live by our own hands."

Luis's words cut to Jadon's heart.

"Perhaps that is the mission of all who live in this country," said Luis. Jadon could sense a sparkling light about Luis's eyes, even in the near darkness. "Please, I implore you, lend us your aid."

Luis grasped Jadon's hand. He was frail and feeble, but his hand had a warmth to it.

Jadon noticed Tsutomu watching the two of them from behind the tree outside the tent.

Luis had opened up to striking conversation with the Revolutionary Army soldiers, and so the camp had recovered some of its momentum. Jadon remembered what John said about Luis being the key to making this dream a reality.

"Did you tell him something? The guy looks different than usual," Penelope asked Jadon. Though she was still devoting herself to her father's care, she hadn't stopped calling him "the guy."

"Professor Escárcega pushed me forward. He said what people need the most are hope and a reason to go on."

"That's certainly true. Especially for you and for all the soldiers here," she said, shrugging.

Tsutomu looked up from his computer. He was consolidating the information the War Room had sent, as well as the state of the unit.

"The biggest coke storage facility slash refinery still hasn't gotten attacked. What's Cortázar thinking?" Tsutomu pointed to a spot on the map. They knew its size and location from the War Room intel. And there was no way the government hadn't sussed it out for themselves.

Bryan and Sebastian gave the screen a look. Jadon thought to himself while he listened to Tsutomu.

"Over a hundred pounds of coke get refined there per day, and over fifteen hundred pounds are in storage. If they brought it all to the US, it'd equate to a hundred million dollars."

"I bet you Cortázar wants to take all of that product for himself once he crushes Los Eternos. That's why he wants the factories intact. If Los Eternos are taken out of the picture, the shortages in supply will cause coke prices in America to rise. It might even impact the whole world," Bryan told Sebastian.

"Actually, reports say coke prices have been dropping since yesterday, probably because Cortázar has been selling the coke they've been robbing off Los Eternos at lower prices."

"So President Cortázar's a coke dealer now, huh? I've heard there are countries in Asia that do much the same."

"He'll be reluctant to destroy it, that's for sure. He's going to want to keep it intact and continue refining coke for money."

"Let's be the ones to attack the place. If we do, the Cordovan cartel is completely finished. After that, we can focus on the military," proposed Tsutomu, and Bryan and Sebastian agreed.

Jadon turned it over in his mind.

"But we haven't got enough to go on yet. We need to figure out the security setup. If we sustain any more losses, we'll be this close to getting wiped out too," offered Jadon. "Bring Chad here. He used to be with the cartel."

Arsenio fetched Chad.

Tsutomu pointed to the cocaine refinery on the map. "Do you know this place?"

"I worked there for half a year before coming here."

"Let me ask again why you left Los Eternos."

"They beat me every day and paid me next to nothing. They chopped off the head of a friend of mine who tried to smuggle out some coke and hanged him as an example to others. I got scared and ran back to my village, but they came searching for me, so I came here," he recounted casually. Then he rolled up a sleeve and pushed his arm out for them to see. Half of its flesh was shrunken like a keloid. Burn marks. "A drunk bastard laughed while he pressed a burning knife into me."

"Tell me more about the factory. The building, the security, everything." Jadon put the map and satellite photos in front of Chad.

Chad leaned in to look. He pointed to a place on the map.

"There's nothing there. The satellite photos show us it's just jungle and more jungle. The War Room didn't say anything about it either."

"The factory's underground. There are underpasses that were dug in the mountains around this area. We traveled through those underground passages," Chad replied, marking Xs on five places on the map. Some were only 320 or so feet apart.

"These are the exits out of the underground, and there's a coke storage room and a refinery in the facility. All of the entrances are camouflaged and difficult to spot."

Jadon and the others looked at each other. "Is that all of them?"

"All the ones I know of. There may be more."

"We've got no choice but to believe him. We can't rely on satellite photos to find an underground facility."

Jadon and Tsutomu drafted a battle plan based on Chad's intel.

"When should we do it?"

"Tonight. The sooner, the better," said Tsutomu. And Jadon concurred. After all, if there was a government spy at the camp, it behooved them to act quickly.

The camp was full of energy—this was the first time they were picking the fight.

■ ■ ■

The unit moved after dark, at Jadon's command. Ten American mercs, and twenty Revolutionary Army soldiers, for a total of thirty men. The rest were defending the camp.

If Chad's information was to be believed, the cocaine refinery was guarded by around twenty men. The rest were the men and women working inside.

The camp was lit dimly by the stars above; one step into the jungle and the shade of the trees cast them in near total darkness. Jadon and the mercs had on night-vision goggles, so they guided the revolutionaries.

When they set foot on the mountain path, his chest ached from the previous battle's sniper shot, but he'd regained his strength.

Arsenio was walking ahead of Jadon.

"Thanks for your help back there. You saved my life. Sorry I never thanked you."

Arsenio just sped up without saying a word.

Tsutomu was walking next to Jadon. "What's this about?"

"Arsenio saved me. I got shot, but he helped me all the way back to camp."

"Is that all?"

"What else would there be?" Jadon replied, watching Arsenio's back.

The jungle was never-ending and silent—apart from the occasional shrill of the birds.

They reached their destination, and just as Chad had told them, the entrance was camouflaged and difficult to make out.

The unit split into two teams. One of them, headed by Jadon, would storm the refinery. The other, led by Tsutomu and Arsenio, would stand at the five exits to prevent escape.

Jadon assigned a few soldiers to each of the exits. At his signal, hand grenades would be lobbed into the underground underpass.

"Sync your watches. We'll begin the attack at twenty-one hours on the dot."

"I don't have a watch," replied Arsenio.

"You come with me. Everyone else, wait by the entrances. When you hear the hand grenades go off, throw some more inside the underpass. Then watch over the underpass's exit. When the cartel men come running toward you, tie them up. There may be other underpasses, including newly made ones. Maintain constant vigilance over your surroundings."

Jadon led several of the mercs and revolutionaries toward the entrance to the underpass.

"Keep your eyes peeled," whispered Jadon. "We're standing right above Los Eternos' largest cocaine factory—and the largest in all of Latin America."

Jadon checked his watch. He threw a grenade into the underpass at exactly 9 p.m.

The boom triggered a series of explosions.

"Let's go."

Opening the door, they heard screams from within as dust and smoke rushed out to meet them.

One man came up a ladder. Jadon stuck a knife to his neck and yanked him away. "How many are inside?" asked Arsenio, sticking his knife to the man's legs. He muffled the man's inchoate shriek with his other hand.

"There's ten fighters, and twenty laborers."

Gunfire had begun piercing the air. The fighters who'd tried to leave via the other exits had come out shooting.

Jadon went down with Arsenio to the underground factory. Another soldier followed them.

The underground was in wild upheaval. Enraged howling and cries of anguish echoed from the other end of the underpass, punctuated by occasional gunfire. Were Tsutomu and his group underground as well?

The subterranean underpass connected several different rooms. Jadon and Arsenio entered the first of those rooms. It was smaller than the armory, but there were stacks of Kalashnikovs and rockets nonetheless. Jadon ordered the third soldier with them to carry the weapons out.

The door to the next room was made of iron, and locked. Jadon pushed Arsenio out of the way and fired an automatic rifle at the lock. Chilled air enveloped them, while the low hum of air conditioning equipment reached their ears. The room was a sturdy storage room measuring about thirty square feet, and inside were rows of shelves stacked with transparent nylon bags filled with white powder. The walls were covered with iron plates.

"This is the coke storage room. Two or so pounds per bag, I'm sure, and there's over a thousand bags. That's more than I was expecting." said Jadon.

"That's several hundred million dollars' worth of stuff. No wonder Cortázar wants his hands on this place!" said Tsutomu, who'd come inside as well.

Jadon and his men advanced down the underpass, passing some rooms with beds inside them along the way. The guards and workers must have lived here too.

They filed into a spacious room—where the refinement took place.

Alongside the refining equipment were desks with weighing scales and other instruments, as well as bagging machines. They looked in the direction of the sound they heard and spotted around ten women gathered together, all in their undergarments—probably to prevent them from smuggling any of the product.

In one corner of the room, the light embedded in the box on top of a desk was blinking, and the timer on its side was counting down.

"Everyone get out of here! They've set some explosives!" shouted Jadon.

Arsenio was standing beside him, staring at the bomb. Two minutes and ticking down second by second.

"Can we defuse it?"

"I certainly can't." Jadon scanned the area. No exit. There was no way to get back to the surface except by going back the way they came.

"One minute, fifty seconds left."

"There's no way we'll make it."

"Take the women and head for a room in the back. Now!" Jadon ordered Arsenio.

"What are you gonna do?"

"There's only seventy seconds left. Hurry!"

Arsenio ran with the women down to the other end of the passageway. Meanwhile, Jadon took a knife to the bomb and pried it off the desk. It was C4 and there was more than enough to completely level the factory.

Arsenio came rushing back inside.

"I thought I told you to escape."

"I got the women out of here. There was another exit to the surface at the back. What do we do about the bomb?"

"We'll put it in the coke storage room. It looks about as sturdy as a strongbox."

The two lifted the box together and dashed down the underpass.

"You open the door. I'll do the rest myself. There's only thirty seconds left."

Arsenio opened the door to the storage room. Jadon mustered all his might to lug the bomb by himself into the room. Then he placed it at the back of the room and leapt back out.

The bomb exploded the split second they closed the iron door. They were blown backward into the opposite wall of the passageway. The door curved outward, creating a large gap with the wall; the blast had broken through the door. Their surroundings were swallowed by darkness.

Earth and dust poured onto their bodies as the whole underpass shuddered on the verge of collapse. Once the shaking stopped, Jadon took out a small flashlight from his pocket. In front of his eyes, an arm was sticking up from the dirt. It wore Arsenio's bangle. Jadon frantically dug away the sediment and uncovered his face. He was breathing. Jadon scraped out half of his body and slapped him awake.

"Do the rest yourself." Jadon collapsed and sat on the ground.

Where's Tsutomu? He was probably someplace near the entrance . . . did he manage to make it out? If he got buried, there's nothing I can do to save him.

Jadon examined the underpass. Two thirds of the cross-section were filled with earth and grit, and the gap with the ceiling was less than a foot. It was just big enough to crawl through.

"The entrance is blocked. There's no choice but to move forward to the other side." Jadon crawled through the darkness, but his path was eventually closed off.

"This is the end of the road. We can't go any further," Jadon told Arsenio, who'd been following him.

The two of them sat side by side against the wall. Only time was advancing now.

"I'd have liked to apologize. To your wife and kid. The events of that day never once left my mind. I always relive the Tragedy in my nightmares."

"I can't let us die in a place like this. I'll avenge my family by my own hands." Arsenio lifted himself up and started digging. At first, Jadon just watched, but soon he started helping by pushing the sediment away.

About an hour later, they heard a sound on the other side of the dirt mound. A scratching, scraping sound.

"Can you hear that? It's coming from the entrance of the underpass."

The scraping grew louder, and they heard people's voices as well. Jadon turned his light toward the sound. It was a wall of soil that exuded that unique mountain mulch smell. When a corner of the wall fell away, Tsutomu's smeared face came into view. It didn't take long for the remaining portions of the wall to get knocked down from there. The revolutionary soldiers were carrying away the obstructing soil for all they were worth.

As Jadon and Arsenio exited the underpass, the area was beginning to turn brighter. Around ten women were sitting close to one another in a hollow on the mountainside. All of them had been kidnapped by Los Eternos and forced to work in the factory. They were wearing dirty men's clothing.

Jadon shifted his gaze from the women to the slope. Twenty or so dead bodies were lined up, half of them in their underwear.

"They're the Los Eternos fighters and sentries of the women. Two of our number lost their lives too. We'll carry them back to camp."

"Did any of the Los Eternos men survive?"

"Seven survived at first, but they all got bludgeoned to death by the women. They used rocks and wood and such. It happened in such a flash, we couldn't put a stop to it. They must have put those poor women through hell."

Around the cocaine refinery, the slope of the mountain had caved in. The underground factory was almost entirely buried.

"Every single one of the bags of coke got blown to bits too. It's almost enough to make me cry." Tsutomu took out some muddied white powder and sprinkled it in the air.

■ ■ ■

At the Presidential Residence in La Caridad, Cortázar had gathered his commanders. After the attack on the Revolutionary Army camp, the eradication campaign against Los Eternos had gained steam. He hastened to capture Moreno.

One of his commanders had a smartphone to his ear, nodding all the while. Then he hung up. "There was a massive explosion in the mountains up north. We suspect it was an explosion at the cocaine factory," he reported.

"Was the cocaine taken out?"

"Reconnaissance is ongoing. There's no report back yet. We're setting up roadblocks and conducting inspections."

"Did Moreno order the bombing?" asked Dourne.

"Most likely. I heard he'd told his subordinates to never let the military lay a hand on his goods."

"Hundreds of pounds of coke, not to mention weapons, all lost," said Dourne.

"It was the largest cocaine refinery in the country. Destroying it means destroying nearly the entirety of Los Eternos."

"I'd wanted the factory for us. We should have taken the initiative to take it sooner," replied Dourne, disappointed.

Cortázar stood up from his desk. His commanders grew nervous.

"What's become of the money that was stolen from my Swiss account?" he asked.

"We'll extract that information from the people we captured."

"Do we still have no lead as to Moreno's whereabouts?"

"No, but it's only a matter of time, sir."

"Bring him alive, no matter what it takes. I want him to spit it out."

"Some of the cartel fighters are surrendering, sir. They have no loyalty to Los Eternos. The vast majority turned to the cartel because they went broke or got kidnapped. If the situation gets any worse for Los Eternos, there will be a flood of people leaving the cartel. We've captured some of them, and we're getting them to talk as we speak. Finding and arresting Moreno is a question of when, not if."

"Then hurry it up. But don't kill him. Drag him to me *alive*," he insisted forcefully.

"Los Eternos aren't the only ones hurting. We've lost nearly a hundred men in the battle against the cartel. They're demoralized. We need to do something."

"Yes—we need to capture Moreno. After we get him to talk, we'll chop him to pieces and hang the parts for the public to see. I should've killed the bastard sooner!" Cortázar sputtered. Then he paused to think.

A current of tension filled the room. Each of Cortázar's commanders stared fixedly at him. What would he order them to do this time?

"What about Luis? Has he still not been found yet?"

Dourne broke the tension. "Due to the terror attacks, we haven't been able to search for him as thoroughly as we'd have liked. But seeing as the Revolutionary Army went to the trouble of rescuing Luis, they must be hatching some plot."

"To think they still had that amount of fight in them. I thought that with the arrests of Luis and the other dissidents six months ago, Nueva Cordova was over."

"I thought so, too, but evidently—"

"Find Luis as soon as possible. How many revolutionaries are still alive?" said Cortázar.

"The camp has been sacked. Some survived, but only a handful."

"The problem is Luis. If we kill him, the rest will scatter. We'll capture him and publicly execute him for high treason."

The misery weighing on Cortázar's psyche spread throughout his body. Luis was a dead man walking, yet he'd busted out of prison. What was he plotting?

"Luis has a daughter. Penelope, I believe," said Dourne.

Cortázar looked back up. "Bring me Penelope. I've let her be until now, but the situation has changed."

"I regret to inform you she's gone missing. The troops went to her home to search for Luis, but she hasn't returned in days."

"Was she connected to his escape?"

"It's being looked into."

"Capture or kill the pair of them before they give us any more trouble. And find out what shape Nueva Cordova is in!" he spat, before plopping onto his sofa.

■ ■ ■

Meanwhile, at the FBI, Adán and Vanessa were glaring at the screen. Empty coffee cups were strewn about the computer desk, with a few boxes of pizza and donuts scattered around the nearby table. The two were watching video of the shoot-out at The Wall. Adán had already watched it over a hundred times.

"This guy's the Border Butcher, Captain Jadon Green, right? He doesn't look like he'd be much for massacres to me."

"He's shouting at the soldiers not to shoot, but his men can't hear him, so they just keep on firing."

"The fire from the refugees' side is heavy too. I'd have shot back if I'd been in the soldiers' shoes. If they hadn't fired back, they'd have just gotten killed," said Vanessa, taking off her headphones and facing Adán.

"Captain Green didn't fire a single shot toward the Mexican side, did he?" said Adán. "He only ever fired into the sky to try to get the others to stop."

"That's what the other records said too. But the Tragedy resulted in 155 dead and 232 wounded on the refugee side, with zero dead and wounded in the single digits on the US side. Of course they'd get torn apart by the world, and by America itself. It really was a massacre," she sighed.

"You could just as easily call this 'the Tragedy of Captain Jadon Green,'" said Adán. "He got labeled the Border Butcher, and was dishonorably discharged. Not to mention how it wrecked his family."

"If we're barking up the right tree, then the whole narrative concerning the Tragedy at The Wall will be turned upside down. Cortázar sent in agents to deliberately *create* the Tragedy. First, there was the gunfire from the parked Mexican car, aimed at the US soldiers. Then, a split second later, Ricardo Sepúlveda fired the first shot from the American side. After that, it degenerated into a shoot-out that resulted in a mountain of corpses. A total of thirty thousand dollars had been transferred to Sepúlveda's account before and after the massacre. Taking all of these things into account, it's Cortázar who should've taken the heat. But it's all circumstantial evidence."

"Ever since the Tragedy, Cordovans have stopped trying to flee the country, having been told by Cortázar that even if they made it all the way to America, they'd just got shot anyway. And President Copeland got attacked for the Tragedy, same as Green. His approval ratings took a nosedive, though they are slowly picking back up. That being said, his chances at reelection are still slim at best. He wants something impactful to happen. Plus, I heard he's still sad his daughter refuses to forgive him."

"All right, so where is Green?" asked Vanessa, her tone serious.

"We've pieced together that he worked at an LA construction site. And that he was living in a nearby motel. Beyond that . . ." Adán closed the file he was looking at.

"Is there nothing we can link to him? Like a robbery where a hundred thousand got stolen, something like that?"

"A former Army captain pulling a robbery because his ex-wife was chewing him out for being late with his child support payments? If that's true, I feel even worse for the guy," said Adán, as he typed. "What if he's peddling coke? You can certainly get lots of money quickly that way. And that's not exactly unheard of in LA, either."

"But he'd need money to start with for that. Maybe he attacked where a deal was taking place to get some money, then got killed after sending it off. Maybe he's swimming with the fishes or buried in the desert."

"Wait, ma'am. Hold on. There's been a steep rise in cocaine prices over the past few days. Apparently, a supply source in Central America got cut off. And when I think cocaine-producing countries in Central America . . ."

"You think Cordova! The country the caravan originated from. The country that caused Captain Green's downfall."

Adán typed Vanessa's words and clicked.

"Look, Cortázar declared he was 'wiping cocaine off the face of Cordova.' And recently there's been battles between Los Eternos and the Cordovan military. Just last night, an explosion of mysterious origin was detected in the jungles. They think it was an underground coke factory."

"That's exactly the kind of thing the refugees in the caravan were trying to escape. They were running from the atrocities committed by Cortázar's regime, and by José Moreno, the head of the Los Eternos cartel," she said, speaking slowly as she marshaled her thoughts.

"Do you think any of it has to do with Jadon's absence?" asked Adán.

"There's no way to tell without more information. But it's the FBI's job to investigate."

"I'd wager that they're not connected. It's just too far-fetched," said Adán. But he pulled up a satellite image of Cordova anyway.

"Just search for something that might give us a lead. Anything will do. I'm going to report to the boss . . . be right back," she said, leaving the room after looking at the screen one last time.

* * *

President Copeland had been pacing the Oval Office for a half hour when he pulled out his smartphone and tapped it.

"What would you like to know, Bob?" came a polite voice.

The man is always like this. He called me "Bob," sure, but why can't he speak a little more casually? It's like he's putting up a wall between himself and others. I've chalked it up to the defense mechanism of a vastly wealthy man, but it's gotten so much worse since his wife and child died.

"The FBI's investigating something relating to the Tragedy at The Wall. Even after all this time."

"Pursuing the truth in all things is commendable. I don't begrudge them. Even if the investigation never comes to light."

"I guess a consummate businessman would say that. But politicians are different. For us, the truth is whatever we want it to be. If there's some other truth out there, we just ignore it or cover it up."

"Do you mean to say history is predicated on a pack of lies?"

"It shouldn't be. History should be our key to the future. If that history is mistaken, it'd distort our view of the present, and negatively affect the future. And I'd hate to see our future become warped by a false past. That's why we need to set the record straight," he said, aware of the contradiction. *John knows well what being in the president's position entails. That's why I made that remark.*

"It's just as you say, sir," said John. "Sometimes the past is harsh enough for people to want to forget. Sometimes they even want to rewrite it. Don't you think you'd like to change that? Correcting the past will lead to an improved present and might even lead to a brighter future."

"The Tragedy at The Wall probably falls under that category too. I'm in my current bind thanks to that twist of fate, and it's cast a dark cloud over the future as well. My slim reelection prospects are one thing, but the worst nightmare is how my daughter still hates me. She thinks she's got history's worst president as her father."

A year prior, his approval ratings had plummeted by 15 percent. He'd done his best to quickly put a lid on the whole affair and move on with his presidency, but he felt that might have been a mistake. He'd only recovered 8 percent approval so far. At this rate, he'd get murdered at the polls. As the election loomed closer, his opposition would assuredly dredge up the Tragedy. His campaign strategists complained that they lost ten thousand votes every time a photo of the blood-soaked bodies at the scene was shown on TV.

"There are also those who rise up because of the past. Jadon's invasion of La Caridad is at hand."

"Vice President Hanna's getting more and more brazen. He came to the West Wing an hour ago to take a look around. I don't doubt he's already redecorating in his head. He wants to own the place before the election even comes around, by pushing for my resignation. And you know what? His being so obvious about it just fuels my fighting spirit. I wouldn't dream of handing the Oval Office to *him*."

"It'll only be a little while longer. Jadon's army will invade La Caridad and establish a new Cordova."

"Is there anything I can do, John?

"Just pray with me, Bob."

Bob hung up. Sadly, even if this operation succeeded, he still couldn't afford to be associated with it. And there would never be a way to tell his daughter that he had helped solve a refugee crisis. He sighed and sat at his desk.

■ ■ ■

6

THE OTHER SIDE OF THE TRUTH

The capo of Los Eternos, José Moreno, was in hiding inside a farmhouse near La Caridad. He'd only taken ten subordinates with him, but they were some of his most trusted henchmen. Of the approximately fifteen hundred men once at his beck and call, some five hundred had been killed by the military, and the rest had either been shoved into prison cells in La Caridad or escaped the organization of their own accord. Those who had been arrested had heard that the former top brass of the cartel had been tortured and executed.

Moreno's mansion was now occupied by Cortázar's forces too. His family had made arrangements to flee abroad, but that was the last he'd heard from them.

"What's become of the coke? The factories?" He'd ordered his subordinates to remove the cocaine they'd had in storage and detonate the refineries. Moreno would sooner destroy them than hand them to Cortázar.

"The plant in the north was attacked, and so the explosives were set. But we can't get in touch with our men there. It doesn't seem like there were any survivors, sir."

"Was the coke transferred out first?"

"They got attacked before they could."

"That was a secret storage refinery. How did its location get leaked to the military? All eight of my factories got attacked by Cortázar's stooges in just the past week. And we lost more than two thousand pounds of coke. Do you know what the street value of that is? Two hundred million dollars. I swear to God, I'm going to slit that bastard Cortázar's throat and feed him to the pigs. Then I'm going to feed his family, his relatives, his friends, and everyone who's ever associated with him in any way to the pigs."

"It's unlikely the government forces stormed the underground facility, sir. We never heard about any such plan from our moles in the military."

"We keep getting attacked and robbed of our weapons, even by people outside the military. How many men do I have left?"

"About fifty, I think. They're hiding in the outskirts of La Caridad."

At that moment, a subordinate entered without knocking to whisper something in Moreno's ear. He blanched.

"Get ready to move out of here, right now!"

"But where will we—"

"Anywhere's fine! Just hurry! We've just been informed that the soldiers have left the barracks and are headed here to attack us. I'm going to feed Cortázar to the pigs one day, I swear it!" he repeated, pulling a knife out. "Let's go to La Caridad. I'm going to slit his throat. Get everybody here."

"La Caridad's too dangerous, sir. One of our hideouts got attacked yesterday, and Cortázar's recalling his units in the north to the capital. They're going to launch an all-out attack against us."

"How did the hideout get leaked!? Are you telling me there's a spy among us?" Moreno let out a pained sigh.

His henchmen strained their ears. They could hear the rumbling of engines, the characteristic rattle of diesel engines. By the sound of it, not only were the vehicles coming closer, there were more than just two or three of them.

Moreno looked through the gap in the curtains, but it was too dark to make anything out. Were they driving with the lights off?

Before he knew it, the sound of the engines stopped. Silence had returned.

The door swung open and a subordinate dashed inside. "It's the military. We're totally surrounded!"

The window shattered and white smoke filled the room as gunfire commenced. Photo frames and vases came crashing down from the shelves.

Moreno and his men crawled along the floor, distancing themselves from the window. Several of them exclaimed over each other.

"It's tear gas. Get to the hallway!"

"Fire back! Kill them all!"

Then, gunfire was heard inside the house, as outside shooting ceased. Suddenly, all was quiet.

They covered their eyes as a powerful light was flashed on them.

"Don't resist, gentlemen of Los Eternos," said a mic-amplified voice. "We've got you totally surrounded. If you surrender, you'll come out of this alive."

"Don't let them fool you! This is do-or-die!"

"Hand over Moreno. He's got a million-dollar price tag on his head. Not only will that spare him his life, you'll also get a cool million out of the deal."

"Everybody who's surrendered gets tortured and killed!" Moreno gripped his automatic rifle tighter and fired at the source of the light outside.

The troops started shooting again. Windows were blown out, and walls were pocked with bullet holes.

Just then, Moreno felt a heavy blow to his head. He turned to look and standing there was a subordinate brandishing the butt of his gun. "You! Did you double-cross me?" he squealed. He tried to point his gun, but it was too heavy; he couldn't lift his arms. Another blow to the head, and he was out cold.

Cortázar stared at Moreno. He was a plump man with half of his swarthy face covered in hair, and he had his hands cuffed behind his back. His shirt stained red, blood was dripping down his face and neck.

Upon seeing Cortázar, he hawked up a loogie and spat.

A hulking man with a sergeant's lapel badge, who was standing behind Moreno, struck him in the back with his gun. Moreno whimpered and pitched forward onto the floor. The sergeant grabbed Moreno by the shoulder, pulled him, and forced him to kneel before Cortázar.

"Don't be so rough with the world's number one drug lord. But when you do him in, pull out all the stops. I want him begging for death," said Cortázar, leering down at Moreno.

"I'll curse you to death. Mark my words."

"Feel free to try, if you have the energy left. Now, tell me, where's my money? Where's the $7.5 billion from my Swiss bank account?"

Moreno glowered up at him. "Did you steal all of my money in retaliation for that? And you call yourself 'President'. You're nothing but a dirty thief!"

The sergeant kicked him in the back. Then, Cortázar's boot pushed down on the back of his head.

Dourne's cold eyes watched, emotionless.

"I have plenty of time, you know. And I am a great and merciful president. If you talk, I'll kill you painlessly."

"Why don't you return *my* money, huh? I swear to God, I will curse you to death!"

"What are you talking about? You stole my money, blew up that restaurant, and started a full-scale war. Don't tell me you didn't know the consequences."

"Stop bullshitting me. You stole my money, didn't you? That's why I had them blow up the restaurant. You're the bastard who wanted this war. I ought to slash your throat and rip out your beating heart, eat it, and shit it out."

"Take him away. Make him spit out where the money is before the night is over."

At Cortázar's command, the sergeant pulled Moreno to his feet and dragged him out the door.

Cortázar waited until the door was closed before taking a glass and a bottle of tequila from the shelf. He went to the sofa and sat beside Dourne.

In front of them stood several captains.

"What a vile little swine. Make sure he learns that the money is meaningless once he's dead. Let's see how long that bull head of his lasts." He downed his glass of tequila all at once.

"Did you find Luis's location?" Dourne asked one of the captains.

"We're still searching. After the attack in the valley, he vanished, along with the other dissidents. But they're all elderly men with no strength in their bones. They can't survive in the jungle for long. Sooner or later, we'll find them."

"Is there any chance they've crossed the border?" said Cortázar. "If they defect to the US, that'd be a headache. They'll bleat about their precious 'human rights,' and that'll land them tickets into America." Cortázar planted his eyes on Dourne.

"No, Copeland is bound to refuse them. The Tragedy at The Wall isn't ancient history to the US quite yet. People would cry foul: why take them in and not other Cordovans? If he's smart, he'll avoid dredging up the past. He's going to keep away from all things Cordova for the foreseeable future."

"But still, it isn't impossible. Plus, was it really Moreno who stole my money? I heard that even if ten of the world's greatest hackers formed a team, they still couldn't crack that account's security. So how could Los Eternos have done it?"

"Super high-grade hackers for hire steal that kind of money all the time. But why would they take *only* your money?"

Cortázar got up and began to pace. Dourne's eyes followed him around the room. Then Cortázar stopped. "You're right. And he must have known what would happen if he stole my money. He asked me whether I stole *his* money in retaliation. Was his money stolen too?" Cortázar closed his eyes. "If, hypothetically, he wasn't the one who stole my money . . . then could it have been the Revolutionary Army?"

The commanders looked at each other.

"When was the president's money withdrawn?" asked Dourne.

One of the commanders informed them of the exact date and time.

"That was *after* the restaurant was bombed. So Moreno bombed the restaurant, *then* had the money withdrawn, all the while knowing there would be hell to pay?"

Cortázar got to his feet. "It's time I paid Moreno another visit."

Moreno was being held in a room in the basement, naked, unconscious, and chained to a chair. There were bruises all over his body and his face was swollen. His head was hanging. There was a twenty-inch hose on the floor, with blood splattered all around it.

"Has he spit it out yet?"

"He's yet to experience the main event. We'll make him sing, sir, don't you worry."

"Wake him up."

The sergeant dumped a bucket of water over him. Moreno came to and glared up at Cortázar without raising his head.

"You called me a filthy thief earlier. It looks like we're both victims of theft. I should have suspected. There's no way you had the know-how to hack into my bank account," said Cortázar.

Moreno lifted his head and spat.

Cortázar peered into Moreno's face. Moreno attempted to spit again, only for Cortázar's fist to send him reeling.

Cortázar pulled a knife from a subordinate's waistband and slit Moreno's throat. Blood splattered all over Cortázar's military uniform. He wiped the the knife clean on Moreno's body and returned it to the subordinate.

Not a sound was heard from anyone in the room.

Cortázar returned to his office. Moreno's final words were etched into his mind, along with the dying expression on his face. *The man was a savage, a subhuman.*

Cortázar's eyes fell on the commanders standing in a row. They all looked frightened of him.

"He wasn't the one who took my money."

"Then who?" asked one of them hoarsely.

"It was those revolutionary weasels. But they no more have the capacity to hack into my account than Moreno did. Then again, how they busted Luis out of prison, and had choppers save them. Even during our assault on their camp, half of them were able to slip away. And they even counterattacked. Until recently, an attack on that scale would have wiped them out. We're being *watched.*"

"Do you mean there are Revolutionary Army spies in the military, sir? But that can't be."

Cortázar pointed up.

"They have a satellite on us. The attack units' movements were telegraphed to the enemy. America is involved."

"So America is aiding the Revolutionary Army? But we've never received any such intel."

"Contact Russia. They must have sources of information within the US government. The president must have issued one or more orders. This is a secret operation unapproved by Congress. If there's even the smallest evidence Copeland had a hand in this operation, I'll have him resign over it."

"I will ask Russia as soon as possible."

"Who's the one *really* leading the Revolutionary Army? I don't mean Luis or Sebastian. Luis may be backed by the people, but he can't lead a military! He doesn't even know his way around a gun! And Sebastian's much the same. He hasn't got the strength or the ability. There must be someone else. Find him!" he shouted. He took deep breaths in order to calm himself down. "Tell the people that Moreno's been executed. Tell the world. The bravery of the Cordovan Army led to the Los Eternos drug lord's capture and execution. Tell them it was Moreno behind the acts of terrorism these past few days."

Dourne had an idea. "What if we were to send the people and the world a message from around here? I can picture it now: 'Cordovan President Gumersindo Cortázar declares the destruction of the cartel and holds a founding ceremony commemorating a new future for the country, in order to further strengthen the unity of the people.' How about that?"

"The Revolutionary Army won't take that lying down," said a commander. "They'll issue a statement and launch an attack on us."

"Then we return fire. If you can't find them after this much searching, they can't be big enough to be worried about."

"I see, sir. So that's what you're aiming for with this founding ceremony for a new nation."

Cortázar interrupted. "Any word from *him* yet?"

"All contact has been cut off since the last attack."

"That doesn't mean he's been found out, does it?"

"We told him to choose death should he be discovered."

Cortázar mulled it over. Suddenly, he looked up at the commanders and said: "Next Sunday, we'll hold a national ceremony in the Plaza. We'll put on a military parade for the United Nations ambassador to see."

"We'll arrange for it at once, sir. And we'll increase the number of people on the hunt for Luis."

"It's going to be a ceremony to pave the way for a new Cordova. This is our chance to show the military off to the world, and it'll intimidate all of the countries bordering us as well." Cortázar smiled a creepy smile.

Dourne remained seated on the sofa, observing impassively.

■ ■ ■

Jadon's group carried the weapons they'd procured from the cocaine factory back to camp. The women who had been Los Eternos slaves helped them transport the spoils of war.

The camp was ready to move at a moment's notice. It was dangerous to stay in the same location for long. Sebastian's injuries hadn't totally healed, but he was spearheading the camp's migration. It seemed he felt responsible for the burning of the former camp and the lives lost in the assault by the military.

Inside a tent, Jadon convened a meeting of the Revolutionary Army's top executives, including Tsutomu, Bryan, and Luis.

"News of today's raid has already made it to both the military and Los Eternos. Los Eternos don't have the power left to strike back against the military, which means Cortázar will set his sights on us. It's only a matter of time before he wakes up to the presence of us Americans."

"But there still isn't anything concrete to tie us to Washington. They'll just think they managed to hire some mercs," said Tsutomu.

Jadon laid his eyes on Tsutomu. "I'd like to invade La Caridad before Cortázar notices us and the camp gets attacked."

"But we're not ready yet. In terms of both numbers of troops and weapons, the military outstrips us by a huge margin. We'll never survive using just the weapons we stole today."

"We can't bide our time until we have everything we'd ever want. We've managed to pull through until now, and we'll manage to pull through again."

"That was just luck. We could just as easily have been wiped out. There's no denying we're not adequately prepared."

"What do you think, professor?" asked Jadon.

Penelope was sitting beside her infirm father as his physician. "I can't express how grateful I am to you all," he stated. "But far too many Cordovans have died. I can't stand the notion that even more may lose their lives."

"Dad, you can't think of it that way. If we give up now, then their deaths will have been in vain. *Mom's* death—"

Jadon glanced at her. "Are you saying you're in favor of invading La Caridad?"

"I'm a doctor. I don't know the first thing about war. But I've seen a whole lot of my countrymen and women die. These past few days, I've interacted more with the dead than with the living. We can't let their sacrifices go to waste. We need to avenge them."

"Have we got a shot at actually winning?" asked Tsutomu, in all seriousness. "I don't want to fight a losing battle."

Bryan, for his part, nodded in agreement.

"It all hinges on how much the professor's rhetoric resonates with the people. If he rises up, there *will* be those who rise up with him. Even some of the soldiers in the government military will cooperate with us."

"And if they *don't* come out for the cause? What then? We'll be inferior to the enemy in every way. I don't want to march off to my untimely demise based on a hunch."

"I don't think now's the time, either," said Sebastian. "The soldiers are exhausted. They don't have the energy to invade the capital."

Moving camp had taken several days, and not only were they short on weapons, they were getting short on food too. But even worse, the pain of losing so many comrades weighed heavily on their minds.

"You don't know that if you don't try!" shouted Penelope. Luis goggled at her. "That's what a revolution is! A bunch of disgruntled people bad-mouth the government. Once that sentiment spreads, you have a group of like-minded people. And that group can only get bigger as the idea gains traction. Nueva Cordova may be licking its wounds now, but by the time we reach La Caridad, we'll be a force to be reckoned with."

"I didn't take you for such an optimist. I thought you'd be the cautious type."

"I'm not an optimist. You people are just being spineless. You started this war. You end it."

"We came here to build a new Cordova. A Cordova of safety and prosperity. And now is that time," said Jadon.

With that, it was decided. They would invade La Caridad and pick up all who agreed with Luis's vision along the way. Sebastian and Tsutomu folded in the face of Penelope's conviction.

The invasion of La Caridad was to be kept secret from the soldiers, as it would upset them; every man and woman there knew they were on the back foot. There was also the concern that the info would be leaked to the military. If they were attacked now, they didn't stand a chance.

"Keep an eye on the soldiers and report back to me if you see anyone acting suspiciously," Jadon told Sebastian and Tsutomu.

That night, Jadon placed a satellite call to Stewart. The phone had stopped functioning during the attack by Cortázar's men in the mountains, but it started working again after returning to the camp. The War Room had told him of the possibility someone was jamming it, but he hadn't divulged that to anyone but Tsutomu.

"Tomorrow, we head for La Caridad. We'll walk through the jungle and along the roads during the day, and camp in the jungle at night. On the way, we'll visit villages where the professor will call for people to join the Revolutionary Army. That should increase our rate of recruitment. Right now, we've got a total of three hundred soldiers. We should have a thousand by the time we reach La Caridad. But this operation won't be easy."

"Your chances of success seem low. We won't be able to provide you with backup without blowing our cover," said Stewart.

"Getting the Air Force to help may be unworkable, but could you use cruise missiles to bomb any military bases? If we claim the Revolutionary Army launched the attack, we could deceive the enemy as to our strength of arms too. And enemy morale would take a blow."

"We can't take any risks. Russia and China have begun to take notice of the situation surrounding Cordova. If they find out Washington is involved, the media and Congress will raise a fuss, and the president will probably need to resign as a result. The Tragedy at The Wall is finally on the wane; it'd be a shame if the president couldn't repair his reputation in time. The White House is a den of calculating types, or rather of self-preservationists. Try to avoid making waves. If this operation comes to light in any respect, the president is finished. And John agrees."

"Roger. We'll manage somehow." Jadon hung up, booted up his computer, and looked up the positions of the Cordovan military and facilities once again.

Jadon turned to inspect the source of a sudden noise. It was Penelope, standing nearby.

"Did something happen to the professor?"

"He's sleeping—or pretending to. His insomnia isn't going away. He just wants to reassure me and everyone else. It'd be more unnatural to be *able* to sleep at a time like this."

"I sleep when I need to," Jadon lied. He hadn't gotten enough sleep in days. But he didn't feel sleepy, either; he was just too tense. Besides, this reality was still preferable to the hell of his nightmares. He felt even more wired than usual.

"Give it to me straight—do we really have a shot against the military?"

Significantly, Penelope had used the word "we." Jadon paused for a second before replying. "It'll be tough. They outnumber us by more than a hundred to one, and they've got automatic rifles, land mines, and RPGs. But we have an ultimate trump card up our sleeves." Jadon looked at her. "We've got your father, the great Professor Luis

Escárcega. The people and the revolutionaries have absolute faith in him. Even in this horrible situation, his presence somehow binds everyone together. Many will join our ranks simply at his request. We'll head for La Caridad starting tomorrow, but how many more soldiers can we recruit by the time we arrive?"

"Can we exit the jungle and go by car?" asked Penelope.

"There are too many checkpoints. If we're spotted, we'll get crushed to smithereens before we ever make it to La Caridad."

"My father, he's gotten so weak. He's running on pure willpower. He could collapse at any second."

"That's why we're relying on you. We want you to be there for him."

"So you want to use him until the revolution succeeds."

Jadon had no response to that.

Penelope averted her gaze. She had something on her mind, but when her eyes found Jadon again, she left without saying anything.

The next morning, everyone was ordered to move out before it got too bright.

The Revolutionary Army packed up camp at the crack of dawn and departed with the women they'd rescued from Los Eternos in tow. By noon, they were on the unpaved road that cut across the jungle.

The road was about ten feet wide, which was enough for the occasional truck loaded with goods to pass by, kicking a cloud of dust in its wake as it headed for La Caridad.

"Let's leave the women here," said Jadon, scanning both sides of the road. "They can hitchhike to their individual villages."

"But if they encounter military vehicles, they'll be in trouble. They'll get raped and killed as former Los Eternos members. Since we've come this far, we ought to take them to somewhere safe."

"They stand out too much. Rumors will spread," said one of Tsutomu's men. "They'll put two and two together and realize we were the ones who attacked the Los Eternos factory."

"The broads are weighing us way the hell down," said another.

Jadon overheard what they were saying.

"There's a village about two hours from here," said Arsenio, showing Jadon the place on the map. "It's a bit of a detour, but that road also leads to La Caridad."

Ultimately, they decided to take the women to the village Arsenio indicated.

Upon entering the village, its denizens gathered to gawk at the rare sight that was the Revolutionary Army. The women regarded the villagers with fearful eyes and huddled close to each other.

"Can we trust these villagers?" Jadon asked Arsenio.

"No idea. All we know for sure is that they hate the military and Los Eternos. They've been assaulted and pillaged by both."

"But they're also afraid of them. They'll do anything if threatened."

A moment's pause.

"They believe in us," said Arsenio. "In the Revolutionary Army."

"Explain to the head of the village why the women need to hide here for a while before they can return to their home villages."

One of the women came up to Jadon. "Everybody wants to fight alongside the soldiers. Me, too, of course."

The group of women eyed Jadon warily.

"You'd only get in our way. Hide here for now and go back to your home villages when the coast is clear."

"We can't return to our villages anymore. We were forced to work in the coke factories, but that's not the half of it. We were violated every single day. Our villages won't accept us back."

"But I can't take you with us to the combat zone in good conscience."

The woman took Arsenio's automatic rifle, took off the safety, and fired at the feet and above the heads of the soldiers. Bullets kicked up clouds of dirt and splintered the bark and branches of trees.

"We've received combat training too!" she shouted, tears in her eyes. "They wanted us to be the ones on the front lines when the military inevitably attacked, so that we could buy them time to run. But now, this country finally has a ray of hope to fight for. And fight we will!"

"You'll have a harsh trek ahead of you. We have to travel through the jungle and over the mountains to La Caridad."

"Two years ago, after we got kidnapped by Los Eternos, we were forced to move to so many different locations, all while carrying very large amounts of heavy bags. We're strong enough to keep up with you men."

"They should accompany us," said Arsenio. "I'll be responsible for them."

"I'll leave it to your discretion. Don't let them, or us, down," said Jadon. Sebastian, too, nodded his assent.

The Revolutionary Army left the village and headed for La Caridad.

The women entered Arsenio's unit holding the weapons they took from Los Eternos.

One hour had passed since they started walking through the jungle. The units in back were beginning to lag behind.

Arsenio went up to Jadon. "Bring the doctor," he whispered. "The doctor" referred to Penelope, as the camp had taken to calling her.

"Is somebody sick?"

"One of the women fell to the ground. It's Nadia."

Nadia Brito was one of the women they'd rescued—the one with a pale complexion. Her movements were sluggish, and she was always hiding behind friends, who seemed eager to protect her.

Penelope was summoned to help, and the men cleared out of the way so she could examine Nadia.

"She's pregnant. She must already be at nine months. She's just so thin, and we couldn't tell through those clothes. If she's forced to walk anymore, it might prove fatal to her and/or to the baby," Penelope told Jadon.

"But she never showed any signs of being pregnant."

"She must have thought she would get left behind. Everyone's scraping by as it is, after all."

Jadon and Arsenio went to Nadia. She seemed to be in a great deal of pain, and totally exhausted.

Jadon relayed Penelope's conclusion. "We'll have you sent to a village, where you can rest for a while and get your strength back. Then you can return home."

"I will follow everyone. My life isn't worth anything. I don't even know whose baby this is. I was raped by more than one Los Eternos bastard."

"'Whose baby? It's *your* baby," Arsenio insisted.

The other women were listening to what Jadon and Arsenio were saying.

"Get this woman to her village."

"I won't go back. I will go to La Caridad with all of you."

"Cortázar's men are looking for us. We have to hurry. If you stick around, you might put everyone at greater risk."

Nadia took out a knife and held it up to her throat. "Then I'll just die here! I don't want to live in this godforsaken country anymore."

"I'll take her with us even if it means carrying her on my back. Then there's no problem, right?" said Arsenio, standing in front of Nadia and glaring at Jadon.

"We'll protect Nadia too," said one of the women. "We've suffered so much already; I can't bear the thought of losing to another bunch of men."

The women encircled Nadia.

Jadon walked away without a word. Even Tsutomu didn't say anything.

Nadia was placed on a cart that Arsenio found, and the women pulled it. For half a day, they continued walking. Just as they'd said, they didn't lose to the men; doggedly, they kept up while holding their guns and carrying their bags.

■ ■ ■

When the Revolutionary Army began making inroads to La Caridad, they had a little more than a hundred fighters, including the women. If every one of them armed themselves, they'd still have nearly a hundred automatic rifles left over. When they entered the jungle, they carried the weapons by hand. True to his word, Arsenio was walking with Nadia on his back.

Come nightfall, after setting up camp, everyone was drained. Some even fell asleep before hitting the ground.

Professor Escárcega was in less than good health. Even with Penelope holding him up and helping him walk, he was running on fumes.

"At this rate, we won't be able to put up a fight when we reach La Caridad. We need ten times more soldiers and weapons," said Tsutomu.

"You can cry over what we haven't got all you like, but it won't solve anything," said Jadon.

"I'll go get people from my village," Chad told Jadon. "There are loads who escaped from Los Eternos. They've received combat training too."

"Can we afford to trust them with our weapons?"

"They're just like me. I joined Los Eternos to survive. What they really want is their country back. We all love Cordova."

"Take some people with you. You can take Arsenio. It's too dangerous to go by yourself." Tsutomu patted Chad on the shoulder.

Jadon waited for Chad to leave the tent. "So you're going to have Arsenio watch them."

"We don't know what's running through their minds. Better that than they run off with our firepower," said Tsutomu.

At dawn the next day, Chad and Arsenio returned with about twenty young tough guys—all exuding plenty of attitude.

Some bore Kalashnikovs, others knives and cutting tools.

"Don't make any problems for us. If something happens, it's your responsibility," Jadon told Chad.

Chad nodded with a confused expression. He'd never been vested with such responsibility before.

"Let's let Chad handle the training for these guys," said Sebastian. "Give them guns, and some food to eat."

Chad nodded some more. "I'll make grade A soldiers out of them, just you wait. Five of them are my cousins. They ran from Los Eternos and hid out in the village."

"Our troubles are only starting, so make sure you look after them, because no one else will. Again, if anything should happen, the responsibility will be yours to shoulder," said Sebastian.

Tsutomu observed their conversation with cold eyes.

As they wound their way to La Caridad, the revolutionaries visited jungle villages, calling out to potential joiners of the cause. More than a hundred farmers enlisted, swelling the ranks significantly. But Jadon's anxiety was increasing. Most of the farmers had never fired a gun. Bryan and Arsenio were teaching them how to handle firearms as they advanced.

The closer they got to La Caridad, the more military vehicles they spotted driving down the road. The checkpoints were many, and the Revolutionary Army had to make considerable detours around them.

One could cut through the tension in the air with a dagger.

The leaders of the revolution, including Luis and Sebastian, were sitting in front of Jadon. The satellite phone and computer were on the table. In just a few minutes, John would be calling in from the War Room. At last, the phone rang.

John's voice was put on speakerphone. "Tell us your situation. The War Room's worried about you."

"The military's assault did a number on us. We don't have the weapons or the boots on the ground. We're trekking through the jungle toward La Caridad while evading the enemy. We don't have enough intel either."

"Are you aware Cortázar has executed Moreno?"

"Can we connect the satellite phone to the computer and make this a video conference or is that unsafe? I have Sebastian, Tsutomu, and Bryan here with me."

"That shouldn't be a problem. This is a secure line."

Jadon switched to video conference mode by connecting his satellite phone to the computer, which had a webcam. The War Room came on the screen. John in his wheelchair was in the center of the shot, with Nick Beasley sitting to one side and Stewart to the other. In the War Room, the inside of Jadon's tent could be seen on the central screen and on each computer screen.

"Two hours ago, Cordova announced that they executed Moreno, who was in their custody."

"Does that mean Los Eternos are dead?"

"I don't know. They may have lost their capo, but the man under him could take over. Or at least, that's how it works in the business world."

"Moreno wasn't just a drug lord, he had around the same amount of power as Cortázar within Cordova," said Jadon. "He wasn't just cultivating and selling coke either. He was using the profits to buy weapons from Russia and China and made money hand over fist selling them to neighboring countries and to international guerrilla organizations. And he was able to do so because of his cunning, and sheer force of personality. He ruled over Cordova through fear and coin. No one else can match his charisma or raw talent. Groups of hoodlums and racketeers may form, but nothing on the level of Los Eternos." Jadon almost couldn't believe the man had been captured and killed.

"Cortázar is planning to announce it to the world by throwing a ceremony and military parade at the Plaza."

"When is that going to be?"

"Three days from now. Cortázar's trying to reframe Cordova's image. He's calling it a new Cordova. He's also planning to give a speech at the United Nations."

"He's going to hold a ceremony, knowing full well we'll attack it?"

It went without saying that the military was deployed and on the watch for them. The ceremony's ulterior motive was clearly to lure in the Revolutionary Army for the crushing.

"Please give us news from your end," said John.

"We're at a point three miles north of La Caridad. Is the transmitter inside me still working?"

"Yes, it is. It's PathNet technology, so of course it's working."

Jadon gave them the lowdown on their circumstances and numbers. The more Jadon spoke, the more the faces of the people in the War Room changed. Clealry, they hadn't expected the revolutionaries' position to be this desperate.

"The capture of La Caridad will require several times more soldiers and weapons than we currently have. Our soldier counts are steadily increasing, but we don't have the time we need."

"So the operation is a failure? Is that what you're saying?"

"We have Professor Escárcega and his daughter with us, so we do have the benefit of heightened morale. And the number of people joining the revolution from nearby villages is increasing. But there's no guarantee the military won't catch up to us. All in all, there is hope, but we can't tell what's coming."

"Cortázar is proving himself more tenacious, cunning, and cruel than we expected. His men are all afraid of him," said John darkly. "We're thinking of sending in choppers to take you out of there if you want. They'd be rescue choppers affiliated with a private military company unconnected to Washington. We can bring the Escárcegas to America to seek asylum."

Luis stood up, moved behind Jadon, and put a hand on his shoulder to signal his intent to switch places with him. He blinked a few times into the webcam. "I have no intention whatsoever of fleeing my homeland. We can still fight. We will come by weapons and allies."

"You are—"

"I am Luis Escárcega. I will make sure this revolution succeeds, even if it costs me my life. All of you have my sincerest gratitude, along with the man who saved me, Captain Jadon Green."

John's expression was a mixture of surprise and reassurance.

"Your words have buoyed our spirits a great deal. While we have to operate from the shadows, know that we are striving to aid you and your nation. Captain Green has informed us as to the situation on the ground. We're currently looking into what we can do from here."

"You've done more than enough for us already. It's thanks to you that I'm alive. From here on out, we will build a new Cordova by our own power. We *will* surmount these hardships."

"The president of the United States will be delighted to hear you said that, sir. We are tracking your and Jadon's whereabouts. Good luck going forward!"

"We'll do our best." Jadon hung up the phone.

"All right, so, having said all that, what do we do now?" Tsutomu asked Jadon and Luis. "Because as it stands, we're a cocker spaniel antagonizing a tiger."

"There is such a thing as a paper tiger. And dogs can be both clever and heroic," said Penelope.

The Nueva Cordova Army pressed on through the jungle. Their plan was to visit a few more villages on their way to the capital, so as to grow their forces. People carrying Luis's letters were already going around to convey his message to the movers and shakers of the various villages.

Yet when farmers saw the Revolutionary Army coming through, they simply kept at their work. People crossing the road looked away from the revolutionaries and picked up their pace. People toting guns frightened them. Only a few of the townsfolk noticed Luis, and they stopped to get a good look at him.

"Do we have a loudspeaker?" asked Luis. "I will speak to them." Jadon handed him a loudspeaker. "People of Cordova, this is Luis Escárcega speaking. We are headed toward La Caridad in order to overthrow Cortázar's dictatorship and build a new nation in its stead. Let us do so together, as one! José Moreno has already been executed, and Los Eternos destroyed. A Cordova where children can live in peace and prosperity is within reach. Why don't we join forces to make our homeland a place where we won't starve or be forced to flee?" he declaimed. The speech was so rousing, some of the Revolutionary Army soldiers were even weeping.

The farmers stopped working the land and listened. Children began waving at the revolutionaries.

"Please continue. This may just be working," Jadon told Luis.

"Half a year ago, I was captured by Cortázar's forces, but now I am free, and with my comrades. Cordova is not a country ruled by fear and poverty because that is all Cordova can be. The true Cordova is as beautiful as it is peaceful. It is as rich in culture as it is in resources. Let us fight, then. Let us fight together, so that we may shape the country into the Cordova we know in our hearts."

A farmer was talking to the soldiers and ended up joining while he still had a hoe in hand. Other farmers would follow his example. By day's end, they passed through ten or so towns and villages, their ranks expanding with each visit. When they made camp in the jungle, they had passed the five hundred mark.

"We'll be fifteen hundred before we launch the attack on La Caridad. But that still won't be enough to face off against the military," said Tsutomu, eyeing a soldier who was sitting out of exhaustion.

"It's still nothing to sneeze at. They're here because they want to fight alongside Luis. The real problem is that we're already out of guns to hand out."

The majority of people they'd recruited were poorly dressed farmers.

Jadon himself had to wonder whether they'd even meet the baseline for being able to fight at all, but he was trying not to think about it.

"For the lion's share of them, this is the first they've held a gun. We don't have the time to train them."

"Not being able to fire straight is proof they were living in peace and harmony," said Luis with Penelope beside him. "That is why they would flee Cordova before they would fight for it. To fight, you must steel yourself for sacrifices."

And Cordovans killing each other doesn't qualify as sacrifices? Jadon nearly said.

Luis's strength was giving out, but he was pulling through by force of will, and with Penelope gallantly looking after his well-being.

In the War Room, there was a faint whiff of hope in the otherwise heavy air. That hope had been provided by Luis's humility and forthrightness. Hearing from the man directly was quite the treat. His sincerity and strength of purpose could make a believer out of anyone.

On the other hand, he looked like such a reduced version of his former self that it was frankly shocking. They'd known what he looked like through photos, but the Luis they had seen a few minutes ago was emaciated, his cheeks hollow. He looked a decade older than he was. All that was left of his former visage was the glint of wisdom in his eyes.

Antonio went up to Billy. "Show me the video file of that chat with Luis again."

"Nostalgic for Cordova, huh?"

"About ten minutes into the video, I saw a young soldier enter the tent and speak to Sebastian Loyola, the captain of the Revolutionary Army."

Billy replayed the recording of the video conference call. Antonio leaned in so close his eyes were almost touching the screen.

"Around ten minutes have passed, my friend."

"That's the one. The short one in ACUs."

Billy zoomed in where Antonio was pointing and increased

the resolution. Antonio all but absorbed the man's face through his eyeballs.

"It's *him*. There's no doubt about it. He raped my wife and the wife of my comrade and slit my daughter's throat. He sliced off my fingers with the knife I used to try to stop him. I could never forget his face even if I wanted to. He's the sickest bastard in the president's elite guard," seethed Antonio, as he clenched his fists. Tears streamed down his cheeks. "What is that man doing in the Revolutionary Army!?"

"Do you know his name?"

"Contreras. His mates called him Contreras. I'll chase him into the bowels of hell if I have to. He may be young, but he's a sergeant in the elite guard."

Billy moved his mouse and clicked, clicked, clicked. He pulled up the War Room's database. Then he put on a video of Cortázar at a ceremony with foreign ambassadors. Young men in white ceremonial uniforms were standing stock-still. "If Contreras is in there, let me know. This is the elite guard. You see them lined up behind Cortázar?"

Antonio pointed at one of them. A handsome young man was glaring at Cortázar, his expression beaming naked envy. "That's him. I'm sure of it."

In his military uniform, Contreras was a conspicuous ball of ambition. Billy put two photos side by side and ran some facial recognition software. "Oh, it's him all right, 99.7 percent certainty. Honestly, though, who would've seen that coming? This guy, a government spy?" Billy proceeded to print out the two photos and the results of the analysis.

Billy and Antonio went to Stewart.

"There's a Cordovan Army sergeant lurking in the Revolutionary Army. He's probably leaking information about them to Cortázar's men. Please notify Jadon as soon as humanly possible," said Billy, showing Stewart the two photos. One was a screenshot of the relevant segment of the video conference call with Luis, the other was taken at the ceremony conducted by Cortázar. Each zoomed in on Contreras's face.

Nick came and took a look, while Antonio told them about Contreras.

"And you're sure?"

"I swear it on these fingers of mine. I have no doubt whatsoever."

"No matter how close the results are to 100 percent, we can't be sure going off just this video. Though they certainly look alike, I'll give you that."

"That's why I looked into the matter a little more," said Billy. "His name is Leandro Contreras, and he's twenty-three years old. He joined the elite guard three years ago."

"So you're saying Contreras is a spy for Cortázar."

"I'm just giving you the facts. Somebody else can make the decisions."

"Get John."

Stewart explained the Contreras situation to John, who listened intently while soaking in the photos.

"If he was a spy for Cortázar the whole time, he could have reported the location of the camp or even jammed the satellite phones."

"If we're wrong—"

"We're not wrong. I swear it on the graves of my wife and daughter, and on these fingers!" he shouted tearfully.

"I'll talk to Jadon." Stewart took the photos from John.

When Stewart called, Jadon was just returning to the camp's command center. Stewart relayed what Antonio had said and sent the photo of Contreras in elite guard uniform to his smartphone. That was Chad, no question.

"This guy is in a Revolutionary Army unit. He told us he'd fled Los Eternos. He's an excellent soldier Sebastian's taken a liking to."

"He's a twenty-three-year-old sergeant in Cortázar's elite guard and a top dog among top dogs in the military. Has there been no sign of the enemy since the camp was attacked?"

"We got attacked just the one time. Ever since then, we've been on the move."

"Where is Chad at the moment?"

"He's out scouting the condition of the road to La Caridad. He should be back by midnight. Tomorrow morning, we'll all be headed to the capital."

"Does Chad know that?"

"Everyone in the camp knows. They're making travel preparations as we speak."

"You can deal with him at your discretion. We can't afford mistakes."

"Yes, sir." Jadon hung up.

Come to think of it, Jadon thought, Chad had been more than capable of sabotaging them. There was the attack on the camp, not to mention the time his satellite phone stopped working, and the sudden severance of the communications link. Chad had followed Sebastian in and out of the command center quite a few times too.

Jadon summoned Bryan and Tsutomu. They were the only two he could fully trust. He filled them in.

"I'm not necessarily surprised, but I still don't want to believe it," said Tsutomu. "If that is the case, then I'm amazed we managed to make it this far since the camp got attacked." He stood up with his gun in hand.

"Strengthen the camp's security. Send out scouts to see if there are enemy troops on the move within a six-mile radius. Everyone else should get ready to fight," ordered Jadon. "If Chad's a spy, the enemy will attack tonight."

Jadon was aware that by issuing those orders, he was just indulging in the comforting illusion of control. If the enemy attacked now, they wouldn't have a chance in hell. He exited the tent to go see the commander of the revolutionaries, Sebastian.

They tripled the guard, but no government attack came.

In the dead of night, Sebastian entered Jadon's tent. "Chad's back. He says he didn't spot any enemy troops."

"And no one was following him?"

"I looked, but no, no one."

"Where is Chad?"

"We have him under guard."

Jadon and Tsutomu went to Sebastian's tent. Chad was tied to a chair with his hands bound behind him.

From his swollen face, it looked like he had already taken a thrashing.

"Hello there, Contreras. You *are* Sergeant Contreras of the president's elite guard, I take it," said Jadon.

"Chad" lifted his head and stared at Jadon with pleading eyes.

"The military attacked our camp, burned it to the ground, and killed around half of the people there. And you're the one who made that happen, aren't you?"

He merely bit his lip.

"Do you know a man by the name of Antonio Alvarado? He was a revolutionary too. Still is, actually. And you raped and murdered his wife, before slitting his daughter's throat. He himself lost an eye and a leg to you, plus three fingers from his right hand."

He didn't utter a sound. That settled it—this was Contreras.

Tsutomu stuck a gun to Contreras's head. "If you're the guy, I'm going to blow your head off."

"And I won't stop him," said Jadon. "If it's all true, you deserve to die. If you've got anything to say, this is your chance."

"My real name is Leandro Contreras. I joined the president's elite guard when I was eighteen. Elite guardsmen can't disobey orders from above because they're by definition orders from Cortázar. That's what was drilled into our heads," he said, choking occasionally as his voice quavered. "I was ordered to infiltrate the Revolutionary Army and leak information. And I did just that, at first. I told them your position and when the most soldiers would be away from camp."

Sebastian struck Contreras, and he fell to the floor—chair and all. "That was for all the comrades who died. But that's not going to cut it. This one's for the injured!"

Contreras and his chair had been righted, only for Sebastian to slug him across the face. Once again, he crashed to the floor. The man's eyes were swollen red and black from internal bleeding.

"I was in the elite guard, but that's in the past. I don't want to go back there. Though you'll probably never believe me," wheezed Contreras, as he slobbered bloody spit. "I was horrified when I saw the ruins of the camp the military assaulted. That wasn't a battle, that was a slaughter. It was Cordovans murdering Cordovans. Plus . . . when I heard the professor and Captain Green speaking, I started to yearn for my true homeland too," he continued, looking at Sebastian with beseeching eyes.

Sebastian was trembling slightly.

"I haven't contacted the military since we started heading to La Caridad. Living with you changed my mind. It made me want to build a better Cordova too. I love my homeland. But I didn't have a choice. My mother is in La Carid—"

A gunshot. Sebastian pulled the trigger a second time. Another flash.

"So many of my comrades in arms because of this little bastard. I just gave him what was coming to him. No one will mourn his death!" he shouted, staring at what used to be Contreras as tears welled in his eyes.

The man standing behind Sebastian stepped forward and pointed his gun at Contreras. "Antonio's my cousin. Let me avenge him and his wife and daughter." He emptied his gun into Contreras's body.

Jadon simply watched as "Chad" was transformed into a bloody pile of flesh and bones. Before they knew it, groups of revolutionaries were crowding around them.

■ ■ ■

The airport lobby was visible on the computer screen. A photo of Jadon's face was posted on the frame.

"Jadon's last sighting was at Van Nuys, ten days ago at eight o'clock in the morning. I double-checked using facial recognition software. He was walking through the lobby with his duffel bags," Adán told Vanessa.

"If you've looked into it that closely, you can inquire with the airline as to his destination."

"That's where the trail goes cold. He didn't buy a ticket with any airline. He didn't even go up to any of the counters and never went through a boarding gate. In other words—"

"He took a private jet."

"There were three private jets out of Van Nuys that day. I checked all three, but the lead with the most potential is John Olson's."

"John Olson, as in the PathNet guy?"

"That's the one."

"Where'd that jet go?"

"To Basin Sands Airport. It's in the Nevada desert."

"The headquarters of PathNet is in San Jose. That's five hundred miles away. He could be starting up a new business, I suppose. Or maybe he's growing a cacti garden out there. If he's going into the tequila business, then count me interested."

"Shall we make a trip?"

"If the boss clears it, sure," said Vanessa, while typing on the keyboard. A satellite image of the Nevada desert appeared on the screen.

"There aren't many buildings near that airport. There's a gas station and an abandoned hotel." She zoomed into the area around the hotel. Adán peered over her shoulder. "Looks ordinary to me. That being said . . . look at those. Are those tire tracks? At the very least, we know a bunch of cars have come and gone around there in the past few days."

"But there are no cars in the image," said Adán. "Could it be an underground parking lot?"

Vanessa dragged the photo, tracing the tire tracks. They all disappeared into the hotel. "Look into how much water and electricity this hotel uses."

"The answer to both seems to be zero. The building doesn't have any electricity or running water. They must be using a generator for the power and either stored water or a used water truck."

"That is, if people are even in there," said Vanessa.

Adán moved the cursor. "I'll pull up satellite images of the hotel from the past few days." He typed for a moment, and images of black cars entering and leaving the hotel appeared. There was an underground parking lot all right. "These are cars from the past ten days. Large transport vehicles can also be seen driving through there over the past six months. Most are with companies affiliated with PathNet."

"I'm curious to know what's inside that hotel," said Vanessa.

"There's no way to look inside from here. Do we send an investigator? Or can we go ourselves?"

Vanessa mulled it over. "From here on out, we're really putting our careers on the line. John Olson's a big shot, to say the least, and he's also friends with the president. But he's not just his friend. He's his *billionaire* friend. He could flick gnats like us away with his pinky finger if he wanted to."

"Well, if we're going to get flicked away, let it be by the pinky finger of a billionaire," said Adán. "We'll be able to brag about it one day."

"You're right. It's the big shots we need to be looking into." Vanessa nodded and stood up. "You book the flight and the rental car. I'll talk it over with the boss."

"There are no regular flights to Basin Sands Airport. We'll fly to LA and rent a car from there . . ."

Vanessa just shrugged and left. Adán squinted into the screen and typed.

Ten minutes later, she was back with Deputy Director Douglas Fellure, who looked at Adán's computer screen.

"Is Jadon in that hotel? With John Olson?"

Adán didn't answer; he stared into the display.

"Did you find something new?"

"I think it's safe to assume Jadon left the hotel some time ago. A helicopter landed on the hotel's roof a week ago, and Jadon boarded that copter. There is no proof he came back either. As for his destination . . ." But Adán stopped there.

Doug's eyes screamed *spit it out.*

". . . It's Cordova, sir. My hunch is that he went to Cordova."

"But Jadon's the Border Butcher. If the citizens of that country ever laid eyes on him, they'd beat him to a pulp and hang him. Many of the people who died during the Tragedy were friends and relatives of Cordovans."

"Ever since a week ago, Cordova has been undergoing a sea change," said Vanessa. "Battles between the government and the cartel have erupted since Jadon went missing. And *something's* behind it all."

"I'll go with you," said Doug. "We'll go to Reagan National, where an FBI plane will be waiting to take us to an airport in Nevada. Then we'll take choppers to the desert hotel."

"But preparations—"

"Can be made on the plane. It's got better computers than here, so access won't be a problem."

"Will you report to the director?" asked Adán.

Doug gave it some thought. "Let's keep this a secret for now. Everything is speculation. We'll tell him when we've got a smoking gun." Doug told them not to be late and left.

"It's true that we can't be too loose-lipped about this," murmured

Adán. "If Green does have something to do with what's going down in Cordova, this is an international incident. Of course, that's not something one man can achieve. And if John Olson's involved, chances are high President Copeland is too." Adán attached a gun holster to his belt and went out the door.

President Copeland took a deep breath. John's report continued:

"I spoke with Professor Escárcega, the leader of Nueva Cordova. I think he will be the next president of Cordova. He says he gives thanks to the president of the United States."

Bob had seen Luis in photos. With his avuncular smile and silver hair, he had the air of a scholar, not a politician. "I hope I can meet him one day."

"He's currently working in tandem with Jadon and the rest."

"Do you mean to say he's taking up arms himself?"

"I don't think he's the type. But he is a symbol for Cordovans to rally behind. He can unite the people under him."

"I wish Professor Escárcega the best of luck."

"The operation is finally entering the last stages of Phase 1. Jadon and the Revolutionary Army are leaving the jungle to head for La Caridad."

"There's an aircraft carrier near Cordovan waters. It's prepared to send fighter planes at a moment's notice."

"You can't come across as being involved, Mr. President. Jadon asked to have Cordovan military bases blown up via Tomahawks, but we turned that idea down. It's just too dangerous because it seems Russian and Chinese satellites are focusing closely on Cordova."

"Is there anything I can do to help? I can't stand the thought that I'm the only one sitting pretty, not sticking my neck out." The president recalled the Tragedy at The Wall—the shooting and the bloodshed. The screaming and the crying. The hundreds lying dead in the sand. And he couldn't forget Patricia's tearful eyes, driving a stake into his soul.

"You already sent out helicopters for us. As a result, Jadon and Luis were able to return to the camp safe and sound. For that, I thank you."

"Speaking of which, it seems Vice President Hanna went and gave one of the chopper pilots a call."

"How did the pilot respond?"

"Apparently, that they'd saved American civilians. He said they'd received an SOS signal during some in-formation emergency flight training and that it was right on the verge of the border. Hanna couldn't press him any further. But where did this civilian rescue operation idea come from?"

"It must have been Jadon's idea. He was discharged, after all. Technically, they *were* all civilians."

"A rescue from a hostile land. Sounds like someone needs a medal or two."

"Nobody involved in this operation wants a medal for it."

"Guess you're right. I'll stop expecting ye olde quid pro quo. Scoring points for reelection is beneath me. I'm ashamed, I tell you. Nevertheless, I hope there's some tiny chance I can repair my relationship with my daughter."

"If we get our happy ending, everything else will fall into place. All we can do is work hard and try to make that happy ending happen," said John, his tone placid throughout, although it was clear he was under considerable pressure.

"When the operation is over, whether or not it is a success, I want to bring it out into the open. It's undeniable that I am interfering with another country and that I am inextricably involved. It's my responsibility. If that causes me to have to resign, then so be it. I'll do so without regrets."

"We'll cross that bridge when we get to it. For the time being, let's just give this operation our all." John hung up.

Bob kept the phone at his ear for a moment. He could almost hear them . . . Off in the jungle, Jadon, Luis, and many more were fighting to build a vibrant new democracy and to make sure that horrible tragedy would never occur a second time.

He put his smartphone in his chest pocket.

■ ■ ■

7

INTO THE CAPITAL

Jadon assembled the unit captains of Nueva Cordova and Supreme Commander Sebastian, to discuss their plan going forward.

It had been drizzling for a few hours. The Central American heat and humidity had them all exhausted and irritated.

Sebastian stood up and explained the future operations of the Revolutionary Army. "Cortázar's going to hold a large-scale founding ceremony and a military parade to commemorate the eradication of Los Eternos and the squashing of our Nueva Cordova in favor of *his*. He wants to show the people and the world that, within Cordova, his power and authority are rock-solid." The assembled commanders listened with grim expressions. "We can't let him get his way, so we're going to attack the ceremony. Ours is the only new Cordova that will be built by Cordovans, for Cordovans."

At Sebastian's words of conviction, a buzz of excitement ran through the tent. Sebastian and Jadon had decided to attack the ceremony the night before.

Tsutomu was looking at Jadon. This was the first he'd heard of the attack.

"I agree with Sebastian," said Jadon, scanning the soldiers in attendance. "If we let this chance slip by, the Revolutionary Army is done for."

"But Cortázar will arrange for the strictest security measures he can. And they know we'll be attacking too. In fact, that's probably the actual motive behind the parade."

"If we don't strike while the iron's hot, Cortázar will successfully improve his image in the eyes of the world. This ceremony will be broadcast through media outlets all over the globe. If things go his way, he'll show the world Cordova is more stable and secure than it actually is, and people will believe it. Then the Revolutionary Army will be painted as nothing more than a bunch of terrorists aiming to destabilize the country and tyrannize its citizens."

"I get that, but we're no match for them. We don't have the troops or the weapons. Cortázar took out Los Eternos and he can take us out too."

"We knew that was a possibility from the start. We've already come this far, and La Caridad is right within reach."

"We should bide our time. We aren't prepared."

Jadon listened to their exchange. Everything the soldiers said was true.

"No matter what, we have to topple Cortázar and establish a new government," spoke Luis, standing up. "So long as he stands at the top, our predicament cannot change for the better. New caravans full of desperate people will try to search for a place to call home, which will lead to another Tragedy at The Wall. This is our final window of opportunity. I'm fully on board with the plan to attack Cortázar's ceremony."

Everyone looked startled. They weren't expecting the professor to sign off on the attack. Penelope alone looked unsurprised.

"I want you back here in an hour. We'll give you all the details about the plan then."

The commanders got up and walked out of the tent. When Jadon came outside, he saw Tsutomu looking his way, so he went to him.

"Are you sure you want to go through with this? I don't want to fight for a hopeless cause, but if we have any chance of winning, then I'll gladly lend a hand."

"We do have a chance. The professor's our key to victory. From now on, he'll be standing at the forefront, and we'll attract droves of people who believe in what he stands for. He's got a charisma that can't be beat."

"Sure, but those believers will be farmers and villagers. Not soldiers. They don't know how to fight. They'll get massacred by the military."

"I hear there are quite a few followers of the professor within that military."

"So you're saying those troops will defect to the revolution? Then why haven't they already? Has a single one of Cortázar's men switched sides?"

"Chad switched sides, in the end. I'd like to believe his final words were the truth, that he wanted to create a Cordova he could love and admire, just like us."

"He was just saying that to save his own skin. Thanks to him leaking information to the military, we lost half of our forces. And he made our morale plummet too."

"But now, morale is as high as it ever was. And we've made it this far."

" 'This far' is the end of the road. You're an Army captain. You know how to assess each side's war potential. I told you—I don't want to die a dog's death."

"I want to trust in them. In the professor."

"You just want to die, don't you? Is this to atone for being the Border Butcher?"

Jadon clocked Tsutomu, who staggered but didn't fall.

"Go ahead. Hit me. Hit me if that's what it takes for you to snap back to reality."

"I apologize. I'll leave you to decide for yourself." Jadon went back inside the tent. He noticed Penelope looking at them but said nothing.

Cortázar was in his office inside the Presidential Residence, pacing aimlessly around the room.

Of the men lined up against the walls, over half were in military uniforms. Cortázar had called for his aides to give them their final instructions for the ceremony.

Meanwhile, Dourne was sitting on the edge of the sofa, observing them all.

Cortázar stopped pacing and trained his eyes on the men in the room. Low-key panic was written all over their faces.

"The Revolutionary Army will attack, that much is certain. This is an excellent opportunity for us. We'll kill the lot of them, including Luis!" he spat. "Keep our soldiers on standby outside town. The elite guard stays here in the building. Once the revolutionaries enter the Plaza, the elite guardsmen will surround them from the inside, while our troops will surround them from the outside. We'll cut off their paths of retreat and crush them once and for all."

"But we have yet to grasp how exactly the Revolutionary Army's main force will move. We've also lost contact with Contreras. It looks as though the tides have turned. We think it's likely Luis has taken command."

"A pencil neck like Luis can't command an army. The only reason you can't grasp how they'll move is your own incompetence. The point of the ceremony is to lure them in. Do not let them escape."

"At the moment, we're summoning all of the units stationed in the countryside. By the time the ceremony begins, over half of them will have arrived in La Caridad."

"Hurry them up. And prepare to receive the influx of troops." Cortázar looked at each of the men in the eyes.

Eventually, most of them left the room, leaving only a few. They were Cortázar's most trusted men.

"Do you think Luis can take command of the Revolutionary Army? He's a yellow-bellied coward who can't even hold a gun. If he had me at gunpoint, he wouldn't be able to pull the trigger." Cortázar looked to Dourne for validation.

"I think so too. Luis can't direct combat. Someone else must be in command."

"But who? It can't be Sebastian. All he'd do is hole up in the jungle and attack our troops whenever the opportunity presented itself."

"It's probably a foreigner. An American, if Copeland's involvement is anything to go by. But Copeland can't meddle openly. The leader might be a mercenary."

"Then we need to find out who he is, and fast. Find and capture him. I'll hang him in public as a foreign saboteur and leave his body out to rot, as a lesson to all who would oppose me!"

Almost everyone in the War Room had come together around John and Stewart, and all eyes were glued to the central screen, which displayed a close-up shot of Jadon's face.

When Jadon moved away from his computer, they could see the inside of the tent. The Escárcegas were seated beside Jadon, and Sebastian was next to them. Arsenio, Tsutomu, and Bryan were behind Jadon. On their computer, they could view the current War Room.

It was a satellite-aided video conference call between a tent in the jungle and a hotel in the desert.

At the head of the War Room's U-shaped table—where the miscellaneous experts were seated—sat John in his wheelchair, with Stewart and Antonio on either side of him.

Jadon had detailed the plan to restrain Cortázar by raiding the ceremony that would be held at La Plaza Fundadores. The War Room decided to give them and the plan their full support. This was their final meeting before the endgame.

"The success of Operation Caravan hinges on the mission that will take place within the next twenty-four hours. We require real-time satellite imagery and all the aid you can give us," said Jadon, addressing his computer screen in a pleading tone—a first for him.

"That's no problem. But Cortázar is already aware the Revolutionary Army is going to attack. In fact, the ceremony and parade are just a trap to lure you in," said psychologist Liz Watson. "Cortázar is a cruel and emotion-driven man, but he can also be calm and tactical. He's especially good at reading and manipulating people. He's even better at using fear and violence to contain any who would defy him. He's a modern-day, wannabe Hitler. That's how he's obtained and maintained that level of power."

"We know it's a trap. But it's now or never. If we miss this chance, Cortázar is free to tell the world what he wants. And he's even planning on giving a speech to the United Nations. He'll declare his tenure a success, citing how he destroyed the cartel, all so the United Nations will tolerate his regime."

"What is the current state of the Revolutionary Army?" asked John.

"Not great. We lack the soldiers and weapons we need. The cartel has been wiped out, while Cortázar's forces didn't take that much damage. The military was far stronger than we anticipated."

"That's not it," said Liz. "Cortázar's forces' willingness to fight is just an expression of their fear, a façade they need to survive. It's a house of cards waiting to be blown away."

"Tell us, how do we blow away the house of cards?"

"I don't know. Only God knows."

"Then drag God down here to tell us or ascend to heaven and tell us yourself."

Silence. Everyone in the War Room was looking at Liz.

"Think outside the box and outwit them," she said. "If you act how the opponent expects you to, that might actually throw them for a loop. And it might give you peace of mind."

"In other words, we can do whatever we need to do, as long as we get the desired results."

"Almost. Just don't forget that the morale of the Cordovan military is far from high. The lower-ranked soldiers aren't that well-trained, and many of them enlisted because they had no other options. There's a great chance some will defect to your side. And once some do, it will open the floodgates. You just have to find your angle."

"Our angle being?"

"You'd know better than we would. I'm not God."

"So you're leaving it to us in the end. We need *real* support here. Without it, we'll get wiped out. They're the ones with all the firepower."

For the first time, they heard despair in his voice.

A hush fell over the War Room. John recalled how frustrated the president felt that there was nothing he could do. The same applied to him right now.

"Professor Escárcega is your ticket to victory," said Liz. "His charisma is alive and well. If he calls Cordovans to action, people from all walks of life will answer, and the psyches of Cortázar's soldiers will be shaken. So just take the time to . . ."

As he listened to Liz's words, Jadon was looking at Luis. The man had his eyes closed; he was thinking about something. In the past few days, the way his body shook had grown more noticeable. His cheeks were even gaunter, and merely walking seemed a painful struggle for him. Jadon had heard that he could barely keep upright for long. Jungle life and the endless march had worn him out both physically and emotionally. His force of will as a commander of the revolution was reaching its limits.

Penelope was by her father's side, eyeing him with anxiety.

"We're attacking the ceremony," Jadon declared to the webcam. "If we let this opportunity pass us by, we won't get another."

"Cortázar will review his troops, but he'll be surrounded by presidential guardsmen, and hundreds of soldiers will be marching alongside tanks and self-propelled artillery," said Stewart. "They'll be on the alert for an attack by the Revolutionary Army and will have deployed troops to defeat them. There will be stricter security measures than ever before."

Nick was listening by Stewart's side, eyes closed and arms folded.

"Cortázar will be our one and only target. Taking him out will take the head off the snake. Many enemy soldiers will surrender."

"But how will you get close enough? You can't just barge in head-on. They've got us horribly outnumbered and outgunned."

"Your psych professor there said that combat isn't decided by numbers. We're just taking her words to heart," said Jadon, glaring at Stewart on the monitor.

Nick, eyes now open, was stifling a laugh.

"We can send real-time satellite images of the Foundation Plaza area. If there's anything else you need, let us know. I promise I'll provide you whatever support we can," said Stewart.

"We're going to be holding a strategy meeting. We leave the logistical support to you," said Jadon.

With that, the video call was dropped.

"All right," said Billy, "let's help our jungle homies out. They're only twenty-five hundred miles away. Meanwhile, we can drink our cold beers, and eat some pizza while we're at it."

No one laughed. Everyone left the table to return to their own stations.

The tension in the tent was downright oppressive.

Atop the table lay a map, and the satellite images sent by the War Room. Surrounding the table were Jadon, Tsutomu, Arsenio, Penelope, Luis, Sebastian, and Bryan. Jadon was relieved to have Tsutomu around. He'd never met a more reliable aide-de-camp than him. If Tsutomu were still in the US military, he would rise up the ranks fast.

"This is what the Plaza looks like as of ten minutes ago."

"It looks the same as always. It's full of residents and sightseers. They haven't started preparing for the ceremony and parade yet," said Tsutomu, as calmly as usual.

"Why a founding ceremony *now*, though? And why did Cortázar decide on it so hastily?"

"On the surface," said Sebastian, "it's supposed to be celebrating the destruction of the cartel and the revolution. The message is that he's rooted out the disturbers of the peace and the threats to Cordova's stability. He's selling himself to potential investors the world over. In the lead-up to the United Nations speech he's got scheduled for next month, he wants to show off his power."

"Does Cortázar know we've come this far?"

"He knows. He's trying to lure us in. That's the other ulterior motive behind the ceremony. Looks like he's quite confident."

"And we're just going to walk right into his trap?" said Arsenio. "They'll have tanks and armored cars. If we take the battle to the Plaza, we'll create a mountain out of revolutionaries' corpses. It'll take them maybe an hour to break us, if that. Nueva Cordova survived the guerrilla combat in the jungle by the skin of its teeth, but there's no way we can hold our own anymore."

Jadon regarded Arsenio. Until now he was always silent at every meeting; he simply did what Jadon told him to do. But today was different. He seemed nervous.

"Going by the satellite photos, neither tanks nor armored vehicles are traveling away from the borders. Given the tensions between Cordova and its neighbors, Cortázar can't afford to move his main forces to La Caridad. He thinks he can deal with us with just small arms."

"Do we have a plan? One misstep, and it's curtains for us."

"We don't have a plan, per se. We're just expecting something to give in the middle of the battle," said Jadon, thinking back on what Liz Watson said. More than likely, enemy troops would defect. But what percentage? Jadon regretted not asking that.

"Are you expecting the assistance of the US military?" asked Bryan. "Or the military of surrounding countries?"

Jadon didn't say anything.

"What do we do if we don't get help from either? I'll fight anyway, of course, but still."

"You're expecting the people to rise up," Arsenio told Bryan heatedly, "but they're not that heroic. People are selfish. All they really care about is themselves and their own families, in that order. They couldn't care less about the nation."

Clearly, Arsenio was talking to Jadon as well. This was the first time they'd seen him get so worked up.

No one rebutted Arsenio. He was right.

Tsutomu, who had been listening with his head downcast, looked up. "Everyone cares about their lives and their families. That's why you abandoned Cordova and headed for America in that caravan, right?" he said, staring at Arsenio. All eyes were on Tsutomu. He didn't usually speak up like this. "And then, when you lost everything, you came back here. The only place you can live with pride and humanity is Cordova. And you realized that. That's why you're fighting to better your homeland."

Tsutomu wasn't just convincing Arsenio, though. He was convincing himself.

"The hearts of the soldiers in the military are also wavering. They love their homeland too. They're just obeying Cortázar out of fear. If they throw down that fear, they'll join our cause," Tsutomu continued.

Arsenio's fists were clenched, and trembling.

"You learn a thing or two from Jadon, or what?" Bryan whispered sarcastically in Tsutomu's ear. "You've got him all riled up."

Jadon spoke before Tsutomu could reply. Discussion time was over. "Once we enter La Caridad, we'll split into three units. Two will head for the Plaza. One of them will attack the Plaza from the front, and the other from the sides. The third will take over media outlets."

La Caridad had one TV station, one radio station and a few newspaper companies. All were controlled by the state. They were supposed to be defended by the military and the president's elite guardsmen, but they'd received intel that only a tiny number of government troops were deployed to protect them.

"Once we've seized the media, we'll broadcast the professor's message to all parts of the country," said Sebastian.

Jadon glanced at the computer screen. Sebastian used the images on the monitor—the satellite images sent by the War Room—to explain. Together, they made use of the information on the latest positioning of the enemy troops provided to them by John to form their invasion plan. On the day of the ceremony, they would attack the capital from three directions with the help of the farmers.

"Keep one path open. Make sure they have an escape route. Otherwise the enemy will fight like cornered foxes."

"When the Revolutionary Army enters the Plaza, the enemy will release the elite guards on us. They're the military's top soldiers. I just hope their path doesn't become our escape path," said Tsutomu detachedly. It seemed he'd steeled himself for the battle to come.

After the meeting, Tsutomu and Bryan were talking. When Tsutomu's and Jadon's eyes met, Tsutomu shrugged in exaggerated fashion. An uneasy sensation came over Jadon. He could sense some kind of veil around Tsutomu. But his faith in Tsutomu didn't waver at all.

That night, Jadon was examining the satellite photos of La Caridad in his tent. Hearing someone come in, he turned to look, and there stood Penelope.

"I'm grateful to you. You gave me a chance to talk to my father," she said stiffly. "Before now, I never had a chance to see him this up close. When we're alone together, we talk at length. It seems he's trying to make up for lost time. He's even telling me things I've never known about my mother. They really did love each other."

Penelope was staring at Jadon. Jadon found himself averting his gaze. "Is the professor doing okay, health-wise?"

It was clear as day that Luis was in less than ideal shape. He was getting by through sheer drive and spirit.

"I'm a doctor. I never hesitate to tell him what's best for him. The question is whether he'll listen."

"Professor Escárcega's real chance to shine will be when the new administration under him sets about rebuilding the nation. The revolutions in the Middle East all failed when it came to constructing new nations in place of the old regimes. There were too many people who jockeyed for power, and not enough who promoted harmony and reconciliation. That's why those countries fell apart and succumbed to civil strife. But the professor's charisma is an unstoppable force in Cordova. No one would dare try to supersede him. He has the support of the vast majority of the people. It's not hard to see why Cortázar would hate and envy him."

Penelope looked downcast. She was hiding something.

"It's my obligation to protect everyone here, so tell me the truth. How bad is the professor's condition?"

"His burning desire to realize the revolution is all that's keeping him alive. And once that desire is fulfilled . . ."

Penelope leaned her hands against the desk. She stayed like that for a while, to calm her mind.

"I'll take you to your tent. Go get some rest."

Jadon helped her out of his tent.

■ ■ ■

The Revolutionary Army left camp before dawn. They walked in hundred-yard-long files. Around five hundred people had to carry their food, weapons, and ammo across the jungle.

"Exercise extreme caution. If the military attacks us, we're dead as doornails," said Jadon. It wasn't the first time he expressed that sentiment, and it wouldn't be the last. They truly were outmatched.

Not long after they departed, it started raining. The downpour beat down on them, and they thought it might be a squall, but the rain refused to show any signs of dying down after several hours. The streaks of pouring rain did let up eventually, but still they were trudging on while soaked to the bone.

Three hundred enemy troops were in position on each of the three main roads to La Caridad, with another two thousand defending the city. The total number of enemy soldiers guarding La Caridad was around three thousand. In addition, they had been tipped off by a fellow revolutionary hiding in La Caridad that there were about three hundred of the president's elite guardsmen too.

The Revolutionary Army would arrive on the outskirts of La Caridad by that evening. They would spend a night in the jungle and craft a strategy with the soldiers who had joined up in that time. At dawn the next day, they would attack La Caridad while continuing to converge.

At day's end, right after the tents had been set up, the second-in-command of Arsenio's unit came up to Jadon.

"Arsenio is nowhere to be seen."

"For how long?"

"Since we got here."

"Did you look for him?"

"He was witnessed leaving the camp, along with Nadia."

"I heard Arsenio is from a village near here. He'll be back soon."

"Then why'd he leave with Nadia?" asked Tsutomu.

"Let's not jump to conclusions. There's no proof he's abandoned the revolution. He was raised in this area. He's got a lot of friends and relatives around these parts. He just went to see them."

"With Nadia? Ever since they got to know each other, he's been behaving erratically."

"Arsenio *will* be back. He's not afraid of death. And he's got a goal he's sworn to fulfill." *The goal of killing me and avenging his family and brethren.* "Don't tell anyone Arsenio isn't here. For the time being, you take command," Jadon told Arsenio's first lieutenant.

When Tsutomu and Jadon were alone, Tsutomu whispered: "We're in a rough position. Our numbers aren't increasing like we'd hoped, and the soldiers we do have are getting sheepish." It was true; the quantity of soldiers who joined due to Luis's call to action was lower than they had expected. "We're a hundred percent on the back foot. Faced with a situation this grim, any reasonable person would have run away a long time ago. I don't feel like staking my life fighting for another man's war. And yet . . . weirdly enough, I don't feel the urge to run this time. Oh well, I tried to psych myself out. Guess it didn't work." Tsutomu shrugged.

"This fight is for a worthy cause. Usually, in war, both sides have their grievances and bones to pick. It's not the people that choose to go to war, it's the state. To most ordinary citizens, war is a thorn in their sides no matter if their nation wins or loses. It's just pointless bloodshed and misery, a mass slaughter-fest where both sides insist they're in the right. And then whichever side wins gets to write history. But this fight is *pure*. They're fighting so they and their children can survive. And you're sticking around because you understand that."

Tsutomu looked outside the tent. The rain was nonstop. It was enough to leave a man sapped and despondent.

An hour later, Tsutomu reported Bryan was AWOL.

"No way he ran away. You two are war buddies, can you guess where he might be?" asked Jadon.

"He has a family and, as of last year, a kid. He also said this would be his last operation before retiring. That being said—"

"So he figured his role here was over? But he left far too abruptly. Don't let the other soldiers catch on that Bryan and Arsenio are gone. If they find out, there'll be an avalanche of deserters."

Jadon regretted using the word deserters. The two were his most trusted men and that hadn't changed.

The rain was getting heavier. The pelting patter of the raindrops against the trees wasn't helping Jadon's anxiety.

* * *

President Cortázar stood before the mirror in his office. He was checking his attire for the founding ceremony and military parade. It was the uniform of an army captain. Once a soldier became a general, they were taken away from the battlefield. Captain was the highest rank of a soldier who participated directly in combat. Cortázar elected to don a captain's uniform so as not to forget the past. *Wearing this says, "Let's fight together." My subordinates understand that we are fighting together, that's why they're so loyal to me. And this way, I can get across my youth and my power.*

"You still can't ascertain the Revolutionary Army's movements? They should be near La Caridad by now."

"Since the last assault on them, they've been moving camp every day. We've put out a reward for anyone willing to sell information about them to us, but we haven't gotten anything actionable out of it. But we know for sure they are drawing near."

"They'll try to pull something at the ceremony. Is everyone combat-ready?" Cortázar asked Dourne.

"Our main forces have been placed around the Residence and the Plaza and positioned just as planned. Snipers have been stationed atop the main buildings around the Plaza. No matter what angle they attack from, we are fully prepared for them," he stated calmly, while pointing to places on the map.

Yet Cortázar's irritation had not subsided. He couldn't put his finger on what was making him so vexed, and it was gradually transforming into nail-biting insecurity.

"Capture Luis alive. Actually, scratch that. If it's too difficult to capture him, feel free to kill him. Just don't let him get away. Capture the commanders of the revolution alive, though. I'll have them spit out where my and Moreno's money is."

"We know, sir. We have tanks and armored cars behind the Residence. If something happens, they can be dispatched immediately," said one of his commanders.

Dourne, who had been ruminating, looked up at them. "The

Revolutionary Army could not have rescued Luis or hacked into his bank account by their own power. Someone or something else must be involved."

"If it's not the cartel, and it's not the revolutionaries, then—"

"It's America. The United States of America is aiding the Revolutionary Army," Dourne averred.

"It can't be," said Cortázar. "Following the Tragedy at The Wall, Copeland took a beating from Congress and the media. He wouldn't meddle in Cordovan affairs. If it got out that he did, he'd be well and truly finished. He'd have to kiss reelection goodbye."

Dourne sighed. "You're right. Copeland is a spineless worm of a president. All he cares about is his image," he hissed.

Cortázar looked into his mirror, stretched his back, and grinned.

I have nothing to fear. The man in front of my eyes is Gumersindo Cortázar, military man extraordinaire, and president of Cordova.

■ ■ ■

The area was suffused in dim sunlight, trickling through the thick jungle canopy. The rain that had cascaded down on them all through the night had stopped, and the dew on the leaves had evaporated, hanging like a mist.

The day they arrived at La Caridad was fast approaching. Jadon scanned the map inside his tent, but there was a commotion outside. He found a crowd of soldiers nearby.

"What happened?" he asked the lookout near the tent.

"I don't know," he replied, his own eyes fixed on a point in the jungle.

One after the other, local people, seemingly farmers and peasants all, emerged from the jungle. Some wielded hoes or sickles, others old guns. More than two hundred had answered the call.

Tsutomu took Arsenio to Jadon. "Arsenio brought us these soldiers-in-the-rough."

"How usable are they?"

"They can fire guns—they just need to be taught how," said Tsutomu matter-of-factly. "We may not have enough guns or bullets, but we'll just take them off of the enemy once we enter La Caridad."

Arsenio bowed his head. "As a commander and a soldier, I'm sorry. I acted without thinking. I wanted to take Nadia to a village. If she continued this march, she'd die. The doctor stated as much herself."

"Why didn't you say anything? You know how everyone's morale will take a dip if a commander disappears on them."

"I thought you'd be opposed to leaving the troops at a time like this, even if only temporarily. I'm not qualified to be a commander."

"How is Nadia doing?" asked Jadon.

"I dropped her off at an acquaintance's place. Now it all depends on her will to live . . . and her luck." Arsenio sighed. Judging by his expression, Nadia was in poor condition.

"I'm impressed you managed to bring two hundred people back with you."

"A fair amount of them idolize the professor. All I did was tell them they'd be fighting alongside him. If I'd had more time, even more people would've joined. Also . . ." Arsenio stopped to think. Then: "I heard rumors going around that a Revolutionary Army battalion is closing in on La Caridad. A battalion of five thousand. And that we're equipped with tanks and self-propelled artillery. There are people who joined because they bought into those rumors."

"But we're the only troops in the Revolutionary Army. Where the hell is this battalion?"

"I myself would like to know. It seems there are people who say they saw it."

Tsutomu didn't look surprised by any of this. Bryan and the other mercenaries must have gone around to all the villages enhancing the truth deliberately.

Jadon ordered Arsenio to return to his troops and to look after the new soldiers.

"We have to face facts here," said Tsutomu, who was watching the revolutionaries cheer the peasants in welcome. "Not only do we not have enough soldiers or weapons, many of the soldiers we do have can't shoot straight. Also, we've got people of all ages, from teenagers to guys in their eighties. Cortázar's men are all trained soldiers. They know how to aim and pull a trigger, and they were trained to shoot to kill. They'll fire at us without hesitation. Can these revolutionaries do the same?"

Luis was hesitant to engage in combat with the military. Even now, on the eve of battle, he was reflecting on possible ways to avoid fighting.

John stopped his wheelchair and turned his gaze to the central screen, where the city of La Caridad could be viewed. The War Room was crammed full of people—John had summoned every staff member.

"Have the post-mission preparations been made?"

"I've written a paper titled 'What's Next for Cordova'," answered Professor Kowalchuk. "First, we'll ask the United Nations for assistance and implement food and medical aid. That shouldn't be an issue. Next, as soon as Professor Escárcega enters the Presidential Residence, we'll announce five hundred million dollars in financial assistance. One of my former students is a high-ranking United Nations official. I consulted with said student and there's no issue there either. After that, we'll request each country's financial support, and lure in mutually beneficial business partnerships. I've already prepared some proposals and materials on the matter. I could use your help on that front."

"Do you think Professor Escárcega will accept our proposals?"

"I've met the man numerous times at academic conferences. He's an idealist but he's not inflexible, and he is extremely judicious," said Eugene, both his voice and his expression brimming with confidence. "Our plan lays out the best revitalization strategy that could possibly be conceived for Cordova through the latest AI advancements. Professor Escárcega holds a PhD in economics, in addition to his political science PhD. He'll accept our proposals with open arms."

The central screen displayed what Cordova's three-year economic forecast would be if the plan were put into effect. Cordova had the potential for a bright future; all the index numbers were soaring.

"And we've made sure that these foreign countries and corporations won't be exploiting Cordova from a position of superiority?"

"We've taken that into consideration. The way we set it up, the scales are either totally balanced or tipped in Cordova's favor. Cordova reserves the right to be the ultimate deciding factor, just as you wished."

"So long as Cordova uses its resources to the fullest, there's no reason it has to be a poor country. Investing countries and businesses should obtain tidy profits within a short span of time. Until now, Cortázar's oppressive regime and Moreno's cartel had Cordova on its knees. Professor Escárcega tried to stand up to them, but he didn't have a leg to stand on, and the circumstances weren't on his side. But that's going to change. We will rebuild the country in a rational and science-based way."

"In a handful of years, the country's GDP will double. By that time, it will be recognized by the international community and be able to receive even more assistance. Then it's just a matter of how egalitarian the distribution of that wealth will be. And a man like Professor Escárcega surely won't tolerate corruption."

"Economics is one of the most important issues to grapple with, along with education and medical care. Until now, Cordova's metrics were among the lowest in the world. The country needs urgent help enacting improvements in these areas."

This meeting's minutes would be delivered to the new Cordovan administration to serve as a handy reference.

"Can your AI devise our soldiers' battle plan?" Nick asked Billy sarcastically.

Billy looked at Professor Kowalchuk, who nodded. In the past few days, Billy and Eugene had been spending their free time together. Nick had overheard them swapping words like battle, weapons, terrain, troops, etc.

"It's possible. Would you like to know more?"

"Wait, you're already using AI for that? Show me."

"It's the same as with chess simulations. You set up the two groups and the battle conditions. Then you simulate the two groups fighting over and over again. But you need to input as much data as possible for the parameters—troop strength, weapons quality, skill level, battle experience, location . . . you get the idea."

"But war in the real world is different from some computer game. The weather, the terrain, the motivations of the soldiers, and various factors that can't be quantified because they all play a role."

"A computer simulation is no different from real life, as long as you have all the necessary data."

"And what are the results?"

"Victory is decided a few hours after the battle starts—and Nueva Cordova is always left in a state of near ruin," said Eugene, before heaving a sigh.

"Does that simulation have Professor Watson's psych analysis plugged in?"

"Yes," said Eugene. "Only . . . the inner minds of the people haven't been factored in. There's not enough data, or rather, there's next to no data at all. And we're not able to sufficiently quantify Professor Escárcega's charisma level either. In order to simulate reality as closely as possible, we need more data."

"So our hope lies in the data gap. And in *Jadon.*"

Eugene didn't reply. Billy smiled and winked.

Following the meeting, John paid Stewart's room a visit. "You're a professional military man. What do you think of this plan?"

"It's not bad. But you can't rely too much on good luck. If luck doesn't go your way, the losses can get out of hand."

"So you think the Revolutionary Army has been relying on luck?"

"Cordova may be small, but it's still a military dictatorship. Fighting a military-obsessed government's forces isn't easy, so Jadon is doing a stand-up job, as are the mercs and the revolutionaries. But now that the cartel is destroyed and Moreno is dead, Cortázar has one enemy left to focus on. And the Cordovan military's weapon and troop numbers are still leagues above the revolutionaries'."

"Do you think they will lose?"

"We do have one advantage," said Stewart, sighing. "Morale. As Professor Watson said, morale is important. The Revolutionary Army's soldiers desperately want to win. Possibly enough to risk dying for the cause. Just how hard they'll fight depends on the strength of Professor Escárcega's charisma," said Stewart warily, sensing John's dismay.

John brooded. "Is there anything we can do?"

"We're doing enough as it is. What you can do is sleep. You haven't slept a wink in days."

"It's raining in Cordova. The jungles are hot and humid. And Jadon's men are fighting through that."

"There's nothing that we can do to affect the battlefield directly. The best we can do is send them information. This was always a fight we can't take part in."

"Of course. We can't operate in the open," John muttered, his wheelchair shifting course.

"The members of the War Room are doing their best to find ways to assist Jadon and the revolution," said Stewart. But John already had his back turned.

■ ■ ■

The camp was a crowded mess of soldiers and transport vehicles; everyone was preparing to leave.

It was still dark out, but despite that, they had twice the number of soldiers gathered compared to the day before. Luis had called out to the soldiers who had returned to the surrounding villages.

By that early afternoon, they were setting up camp in the village right on the border of La Caridad and preparing to attack.

Penelope went up to Jadon. "You have to stop him. My father is preparing to advance alongside the soldiers. The battle is tomorrow, right? His body can't withstand the march or the combat. And he'll only be getting in the way. He needs to stay here."

"Can't you appeal to him as his daughter, as opposed to his doctor?"

"He just won't listen. That's why I'm asking you. He trusts you. He might listen."

Jadon went to Luis, who was sitting on the ground and tying his laces. He noticed Jadon and smiled. But it was a forlorn smile, tinged with exhaustion. Jadon crouched in front of him and tied his laces for him.

"There's a trick to it. It's the first thing they teach you when you join the military."

"I am grateful to you. You've given me and the people of Cordova a reason to hope."

"I didn't give them hope. They grabbed it with their own hands." Jadon looked up at him. "But hope isn't enough. You'll just wear yourself out. The end goal is to realize the future we envision."

"We're approaching La Caridad. The end goal of the people is starting to loom on the horizon."

"You have an important role to fulfill—rebuilding the country after the war. That's the end goal of the people. That's the reason we rescued you."

"That's why I have to go with them. Without victory, there will be no rebuilding. If I don't stand at the front, do you think the people will follow?"

"Cortázar's forces are waiting for us. It'll be nothing but a series of battles from here on out—extremely fierce battles, at that. It won't be like those skirmishes. You're just going to get in our way."

Luis stood up and took a gun off a young soldier nearby. He lifted it up and down a few times to feel its weight, then returned it.

"Fighting won't be easy for me. Like you said, continuous battle awaits us. But fighting isn't restricted to shooting guns. Do you remember what the War Room psychologist said? There are many who will unite under us upon seeing me or hearing my voice. You even said it yourself. I want to be shoulder to shoulder with them," said Luis, staring at Jadon.

Jadon could sense the fire in his words. He had no rebuttal. Of the political dissidents who had escaped from the detention center, Luis alone exhibited the power to draw hearts and minds. Jadon recalled how confidently John had declared the revolution could not succeed without him.

"Wear this," said Jadon, taking off his bulletproof vest to give to Luis.

"None of the other soldiers have the luxury of wearing one. I want to be with them in spirit too."

Penelope and Jadon exchanged looks. *Once he says something aloud, he never goes back on his word.*

"Please promise me you'll follow my orders and you won't leave our side. You are indispensable for the post-war rebuilding of the country."

"I'll make you that promise. However, you must understand that to Cordova, everyone here is indispensable."

Jadon sighed lightly.

"I'm coming too," declared Penelope. "And I'm not taking no for an answer." Just like her father, she wasn't the type to go back on her word.

Arsenio approached. "We're ready for departure," he reported.

"At sunrise, we exit the jungle and take the main road, where we'll board the trucks. The march into town will be easy, but the military will see us coming, so we have to move quickly."

When Jadon's group left the tent, the clearing was full of the ragtag soldiers of Nueva Cordova. The eyes of more than a thousand men were on Jadon.

"Now is the time. We're heading for the capital. We're going to build a new Cordova. A Cordova your children can take pride in. A Cordova of peace and prosperity!"

The soldiers listened wordlessly.

"Those of you who want to help shape Cordova into a country no one has to run from, let me hear you!" cut in Tsutomu, raising his fist. This was a first, coming from him. "A country of peace! A new Cordova!"

Cheers erupted from the crowd.

"I can't hear you," said Sebastian. "Do you *really* want to save Cordova?"

The numbers cheering multiplied several times over.

Penelope helped Luis to Jadon. Luis was short, but his voice was towering with zeal. "Let's create a nation for a people reborn. For us! For the Cordova we will build is one where the children can live and laugh with full bellies and sparks in their souls. Let's fight for the next generation!"

At Luis's exhortation, the soldiers raised their fists and clamored. Yet more of the men were lending their voices to the cheering.

"Imagine the faces of your children, your wives, your parents. The faces of your loved ones. Let's make this a country where they can be safe and happy. Stake your lives for their smiles."

At first, Arsenio had been looking on dispassionately, but then he yelled, "For your children, and for your loved ones!"

Their voices resounded through the early-morning rainforest. Then, they began their march toward La Caridad.

Doug, Vanessa, and Adán took a helicopter to Reagan National, where they boarded an FBI plane.

"Wow," said Adán. "Never been on a private jet before."

"Me neither," said Vanessa. "You should count your lucky stars. You're technically still in training, but you got to work on a high-level investigation. And as the main agent on the case too."

"It's only because my superiors are so awesome and talented that I'm on this ride."

"Let's not pop the champagne just yet," said Doug. "If you screw this up, you might be catching a bus home. Do you know the names and backgrounds of everyone at that desert hotel?"

Adán took a file out of his bag and read it aloud, "The leader is most likely the former CEO of PathNet, John Olson. He is a friend of President Copeland, and his largest donor. Colonel Stewart Gobel is Captain Jadon Green's former superior. His late daughter, Catrina, was John's wife, making Stewart John's father-in-law. Catrina Olson and her daughter, Rose, died in the Nice terror attack, where John Olson and Stewart sustained serious injuries. John Olson lost his lower legs and is in a wheelchair. Professor Eugene Kowalchuk won the Nobel Prize in economics two years ago for marrying AI and economics. He is a pioneer in a new field called optimal national economics. Other notable people include a psychologist and the head of a mercenary training company, plus William 'Billy' Ganaway, a genius hacker. He is serving a term in prison but is on parole for community service. In addi—"

"So we've got a businessman, a man of war, scholars, and even a convict. The hell are they all doing in a hotel in the middle of the desert?" murmured Doug. "And where's the main attraction, Captain Green?"

"If he's not in the hotel, then . . ." Adán hesitated to say it. All three of them were of the same mind, but they had no real proof.

The jet flew from east to west, as if chasing the sun. With the file on top of his lap, Adán thought back on the past ten days. He could hear Vanessa's soft sleep-breathing from across the aisle. Ever since they'd seen the video of the Tragedy at The Wall, neither one of them had gotten much sleep. Adán pondered about the people at the desert hotel. What was the common denominator between, as Doug put it, a businessman, a man of war, some scholars, and a convict? Jadon was likely to be in Cordova.

What if the common thread is the Tragedy at The Wall? It's like I've got all the pieces of the puzzle, but I can't figure out how they connect . . .

Adán slept until a bright shaft of light snapped him awake. Looking out the window, he saw a clear and cloudless sky. White sands and green foliage dotted the land.

"We'll reach Nevada in an hour," said Vanessa, sipping her coffee. "I never took you for the type that can sleep anywhere. I wish I could."

The jet landed in the Nevada airport. Three CH-47 choppers were on standby at the airport's edge. The three of them boarded the first. Four fully armed FBI special agents were sitting there.

"Four special agents to each chopper!" Doug shouted over the sound of the propeller blades as he fastened his seat belt. "We've got ten agents to help with the tech too!"

"But why? Are we going to war?"

"They're with the FBI Tactics Team," said Vanessa into Adán's ear. "You're the one who said the hotel's got a man of war and a convicted criminal."

Doug held the radio. "This is not a battle," he told all three copters. "When we land, we'll have been spotted already. We're dealing with the guy behind the company that gave us and the military a lot of their high-tech gadgets. None of them are threats. Your Tactics guys are here to show them we mean business. I want you following my orders. Do not act without my say-so."

Thirty minutes later, the choppers were hovering above the hotel. If the people inside the hotel were who the agents thought they were, then they'd already noticed their presence and were taking whatever countermeasures they'd laid out beforehand. The copters landed on the stretch of desert in front of the hotel. Doug, Vanessa, and Adán strode toward the entrance, the twelve FBI Tactics Team agents following behind.

Upon entering, the deputy director stopped in his tracks. At the front of the empty hallway was a check-in counter, and there stood around ten men and women. The man in the wheelchair at the center of the crowd was John Olson, who was flanked by Stewart Gobel and Eugene Kowalchuk. The rest of them were also familiar faces from Adán's files.

Doug took a step forward and flashed his FBI badge.

"What business does the FBI have out here in the desert?" asked John.

"Mr. Olson. We've come here today because of some suspicious activity we spotted with our satellite images."

"Aren't you going a little overboard with the fully armed agents? It's like a scene out of a movie."

"You're one to talk. A secret cabal in the middle of the desert is something you only see in fiction."

"Do you have a search warrant?"

"We came to investigate the situation in the vicinity. This is part of that investigation. Please cooperate."

"Then why so many armed agents?"

"Because I heard the area's unsafe. We may be FBI, but we need protection too."

"Protection from what? Coyotes? Rattlesnakes?"

"We heard the place is infested with something more dangerous than a coyote or two. That's why we're running a search." Doug scanned the hall. "Is that the banquet hall all the way down there? Could you show me?"

John beckoned him over. Beyond the doors lay a wide and spacious room, with a U-shaped table at the center and large screens lined up at the front. It looked like the exhibition hall of an IT company, but that wasn't what they were looking at. The tension in the room was excruciating. Dozens of men and women were busy working. They did take note of Doug and his agents, but they were engrossed in their own tasks. The place had an almost sacrosanct vibe to it, such was their devotion.

In his gut, Doug felt something halfway to apprehension. He almost wondered whether he was making a big mistake. Perhaps these people's mission was righteous—was the FBI hindering a noble undertaking? But his sense of responsibility to his own mission and to the FBI won out.

John's voice snapped him back to reality.

"This is PathNet's most bleeding-edge information research institute. It's been in operation for half a year. We're running verification tests and conducting research on next-generation information and communication technology that makes full use of AI, in conjunction with PathNet's central research center in San Jose."

"That's news to me. Surely it's not yet a full-scale operation?"

"It is. We are opening the door to a new era by connecting the world with outer orbit."

Adán looked around the room, amazed. "This place reminds me of the MIT lab when I was in college. It's got that open, relaxed feel to it," he whispered to Vanessa.

"You don't mind if we take a look around?" Doug signaled, and from behind the Tactics Team agents emerged the ten tech-expert agents.

John sighed and pushed himself before them. "Could I ask you to wait a moment? I'd like to consult with my friend." He took out his smartphone, looked at the clock on the wall, and sighed slightly before dialing a number.

Before the first ring of the ringtone was over, "Something bad happen? You hardly ever call me."

John turned his back on the agents and spoke: "I'm sorry to have to call you at a time like this, Bob."

"I'm still in the Oval Office. No way I can sleep tonight. It's already begun, hasn't it? What I would do to fly over there."

"We have an emergency. We'd like to be able to concentrate on supporting Green and his men, but something is keeping us from doing so at the moment. That's where you come in."

"Got it. I'll settle things."

John had been talking under his breath but now he handed the smartphone over to Doug, who took it with a raised eyebrow. When he put it to his ear, the look on his face changed. He straightened up, and listened to the president with an occasional "yes, sir" and "I understand" thrown in.

"Yes, sir. But I would like an explanation from you later," he said. Then he returned John's phone. "All right, everyone, we're going back. Let's keep this little excursion a secret. Don't divulge anything you've witnessed today."

"But, sir, we—"

"Zip it. We're out of here," he said, silencing the young agent's protests before making for the exit. His twenty-four subordinates followed hurriedly after him.

Billy stuck his tongue out and flipped them the bird behind their backs. Stewart slapped him.

John's mind was racing. *How did they find us in this desert hotel? The FBI's tech-specialist agents must have been on our backs this whole time. Have I made a grave error that will sink the president?*

"Let's get back to work," said Stewart, snapping John out of his reverie. "The operation will begin in just a few hours."

Doug exited the hotel and kept walking. Even he didn't know why a single phone call had him heading back, especially after he'd crossed the continent to reach the middle of nowhere. That one call had the authority—no, the sincerity and enthusiasm, to sway him.

"Are you really okay with turning back so readily?" asked Vanessa, who'd caught up with Doug.

"You can stay if you like."

"Who was on the phone?"

"It was President Copeland," he said bluntly.

Vanessa froze for a moment, before catching up once again. "Are you sure—"

"I know that voice. It was him. I voted for him after listening to a speech of his. He said he'd explain everything when the time came, but that for now, he'd like us to go back. He even said 'please'," he said excitedly, as though trying to convince himself it had really happened.

Then they got back on the choppers.

"What the hell kind of sorcery did you just use?" Stewart asked John as he returned to his seat.

"I asked for a little help from the Eastern Seaboard."

John switched the image on the central screen. Now it showed the roundabout in front of the hotel and the three helicopters parked there. They also saw Doug climbing aboard a chopper, talking to a female agent.

"Well, that's one thing settled. What're you staring at? Back to work! The people down in Cordova are putting their lives on the line. We can't afford to make any mistakes. Concentrate!" shouted Stewart.

With that, everyone recovered their senses and went back to their workstations.

"Why did the FBI come here? That Doug Fellure rolled through with all the confidence in the world. How did they find out about this place, and what else have they figured out?" John whispered to Stewart.

"Now we can be sure America's intelligence agencies aren't just for show. They could smell we were doing something fishy," he said.

Everyone who overheard looked at Stewart.

"In two or three days," stated John, "we're closing this place down and moving to New York. That's where Operation Caravan will proceed to Phase 2. Until then, we're going to support Jadon and the revolution in any way we can. And we're going to bring them back home to America, no matter what it takes. If we don't, then . . ."

John glanced at the screen. The three copters were taking off.

"How did they find us here, and what do they know?" murmured Stewart.

Billy was pounding on the keys as laboriously as a concert pianist. "You know the term cyber warfare? Turns out you can wage war without firing a gun or even casting a shadow on the battlefield. That's where war is these days. So let me join in on the fun," Billy had told John the night before.

"You've done enough work for us already. Your hacking into those two bank accounts secured a whole year's worth of funding for Cordova."

"But Jadon and his men are bleeding while I'm here typing. Believe it or not, I want to help. There must be even more I can do for them."

"Don't ask me; why don't you ask Colonel Gobel or Mr. Beasley? They feel the same way you do, in that they'd sooner spend the night in the War Room racking their brains as to how to help the revolutionaries than tuck in for the night."

Some of the experts had been working twenty-four-hour days, to the point of bringing a cot to a corner of the room, or slipping into a sleeping bag placed under a desk. They were analyzing the Cordovan military's movements and scope through the satellite images and sending the intel to Jadon.

Billy went up to Nick. "If I were to hack into the Cordovan military's communications network, what would happen?"

"Nevada is two thousand five hundred miles from where the war is."

"But the weapons they're using were manufactured by developed countries. Missiles are equipped with digital devices, and their communications equipment is internet-connected. For lots of weapons, if you were to take out the PathNet technology, they'd become useless museum pieces."

"You may be on to something. We could spread false information to confuse the military, and if we can direct the enemy's electronic hardware from here, it'd be a huge help to our soldiers," said Nick.

Billy gave it some thought. "It doesn't seem too hard to do. For *me*, anyway . . ." he murmured, before returning to his desk.

■ ■ ■

8

THE FINAL BATTLE

Two hours had passed since they started trekking through the jungle in the wee hours of the morning. Luis was pushing himself hard to keep up, walking with his daughter's aid.

"It's not long now. You can do it. As soon as we make it to the road, the trucks will be there."

It was quite bright now; the Revolutionary Army had emerged from under the dense canopy at a point twelve miles north of La Caridad. A parched road leading to the city appeared—Foundation Road (Ruta Fundadores).

"The trucks will be here soon. Let's take a break for now." Jadon set up camp and bade the top executives of the Revolutionary Army assemble.

Sebastian, Jadon, Tsutomu, Luis, and Penelope sat in front of the map. La Caridad was near the map's center.

Jadon listened and contemplated as everyone voiced their opinions:

"According to the War Room, the enemy is mobilizing border troops toward La Caridad. Obviously they're hunkering down against us."

"Maybe it's to up security for the ceremony and military parade. They're having foreign dignitaries, including United Nations reps. If a battle broke out then and there, it would rattle Cortázar's authority."

"But Cortázar is more preoccupied with crushing the revolution."

"So you think he's absolutely certain we're coming for him?"

Jadon raised his head and eyed the group. "The ceremony will take place tomorrow afternoon. If the War Room's intel is right, Cortázar will watch the parade on a viewing platform alongside the dignitaries and senior United Nations officials he's invited. Cortázar only rarely makes public appearances, so this presents a unique opportunity to capture him. Though, in his eyes, this will serve as a chance to kill us all."

"Security will be strict. It won't be easy to reach the square, which is where Cortázar's going to be."

"We'll arrive at the edge of La Caridad by noon, enter the city when the ceremony starts, and push toward the Plaza. Cortázar will escape inside the Residence, where his elite guardsmen can protect him."

"Enemy troops will be waiting for us inside the city. If we engage them in our current state, that'll put us at a disadvantage. We're still not anywhere close to rivaling them in numbers," replied Tsutomu.

"You're the one who said war isn't just a numbers game. And I happen to agree with that."

"The number of men and quality of weapons do play a role though. The soldiers' morale also matters, but in this case the gap in strength is just too big."

"The time the ceremony starts isn't going to change. You've got to do something about the situation by the time we attack."

The Escárcegas, sitting beside Jadon, just listened without a word.

The soldiers waiting on the roadside started making noise.

They filed out of the tent to find a cloud of dust kicking up. There was a line of about fifty large trucks headed their way.

"Everyone, get your weapons. It's the enemy."

The soldiers raised angry yells, and the camp was in disorder. Jadon and his men ran out onto the road with their guns. The gathered revolutionaries stared down the road with their own firearms in hand.

"It's not the enemy; those are our trucks. Don't shoot!" someone shouted.

The trucks contained gun-toting men in various clothing. Bryan Fuller and some of the other mercs were waving their hands out the windows of the truck in front.

Revolutionaries on both sides of the road cheered. Tsutomu brought Bryan to Jadon and the rest.

"We made it on time. But we still haven't got enough soldiers or weapons. If only we'd had the time."

"This is enough. We may not have enough guns or ammo, but we can manage."

"We took a little with us. It's stuff we stole from the enemy."

Bryan filled them in on how they spread the rumor that the Revolutionary Army was mobilizing, while also attacking government troops stationed at the border for their weapons.

"We also told people it was soldiers from a neighboring country that attacked those guys. For the time being, those garrisons won't be able to leave the border. Cortázar can't call them back anymore. He can't shore up La Caridad's defenses," said Bryan, pointing to various places on the map.

The country's borders were always in a state of high tension. Several times a year, skirmishes at the border inevitably yielded casualties. Most of Cordova's tanks were already deployed. And if those tanks couldn't be summoned to La Caridad, it gave the revolutionaries' chances a significant boost.

Outside the tents, the soldiers were still cheering in welcome of their new comrades.

At the Presidential Residence, Cortázar could have heard a pin drop.

He was pacing around his office with his army captain's uniform on. Meanwhile, Dourne was on the sofa, watching.

Cortázar stopped in his tracks. Moreno and Los Eternos were no more, and the preparations to strike against the Revolutionary Army were in place. But what was this sense of *foreboding*? Whenever he stopped moving, he could feel the lump of anxiety reemerge inside him.

From the veranda outside the office, one could look upon the whole Plaza, where people were making the final arrangements for the ceremony and military parade scheduled for noon the next day. Orders were occasionally issued to the workers at the site through the loudspeakers.

The door swung open, and a soldier stepped inside. "We've been informed that the Revolutionary Army is getting ready to leave the jungle for La Caridad. There are around two hundred of them. They are all armed with Kalashnikovs or M16s."

"Two hundred, eh? That's fewer than I was expecting. Is Luis with them?"

"He is, or so we heard. The leader of the Revolutionary Army is Sebastian Loyola."

Cortázar glanced at Dourne.

"We will lure them to the Plaza. In the run-up to that, we will dispose of their leaders. I'll tell them that there's a bounty in it for anyone who takes Luis's head. Without its leaders, the soldiers will run around like headless chickens. And the snipers have already taken their positions," said Dourne.

"When the Revolutionary Army enters the Plaza, our soldiers and the elite guards will spring their attack. We will make a show of the Revolutionary Army's annihilation so that the people get a good look and learn their lesson," said Cortázar. They'd discussed this many times before.

"Let's call back some of the border garrisons, just in case."

Cortázar nodded and went out the door at the other end of the office onto the veranda. The viewing platform for the military parade had been fully constructed, as well as the ceremony stage. The perimeter of the Plaza was heavily guarded.

United Nations officials will be at the ceremony when the revolutionaries come barging through. They'll see it as an act of terrorism. And then the righteous government of Cordova will put an end to their campaign of terror. A new Cordova will be born, all right. A Cordova that is mine.

Cortázar stretched his back and clicked his heels to bolster his spirits.

The line of trucks carrying Jadon, Luis, and the soldiers was driving down Foundation Road for La Caridad. Including the new soldiers, there were more than fifteen hundred of them.

Luis's calls to action, conducted from a jeep, continued even as they made their way to the capital. People's reactions became more and more pronounced as they got closer to their destination. Cordovans dashed from their homes at the professor's voice. Whenever the jeep came to a halt, it would get surrounded by adoring crowds. The news of how Luis had been freed from his confinement at Cortázar's hands by the Revolutionary Army he now led, and how people were joining the revolution from each and every region of Cordova, was spreading across the land.

Jadon could still only marvel at the sheer magnetism Luis exerted over the nation.

"Let us raise up our voices, my brothers and sisters. It is silence and meekness in the face of evil that give rise to refugees, and that caused the Tragedy at The Wall. We must rise up and build Cordova as we see fit."

The closer to the capital they came, the stronger and hotter the fire in Luis's voice. Penelope was providing him the necessary support, looking after his health so devotedly one might surmise she was making up for years of absence and resentment.

At the same time, Jadon was taking notice that she herself was a beloved and popular figure among Cordovans. It wasn't that she was Luis's daughter. She'd earned her high esteem by helping to build hospitals and schools throughout the years and by contributing to the medical care and education of her people. She was especially well regarded by women and children.

When they left the jungle, the number of troops increased even more. People who couldn't get on trucks followed on foot. Most of them were farmers or townsfolk who had never held a gun in their lives. Needless to say, they didn't possess any firearms, nor did the Revolutionary Army have any to give them.

"It's like they think they're going on a picnic. Like we've already chased Cortázar's soldiers out of the capital. Do they think they can take knives and sickles to a gunfight? At this rate, we'll have a bloodbath on our hands," sighed Tsutomu, a grave look on his face.

"Nueva Cordova will serve as the advance contingent. We'll use the weapons we take from the soldiers we defeat. That's why we need to get them used to handling guns."

"Sebastian and Bryan are training them with that in mind. But—"

"The Tragedy at The Wall will never happen again," said Jadon, his words full of determination.

What little training they could conduct in the time they had continued even as the Revolutionary Army neared La Caridad. The new soldiers were drilled on the basics of how to handle guns and how dangerous they could be, how to toss grenades and how to work RPG launchers, how to tell what direction bullets were coming from, and how to hide from gunfire, all to vest them with the absolute essentials and thereby save some lives.

Jadon announced that he was the Border Butcher of infamy for the peasants, townsfolk, and soldiers to hear. "Look at me. Your brethren died before my eyes, shot through the head and stomach. Feel free to hate and detest me. You can even pull your triggers and end me altogether. But this is your one and only chance."

The farmers and soldiers just listened, dead silent. The air around him was charged with a strange tension.

It was a small village near La Caridad where they camped out for the last time. Revising their strategy, they would advance toward La Caridad the next day. The soldiers were exhausted and the majority were fast asleep.

A single step outside the camp, and it was complete darkness. The cries of small animals could be heard coming from the jungle.

Jadon parted with Tsutomu and returned to the command center tent. He sat on the cot in the corner. Then, a figure stood at the entrance of the tent. It was too dark to see, but he could tell it was Penelope.

"You're always on your toes, aren't you? You can put the gun away." She took a seat beside him.

"You should get some sleep. Tomorrow we're riding straight to the Plaza."

"That's why I'm here. There's something I've been meaning to tell you," she said, her voice quivering a little. "I get so sad whenever I watch you." Jadon could feel her eyes on him. "I get the feeling a part of you is just looking for a place to die."

"I'm already dead. I died a year ago, at The Wall."

"But I want you to *live*. For the sake of the people of Cordova."

"I'm the Border Butcher. So many women and children died because of me. So I'm ready to die at any moment."

"You're wrong. You fostered seeds of hatred among the soldiers of the Revolutionary Army on purpose, to raise morale."

"I just don't want to keep fooling myself in order to cling to life. I'm the Border Butcher, and no amount of running or hiding will change that."

Penelope went quiet, and a moment of silence enfolded them. Her entire body was shaking slightly. Was she crying?

"Do as you like," she said. "But it doesn't have to be this way. You'll come to regret that attitude."

"I've already experienced all the regret in the world."

"The people of Cordova think of you as their *ally*. Or at least the people in this camp do. And if someone doesn't, they'll have me to answer to."

Once again, silence. All he could sense was Penelope's breathing. Until, at last, she stood up. Her silhouette departed the tent.

Jadon sat there for some time, staring into the darkness that had swallowed her.

The Revolutionary Army had one final meeting in the small village near La Caridad. An hour later, they would head for Foundation Plaza.

The tents were full of people, and everybody's faces were brimming with equal parts excitement and apprehension.

Jadon was sitting in front of the Escárcegas. "When we enter La Caridad, think of the place as one big battlefield. I'd like for you to stay behind the combat units and avoid any dangerous areas."

"I want to fight alongside you," said Luis, gazing at him resolutely.

"As much as I'd appreciate that, it's too risky. Just make sure you follow my instructions. Only under that condition can you come with us." Jadon looked at Penelope. She was clearly afraid her father would get in Jadon's way.

Tsutomu and Sebastian entered the room. Tsutomu's tablet contained the latest satellite images of La Caridad, just as Jadon had requested from the War Room.

He saw the Escárcegas there and pulled an uneasy expression.

"What?" said Luis. "Please, you can tell us. I want to know what's going on."

"We have a problem. Look at the latest images from the War Room." Tsutomu showed Jadon using the tablet. The images were sharp enough to tell them where the government's troops had been stationed. "They've got their men surrounding the Plaza and Residence.

Also, there are signs that the border garrisons *are* moving toward the capital. Cortázar must have summoned them to La Caridad. Yet there aren't that many troops in the city. It's like they're *asking* us to invade La Caridad."

"So they lure us in and then cut off our means of escape?" said Jadon as he examined the images.

"The troops' positioning is also weird. There's not many in front of the Plaza, but there's lots on either side." Then Tsutomu placed seven different X marks on the screen. "That's where they've got snipers waiting for us. Seven's too many, and they're mostly on buildings by the main road."

Jadon turned to Luis. "Cortázar knows you're with the Revolutionary Army. And they know you'll stand at the fore and come attacking."

The Escárcegas looked at Jadon and Tsutomu like they were crazy.

"I agree. The snipers are aiming for the leader of the revolution—Professor Escárcega. He knows how influential you are, and it seems he's willing to do whatever it takes to snuff you out. Before we can enter the square, those snipers need to be taken care of." Then Tsutomu looked at Jadon.

"It's not going to be easy. Cortázar's far from dumb. He must be anticipating we'll attack the snipers."

"Then we just push through. We're willing to stake our lives."

At that, Jadon nodded.

"An advance contingent of several soldiers will infiltrate La Caridad and eliminate the snipers. Please proceed with the main force after you get the all-clear," Jadon told the Escárcegas before turning to Tsutomu. "Choose who you want to take, including the sniper."

Ten minutes later, Tsutomu reappeared with four revolutionaries. He was carrying a sniper rifle on his shoulder—the rifle Jadon had seen on the plane from LA.

"So *you're* the sniper, huh? Guess you're a cut above when it comes to shooting too."

"I'm not bad. When I was in the military, I was a candidate for the Olympics at one point."

"And? What happened?"

"On the day I was set to depart for the competition as a rep for America, the order to deploy to Afghanistan came down."

"That's a shame."

"It was just the qualifiers anyway. And I don't know if I would've had the attention span for it. Competitive shooting requires concentration and patience—plus it's such a different animal from battlefield shooting. I've got my own style of shooting, you know?"

"Whenever there's something you need to tell me, don't hesitate to call me. I won't call you; instead, I'll send the latest info from the War Room to your tablet." Jadon took the tablet from Tsutomu's hands. He wanted to double-check the snipers' positions. Then, when he was about to hand the tablet back, his finger touched the screen and the screen changed.

Ten men were visible, with Cortázar at the center. Half of them were wearing military uniforms.

"That's a photo of the inauguration ceremony of a cabinet minister. It's Cortázar and his aides. I just want to study the face of the guy we'll be fighting," said Tsutomu, taking the tablet back.

They hadn't seen many pictures of Cortázar with his aides.

"I've got his face so seared into my brain that I could tell if it's him even if he were to wear a disguise."

Behind Cortázar stood a tall man in sunglasses and a suit. He had thick eyebrows and a stubble beard. Jadon spotted the circle on the man's face and realized who this was. He was a dead ringer for the man in the photos he'd had his former subordinate send over on the day he left for Cordova.

Jadon set his eyes on Tsutomu and spoke under his breath: "Do you plan to kill Cortázar?"

"We'll arrest him and take him to court. Just like the professor said."

"Cortázar knows what he's done. He won't let himself get caught without a fight. In which case . . ." Jadon gulped down what he was about to say.

"He wouldn't be the only dictator in history to get killed by his citizens. There was Ceaușescu, Gaddafi, Saddam Hussein . . . and Assad and Kim Jong-un know that if their dictatorships collapse, the people will corner and kill them. That's why they're trying to maintain their current systems so desperately. Their most feared enemies are their own people."

"That's why Cortázar's not backing down. It's a matter of life or death for him."

"That's what regime change is," said Tsutomu, shoving his tablet into the bag over his shoulder. He took a few steps before stopping and turning to Jadon. He straightened up. "My last name's Saegusa, by the way. I'm Tsutomu Saegusa." Then he smiled and crossed into La Caridad with his men.

The air conditioning was on, but it couldn't beat back the suffocating heat of excitement. For an hour, most of the people working in the War Room were gathered around the U-shaped table, and all eyes were on the central screen, viewing the real-time satellite imagery of La Caridad.

The blue dot in the center was Jadon. He was staying in a village near La Caridad.

Stewart's satellite phone rang. It was a call from Jadon. He put it on speaker so everyone could hear.

"Tsutomu took four soldiers with him to La Caridad to take out the snipers around the Plaza and along Foundation Road. They want support."

"Does Tsutomu not have a satellite phone?"

"This one's the only one we can use. But Tsutomu's got a tablet that works here. I can relay any relevant information to him."

"Sync the satellite images to Tsutomu—he has a tracking chip inside him as well," ordered Stewart.

The screen changed. Now it was fixed to a point two and a half miles from the square. That must be Tsutomu's position.

"I'm passing the phone to Nick."

"Zoom in," said Nick, and the image zoomed in and turned sharper. Several soldiers were being led by Tsutomu.

"We found him. You should be able to see the same images on your computer too. Are you still in contact with him?"

"No issues on that front," said Jadon.

Tsutomu was on the central screen now. A figure was visible atop the building on the corner to the right.

"That's a sniper. He's hiding behind the building facing Tsutomu and the others, and Tsutomu's not aware of his presence," Nick told Jadon.

When Jadon relayed the info, Tsutomu stopped. Together with his two subordinates, they entered the building and ascended to the roof. Then they snuck up behind the sniper, and a few minutes later the sniper was down.

While Tsutomu and his men were busy removing the snipers from the picture, they kept moving closer to the Plaza.

Music could be heard from Tsutomu's smartphone—they were close.

It was quiet inside the private FBI jet. Adán, Vanessa, and Doug transferred from a chopper to the jet at the Nevada airport, and since then not one word had been uttered. But all three were doubtless thinking the same thing.

"What are we going to do?" Adán asked Doug. "We can't produce any results."

Vanessa was looking at Doug for an answer too.

"We can't say it was all we were hoping for, but we did get some results. I heard the president's voice. Directly."

"What did he say, sir? Did he really say nothing besides wanting us to return today? Did he say please?"

"He said he'll tell us everything eventually. He also said the FBI is a capable and reliable agency to be proud of and that you two have done a great job."

"What have we done that's so great?"

"I didn't tell the president anything, apart from 'yes, sir' and 'I understand.' You heard, didn't you?"

"He must be praising us because we dug up that hotel. Nobody knew about that place," said Vanessa. "What is that place, anyway?" She sighed.

"There's plenty more we've uncovered too. The way we managed to find the desert hotel from the video of the Tragedy is just one. The most important thing we found out was the fact that the Mexican side was the first to shoot, and that the American soldier who fired back is already dead—with a slit throat."

"That soldier received a total of thirty thousand on the days before and after the incident. It was transferred to his account from an account with a company affiliated with Cortázar, Azure Ocean in Florida," said Adán. "In other words, the Tragedy at The Wall was orchestrated by Cortázar to keep Cordovans from fleeing the country." Adán looked at Vanessa for confirmation. "I'll even testify before the president if I have to. The Border Butcher, Captain Jadon Green, is now doing something in Cordova, a year out from the massacre. And at the desert hotel, one of the world's wealthiest people is gathering men of war, scholars, and even criminals like Billy. All probably with the president's consent."

"I want you to write a detailed report, even if it's just the first half. Consider it your first assignment," said Doug.

"Do you want the second half to be blank?"

"Let's wait a little while longer, until the president gives us a call."

Adán took a computer out of his backpack and turned it on.

Billy was rigorously punching the keys. He would sometimes spare a glance at the room's central screen to check in on the situation in Cordova.

"I've hacked a communications computer for a Cordovan military missile unit!" said Billy. Everyone in the War Room looked his way.

Stewart and Nick rushed to his side and peered at his screen.

"Can we fire the enemy's missiles freely now? Can we select the targets?"

"We can do both. We can even blow them to pieces, if that suits your fancy."

"But Cordovan missiles are manual. They can't be operated remotely." Stewart used a separate computer to pull up satellite images. Billy took a look.

"What you just hacked is the missile unit of one of Cordova's border countries."

Along Cordova's border, mobile missiles were set up on both sides. And Billy had hacked into one of those missile units.

"We could use these missiles to attack Cordova's military and finish them in five minutes flat."

"The effective range of the missiles can't be more than around six miles," said Nick. "But we can attack the forces that are on their way to the capital." He pointed at a spot on the image. Cordovan soldiers could be seen making a move at the border—several trucks were on the road.

"No. I can't aim for trucks with people in them."

"That's fine, we just need to *delay* them. Destroy the roads, the bridges, the tunnels, whatever it takes," said Nick, pointing at the places to blast.

"I'll try destroying all of the ones in a six-mile radius, but we don't know how accurate these missiles are," Billy had his hand on the mouse.

"Fire. That's an order."

"The missile was fired at a bridge. If this were peacetime, this would be more than enough to spark a war between the two countries."

The missile flew over the soldiers' heads. They just watched, stupefied.

The satellite video was filled with flames and white smoke. Missiles were demolishing the bridges and tunnels leading to La Caridad.

■ ■ ■

"The clearing of the road to the Plaza is complete. Now we can ride straight there," Tsutomu reported to Jadon. Roughly two hours had passed since he'd gone to eliminate the snipers. Preparations had been made in full, and the Revolutionary Army could now proceed to La Plaza Fundadores.

Jadon commanded about a thousand men—the main force of Nueva Cordova—and they were waiting in a village on the outskirts of La Caridad. Sebastian's units were occupying the TV and radio stations, as well as newspaper companies. As he was more familiar with the city's geography, Sebastian offered to command that separate operation—it wasn't quite as glorious as the march on the Plaza, but they all knew it would be key to their success.

Tension was thick among the soldiers. Even the typically cheery farmers among them couldn't hide the anxiety from their faces.

La Caridad's Foundation Road split the town in two, stretching all the way toward the Plaza.

Jadon called for Arsenio and ordered him to take command of a unit. "We'll divide the troops into two—a main attack force that'll hit the square head-on, and a rear unit to follow up. The main force will go down Foundation Road as a decoy. We'll be colliding with the enemy head-on, so it'll be dangerous. We'll then draw the enemy to the center, where the rear unit will attack their flanks. Whoever gets to the Presidential Residence first can go in to apprehend Cortázar," said Jadon to his commanders.

In terms of numbers and weapons, the odds were overwhelmingly in favor of the enemy. While Nueva Cordova had added a significant number of people to their ranks in the last few days, they were still outnumbered by more than 100 percent. Moreover, their weaponry was an assorted collection of guns, and they hadn't trained with them enough.

"On my signal, the main force will march down Foundation Road. We want to be noticed, and we want five hundred to look like one or two thousand, so be showy about it."

Arsenio nodded.

Thirty minutes later, the Revolutionary Army units had gathered at the section of Foundation Road at the entry point of La Caridad.

A viewing platform had been built in front of Foundation Plaza. Cortázar was watching the military parade alongside United Nations officials and key figures in Cordova's political and business worlds. Dourne was standing in the back. The parade was in its final stages.

Cordovan Army units marched before them. It was a relatively small military, but it was a force that danced to Cortázar's tune. It was the fighting force of the nation of Cordova, but also of Cortázar himself. And the United Nations officials and big shots of Cordova seated next to him were very aware of that.

Upon the parade's conclusion, another began—the parade of the president's elite guardsmen. A unit of two hundred elite guards was participating. The remaining hundred guardsmen were still on security duty for the Residence and the president himself.

A soldier in captain's uniform, led by an elite guard to Cortázar, whispered in his ear: "The Revolutionary Army is congregating at the entrance to La Caridad. There's about five hundred of them."

"That's more than I heard yesterday."

"More farmers and townspeople have joined them, sir. They probably don't even know how to shoot their guns. Some are even reported as not having guns at all. That won't do the revolutionaries any good."

"Show no mercy. Crush them all. But keep Luis alive for me. I'll hang him in the square, as planned. Tell that to the sniper. He can wound him, but make sure he doesn't kill him."

"We have lost contact with the snipers," said the soldier, who butted into the conversation.

Cortázar's heart dropped. That lump of dread that had accreted over the past week or two came bobbing up.

"Send a recon scout. Now. He is to report back as soon as possible," Dourne ordered the captain in muffled tones.

The United Nations officials were casting suspicious glances Cortázar's way.

"I used this army to eradicate Los Eternos," Cortázar told them smilingly. "And I am focusing all my efforts on crushing every other drug cartel in Latin America."

The Revolutionary Army was waiting at the entrance to La Caridad. The government attack they were expecting was not transpiring. Was their plan to lure them to the Plaza?

The wide Ruta Fundadores stretched invitingly toward La Plaza Fundadores.

The Cordovan anthem could be heard; the military parade was still on.

Jadon was waiting for Tsutomu to come back. He had heard the reports that the snipers had been taken care of but made the call that they should wait for his return. He wanted to ask Tsutomu how things looked in town. The satellite hadn't picked up any soldiers anywhere, but they might be hiding inside any number of buildings.

"Tsutomu's still not here? The unit will wait here until he gets back."

Jadon put the radio aside—he was eyeing the street that led to the square. There were many residents and cars coming and going, albeit fewer than normal. These people should have heard of the coming of the Revolutionary Army. Were they so used to shoot-outs that they weren't particularly ruffled by it? Or did they sense something in the air and refrain from heading outside as a result?

A handful of revolutionaries came walking in the light of the sun. The soldier with the sniper rifle on his shoulder was none other than Tsutomu.

"That's nine snipers down. No casualties on our side," Tsutomu told Jadon.

"That's two more snipers than the War Room told us there were."

"We beaned all the snipers we spotted along the road to the Plaza. It never hurts to be careful; there's no way to know the exact number."

"We can't let the professor stand anywhere he could be easy pickings." Jadon looked at his watch. It was time for the ceremony to be winding down.

Tsutomu let Jadon in on his intel regarding the situation in town up to the Plaza area, then headed to the Plaza again for some recon with his subordinates.

Brass band music could be heard from the square—the parade had yet to conclude. If they engaged now, innocent civilians would get caught in the crossfire.

"We're going to take Foundation Road toward the Plaza," Jadon told Stewart. "If anything comes up, let me know. And keep sending me satellite images." He hung up.

On Jadon's orders, Nueva Cordova began marching down the road.

It the War Room, everyone's eyes were glued to the central screen. At the display's center stood the Presidential Residence, with the Foundation Plaza in front. The group moving across it could only be the military parade.

The situation seemed to line up with Jadon's report. They could hear the music of the parade through the satellite phone.

"A viewing platform has been constructed in front of the Presidential Residence for the parade. The person at the center of it is probably Cortázar. And to think, it would be so easy to just take him out with a cruise missile off a carrier strike group in the Caribbean," said Billy.

"That would drive America's conscience and trust levels into the dirt. The world would rake America over the coals as a country that goes around assassinating the leaders of other countries willy-nilly. This regime change must come at the hands of the people of Cordova," replied Stewart.

John was in his wheelchair, not stirring an inch as he gazed at the screen.

As soon as the military parade was over, people filed out of the Plaza so quickly they practically vanished into thin air. The VIPs formerly on the viewing platform were also gone.

"Something's not right. Get Jadon on the phone." Stewart's words made the War Room palpably nervous.

The military parade was over, and Cortázar was back in the Residence. Following the ceremony's end, the United Nations officials and foreign dignitaries were heading toward Cordova International Airport via private cars, for Cortázar agreed with Dourne's counsel that if they were harmed, Cordova would be held responsible.

He had received reports that the Revolutionary Army had entered La Caridad a half hour prior. Supposedly, they were fifteen hundred in number. The number was rocketing up every time he received new information and now it was more than double the number he'd been told merely a few hours ago. Yet, they were still no match for his army.

Cortázar entered his office with Dourne and a few aides.

"The Revolutionary Army is approaching La Plaza Fundadores," reported a tall commander wearing the lapel badge of a captain.

"They're moving too fast. What happened to the snipers? I thought I ordered recon scouts be sent," said Dourne. His tone, normally always so calm and collected, bore a tinge of irritation.

"We're having no luck contacting them, sir. We sent two more than planned, but none of them are responding," answered the captain.

The original plan was to use snipers to shoot Luis and the leaders of the Revolutionary Army, which would cause confusion and delay their march. In the meantime, the border garrisons would arrive and surround and attack the revolutionaries. But that plan was falling apart.

"What's become of the border garrisons?"

"There are reports that the bridges and tunnels they were set to cross have been destroyed in order to delay them, sir."

"Tell them to hurry. And deploy the troops guarding the Residence. Encircle the revolutionaries and hit them with a concerted assault."

"Let's send out the Reserve Corps as well," said Dourne, pointing at the map on the desk. "They can't have been detected by the satellite. We can catch them off guard."

"Yes, make it happen. We'll crush the revolutionaries in one fell swoop!" Cortázar cried.

"I will dispatch the Presidential Residence Unit and the Reserve Corps and wipe out the Revolutionary Army," the captain repeated, before exiting the office.

Arsenio was in the truck at the lead, as commander of the truck unit. Jadon and Luis's truck was a few vehicles behind. Penelope was next to them. This was done in consideration of Luis's safety.

The truck unit moved at a bicycle pace. Then it decelerated and stopped altogether. Tsutomu, who appeared from a byroad, came running up to Jadon's truck.

"Something weird is going on. The enemy troops are on the move. The ones coming out of the Residence are traveling outside the square, probably to get behind us. They might attack you from both sides as soon as you enter the Plaza."

"Was Cortázar at the Plaza?"

"He's already run off to the Residence. There isn't a soul to be seen in the Plaza itself. They've just got the national anthem playing through the speakers."

Jadon booted up his computer and the real-time satellite feed. The arrangement of enemy troops really had changed. The soldiers who had been waiting behind the Residence were no longer there. And nobody was in the Plaza to lure the revolutionaries there.

The satellite phone rang.

"Any trouble to report?" asked Stewart. "The enemy's in a flurry of activity. They may be plotting something."

He was saying the same thing as Tsutomu. But Jadon couldn't afford to just stop here.

"I'll go to the Plaza to check it out for myself. Arsenio, your unit will act as a detachment force; take an alternate path before the enemy attacks and cut in behind them," ordered Jadon, screwing up his resolve.

Before they knew it, the national anthem was gone from the Plaza. *Does Cortázar know the Revolutionary Army's every move?*

The War Room was in an uproar.

"Get me Jadon!" barked Stewart, eyes fixed on the central screen.

The troop transport vehicles of Cortázar's forces were coming out of the underground parking lots in the buildings on either side of the square, and there were around ten of them. That meant Nueva Cordova would need to contend with over a hundred enemy soldiers.

The transport vehicles left the Plaza and traveled behind the Revolutionary Army, while at the same time, government troops from the Presidential Residence were carrying sandbags to the square.

"They must have parked those troop carriers underground so the satellite couldn't spot them. They're keeping their trump cards hidden until the last possible moment. At this rate, the revolutionaries will get surrounded the second they enter the square!" said Stewart, even louder now.

The revolutionaries stopped right before the Plaza proper. Had they caught sight of the troop carriers themselves?

"Please, don't lose track of Jadon's signal," John half-prayed.

The Revolutionary Army had parked a truck on the road leading to the Plaza, approximately three hundred feet away. Just as Tsutomu had reported, there was no one in sight.

"Why are we stopping? The Plaza's a jump away," asked Tsutomu.

Jadon meticulously scanned the surroundings. Something was *off.* He thought he spotted something moving on the square.

The satellite phone rang. He switched it on and in that very moment, he shouted on reflex: "Watch out! Enemy troops are lying in wait for us!"

Before he was even done saying those words, they heard gunfire ring out.

The sound of low rumbling engines soon joined the gunfire noise. A handful of troop transport vehicles rode along the multiple roads leading to the square. When they braked near the center of the Plaza, soldiers in excess of a hundred jumped out firing their guns as they approached the revolutionaries and citizens around the square. Civilians were screaming and crying as they fled this way and that.

"Return fire, soldiers!" said Jadon, but the revolutionaries were ahead of him. "Get out of your cars and continue shooting. Reinforcements will arrive soon. Just grin and bear it until then."

But the oncoming fire of the government troops was ratcheting up. They were more numerous and quicker to act than they'd anticipated. Had the border garrisons made it to La Caridad already?

Beside him, Tsutomu was diligently shooting his sniper rifle.

"Tell the reinforcements to hurry up. Go around the enemy and cut in at their flanks," Jadon ordered Arsenio by radio.

"I can't make a move, the enemy's attacking. We should withdraw and regain our footing."

"We're not going anywhere, they'll just smash us into the ground."

The enemy troops' fire was coming in hotter and heavier than ever. They had the revolutionaries trapped both in front and in back.

Moreover, they'd even started hearing bullets coming at them from either side. If they didn't do something fast, they'd be surrounded.

"The reinforcements still not here? At this rate we're just going to take a beating," said Tsutomu as he fired his rifle.

Government forces came shooting from the Plaza's center, while more approached from behind.

"We're never going to hold out like this. Where *are* they?"

"They're keeping the rear units from getting to us."

That was when they heard cheers of success—along with more gunfire and more grenades. There were voices of men and women they hadn't heard before.

"It's the civilians. The residents of La Caridad are rising up, and in the hundreds. And their numbers are increasing!" said Arsenio through the radio.

The city was in chaos, as groups of revolutionaries, government troops, and civilians wove together. This was now urban warfare.

Consequently, the tide of battle at the Plaza shifted, and the hunted were now the hunters.

"The enemy units on the sides are being slow too. Advance through the square and attack the Residence," ordered Jadon, and with that, the soldiers of Nueva Cordova began marching toward La Plaza Fundadores.

Order had returned to the War Room. An hour or so ago, a fierce shoot-out had flared up in the Plaza's vicinity, in an area where the troops of both sides and civilians met head-on.

The satellite phone had been switched on before they reached the fight. They could hear automatic rifles, as well as intermittent rockets and grenades detonating, but it had yet to reach the fever pitch of a battle.

"Where's Jadon?"

"They haven't entered the Plaza yet," said Stewart. No attempt to call out to Jadon was met with a response. The phone was left on the seat of his truck.

The central screen gave them a glimpse into goings-on in the Plaza and the surrounding quarter. Many government soldiers lay out of action on the streets. Animated crowds of civilians were surging through, and Cortázar's men felt the brunt of their discontent. The ordinary residents of La Caridad mobbed the soldiers, robbed them of their weapons, and joined the fray. Many a civilian's body littered the streets as well, having been shot down by the regime's troops.

"Please enlarge the image. Can we pick up the video and audio of Cordovan TV stations? If everything went according to plan, the Revolutionary Army should already have occupied the stations," said John to no one in particular.

Across La Plaza Fundadores sat the Presidential Residence. Fifteen hundred revolutionaries and civilians were waiting for their orders across the road from the square. More than half of the soldiers of Nueva Cordova were men who had learned how to handle a gun within the past week.

Jadon and Arsenio were eyeing the Plaza from behind a truck. Sandbags had been piled up at the entrance to the square, situated alongside machine gun emplacements. Furthermore, Cortázar's elite guardsmen were on the move. That was why Jadon ordered everyone to remain on standby in front of the Plaza.

Heavy gunfire pierced the air, and Jadon and Arsenio ducked instinctively. It was the machine gun emplacements. They were trying to intimidate them.

"So long as those emplacements are there, we can't cut through the square. We need to take them out of the picture before we can make it to the Presidential Residence."

"We'd need a tank to pass through unscathed."

"We'll get in closer and lob a grenade or two. It'll be touch and go, but it's the only way," said Jadon as he looked through his binoculars.

"Don't be ridiculous. You *will* get hit. Let's bypass the Plaza altogether and infiltrate the Residence some other way," pled Arsenio.

The cacophony of the close-range hail of gunfire would not end. The even more ear-shattering explosions that ripped every so often were courtesy of the rockets and grenades.

"Both wings of the Residence are guarded by Cortázar's elites. We'll never get in that way."

"If we go now, we can manage. If their numbers increase any more than this, and if our numbers decrease any more than this, we—"

Suddenly, shouts of joy from behind them—female voices included. The growl of an engine, the honking . . . The pair glanced back to find a large truck hurtling down the road toward the square. The closer it got, the more it accelerated.

"Oncoming!" yelled Jadon. The soldiers nearby leapt out of the way.

The truck smacked over the curb and charged down the Plaza.

When the truck and the machine gun collided, a towering pillar of fire was born with a boom, its flames spreading across the square. The truck had been loaded with explosives. The fire reached the emplacements, and government soldiers came crawling out. A man lay about a hundred feet away from the site of the explosion. He was the driver, and he'd jumped out a safe distance away.

The man staggered onto his feet as he rose off the ground. It was Tsutomu! Jadon ran to his side, grabbed his arm, and brought him back to their truck.

"You goddamn idiot, are you asking to get killed!?"

"I just want to get home alive," said Tsutomu.

Another explosion. The entrance to the Plaza was now on fire.

"The truck had a leaking oil drum."

The gunfire from the government's side had paused for a moment, but now it was starting back up.

"C'mon, let's go attack the president's building!" shouted Jadon.

* * *

The racket of the gunfire around town was unceasing, gaining intensity with each passing second. The occasional explosions caused by the rockets didn't help matters either.

The Presidential Residence was in an uproar, which was only getting worse. Cortázar could almost hear the spittle coming out of the mouths of his commanders as they issued their orders. More and more soldiers were entering and leaving, and more than a few were wounded. Meanwhile, Cortázar just stared, dumbfounded.

"Call the troops stationed in La Caridad back here. The Residence's security is getting too thin," ordered Dourne, in place of Cortázar.

"We've already issued those orders, sir. It's just that it's taking them longer than normal to arrive. Civilians and revolutionaries are sabotaging them by obstructing their passage."

The residents of La Caridad were blocking the roads with their cars, burning the tires of military vehicles, and doing whatever else they could to stymie their efforts.

I may have made a fatal mistake, thought Cortázar, fear and dread had metastasized from his heart to the rest of his body. "Place the elite guardsmen at the edge of the Plaza, and do NOT let the revolutionaries enter it!" he shouted, as much to cast aside his anxiety as for any other reason. "Mobilize the tank. Bring it to the Plaza to attack the revolutionaries," he added—he'd almost forgotten he had it in his arsenal.

■ ■ ■

Each unit of the Revolutionary Army had come together, alongside an ever-growing onrush of civilians, and they were making their advance into La Plaza Fundadores. The square was now a tumultuous place, and a noisy one, with the rumble of diesel engines looming louder and heavier.

"I thought there weren't supposed to be any near the president's building!?" shouted Jadon despite himself. But the engines drowned his words in their din. A tank rolled into view from the parking lot of one of the Plaza's adjacent buildings. It crossed the road and into the square.

"The War Room never made any mention of this. The tanks were supposed to be placed on border security duty twenty miles from here."

Not one second after they heard the cannon fire, a large truck went up in smoke. A number of Revolutionary Army soldiers were knocked to the ground. The tank trampled over their bodies as it drew up toward Jadon and his men. Behind the tank marched dozens of government troops, guns in hand.

Arsenio was firing an automatic rifle at the tank.

"Don't waste your ammo," said Jadon. "Haven't we got any RPGs?"

No one replied. Before the attack, he'd seen more than ten RPG boxes.

"The enemy's onslaught is ramping in intensity. Let's retreat for now!" Arsenio shouted at Jadon.

"He's right. We need to withdraw. If we don't, we're done!" said Tsutomu.

"If we can just take down that tank, we can move forward. Go take the Escárcegas someplace safe. I'll draw Cortázar's forces elsewhere."

"Captain, don't—"

There was no time; Jadon hugged Tsutomu and pulled him behind a truck.

The shell exploded at close range, its blast slamming them against the cobblestones.

The blue dot on the central screen represented the signal emitted by the transmitter capsule they'd stuck inside Jadon.

The War Room was in the grips of an uncanny silence.

"Jadon is near the entrance to the Plaza. He's near a burning vehicle."

"Can you enhance the image? The resolution is terrible."

"It's the satellite, sir. The one we've got over Cordova is an old model."

"Either get in touch with Jadon or pick up his voice. Tell me how the battle is going."

"All we have is the satellite phone."

Billy put the satellite phone on speaker and placed it on the table to pick up Jadon's voice: "For God's sake, you got a death wish? Keep your head down and stay behind the car! There's a sniper on the veranda of the president's building!"

"We turned on his phone remotely."

"Is there anything we can do?"

John tried to catch Jadon's attention, just in case, but there was no reply. All they could hear was gunfire and the orders Jadon was shouting at his subordinates.

"Do they have the upper hand? Or are they on the back foot?" John asked Stewart.

"Jadon's doing an admirable job," he replied, shifting his gaze to the central screen, "but Cortázar's unleashed a tank that was hidden in the building's underground parking lot. And that's not all—there are hundreds of troops and elite guardsmen inside the central government building who are fresh and ready to go. That's the building Jadon and his men aim to invade."

"That's all well and good, could someone please tell me if they are winning or losing?" said John, voice dripping with irritation.

"Cortázar has the upper hand at the moment. Jadon's forces are trapped in the Plaza. If the situation doesn't shift, they'll get annihilated. More of Cortázar's elite guards will be deployed to the battle zone."

"Please, warn them of the enemy reinforcements."

"I'm trying to reach Jadon through the phone, but he's not replying."

"Is there anything we can do?"

"Yes," said Stewart. "We can sit here and watch. And pray. We can pray."

With those words, the hushed chatter of the War Room was brought to a halt.

"I'll deal with the tank," said Tsutomu, who put aside his sniper rifle and retrieved a large carry bag from the truck's backseat. It was the bag that had been placed next to the wooden weapon boxes on the plane they took from LA. Tsutomu pulled a fifteen-square-inch case from out of the bag, and inside the case was a drone fuselage alongside four propellers.

"Is this the time to take your RC copter for a joyride?"

"This thing cost $100K. It's no RC copter. It can automatically avoid obstacles while maintaining altitude using a high-precision camera, sound recorder, speaker, acceleration sensors, electronic compass, GPS . . . you name it, it's got it," said Tsutomu as he put the parts together. A few minutes later, the three-by-three-foot drone was assembled.

"Can we stick guns on it?"

"It's equipped with two small missiles. You can set the targets with the remote. You can also swap them out for a machine gun."

"So it's a portable fighter plane."

"The remote's got its own screen, which is linked to the drone's camera. You can get a pretty accurate lock-on with the thing too."

The screen had a crosshair reticule. This was the sighting device for the missiles.

Tsutomu worked the controls, and the drone rose through the air.

"Bye-bye, tank," said Tsutomu.

"Aim for its treads. Tanks like that one are made to be sturdy around the ceiling hatch. You can't destroy that part with just two missiles. Hit it in the treads so it stops moving."

The drone was rising rapidly, unbeknownst to the enemy. The tank stopped at the center of the square, its turret pointed straight at Jadon and the revolutionaries.

"Firing missiles," said Tsutomu.

One met its mark, then the other, and the twin explosions covered the surrounding area in cobblestone debris, amid which the tank's treads could be seen. The military men behind it retreated while firing their automatic rifles.

A soldier jumped from inside the tank, followed by another fiery BOOM. One of the missiles had destroyed the engine.

"Bringing it back now," said Tsutomu. The drone shed altitude and came whirring back. "Time to load some more missiles and get it back out there. Make it happen," he ordered a subordinate, parking the drone a few yards away. The subordinate rushed to collect the drone. Ten or so minutes later, it was reloaded and ready to take to the air once more.

The drone blew up the various machine gun emplacements on roofs, streets corners, and alleyways. Ever since it incapacitated the tank, the one little drone had done more than enough to turn the tables. The Revolutionary Army was now on the offensive.

The Presidential Residence of Cordova was suffused with unclean air. Cortázar plugged his ears against the nonstop booms and gunfire outside. The presence of his subordinates was all that was keeping him from losing his cool.

"The border garrisons aren't here yet? What about all the troops we recalled to La Caridad!?" he yelled at his commanders.

"The bridges and roads keep getting destroyed, sir. They're going to arrive later than anticipated."

"How much later?"

"We don't know, sir."

Cortázar managed to tamp down the urge to punch the commander in front of him, albeit barely.

"That must be the work of the revolutionaries," said Dourne. "We should have called the troops here sooner."

Cortázar refrained from raising a hand, but not without effort. *Don't tell me that like I don't already know!*

"Send in the elite guard."

"They're already defending the Plaza."

So they're the ones fighting the revolutionaries right now. "Send in the chopper. And notify me of the situation on the ground."

Cortázar plopped down on the sofa. He wanted to lie down, but he could hardly afford to let his subordinates see him vulnerable.

Tsutomu was working up a sweat operating the drone. It fired at machine gun emplacements, snipers on the verandas of the Presidential Residence, and mortars, shooting both bullets and missiles at enemy troops wielding RPGs. After each attack, it quickly gained altitude to evade enemy fire.

"Keep it down! Can you hear that?" shouted Jadon.

It was a low-pitch rumbling noise. A black shadow appeared over the Residence. A Russian military copter!

"They're siccing a chopper on us."

The copter began to descend. Jadon shot his automatic rifle at it several times, but it raked the revolutionaries with machine gun fire as it flew over and past them. A bullet grazed Tsutomu's side and raised a small cloud of soil where it hit the ground.

The remote control was sent flying from Tsutomu's grip. The drone veered wildly off course, bumped into the side of the chopper, and crashed to pieces. Tsutomu's right arm was bleeding.

The chopper turned back around and rained another salvo of bullets on them as it passed overhead.

"There's a sniper rifle in the truck! Someone get it for me!" Tsutomu shouted, as he stanched the bleeding.

That moment, a young revolutionary dashed off. It was Gerardo, who promptly fetched Tsutomu his rifle while the chopper fired relentlessly at revolutionaries and civilians alike.

The rifle's barrel quivered in Tsutomu's hands. His arm was refusing to cooperate.

The chopper was closing in for another round of killing. Jadon yanked the sniper rifle out of Tsutomu's hands, aimed, and pulled the trigger. Yet the chopper flew and fired unimpeded, returning yet again.

"I know you can do it," said Tsutomu. "When sniping, shoot the target's body first since it's easier to aim for than the head. *Then* you can nab them in the head. Breathe deep and center yourself. Line up your sight and pull the trigger. Pull it softly, like you're stroking a lady's hair . . ."

Jadon stood up as he took in Tsutomu's advice. Meanwhile, the chopper dipped lower still and zoomed toward them.

Jadon had the pilot's face in his sight. The instant he pulled the trigger, the man pulled back in his chair.

The chopper shuddered violently and careened down toward the Plaza, where it smashed into a heap of flaming metal to the cheers of the nearby revolutionaries.

Jadon took a look at Tsutomu's wound. The bullet wasn't lodged inside him, but he still needed treatment. "Withdraw and get yourself looked at. You can't handle a firearm in this state."

Tsutomu nodded, took the sniper rifle, and cleared out of the Plaza.

Guns were being fired from near the Presidential Residence on the Plaza. And the Revolutionary Army was already closing in.

The battle unfolding on the square at the core of the nation was heating up. Bullets were zipping into the Residence, and most of the glass windows facing the Plaza were already in pieces. The only window in the building that was bulletproof was the one window in the president's office.

The smell of gunpowder pervaded the room, along with the incessant noise of the shooting and the hollering of the soldiers.

BOOM! A sizable explosion triggered a chorus of shrieking. Was it a grenade? A rocket? Was it the enemy scoring a strike against him, or his forces succeeding in repelling the revolutionaries? Cortázar was a ball of anxiety.

At first, Cortázar's men were confident they had the advantage. Then, he started getting reports that the revolutionaries were gaining some ground on them.

"Could the revolution have marshaled reinforcements somehow? Their numbers are increasing."

"They're civilians," replied Dourne. "It appears as though the residents of La Caridad are joining the struggle, taking weapons off of the bodies of soldiers on both sides."

The sound of the gunfire on the Plaza continued to magnify, reaching an almost maddening pitch.

"Transfer the remaining members of the elite guard to the back of the Residence, and don't let the enemy approach that area. On the off chance we lose, you can escape out the back," said Dourne as he examined the magazine of his handgun and holstered it in his belt. He took the rifle of the soldier next to him and pulled the magazine out of the magazine band at his waist before pocketing it.

"Deploy the elite guard. The revolutionaries are to be chased off the Plaza! Do NOT let them inside the building!" Cortázar shouted at his officers, who proceeded to dash out of the room in a frenzy.

The footfalls of the elite guard reverberated through the halls. Was the enemy nearing the Residence?

Cortázar rose to his feet and aimlessly paced the office.

■ ■ ■

"What the?"

Cortázar had turned on the TV, and Luis was on it. He was gaunt, and his hair was white, but it was unmistakably him. The backdrop behind him was, in all likelihood, the jungle. This must have been taken while he was at the Revolutionary Army camp.

"Let's rebuild our homeland of Cordova together. With our strength combined, we'll transform this nation into one where no one has to flee its borders, a nation where its citizens can live with pride and where its youngest can grow up in safety and prosperity. And in order for that tragedy to never befall us again . . ."

The video was looping on repeat. Nueva Cordova had seized control of the airwaves. Both TV and radio stations were spreading their message.

"Send troops to stop the broadcast! I thought the ones defending the TV stations were my elite guards?"

"Your guards are already on duty defending the Plaza, sir. It was the military soldiers defending the stations."

They could hear gunfire from the Plaza, and it was intensifying.

"You mean they can't hold out against a Revolutionary Army that's at most a thousand people strong!?"

"Their numbers are increasing. La Caridad residents are joining their ranks. We believe they've nearly doubled in size."

"Well, what about the snipers? I thought that if we could just take out Luis and Sebastian, the rest would be just sheep without shepherds?"

"The snipers have already been—"

"Roll out the tanks! And we still have copters, don't we? Don't let those revolutionary dogs into the Plaza! Tell the guards to defend it with their lives!" Cortázar yelled as he dashed to a room where he could view the Plaza.

Several cars were overturned on the sides of the roads. Some of them were up in smoke, while others were still on fire. More than a dozen soldiers wearing Cordovan military uniforms were lying nearby.

"Those orders have already been issued, sir. But it will take time. Also, some of our units aren't responding to orders."

Units disobeying orders? What's going on?

"Where's Dourne?" asked Cortázar, who didn't see him anywhere.

"He is believed to have already evacuated, sir."

Cortázar could see that being true. He hadn't seen Dourne in a while. The dictator could feel something inside him crumble to dust.

After the chopper was shot down, the battle in the Plaza turned in favor of the revolutionaries. The elite guards whose job was to defend the Presidential Residence were deployed, but Nueva Cordova far exceeded them in numbers, especially now that ordinary civilians were joining the revolution. There were even reports that some Cordovan soldiers were deserting their posts.

All over the Plaza, Cordovan military men and the president's elite guards were lying dead. Luis was looking on the scene with blank amazement. "Captain Jadon Green, could you please put a stop to the shooting—even if it's just the revolutionaries who stop firing?"

Jadon turned his head to find Luis gazing his way. Penelope was holding him up.

"No can do. You have to face the reality unfolding before your eyes. This is war. And the battle won't end until only one side's left standing."

"Are there no more drones left? I can't take any more killing."

Jadon looked to the center of the Plaza. Drone fuselage fragments and propellers lay scattered.

"We've got a spare," replied Tsutomu, as he fired his M16.

"Let me talk to them through the drone's speakers," said Luis. "I'd like to call out to the government soldiers from above the Plaza."

"We used a drone to attack them earlier. They might shoot it down." Tsutomu looked at the wrecked drone parts littering the square. For a second, he seemed hesitant but then he ran toward the jeep and rushed back with a small backpack. He took the drone out of the bag, and began assembling it, after which he handed Luis a microphone.

"Just talk into that, and the speakers inside the drone will project what you say. It'll send your audio to state TV and radio too. With this, you can address every corner of Cordova."

"Thank you."

Tsutomu adjusted the volume control to the max setting. The soldiers of the Revolutionary Army watched attentively as the drone took flight. Meanwhile, the regime's troops kept on firing. Eventually, the drone hovered in place over the center of the Plaza.

"Attention, soldiers on both sides! Why must we continue fighting? Why must we continue this senseless slaughter? We Cordovans are all brothers and sisters. Let's hold hands instead of guns and build a brighter future for Cordova together." Luis was doing his best, but his voice was getting drowned out by all the gunfire.

"They can't hear us," Penelope shouted at Jadon, a pained look in her eyes. "Is there anything we can do?"

"The drone's too high up for them to hear."

The drone dropped altitude. Tsutomu was operating the remote control frantically. "If I make it go any lower, it'll become a target. It's in a precarious position as is," he stated, though he dipped it even lower anyway.

At last, Luis's voice began to be heard.

"Lower it even more. Everyone stop firing!" Jadon shouted at the revolutionaries in back. Slowly, the revolutionaries started unhanding their triggers. Consequently, the din of the gunfire diminished, though the military was still continuing to shoot.

"My name is Luis Escárcega and I am a fellow citizen of Cordova. I am your brother, as you are each other's. I implore you, please, stop firing," he said, his words raining down on the Plaza. It worked like a charm; the gunfire was tailing off. Many among the Cordovan military troops took to simply staring at the sky.

Before long, the gunfire had totally abated. A brief moment of silence visited their surroundings. But that lull proved fleeting, as the firing resumed.

"Lower the drone. They still can't hear him loud enough."

"But if it gets shot down, it's all over. This is the absolute limit," muttered Tsutomu, who was manning the controls. The drone dipped yet lower.

Cortázar was in his office, alongside several officers of his elite guard. He recalled ordering the deployment of the guard, but he couldn't remember anything that happened afterward.

"What happened to the chopper!?" The sound of the propellers was suddenly no more.

"It got shot down, sir."

Looking past the officer and at the Plaza, Cortázar could see the helicopter's flaming wreck.

"My name is Luis Escárcega and I am a fellow citizen of Cordova. I am your brother, as you are each other's . . ."

The voice, he noticed, was coming from a small object floating in the sky. A drone! A drone with speakers . . .

"Shoot it down!" he shrieked, taking an officer's gun and putting a hand on the door to the veranda.

The officer grabbed his hand.

"The revolutionaries are approaching. I believe it'd be wise to evacuate the premises."

"Have preparations been made?"

"They haven't made it to the back of the Residence yet. Hurry!"

Maybe it was just his imagination, but Cortázar could swear he heard less gunfire out there. Nevertheless, the battle was still on.

"There are unscathed units at the border. We should consider withdrawing for now to join those units and plan a counterattack." The urgency in the officer's voice was escalating. Given their current predicament, they really had no other options.

Cortázar made up his mind and handed the gun back.

"My name is Luis Escárcega and I am a fellow citizen of Cordova. I am your brother, as you are each other's . . ."

Luis's voice reverberated throughout the Plaza. His manifesto was making it to the TV and radio broadcasts as well, and all of Cordova was lending an ear. If Cortázar was still at the Presidential Residence, he was no doubt getting an earful as well.

The gunfire coming from the military and the elite guard had gradually subsided, but it had yet to completely die off. They had been ordered to resist to the bitter end.

The grisly landscape of the Tragedy sprang to Jadon's mind once again. The whizzing bullets, the wails and the screaming and the crying. The bodies crumpling while the crowds fled in panic and terror. The parents and children who clung to corpses with exposed entrails. In his dreams, he'd waded in the blood-red darkness countless times. It was a gut-churning spectacle he never wanted to witness again. A single gunshot was all it took to spark fear and rage, and set a mad spiral in motion. That was what gave rise to the Tragedy.

"Stop firing. I want everybody here to stop firing!" Jadon found himself getting to his feet.

"Please don't do that, Captain Jadon," said Arsenio from behind him.

Tsutomu grabbed Jadon by the arm. Jadon shook him off, lifted his automatic rifle with both hands, and marched into the center of the Plaza.

"Stop! No more pointless killing!" Jadon shouted at his comrades in arms. The revolutionaries stopped firing for a moment, but the military didn't.

Jadon raised his gun up and walked toward the center. He got hit by blows to the chest and the pit of his stomach, and he was about to stumble and fall but managed to keep his balance. He had a bulletproof vest on, but it still hurt like hell.

"What are you doing, captain!? Please, come back!" cried Arsenio.

"Soldiers on both sides, throw away your guns," pled the drone. "Cordova is a land of plenty. Its forests are lush and its blue oceans sparkling. Let's join forces and create a country of which our children can be proud. A country they needn't ever flee." Luis's voice reached more than just the Plaza, but the entire city of La Caridad.

Jadon buckled and fell to his knees. Blood gushed from his arm. But he stood back up and flung his gun onto the Plaza. Then he took off his cartridge belt and tossed it aside.

The gunfire of the government forces gradually receded. But the shooting, though sporadic, continued.

Jadon staggered back onto his feet and started walking again, only for yet another bullet to strike him in the chest. He fell on his back.

Luis rushed to his side, Penelope chasing after him. The two of them tried to help him up, but he managed it himself, throwing away his bulletproof vest to add to the pile.

At that point both armies had ceased shooting. A hush enveloped the square.

One after another, the soldiers of the Revolutionary Army appeared from behind overturned cars, stone walls, and the statue at the corner of the Plaza. They put down their rifles, handguns, and daggers on the cobblestones.

The soldiers of the Cordovan military took that as their cue to set aside their guns as well.

Soldiers from both sides came to the Plaza's center, while the square started to fill up with more of those who laid down their arms.

Jadon looked ready to collapse, but Penelope kept him aloft. He scanned the Plaza and shouted: "Professor Escárcega is here. The battle's over!"

Not a sound disturbed the scene at the Plaza. The soldiers' eyes were all on Luis.

Penelope helped Jadon come to Luis's side. Jadon raised his right arm in solidarity.

The Plaza cheered.

One corner of the Plaza got especially boisterous—Sebastian and his soldiers had Cortázar and the officers in his entourage surrounded and were marching them toward the square.

Cortázar's countenance was ruddy and congested with blood, but even more striking was how twisted in fear and anger it was.

Tsutomu looked at Jadon and smiled. "You can have an escape route, but it's important to keep watch over it too."

Luis made for Cortázar, but Jadon grabbed his arm. Luis just smiled at Jadon, softly shook him off, and walked up to the former president of Cordova.

"The building of a new Cordova is now underway. We'll make a nation its citizens love and take pride in. No one will ever need to flee again," Jadon heard him say in his dulcet tones.

Cortázar just glared at him without a word. Then, Cortázar shoved Luis to the ground. He grabbed a gun from one of the Revolutionary Army soldiers trying to get him back up and turned it toward Luis.

A gunshot roared. Luis's body collapsed backward.

"NO!" screamed Penelope.

Cortázar pointed the gun at her.

Jadon leapt to embrace her.

The muzzle flashed.

His face utterly contorted, Cortázar scowled at Arsenio.

Once again, Arsenio's gun discharged.

■ ■ ■

Penelope pressed on Luis's chest, desperately trying to stop the bleeding. With every breath, he was coughing up more blood. The bullet had pierced his lungs.

Luis's mouth moved, but his voice was too muted. Jadon put an ear to his mouth.

"Get a doctor! Someone bring a stretcher!" came somebody's voice.

Jadon put a finger to Luis's neck. No pulse.

He put an arm over Penelope's shoulders and spoke. Penelope nodded even as she sobbed.

The citizens who had run from the Plaza were now filing back in.

The people who had seen or heard Luis on TV or on the radio came rushing to the square as well. The streets of La Caridad were now packed, and the crowds were only getting more massive. Before they knew it, every inch of the Plaza was taken up, with one exception—the empty circle around the stretcher carrying Luis.

"Isn't this whole atmosphere a little, *you know?* I mean, we're Americans, and you're the Border Butcher," whispered Tsutomu into Jadon's ear.

The War Room was dead silent. On the central screen, they could see Jadon and another person—an old man with a white head of hair—on a stretcher.

"This isn't good. That's Professor Escárcega who got shot. How's his condition?" asked John quietly.

No one replied. There was no audio to the satellite video, so it was difficult to glean any additional information.

"It seems he's dead, sir. The AI is reading Jadon's lips," said Billy.

"Who shot him? Do we know?"

"Cortázar did. But then he got shot in retaliation."

"Cordova has lost its unifying force. At this rate, the war will resume," they heard Antonio murmur with palpable woe. His face was a cloud of despair and dismay.

"The cornerstone of Phase 2 of the plan is gone. What do we do now?" Billy looked at John, but everyone was at a loss for words.

"Did anybody anticipate this could happen? What about the AI? I thought you people were supposed to be the real smartest people, not misfits like me," quipped Billy.

"Professor Escárcega has passed away," said John. "Does anyone have a plan for what to do without him?"

A photo and career biography came on the central screen.

"That's the AI's answer," said Professor Liz Watson, getting up from her chair to explain. "I didn't come out with it before, since no one wanted to think about Luis dying, but I think the AI has chosen our best option."

"That is unexpected," said Professor Eugene Kowalchuk. "I'll draft a new plan for Phase 2 with a different president." Eugene returned to his seat, and Billy followed after him.

It truly was a wrinkle no one had seen coming.

At Jadon's urging, Penelope knelt at Luis's side. She put a hand on his face and muttered something he couldn't catch. She wasn't crying anymore. She was praying.

A little while later, Penelope was back on her feet. She shouted at the people standing in the square. "I am Penelope Escárcega, Luis's daughter. I will follow in my father's footsteps. If you, the people, so choose, I will realize his vision and build a new Cordova."

Her limpid voice carried across the otherwise silent square. She exuded a dignity that conveyed not only her fixity of purpose, but also her nobility and grace.

"On this day, too much blood was spilt upon this Plaza, too many lives lost. My father, Luis Escárcega, was one of those lives. But his will and warmth abide in us, the people of this nation. He loved Cordova and all Cordovans, and for the first time, I feel his true spirit of love. But I'm not the only one who will walk in his footsteps—the people gathered at this Plaza here today will too. Let's build a new Cordova *together.*"

A few seconds later, cheers erupted, which soon became chants of *Penelope! Penelope!*

Eventually, men nearby lifted Luis's stretcher. "Open the way. We're taking Professor Escárcega to the Presidential Residence," said Sebastian.

A segment of the crowd parted to let them pass. Penelope and the stretcher were at the front of the line that filed into the building.

Adán and Vanessa were in their usual room at the FBI Academy. Adán was absorbed in writing the report on the Tragedy at The Wall. Vanessa didn't say a word about Adán's training—the experience he was gaining through this was leagues more valuable.

"Come here a sec," said Vanessa. "Quick."

A tall, raven-haired Hispanic woman was standing before a mic on their TV screen. Her chiseled features were smeared with soot and dirt, but her beauty shone through. She was wearing dirty, worn-out military garb and army-issue shoes. She turned her eyes to the camera and spoke, her English polished and elegant. She was probably aware this footage would be going out to the world. As for where she was being interviewed, it seemed like some kind of lobby, but the glass panes of the doors and windows in the background were broken, and there were bullet marks all over the walls.

"Our nation will be reborn. From this time onward, a new Cordova will spring from the ashes. We shall run no longer. We refuse to abandon our homeland. No matter how poor we are, no matter the pain, we will not leave these borders, for we do not have despair and fear ahead of us, but hope and possibility. We will build a country where our children can live in peace and joy through our own power."

"That's the country where the caravan originated!" said Vanessa. "Where people were fleeing because they were ruled over by a cartel and an oppressive regime."

"Yes, that's Cordova. Chances are that's where Jadon is. What's happening over there?"

"Looks like there's been a revolution. The government's forces have surrendered to the Revolutionary Army."

"Then is President Cortázar out of office now?" he shouted, despite himself, leaning in out of excitement.

"How am I supposed to know? I don't think anyone has said it yet."

The woman on the TV continued. "The leader of the Los Eternos cartel has been killed, and the organization is no more. The administration of Gumersindo Cortázar has also collapsed, but a new administration is already functioning in its place. The new government's framework has been decided upon, and the reins of power have been transferred. The people of Cordova can now go about their daily lives without fear, for this nation will no longer be a font of refugees, but a place where everyone can operate in safety and with peace of mind.

We will also be taking a step forward into greater harmony with the international community. Fellow nations of the world, I humbly ask you for your kind assistance."

"Who is this lady?"

"That's Dr. Penelope Escárcega. She's a doctor, but now she's the interim president of the provisional government. This must be her inaugural address."

"The revolution has come, but only at the expense of many men and women. We would like to thank the Revolutionary Army of Nueva Cordova, as well as the civilians and the people from other countries who gave those soldiers their aid. We will never forget your service to this nation, nor the gallantry of a brave army captain and his comrades, who helped bring this miracle to Cordova . . ."

"Wait, a 'brave army captain'?"

They looked at each other.

"No way that's Captain Green . . . He's the Border Butcher. They would have torn him to pieces the second he landed there."

The news footage switched to La Plaza Fundadores. Tanks were on fire, military trucks lay on their sides, and the wreckage of a helicopter was issuing smoke in the center of the square. The soldiers of the new government were collecting bodies. All of it spoke volumes as to the intensity of the fighting.

"*Could* Green have something to do with all this?" asked Vanessa. "If only there were some way to find out . . ."

The news piece had run its course. Adán dashed for the computer and started typing up a storm. "I'm downloading the video of that piece," he explained. "There was a battle there. That woman's father must be Luis Escárcega, the face of the Revolutionary Army. They might've caught our 'brave army captain' on camera."

Vanessa peered over his shoulder. Together they scanned the video for some time.

"Guess he's not on here," said Adán. "The video's only five minutes long, so let me try downloading some more footage—"

"Wait," said Vanessa, gripping his arm before he could close the video file. "Zoom in on this bit here. The guy behind the woman. Good, now up the sharpness."

"It's Green. This man is Jadon Green!" shouted Adán.

"And that's Luis Escárcega next to him. Green is helping him."

"Make it sharper. If that is Captain Green, then why was he part of the Battle of Cordova? And why was he, the Border Butcher, commanding the Revolutionary Army?" said Vanessa.

Adán moved the mouse and zoomed in. The man in question became easier to make out.

"That's Jadon, there's no doubt about it. He went from the desert hotel to Cordova. Does that mean that John Olson and the rest of the people at the hotel were assisting with the revolution?"

"President Copeland did say he'd explain it all when the time is right."

"PathNet CEO John Olson teamed up with President Robert Copeland and used Captain Jadon Green to help Professor Luis Escárcega and his Revolutionary Army. It's all coming together. But if this ever came to light, the US would be in violation of—"

"The Tragedy at The Wall was a massacre orchestrated by Cortázar to prevent his own people from escaping. Which would make Green a mere victim of circumstance."

"Let's gather all of our evidence. We've got part of it down already. The first shot came from the car parked on the Mexican side. That was probably a paid agent of Cortázar's. Private Sepúlveda also took money to fire the next shot, which triggered the shoot-out in earnest. That much we can prove, down to the money trail," said Adán.

"I'll go call the deputy director," said Vanessa, patting him on the shoulder before taking the picture of Jadon with her out the door.

President Copeland mouth was running by itself. "Was it a success?"

"We just got word from Jadon. He is currently in the Presidential Residence of Cordova, alongside Professor Luis Escárcega's body and the interim president, Dr. Penelope Escárcega," exulted the normally calm and collected John, unable to contain his joy.

"Dr. Penelope Escárcega? She's the professor's daughter, right?"

John went into Luis's unfortunate demise, and how Penelope took over for him. He also relayed the words of Professors Watson and Kowalchuk.

"So does that make Dr. Penelope her father's successor? She might be just the person for the job. She's a doctor and a philanthropist. She's a well-known and popular figure in Cordova. She's also got the touching backstory of losing her presidential candidate father, so that's the sympathy vote locked in. Moreov—" The president stopped while he was ahead. His political instincts were leaking out. "Let's just pray to God everything goes okay. Is Jadon injured?"

"He took a licking, but his injuries seem to be light."

The president's tone reverted to serious mode. "Is there anything I can do for the guy?"

"No. The American government wasn't involved at all, remember? But I would like to give Jadon his due reward. He did so much for us."

"Maybe I can restore his standing with the military. If that's okay with him, of course."

"But the operation never happened, Mr. President. Only a select few outside of the War Room know of it. There is an ocean of things you can do for him, however."

"Where is he going after this? After the operation's over and done with, I mean? Is he going to your place?"

"The War Room will disband as of tomorrow. This building will go back to being an abandoned hotel. But we do have a new office on Wall Street. And this time, it's on the books. I'm busy with the moving process at the moment. And our team, which will stay almost exactly the same, is moving to the new War Room as well. It's the start of the second phase of our project, the beginning of the Cordovan Renaissance. The next time I meet Jadon, it will be at the PathNet adviser's office in San Jose."

"I'd very much like to pay a visit too."

"You're welcome anytime."

"Am I welcome as president, or as your friend?"

"As my friend, naturally."

With a knock on the door, a secretary entered the room. The president hung up the phone.

"Mr. President, FBI Director Wolcott would like to see you."

"A phone call won't cut it?"

"He's here, sir, along with Deputy Director Fellure. It seems there's something they'd like to discuss with you in person. They told me to tell you that 'the time to talk has come,' and that they'll wait until you're ready for them."

"Tell them I'll meet with them right now."

"But sir, your promise to Vice President Hanna . . ."

"Tell him I'll go see him when I'm done talking to them."

"You'll go see him, sir?"

"That's right. But I don't know when that'll be."

FBI Director Randy Wolcott and Deputy Director Doug Fellure entered as the secretary left. Their meeting lasted two hours. The president thought he would have to do some explaining, yet the FBI leaders spent most of their time together with explanations of their own. After they left, the chief of staff came in.

The president spoke about his chat with the FBI directors. The chief of staff listened with a solemn look on his face, but he was clearly terribly excited, given how his cheek muscles kept twitching.

"America still remembers the Tragedy at The Wall. I'd like to raise my approval ratings by five points by the time the election rolls around," the president concluded. "The problem is how we communicate what happened to the public."

"A year after the Tragedy, the Cordovan dictatorship collapses, and a democratic administration led by Professor Escárcega's daughter is born from the ashes. The drug cartel Los Eternos was also eradicated in the process. The public will look on our administration favorably now."

"And that's even without making my involvement known."

The president shook his head. So far, he'd taken great care to hide his involvement, but now he'd let it slip.

"Let's just keep this mum. Otherwise the press will play it up. If the president goes out of his way to deny his involvement, there's not a man alive who'd take him at his word."

"Suppose you're right—"

The secretary came in and pointed at her watch. Three hours had passed since he'd told her to postpone his scheduled appointment with Vice President Hanna.

The president nodded and got out of his seat.

Jadon was in the office of the Presidential Residence. Luis's body lay on the sofa, covered by a Cordovan flag. Penelope was sitting at the desk. She was listening to what Sebastian and the executives of the Revolutionary Army had to say, along with the surviving cabinet ministers of what used to be Cortázar's government. The political dissidents who'd allied themselves with Luis were also discussing what steps they should take for the future.

"We need to call on the public before the day is over. Please call the executives of the TV and radio stations in La Caridad and have them come over to the Presidential Residence."

Penelope's orders were shrewd and effective. She had been paying heed to their words ever since the revolutionaries freed them from the prison camp. Either that, or she had read Luis's books and papers before that.

Jadon's phone vibrated in his pocket. The Presidential Residence had Wi-Fi.

"Tell us what's going on," said Stewart, emotion bleeding into his voice for the first time.

"You've got front row seats through the satellite video, don't you? You saw what we did."

"I'm asking you because we *don't* know. What's going on there?"

"We've accomplished our objective. And the objective of you and John is complete too."

Stewart fell silent for a moment, but words returned to him soon enough.

"Our objective was to build a new Cordova, and nothing else. Has Cortázar been eliminated?"

"Professor Escárcega got shot by Cortázar and died. Then Cortázar got shot by a soldier with the revolution. Dourne, as well."

Jadon could tell Stewart's heart had skipped a beat. A few seconds later, Stewart spoke.

"How sure are you?"

"Did Tsutomu not contact you? He's your subordinate more than he is Nick's, isn't he? He used to be Delta Force. And you were connected to the Delta Force yourself. The primary objective of the operation was to kill Raminez Dourne, real name Adel bin Saud." Stewart had no reply, so Jadon continued. "I've got friends in military intelligence too. This operation was outlandish from the start. You and John may despise terrorists, but European terror attacks have nothing to do with Central American dictatorships. And the whole affair was too expansive to chalk it up to a billionaire's whims. So I asked my friend to look into it before I got here."

"What did you find out?"

"That among the masterminds of the Nice terror attack, one of them had yet to be found."

Stewart was breathing hard now. "And?"

"Cortázar's political adviser was one Raminez Dourne, or rather, Adel bin Saud."

"Who told you that nonsense? Your information is all wrong," Stewart lied.

"It's fine. I don't hold it against you or John. I couldn't care less. I did what I did for my own sake."

Jadon hung up.

He exited the president's office and descended to the first-floor hallway. The bodies of the Cortázar administration executives were lined up along the walls, with Cortázar at the center. Jadon looked at each of the corpses in the face, stopping in front of one in particular. His was the face he'd seen on Tsutomu's tablet. Bullet holes had marred his forehead and chest. Something Tsutomu had told him sprang to mind: *Shoot the target's body first, since it's easier to aim for than the head. Then you can nab them in the head.*

He took a photo with his phone and pressed Send.

■ ■ ■

EPILOGUE

"The Tragedy at The Wall was engineered," said a female reporter, live from La Plaza Fundadores in La Caridad. "This afternoon, the FBI submitted the results of their investigation to President Copeland, stating that former President Gumersindo Cortázar of Cordova, who was confirmed dead a few days ago, deliberately staged the incident in order to curb emigration from his country. In the evening, President Copeland officially announced those findings to the world. Furthermore, the president will shortly be formally rescinding the dishonorable discharge of the commanding officer at the scene of the Tragedy, Captain Jadon Green. The president of Cordova's transitional government, Penelope Escárcega, has also officially confirmed that. President Escárcega is scheduled to pay a visit to Washington, DC, to meet with President Copeland, after which she will travel to New York to deliver the first-ever speech by the president of Cordova at the United Nations. She is expected to request the assistance of the United Nations to rebuild her nation."

The Presidential Residence could be seen at the other end of La Plaza Fundadores.

The marks of bullets and blasted shells stood out around the Plaza and on the walls of houses and buildings all over town, and the walls of the House of Assembly and the Presidential Residence were no exception. Apart from that, however, the old vibe of La Caridad had returned. People were ambling down the streets in full force. From their expressions, one would never guess that a fierce battle had only recently taken place there. On the contrary, the citizens' faces were filled with hope and excitement for their new president and for Cordova's promising future.

"The FBI's contribution to the investigation was invaluable, and at its center is a pair of agents named—"

Adán turned off the TV. He didn't need to watch his and Vanessa's interview.

The leading papers from coast to coast published excerpts from Adán's investigation report, and now everyone was holding the FBI's investigative skills in high esteem. The day after they'd submitted the report to the president, the press gave the news wall-to-wall coverage. The higher-ups must have leaked it on purpose.

"Why'd you turn it off?" asked Vanessa, turning it back on. "You did great on camera!"

The timing was perfect—the piece showing their interview at the FBI Academy was just starting. A few minutes later, Vanessa turned it off. "I really need to diet, don't I? I've been stuck doing desk work for more than two weeks straight. And we ate nothing but pizza and donuts the entire time!" Before exiting the room, she vowed to hit the gym and work up a sweat.

Adán looked at his computer screen and clicked on the news show recording.

It was a whirlwind of activity in the Oval Office. More than ten camera people were inside taking video, and the chief of staff, secretary of state, and various other important cabinet members and White House staff were standing side by side with nervous expressions.

President Copeland was about to speak to the United States of America and the world.

"Are you ready, Mr. President? We're ready when you are," said the director.

At her query, Bob adjusted his tie and gave her a nod. Straightening himself up in his chair, he fixed the position of his mic, lightly slapped himself two, three times on the cheeks, and turned to face the cameras.

"Regime change has occurred in the nation of Cordova. Cordova is the country where many of the unfortunate souls who lost everything at the Tragedy at The Wall originated from. Our nation also suffered greatly in the wake of the Tragedy. But I have received a new report from FBI Director Wolcott. The details of that report have already been made public by the FBI, and the world has taken notice. Based on that fact . . ."

Then he pushed his documents aside. Today he would express his thoughts to the American people frankly and openly. He sighed a faint sigh, and looked into the camera with a steely gaze. "As president of these United States, I had to make a tough decision." He straightened his back a little more. The office was dead quiet. He was going off script; they didn't know what he'd say.

"I, United States President Robert Copeland, hereby declare my intention to remove the US-Mexico border wall. The Tragedy started well before the massacre. It began when people were forced to turn their backs on their country, becoming refugees or illegal immigrants. Every human being has a homeland. The country their ancestors built, the country they grew up in, or where their families live. To have no choice but to give up all hope of making a life of dignity for oneself . . . that state of misery is the root of this crisis."

Just then, the president spotted a child at the office's entrance. It was Patricia, and she was mouthing something at him.

He thought it looked like she was saying: *"Sorry, Dad. I love you."*

"The misunderstandings that incident has generated are many, and we must set them straight in short order," the president continued. "I will be holding a discussion between the heads of various Latin American states, including Mexico, and I promise you today that we will hash out a policy that best serves the entire region. I will flex the full extent of my power to tear down not just the wall dividing us from other nations, but also the walls we've erected in our own hearts."

Her cheeks blushing red, Patricia clapped for all she was worth. The staff and camera crew seemed to share her sentiment, for they joined her in applauding his words.

John and Stewart stood alone in an otherwise empty War Room. All the equipment had already been sent to the new War Room located in New York. The name had stuck, though this time, the only battlefield they'd be engaged in was the economic one. They were determined to make Cordova a land of wealth and prosperity. New specialists would be joining the crack team, but that aside, the lineup was almost identical to the one in Nevada.

The red desert sands sprawled outside the window. The same scenery as when Jadon left for Cordova.

"It's all over now," said Stewart softly.

"I wonder, have I done right by them?" said John, asking at last the question he'd bottled up inside. "Will the souls of my wife and daughter rest in peace now?"

"I can't answer that, but I know that at the very least, we can all take a step forward now."

John didn't know how to grapple with Stewart's remark. He recalled Stewart's hospital visit from a year and a half ago.

The doctor had been recommending a rehabilitation regimen, but John didn't have the ears to hear. All he thought about was his wife and daughter, every minute of the day. Whenever he closed his eyes while in bed, he could feel his daughter on his lap, feel his wife's warm gaze.

And he seethed with an all-consuming hatred for the terrorists that did this to them.

"The main culprit of the attack is still around, you know," said Stewart, who stood by his bedside, after a long silence.

At first, John didn't understand what he meant by that. "Wasn't he shot dead by police after the crime?"

"That's just the guy who did it. I'm talking about the mastermind behind it all. The guy who raised the funds, drafted the plan, and set it all up."

John flashed back to that awful day. The image of his wife huddling over his daughter to protect her was seared into his mind . . . along with the explosion of flesh that followed. And the bloody heaps of crushed bone they were reduced to as they hit the ground.

"Ever since it happened, I've been scouring every American intelligence agency for relevant information. The terrorist mastermind has been acting as a political and military advisor to the heads of several Central American countries."

John was shocked to his core. He squinted at the photo on the table. It showed dozens of fancily dressed men and women at a dinner party.

"That's a picture taken during a birthday party held for the president of Cordova, a country in Central America. His name is Gumersindo Cortázar," said Stewart. Then he pointed at the tall man standing behind Cortázar. "This is Raminez Dourne. His real name is Adel bin Saud. He's one of the masterminds behind the Nice terror attack."

John's eyes were glued to the man. His hair was long enough to conceal his ears, and his eyes were narrow. His tightly pursed lips exuded his cruelty, which was backed by a powerful will.

John and Stewart worked themselves ragged investigating Dourne, but they couldn't find a way to get any closer to the terrorist backer who had wormed his way into the dictatorship of Cordova. Half a year later, the Tragedy at The Wall broke out, and it was then that the two hatched their plan. It had all been to kill Dourne.

John wheeled his chair to a corner of the room and looked up at the wall. That was where the War Room's central screen used to be. Now it was just a blemished old wall.

Had he succeeded in avenging his family? Were the two of them satisfied? Was this even what they would have wanted? These were the thoughts that ran incessantly through his mind since the plan was set into motion. "Can we be said to have deceived Captain Jadon and the president? Or worse still, the whole world?"

"We *saved* them. Jadon has a whole new life ahead of him, and the same goes for Copeland. And we've saved the people of Cordova too."

"But so much blood was shed . . ."

"There can be no progress without sacrifice. But that was the price that needed to be paid to restore their pride and self-confidence. Now they'll never feel the need to flee."

"That's how I'll view it. And for their sakes, I'll do my damnedest to help build a new Cordova."

And John meant it from the bottom of his heart. His new mission was to rid the world of any and all refugee crises. He would be there to offer all those who had to escape their own homelands a helping hand.

"Would my wife and daughter be happy with our actions?" he muttered under his breath but shook his head clear. While his initial goal may have been to kill Dourne, he was now honestly wishing lives of security for the people of Cordova, and inwardly he vowed to exert every possible effort to making the new Cordova a reality.

"Does Jadon know of our agenda?" John's eyes fell on the photo on the smartphone that Stewart had handed him. In it, Dourne was lying with bullet holes in his head and chest.

"He doesn't need to. He'd have agreed with us anyway," he said detachedly.

John shook his head in sorrow. Before leaving the hotel, he made a phone call.

"Shirley Goodrum-Green?"

"This is she," her voice soft yet inquisitive.

"Shirley, this is John Olson," he started, "I need to share some information about your ex-husband, Captain Jadon Green. It's of the utmost importance. Would you happen to have a moment?"

"Oh no," she said, resigned. "What kind of trouble did he get into now?"

"Actually," he said, his tone upbeat and proud. And with that, he began telling her of Jadon's real role at the Tragedy at The Wall and the pivotal part he had played in the making of Nueva Cordova, highlighting his bravery and selfless service to the mission. He could tell she was relieved beyond words.

"Thank you for telling me the truth about Jadon," she said, her voice broken with emotion. "I'll let Paulina know her dad is a hero!"

John smiled.

Outside the hotel, a car was waiting for them in the traffic circle. Stewart helped John get in, and the car silently drove off.

He glanced ahead; the red desert sands extended beyond the horizon, where the sun was setting. After the sanguine sun was done shining its final, lancing rays of the day, its redness swiftly leaked away. The giver of light gave way to ever-deeper, ever-blacker night.

"I will give my all to rebuilding the country," he vowed to himself, one last time.

Jadon got on his feet and looked around.

The skies were clear, and the sheen of the green jungle surrounding Cordova International hit his eyes hard.

He was waiting for Arsenio. The charter plane John had sent for him was ready for takeoff. As soon as they got on, it would take three hours to reach Van Nuys. The mercenaries were already onboard, drinking champagne.

It was time, but Arsenio wasn't showing up. Jadon had told him when the jet was set to depart. He looked toward the stopped car some distance from the plane. Already more than an hour had passed since Jadon had said, "I want you to wait a little."

"Arsenio still ain't here yet?" asked Tsutomu.

Jadon hadn't told Tsutomu a thing about Dourne.

"What went down between you two?" Tsutomu continued. "He was always giving you that funny look. I asked a while back, but you never said anything."

"You're the one who said everyone's got a secret." Jadon looked up at the skies again. The heat was enveloping.

Jadon pondered whether he'd done the right thing. This war had cost hundreds of people their lives. No, more than that. Had it been worth it? He hoped so. At the very least, he knew Cordovans were now freed from the constant state of fear that used to be part of life in the country. Now they could spend their days with hope and pride. And they could grant their children a future worth believing in.

He thought about John and Stewart. Did they have him dancing in the palm of their hands this entire time? But Jadon shook his head— even if they had, it didn't even matter anymore.

That moment, a car horn sounded. A car was zooming down the runway at blistering speeds, horn honking all the while. And it was coming for Jadon and the rest.

Tsutomu clutched the handgun in his holster. The other men in ACUs pointed their guns.

The car screeched to a halt a couple of yards away from Jadon. The door opened, and out came young Gerardo. Breathless and winded, he came up to Jadon and saluted him.

"I have a message for you from Mr. Fernández: 'Just go home already. I haven't got time for you.'"

"Did something come up?"

"Miss Nadia suddenly went into labor. He won't leave her side for a second. The two of them are together now." Gerardo laughed as he spoke.

Jadon looked up at the sky. The harsh rays of Central America raked his eyeballs. He squinted. His button-down was damp with sweat. He wanted to get back to America, so he could take a nice cold shower.

"You really are leaving?" groused Penelope, who stepped out of the car. Her schedule was packed but seeing him off was just another important duty of the president of Cordova.

"I want to keep myself out of the view of the Cordovan public."

"You heard about President Copeland's speech and the FBI's report yesterday, didn't you? You were never in the wrong to begin with. The Tragedy was nothing more than a trap Cortázar set for America."

The findings that FBI Special Agents Adán Solano and Vanessa Smith had presented were covered by all the leading papers of the country. They'd even appeared on TV.

"Did my father really say he wanted me to inherit his vision?"

"It sounded that way to me."

"I want you to stay in Cordova for a while, to serve as my adviser on how to maintain the peace. Sebastian wants you to stay as my adviser too."

Sebastian Loyola was now the commander of the new Cordovan military, and in charge of guarding Penelope.

"My role here is over. There are more qualified people out there than me. John will come here soon. Just consult with him. He's a good guy. Real smart and real generous. And most importantly, he's got all the money. That's why—"

Jadon's sentence was snuffed by Penelope's lips.

Tsutomu sighed.

When Jadon snapped back to reality, Penelope was already striding back to the car.

Tsutomu prodded Jadon forward, and they began walking up the landing steps.

Time to go spend some quality time with Paulina, Jadon thought, smiling. The jet took off, the magnificent green of Cordova shining below them.

NOTE

ROBERT D. ELDRIDGE, PHD

On Feb. 5, 2020, US President Donald Trump delivered his third State of the Union Address before both chambers of Congress. In the 1 hr., 18 min. speech, Trump discussed immigration, including crime committed by illegal aliens, the cost of taxpayer-funded healthcare for illegal aliens, and border enforcement. Trump's second SOTU, delivered in 2019, spent even more of its time—nearly one-third of the entire speech—on illegal immigration, with a focus on the migrant "caravan" issue, which is at the heart of the book you have before you by the prolific writer Tetsuo Takashima.

I first met the author in May 2007. He and I were speakers in a course taught at the Osaka University School of International Public Policy, where I was a tenured associate professor. I had co-founded the course in the fall of 2001 with a university colleague, Dr. Hoshino Toshiya, now Japan's ambassador to the United Nations, and representatives of the Osaka Provincial Liaison Office, which represents the interests of all three services making up the Self-Defense Forces (Jieitai) in Osaka Prefecture.

The class, called the Workshop on International Security, brought together leading experts, government officials, and military officers to discuss aspects of international or regional security issues. Beginning in 2005, following the December 2004 earthquake and tsunami in Indonesia and South and Southeast Asia, we began looking more and more at natural disasters.

Takashima stimulated the students and faculty with his lecture that day, based on a number of books he had written to date, including *Kyodai Jishin no Hi: Inochi o Mamoru Tame no Hontō no Koto* (which I later translated into English as *Megaquake*) about how Japan would fare if a disaster similar to the Indian Ocean tsunami hit the country. It was five years after his book came out, and four years after our joint lecture, that I was in Sendai helping to respond to the Great East Japan Earthquake. When I returned from the mission, I asked Takashima if I could translate his book. He granted permission, and it was published in 2015 by Potomac Books. As a result of the March 2011 earthquake, our intellectual exchanges were renewed.

What I especially appreciate about Takashima is his approach to research and writing, namely his fieldwork—being on the ground to experience things for himself. I saw him when he came to Okinawa for research on his books about the police there, for example, and was able to pay him back a little bit by showing him around and making introductions. Moreover, because I find his views and thinking so insightful, I arranged for him to give two talks in Okinawa during one of his trips to the operational forces of the US Marine Corps at the headquarters of III Marine Expeditionary Force and another one to the disaster planners of Okinawa's 41 local municipalities.

Takashima has had an interesting career. He was born in 1949 in Okayama Prefecture, between Kobe and Hiroshima. He still lives not too far from Okayama, in Tarumi Ward, Kobe, in the very western part of Japan's fifth-largest city. After studying in the Engineering Department of Keio University in Tokyo, he began working as a researcher for the Japan Atomic Energy Research Institute created in 1956. Subsequently, he moved to the United States, where he conducted further studies at the University of California. Upon his return to Japan, he began writing while managing a private preparatory school. *Fallout*, his debut novel, won the 1994 Shosetsu Gendai Mystery Newcomer Award. Other novels include the action thriller *Intruder*, which won the 1999 Suntory Mystery Award. Takashima, who has written more than thirty novels in the disaster, action, thriller, suspense, mystery, and juvenile fiction genres, is years ahead of everyone in thinking about natural and man-made disasters. We should listen to his advice, through his writings, speeches, blogs, and other activities.

This book, *The Wall*, is about a refugee crisis originating in a fictional Central American country called Cordova run by a dictator. A migrant "caravan" flees Cordova and heads to the United States, leading to a conflict at the US-Mexico border in which many of the refugees are killed. Although the plot is fiction, it is also real, and represents the daily struggle and fears of refugees around the world, and those who live in oppressive states or dysfunctional countries.

Takashima began writing the book two years ago, as a result of the international refugee crisis in Europe and the debate in the United States, which picked up speed after Trump took office and proceeded to ban people from certain countries from entering the United States and called on Mexico to pay for a wall to be built on the border between the two nations. Trump's policies, described by many as inhumane, have brought many new tragedies, but these policies and the situation that preceded them did not start with Trump. They existed before. An example of "man's inhumanity to man."

Through this book, therefore, Takashima expresses the hope that a more humane immigration and refugee system be found worldwide, including in the United States, where he lived earlier in his life, not too far from the border with Mexico in southern California. "All nations must take a greater interest in refugees and immigrant matters," Takashima told this writer recently, "as there is much good that can be done." I hope that the reader finishes the book with that feeling as well.

Robert D. Eldridge is the former deputy assistant chief of staff, Marine Corps Bases Japan, and was a tenured associate professor at the School of International Public Policy, Osaka University, in Osaka, Japan, from 2001–2009. He earned his PhD in Japanese political and diplomatic history at Kobe University and is the author, contributor, editor, and translator of approximately 100 books on foreign policy, international security, and humanitarian disaster matters, including Operation Tomodachi.

AUTHOR'S NOTE

1980S.

El Paso, New Mexico, USA

In the spring of the year I graduated from university, I visited the embankment of the Rio Grande River. The towns, and the river itself, often appear in Westerns. Upon crossing the river, I found myself in the Mexican city of Juárez.

On the opposite bank, I spotted many young Mexicans sitting around. "They're waiting for their chance to enter America," my American companion informed me. They had only to cross the river to set foot in a country of wealth and prosperity. Working in America was their dream. Being Japanese, the whole idea was difficult for me to comprehend.

From that time on, immigration to the US from Latin America (including Mexico) has led to various issues. Illegal immigrants take American jobs, and crimes do occur. On the other hand, without the cheap labor force, the US would be in a bind. There were a ton of contradictions to unpack. The one truth everyone could agree on was that Mexico was poor, and the US was rich. What was behind this wealth gap in a place with the same landscape and climate? Was it the state or the people at fault? Perhaps it was both. I just didn't know at the time.

This state of affairs has persisted for nearly half a century.

2017.

"I'll build a wall on the Mexican border!"

Partially on the back of this statement, Donald J. Trump became the 45th president of the United States.

The next year, the "caravan" became a hot button issue. A group of refugees from the poorest countries in Latin America—their homelands full of gang violence and corrupt politics—traveled a long way in search of better lives. That number swelled to the thousands before the group reached the US–Mexico border.

THE SWELLING RANKS OF REFUGEES ALL OVER THE WORLD.

The problems that come with illegal immigrants and refugees are spreading to EU countries. While asylum seekers escape from civil wars and dictatorships in Africa and the Middle East in order to protect themselves and their families, the tax burden and security concerns regarding refugees are sparking political instability across the nations of the EU. The UK's departure from the EU was also triggered in part by the rise in immigration.

Why do people from the Middle East and Africa aim for Europe? One reason is the political instability in their countries of origin. Many people have been killed or injured due to civil strife. Another reason is the wealth gap, which has grown ever larger over the past century.

People from poor countries tend to flow into rich countries. But how does this gap arise to begin with?

Other problems include high crime rates, drug cartels, and low-quality education in their homelands. Moreover, corruption is widespread, and the public doesn't trust in their governments or politicians. The police and the military typically fare no better either.

Currently, the issues of immigration are spreading across the globe.

EVERYONE LOVES THEIR HOMELAND.

Many refugees try to cross the Mediterranean from Africa and the Middle East by boat, or get to the EU on foot. And many lives are lost, including women and children.

It's a matter of course—everyone loves the homeland where they were born and raised. So why must they abandon their homelands and head toward foreign lands, risking their lives in the process? It's not as though those foreign countries will welcome them with open arms.

"It's in search of a better life." "It's to avoid the civil war in my homeland. I want to live." "I want my family to be safe and secure."

There may be various reasons, but the foremost is the sense that one's life is always in danger in the homeland, and that there is no hope in sight for oneself or one's children.

FOR A HOMELAND WHERE THE CHILDREN CAN BE SAFE AND SOUND.

Immigrants should not have to abandon the countries where they were born and raised. They want to live in their homelands, and they want their homelands to be places where their children can grow up in safety and security, to be places their children can take pride in. They aren't escaping to other countries, so much as they're seeking a nation that's easier to live in. As such, reconstructing their homelands is the best solution to the immigration/refugee crisis. No one would abandon a home-nation they can take pride in, and where they can raise their children with peace of mind.

We shouldn't be creating walls. We need to be revitalizing people's homelands, and tearing down the walls in our hearts.

A NEW DEMOCRATIC STATE.

Companies, mercenaries, scientists and economists joining forces to create a new nation, based on advanced AI. Wiping out drug cartels and defeating a dictatorship, and then aiming for a more rational and livable democratic country by way of AI. It is the establishment of a new nation that could not be accomplished during the Arab Spring. This book depicts one example of that process coming to fruition.

ACKNOWLEDGMENTS

First of all, I dedicate this book to my mother, Miyoko Takashima, who passed away in January 2020. Although I couldn't always be with you, I always thought of you . . . and think of you now.

I am deeply grateful to translator Giuseppe di Martino, editor Brunella Costagliola, proofing editor Francis Lewis and designer José A. Contreras for their amazing translation, editing and cover design. In addition, I would like to extend my sincere gratitude to Akira Chiba, publisher of Museyon, for giving me this opportunity.

I would like to thank my assistant, Takaki Kondo, for gathering information and helping with public relations, and director Toshinari Yonishi for making a powerful video trailer. A great big "thank you" goes to Akemi S. Miller, designer of the New York collection, for her help in distributing this book to the world as she leads the way to Hollywood!

Also, thanks to Satomi Shimoji and Luis Sanchez of Okinawa for their assistance in providing translation consultation for the English promotional trailer. I will visit Okinawa again! And thanks to Yoshiaki Takahashi with New York BIZ newspaper for spreading the word about the book.

Finally, I would like to thank my late friend Brian, Koji Ishijima, for supporting my dream. I'm sure you are happy now, too.

My goal is that many people around the world read my books and ultimately see them adapted into movies. I hope that *The Wall* will be the first step to fulfilling this ambition.

I long for the world's refugees to return to their home countries and lead peaceful everyday lives in nations where children can live safely and happily without starving.

I would be more than happy if this book helps pave the way a little.

Summer 2020

TED TAKASHIMA

After working as a scientist for the Japan Atomic Energy Research Institute, Ted Takashima moved to California, where he studied at the University of California. He has published more than thirty novels in the action/thriller/suspense/mystery genres in Japan. His novels include the action thriller *Intruder*, which won the 1999 Suntory Mystery Award, and *Pandemic* (2010), which foretold the global spread of COVID-19 in 2020.

SPRING 2021

THE GENE OF LIFE

BY TED TAKASHIMA

ISBN 9781940842516